JESS FELT THE STIRRING OF OLD FEARS AND FORGOTTEN MEMORIES.

She shivered, chilled by a wave of long-suppressed dread. For the first time in years she heard the scream of brakes, the crash of metal on metal, the smell of burning rubber and spilled fuel. With sudden startling clarity, she saw the unfamiliar face of a strange man peering down beneath the bumper of the car, intruding into her hiding place. Although she knew the face belonged to Grandpa Gene, she saw it with the terrified eyes of the child she had once been. Instinctively, inside the memory, she crawled away, hiding, protecting herself from discovery.

The vivid memory faded, but the tendrils of the past reached out, sending her a last frantic warning, yelling inside her head that she must never tell anyone the truth or something terrible would happen.

With savage anger, Jess pushed the warnings away. After all of these years, it was time to confront her past. She looked up and stared straight into Dan's eyes.

"My name is Liliana," she said, the name tasting foreign on her tongue after so many years of silence. "I'm not Jessica Marie Pazmany, I'm Liliana."

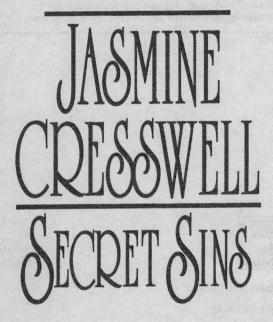

JASMINE CRESSWELL
SECRET SINS

MIRA BOOKS

ISBN 1-55166-261-2

SECRET SINS

Copyright © 1997 by Jasmine Cresswell.

All rights reserved. Except for use in any review, the reproduction or utilization of this work in whole or in part in any form by any electronic, mechanical or other means, now known or hereafter invented, including xerography, photocopying and recording, or in any information storage or retrieval system, is forbidden without the written permission of the publisher, MIRA Books, 225 Duncan Mill Road, Don Mills, Ontario, Canada M3B 3K9

All characters in this book have no existence outside the imagination of the author and have no relation whatsoever to anyone bearing the same name or names. They are not even distantly inspired by any individual known or unknown to the author, and all incidents are pure invention.

MIRA and the star colophon are trademarks of MIRA Books.

Printed in U.S.A.

For Allison Claire Stange
In loving memory

ACKNOWLEDGMENTS

Several people were kind enough to share their expertise with me—usually at short notice. I would like to thank Dr. Franklin G. Harris of New Orleans, who offered many valuable insights into the professional life of a psychiatrist. Stanley Deka, retired lieutenant with the Cleveland police force and father of writer Constance Laux, explained exactly how a catastrophic road accident would have been handled in 1969. And Kay Hooper, writer and friend, provided pages of information on the flora of North Carolina. Of course, they are not responsible for any mistakes I may have made in using their information.

I would also like to thank my editors, Jane Robson, Amy Moore and Ilana Glaun, who all worked so hard to make *Secret Sins* the best book it could be.

Prologue

Cleveland, Ohio
December 9, 1969

Gene Zajak had been a cop for thirty years, so he'd seen his share of dead bodies, especially dead bodies piled up in car wrecks. But this accident was a real doozy. Eight cars, one flipped over, five with doors that couldn't be opened. At least four dead, and that was before the medics pried out all the bodies. Smashed glass and car parts scattered all over the icy road. The stench of blood and fear and burning rubber. The inevitable crowd of dazed witnesses and numb, bleeding survivors. Yeah, this one was a doozy, all right.

The Ford Mustang that caused the initial crash had gone out of control in peak rush hour, and there had been no place for drivers to go—except into each other—when the Mustang skidded on black ice and jumped lanes into the oncoming traffic. The accident had happened less than fifteen minutes before, and traffic was already jammed up for a mile in either direction. If everything went real smooth, with no screwups, Van Aken Boulevard might be cleared of debris in another two hours. Hell of a Friday night, Gene thought.

Two hours of being stuck in traffic in the cold meant lots of drivers with frayed nerves and heated tempers. Shaker Square had to be the worst place on the east side to have an accident of this type. As soon as the medics from the fire department finished ferrying out survivors, Gene decided he'd put another couple of uniforms on crowd and traffic control. They could divert some of the homeward-bound drivers to Chagrin or Shaker Boulevard. Otherwise, there'd be another traffic jam from all the cars with stalled engines.

It was cold enough to freeze your balls off. Gene hunched into the acrylic fur collar of his jacket and walked down the line of wrecked cars, checking to see if any of the emergency crews needed more help, making sure nothing important had been overlooked. In his experience, with a dozen cops and firefighters from two rival jurisdictions trying to work together, the chance for a major fuck-up was high. So far, thank God, everything seemed to be working out okay.

He held back a hysterical onlooker as firefighters finished freeing three teenagers from the back of an old Plymouth station wagon. They were all alive when they were put in ambulances and rushed to Saint Luke's. If the ambulance crews could keep them breathing until they reached the emergency room, the kids had a fighting chance. The teen who'd been driving hadn't been so fortunate. He was lying on the sidewalk, covered with a tarp, one of the four people already pronounced dead at the scene.

Gene hunched deeper into his jacket. You didn't stick it out in this business for thirty years if you had a queasy stomach, but an accident like this made even a tough old cop feel sick. He reached the last car in the chain of shattered vehicles, a late-model Chevy Impala. The driver, a man who was anywhere between thirty and forty, was spitted on the steering wheel and very obviously dead. Fire fighters were working frantically on the woman in the front passenger seat, trying to move her without ripping her flesh on broken glass and twisted metal. She was breathing, but it looked as if her head had gone through the window on impact. One side of her face was torn open, her eye gone. Gene rated her chance of surviving at right around zero. Neither she nor the driver had been wearing their seat belts. Almost nobody did, of course, despite all the efforts at public education. Call him a cynic, but Gene suspected it would be a snowy day in hell before drivers in America got smart enough to realize that losing your life or limbs was a lot more inconvenient than clicking together the buckles of a seat belt every time you got into your car.

The woman stopped breathing. She was dead, but the firefighters weren't ready to give up on her. Gene decided he'd seen enough. He walked to the back of the Chevy, which had been broadsided and pushed into the rear of the delivery van ahead of it. The impact had been so powerful that the front end of the car was crumpled and twisted almost beyond recognition, but the back wasn't damaged. Gene ran his hand over the iridescent silver-blue paint glowing in the light of the street lamp. Poor bastards, he thought. Looks as though they just drove the damn thing off the lot. Well, at least they wouldn't have to worry about making any more car payments. Death had its advantages.

He was just about to walk up the road to the front of the line, when he saw something sticking out from under the rear of the Chevy, wedged up close to the tire. He stopped and looked again, startled into giving a little grunt when he realized that it was a tiny foot wearing a snow boot. As he looked, he saw the foot move.

Gene was on his stomach in a second, peering under the car, almost afraid of what he was going to find. It was a child curled against the tire, not only alive, but conscious, with no visible sign of injury, and he thought for one unbelievable moment that he was going to cry. He hadn't realized until then just how badly the blood, the pain and the death were getting to him.

"Hello," he said, his voice gruff. He coughed to clear his throat, trying to sound more friendly. The kid looked scared half to death. "My name's Gene. Gene Zajak. Can you tell me your name?"

The child, who couldn't have been more than four, stared at him in blank, unblinking silence. He thought she was a girl, although it was hard to tell given that she was bundled up in some sort of a kiddie snowsuit. Christ, he thought, that woman with the eye hanging out onto her cheek is probably this kid's mother. And the guy with the steering wheel through his gut is probably her father.

He was afraid to grab her hands and yank her out. In her bulky outfit, it was impossible to be sure that she wasn't wounded. "It's kind of dark and scary under the car," he said. "What do you think? If you'd come out from there, we could go someplace where it's more comfortable. Check to make sure you didn't get hurt. Does that sound like a good idea?"

Her eyes flickered briefly. He was fairly certain she'd heard and understood, but she didn't move, didn't respond in any way. Maybe her legs were broken. How the hell did she get under there, anyway?

"I'm a policeman," he said. "I often help kids who are hurt." He tried to edge a little closer, and she instantly scooted deeper under the car, moving like greased lightning until she was brought up short by a piece of fallen chassis. Gene just managed to grab one of her feet before she disappeared behind the broken front axle.

If she could move that quickly, with that much coordination, she probably didn't have any fatal injuries, which was a relief to know. The snowsuit padded her body pretty well, so Gene slid her gently along the ground until he could pick her up. She didn't scream, didn't make any sound at all, but her body was rigid with fear when he took her into his arms and carried her to the side of the road. He hugged her a little tighter, trying to tell her that she was safe and that she would be taken care of. He'd see to it. If anything, the terror in her gaze simply increased.

Gene had two married sons and three young grandsons, so he was used to kids and knew that most of the time they were about as much fun to be around as the hounds of hell. But for some reason, this button-nosed dot of a thing reached straight into his heart and hung on tight. By macabre coincidence, tonight was the second anniversary of his wife's death, so maybe he was trying real hard to find some hint that life offered hope and the potential for happiness, as well as pain and sorrow and suffering. This little girl who'd survived the car wreck was his proof that sometimes miracles happened, that sometimes life could be snatched from the jaws of death.

He untied the hood of her snowsuit and swiftly checked for head injuries. No sign of any bumps, cuts or contusions, just a smear of oil on her cheek and a riot of baby-soft curls escaping from two tight braids. Gene wasn't much on girls' hairstyles, but he thought braids were a strange way to fix this kid's hair. He tucked a wisp of curl behind her ear and smiled at her. Geez, she wasn't just cute, she was beautiful. He squished her nose gently with his fingertip, wondering how long it would be before her next of kin could arrive to claim her. He hoped she had grandparents, aunts, cousins, a whole tribe of relatives who'd be able to make up for the parents she'd lost.

"It's going to be okay, sweetie, honest it is. Could you tell me your name, honey?" She didn't answer, so he tried a couple of guesses. "Let's see, is your name Linda? Or how about Debbie? Or maybe it's Lisa."

Her blank gaze never altered, which wasn't surprising, given that she was undoubtedly in shock. And yet something about that wide-eyed stare bothered the heck out of him, Gene realized. Because it wasn't blank, he thought suddenly. The kid wasn't just numb with shock, she was stiff and stony-faced with fear and defiance.

But then, why wouldn't the kid be afraid? She'd just survived a traumatic accident and been rescued by a total stranger. She had every reason to feel scared, hostile and wary.

"Okay, kid, no need to talk if you don't feel like it." He knew he ought to find a doctor or nurse to check her over, in case she had internal injuries. Gene hustled her past the Chevy Impala, screening her from any view of the interior and the mangled bodies of her parents. She struggled to see over his shoulder, seemingly determined to look into the smashed-up car.

"Stop wriggling, honey, I don't want to drop you. Everything's going to be all right." He spoke in the sort of hearty voice grown-ups often used with kids when they were lying through their teeth. "I'm a policeman, remember, and I'm here to take care—"

At that moment, the child started screaming as if all the demons in hell were after her. "Let me go!" she cried, pounding her tiny fists against his leather jacket with all the puny strength she could muster. "Let me go! I want my mommy!"

Well, at least she had excellent command of her vocal cords, Gene thought, and plenty of breath for yelling. He grabbed her flailing hands and held her clamped to his chest so that she couldn't hit him anymore. A fire fighter from the Shaker Heights fire department came up, having probably heard the screams. "What's the matter?" he asked, rubbing his eyes wearily. "Has the kid been checked out yet?"

"Not by a professional."

"I can look her over if you like."

"Sure." Gene handed the little girl to the man. "I don't think she's badly hurt," he said. "In fact, I don't think she's hurt at all. Give her a quick once-over, will you? I'm going to see if I can find some ID for her, maybe even a home address."

The firefighter shot him a questioning look and Gene jerked his head in the direction of the Chevy. "Her parents are in there," he said.

The fireman didn't bother to ask if they were alive or dead; the answer was self-evident. He grunted, and got busy with his blood-pressure monitor. Gene walked back to the Chevy. The body of the kid's mother was being moved to the side of the road, and a young cop and a medic were attempting to prise the shaft of the steering column out of her father, so that his body could be carted off to the morgue.

"How's it going?" Gene asked, reaching in through the shattered passenger-side window and trying to open the glove compartment. The lock was jammed shut and wouldn't budge.

The cop, obviously a rookie, was spattered with blood, and green around the gills. Gene could tell it was touch and go whether they'd unhook the guy from the steering wheel before the young policeman threw up. "We may have to cut through the steering wheel to get him out, sir."

"The fire trucks will have the equipment you need," Gene said.

"Yes, sir. Soon as they can spare another man, they're bringing it over."

"Good, and get someone to open this glove compartment while you're at it," he told the officer. "We need to ID these people as quick as we can. There's a kid to identify. Can you reach inside the driver's jacket and get to his wallet?"

"No way, he's damn near welded to the wheel. But we have this." The cop handed over a black patent-leather purse, badly misshapen. "We found it on the floor," he said. "Looks like the car's a rental, but there's a bunch of stuff in the bag, including airline tickets. Guess these folks were coming from the airport. Some trip they had, huh?"

"Yeah, some trip." Gene snapped open the purse and found the tickets, which had already been used and were made out for a one-way journey from New York's La Guardia to Cleveland's Hopkins airport. The travelers were identified as Rudolph and Elena Pazmany, and the child traveling on the half-fare ticket was Jessica Marie Pazmany.

Looked as though he had a name for the kid. Jessica Marie Pazmany. Hungarian. There were a bunch of Hungarian families in Cleveland, lots of them refugees from the 1956 uprising against the Commies. Perhaps these folks had come to visit relatives. Gene carefully checked through the rest of the purse and found a wallet with five dollars in cash, a pack of tissues and a ballpoint pen attached to a little notebook. There were no pictures or anything personal except a recently issued driver's license tucked into the side pocket, showing an address in Queens. When he flipped open the notebook, there was only one entry, a neatly printed address in Cleveland Heights for a woman by the name of Magda Mizensky.

Mizensky. Another Hungarian name. Gene breathed a sigh of relief. With any luck, he'd found a local contact who would be able to point him in the direction of Jessica's next of kin. Maybe Magda *was* the next of kin. In any case, with a few phone calls and a bit of legwork, he should be able to turn up a cousin or an aunt willing to act as Jessica's legal guardian. He sure as heck didn't want her to end up at the mercy of the overburdened caseworkers over at Child Welfare. He'd seen some of the temporary-care facilities—they were clean, but that was about all you could say in their favor.

Jessica was sitting on the fireman's lap, drinking Gatorade, when Gene made his way back to the emergency-rescue van that was serving as a triage center. "Guess everything checked out okay with the kid, then?" he asked.

"She's fine. Found a few bruises, but nothing serious. Vitals are all normal. No symptoms of a concussion or any internal injuries, so I'd say she's one lucky little lady."

Yeah. Lucky as hell, Gene thought. Aside from the fact that her parents had just been wiped out in the blink of an eye, you could say little Jessica Marie was one of fortune's favored few.

"Where's she going now?" the fire fighter asked. "I can send her to the hospital if you need a few hours to find some family, someplace for her to stay."

Gene shrugged. "I'll take her to the Women's Bureau of the police department. If they can't find anywhere else, she can stay with me for tonight. My daughter-in-law loves kids and she's approved as an emergency-care provider."

"The kid's all yours, then." The fireman set Jessica down and went off to answer a call for help from one of his colleagues.

Gene squatted so that he was eye level with Jessica Marie. She returned his gaze with guarded curiosity. "Would you like to come home with me tonight?" he asked. "I've got two little boys who live at my house and they have great toys. They're my grandsons, and their names are Todd and Matt. Their mom and dad are called Barbara and Frank."

He sounded like a damned game-show host awarding the big prize, Gene thought. But what the hell did you say to a kid whose mom was en route to the morgue and whose dad was still skewered on the steering column of their rental car?

Jessica stared at him for a long time, then, finally, she spoke in a low voice, "Will you take me to see my mommy?"

Hell of a question, Gene thought. It was so cold he couldn't feel the end of his nose, but he realized he was sweating. He drew in a big breath of icy, fume-laden air. "Listen, Jessica, I don't think that's such a good idea. Maybe later."

Her eyes flickered again, and she gave him another of those strange assessing glances. "Is my mommy dead?" she asked, her voice very frightened.

The question tore at his gut. Gene took her into his arms and held her close, cradling her head awkwardly against his chest. His grandsons weren't much for hugging and he discovered he'd kind of lost the knack. "I'm sorry, honey, real sorry, but the truth is, your mom *is* dead. I wish I could tell you something different, but I can't." He figured he ought to say something about angels and heaven and going to live happily ever after with Jesus, but he couldn't bring himself to utter the words he didn't believe.

The kid lifted her head from his chest. For quite a while, she just stared at him, and he had the uncanny feeling that she was trying to determine if he was lying. Eventually, she seemed to decide that he was telling the truth. Her bottom lip wobbled and she started to cry, big, silent tears that made him wonder for about the thousandth time how fate chose its victims and why life needed to be so damned unfair. He patted her back and mumbled clumsy, incoherent words that were meant to be consoling, but which made him angry because of their sheer, hopeless inadequacy.

When she finally stopped crying, she didn't ask about her father, perhaps because she couldn't bear to hear any more bad news. Gene was enough of a coward that he was relieved not to have to tell her that it wasn't only her mother who was dead. He took his handkerchief and mopped up her tears. "Okay, all done for now," he said huskily as he began walking toward his car. "You ready to come home to my house?"

She nodded, but she didn't speak, so he filled the painful silence with a spate of chatter. "You're going to like my house," he said. "It's got a great big backyard with a couple of real old maple trees in it. Matt and Todd love to play in the backyard."

She sucked for a moment on the bobble at the end of her hood string. "How old are Matt and Todd?" she asked.

"Todd is seven and Matt is four. How old are you?"

She seemed to have decided to talk, at least a little. "I'm four," she said. She pulled off her mitten and held up four fingers. "I'm this many years old. I'm a girl."

"You're the same age as Matt. He likes to eat Oreo cookies dunked in milk. How about you? Are you hungry?" *Goddamn stupid question.*

Jessica didn't answer, just stuck her thumb in her mouth and suddenly looked exactly like what she was, an exhausted, bewildered toddler. She wriggled anxiously as he unlocked the door to his Oldsmobile and settled her into the front passenger seat. She clutched at his hand. "You won't make the car crash, will you? Not like...not like before." She gulped, and tears came to her eyes again. "I didn't want them to die, I didn't."

"I'll drive real careful," he said, leaning across to snap her into the seat belt. He smiled and patted her on the knee. "I'm going to take you home to my family. We've got five people living in my house. There's me and Frank—he's my son—and Barbara, his wife, and I already told you about their kids, Matt and Todd." He recited the names in a litany designed to tame the horror of the night into something normal, a group of people she could recognize as a family like the one she'd just lost. He gave Jessica's seat belt a final tug to make sure it was snug. "There you go, honey. Now you're safe."

She looked at him out of dark blue eyes that seemed too big and too sad for such a tiny face. "Seat belts keep you safe. My mommy always said that."

"Did she? Well, she wanted to take good care of you, Jessica Marie, that's why." Pity she hadn't taken equal care of herself, he thought savagely. If she'd been wearing a seat belt, she might be alive this minute instead of stretched out on a slab in the morgue. Gene locked and closed the passenger door and moved toward the driver's side.

Liliana watched the policeman walk around the car, her tummy feeling all sick and hoppity inside. She wondered if she should tell him that her name was Liliana, not Jessica Marie. But she was scared. Mommy had told her that nobody must know her real name, or Daddy would find her. And she sure didn't want Daddy to find her. That's why *they'd* run away with her—Uncle Ralph and Auntie Lena—so's they could hide from the police Daddy would send to look for her. Was Gene one of Daddy's bad policemen? she wondered. He was driving off with her in his car, but he hadn't said a word about Daddy. She didn't know what to do, but it didn't seem like a good idea to tell Gene her name was Liliana. If she did, he might make something bad happen to her. Even worse than what had happened to Mommy.

Gene got inside the car and smiled at her. Her tummy went hippity-hop again. Gene's smiles were nice and friendly, not mean like when Daddy smiled. Still, she knew Auntie Lena and her mommy wouldn't want her to trust a policeman. She wriggled nervously behind her seat belt.

"All set, Jessica Marie?" The name sounded funny because it wasn't hers, but Auntie Lena had said it was a way to keep her safe, and Mommy wanted her to be safe. So she nodded and stared straight ahead, not saying anything. She would let him call her Jessica Marie because that was what she needed to do to keep hidden from Daddy. But deep inside, she knew she was Liliana, whatever the policeman called her. She would always be Liliana inside, even though she had to let all these people call her Jessica Marie.

Liliana. She whispered it to herself as the car drove off into the darkness. *Liliana.*

She would never forget her real name. Never.

One

Denver, Colorado
May 24, 1996

Jess tried all through lunch to make herself accept Timothy Macfadden's proposal. She managed to hold up her end of the discussion about the house they would buy and agreed with him that she wanted two children. But every time she tried to say the fateful words, *Yes, I'll marry you,* they stuck in her throat, a lump of undigested panic that wouldn't go up or down. When the waitress brought their coffee, she finally gave up and told him that she was very sorry, but she couldn't marry him.

Tim, of course, was patient and understanding, which only made Jess feel worse. He finished his coffee—Tim wasn't a man to waste a perfectly good cup of coffee just because the woman he'd been dating for eleven months had turned down his proposal. Then he put the tasteful diamond ring back in its tasteful Tiffany box and assured her he would always be her friend. The frightening thing was she believed him.

Jess wondered why she was such a sick person that she felt weak-kneed with relief when he aligned his spoon neatly in his saucer, picked up the bill and walked away from her, presumably forever. Seventy-five thousand bucks a year, a solid career as an architect and the nicest dog in Denver. If all that wasn't good enough for her, what the heck was she waiting for? But at least the lump in her throat had finally gone away, and her stomach had stopped churning. She was obviously crazy, but it seemed that her nervous system was allergic to the multiple perfections of Timothy Macfadden.

As if rejecting one of Denver's most eligible bachelors wasn't enough trauma for one day, problems piled up all afternoon. Normally Jess loved her job as assistant director of the Colorado Tourist and Convention Bureau, but not today. By midafternoon she learned that she'd lost a regional meeting of the Home Builders' Federation to Jackson Hole, Wyoming. And at five-thirty, she got the *really* bad news: in the year 2000, the International Society of Podiatrists was going to celebrate the millennium by hosting their biggest gathering ever—in Geneva, Switzerland. Switzerland, for heaven's sake! If they wanted mountains and scenic views while discussing hammertoes and bunions, couldn't they have picked Colorado?

Jess sighed as she switched off her computer and cleared her desk for the night. Competition in attracting convention business was becoming so intense that she was sure the first astronauts to land on Mars would be greeted with a free welcome cocktail served by a green man wearing the neatly striped uniform of the Martian Tourist Board.

She locked her file cabinet, wishing she could go home, watch a "Murphy Brown" rerun and eat a large chocolate bar. Refusing a man like Tim Macfadden was enough to make any self-respecting woman want to rush home and eat chocolate. Unfortunately, her workday wasn't over yet. She had to freshen her tired makeup, glue on a perky smile and pump herself up to sparkle at the governor's reception. A Japanese trade delegation was exploring investment opportunities in Colorado, and she was required to put in an appearance.

An hour later, Jess was at the governor's mansion. She had attended so many functions here over the past couple of years that she made her way toward the dining room with no more than a passing glance at the elegance of the paneled reception rooms and the cool opulence of the marble rotunda with its classical statues and magnificent grand piano. A quick glimpse of her reflection in one of the gilt-edged mirrors convinced her that before she had any hope of doing a credible imitation of perky, she needed a drink. And tonight, Perrier wasn't going to cut it. Tonight, even a triple bourbon might not cut it.

She was halfway to the bar set up in the dining room when she saw Dan Stratton striding purposefully toward her. Her stomach instantly plummeted into her shoes. After refusing Tim's proposal and losing the podiatrists to Geneva, she would have sworn that life couldn't get any worse. When she saw her ex-husband heading straight for her, she knew that she hadn't even begun to plumb the miseries in store for her. This day would go into the record books as one of her all-time worst.

Dan, of course, looked terrific. In a universe with even a smidgen of cosmic justice the man would, at the very least, have gone bald and developed a paunch. Cosmic justice, as usual, had fallen down on the job. In the three years since they'd separated, Dan's appearance had become more charismatic, more fascinating, more ruggedly sexy than it had been on the day she left him. Nature's way, she assumed, of preserving the gene pool for feckless idiots.

She watched with an emotion somewhere between amusement, admiration and numb resignation as he smoothly avoided waiters, guests, reporters and their host.

It took a certain amount of chutzpah to blow off the governor of the state of Colorado, but, then, Dan had always possessed a superabundant supply of chutzpah.

He stopped about two feet from her and smiled his familiar crooked smile. His thick, dark hair gleamed in the light of the chandelier. His wonderful gray-green eyes glinted with wry self-mockery. "Hello, Jess."

His husky voice curled around her with subtle invitation. His smile sent a heated promise that, if she succumbed to his lure, he would personally see to it that she enjoyed the sexual experience of a lifetime. Two years of marriage to Dan Stratton should have been enough to provide any reasonably intelligent woman with permanent immunity to his charms. In her case, it seemed the inoculation had failed. She could feel her bones melting as she stood there gazing at him. She just barely managed to restrain herself from panting.

Jess wondered if she was hormonally challenged, or just plain dumb. At lunchtime she'd rejected the honorable Tim, and now she was slavering over disreputable Dan. Was she nuts? How could she forget the misery of living with a man who was so busy waiting to be discovered as a movie star that he never had time to take care of the basic details of life? Like washing his socks, or finding a temporary job so they could buy enough groceries to last until her next paycheck.

The memory of living for two years on tuna fish and spaghetti was enough to put some steel back into Jess's spine. She drew herself up to her full height and gave her ex-husband the sort of smile she reserved for elderly businessmen who tried to pat her fanny. "Hello, Dan. You're looking well."

He ignored her freezing smile and gazed deep into her eyes, probably seeing far more than she wanted him to.

"You're looking beautiful," he said simply. "I've missed you, Jess."

His capacity to deliver lines like that with ringing sincerity was one of the reasons she'd put up with tuna and spaghetti for two years. That, and his ability to make her laugh. For the first year, she'd even considered the laughter a worthwhile trade-off for the dirty socks and Dan's total failure to assume any responsibility for their financial well-being. Thankfully, she was now not only older, but also wiser. Compliments, however velvet-smooth, didn't make up for a lack of real honest-to-God caring. When you turned the whole of life into a joke, it was easy to forget that some things aren't funny.

"Why are you in Denver?" she asked crisply. "I assume you're not part of the Japanese trade delegation."

"No," he said. "I'm here to see you. We have to talk, Jess—"

"Sorry, Dan, but I'm not in the mood for reminiscing about old times. Now, if you'll excuse me, I have work to do."

"This is important, Jess. How long before you can get away? We really need to talk."

"*We* don't really need to do anything, Dan. What *I* need to do is to work this room, to explain to these people some of the unique advantages of doing business in the state of Colorado. That's what I'm paid for—"

"Let's make a deal. I'll help you sell the trade delegation on the wonders of Colorado, and then, in return, you agree to come out to dinner with me."

She shook her head, although she knew that if he set his mind to it, Dan could sell Alaskans on the idea of buying Rocky Mountain snow. "No, thanks, Dan. Goodbye. And don't follow me, or I'll tell one of the security guards you crashed the party."

She turned to go, but Dan intercepted her. "You always did assume the worst about me, didn't you, Jess? As it happens, I was invited to this reception."

She raised an eyebrow. "How astonishing."

Dan's mouth tightened. "Stop sniping, Jess, this isn't about us. Matt sent me. You need to hear me out, someplace we won't be interrupted."

She looked up, alarmed by the sudden edge to his voice. "What is it? What's wrong? Is everyone okay at home?"

"Yes, they're more than okay. I'm sorry, I didn't mean to worry you—"

"Come to think of it, I haven't spoken to them for a couple of weeks. You're sure they're all right?"

He nodded. "They're great, all of them. Matt and Nancy arranged a huge family picnic last weekend, and everyone seemed fighting fit."

"You went to see them? In Cleveland?" Dan was a dyed-in-the-gas-fumes New Yorker. Seeing him in Denver, fresh from a side trip to Cleveland, was a little like seeing Santa Claus and the reindeer frolicking on a Florida beach.

"Matt invited me to come visit. You know we're friends."

Yes, she knew Matt and Dan were still friends. She considered that a rare lapse in judgment on the part of her adoptive brother. "Matt doesn't need to use you as his messenger," she said. "If he wants to speak to me, he can always pick up the phone."

"Not this time."

There was no longer any doubt about the edge to her ex-husband's voice. Jess's fingers tightened around the strap of her purse. "Dan, if there's a problem with somebody in my family, please tell me."

"There's a problem, but not the sort you're imagining."

"Mom and Dad are all right? I know the doctor was nagging Dad to stop smoking, threatening dire consequences if he didn't."

Dan smiled. A genuine smile, she was relieved to see. "I'm sure. Your dad hasn't smoked a cigarette in five weeks and he already looks ten years younger than the last time I saw him."

"That's great. Wonderful, in fact. And Mom?"

"Your mother's all fired up about the new school superintendent, so she's considering running for a seat on the school board. And your nieces and nephews are flourishing, although I'm not sure I can say the same about Todd. Your brother and sister-in-law looked distinctly frayed around the edges."

"They're usually placid as can be. What's wrong with them?"

"Their daughter. Your niece." Matt grinned. "Kelly's taken to wearing a ring through her nose, and she has a boyfriend with a skull and crossbones shaved into his scalp. Todd isn't sure he's going to survive her remaining three years of high school."

Jess laughed, trying to visualize her conservative older brother with a daughter who wore jewelry in her nose. "The joys of being parents to a teenager! I don't envy them the next few years. How about Matt's boys? I haven't seen them since Thanksgiving."

"The twins are…energetic," he said. "I think that's the diplomatic word to use."

"That bad, huh?"

"Worse." He grinned. "Hey, they're great kids underneath all the noise. I also got to see an assorted bunch of aunts, uncles and cousins who trooped out to Matt's house just to inspect me. I had the impression they expected me to have grown horns and a tail since you divorced me."

"You should have told them you did that long before the divorce."

For a moment, Dan looked stricken, but she chose not to apologize. Dan might be one of the world's sexiest hunks, but he'd been a lousy husband, his self-absorbed indifference to her needs bordering on cruelty. And that was before he started cheating on her.

He spoke doggedly. "I'd tell you I'm sorry about the way I behaved, Jess, but I'm sure you don't want to hear it."

"You're right. I've heard all your excuses and apologies before. Multiple versions of them, in fact. So, if you'll excuse me—"

"Jess, I already told you I'm not here to hash over the debris of our marriage. This is about you. When Matt heard I was coming to Denver, he made me promise that I'd meet with you and explain a problem he's run into. Give me the chance to explain the situation the way he wanted me to. Hear me out, Jess."

Fear fluttered in the pit of her stomach. "If you're trying to scare me, Dan, you're doing a fine job of it."

"I didn't mean to scare you. The opposite, in fact. Jess, let's circulate, do our stuff, and then go find some place quiet to eat dinner."

For all his faults, Dan would never try to wrangle a dinner with her by suggesting Matt had a problem when he didn't. Obviously Dan was the bearer of bad news. Jess toyed with the idea of insisting that he explain immediately but, unfortunately, she knew he was right. A reception at the governor's mansion wasn't the time or place to discuss a family crisis, particularly since she was at the reception to work, not play.

"All right," she agreed. "We'll have dinner. But I need to speak with a couple of the trade delegates first."

She made the rounds, finding herself perversely grateful to have Dan at her side. As far as she knew, he hadn't spent more than a couple of weeks in Colorado in his entire life, but he threw himself into the role of official state booster with enthusiasm. With so much, in fact, that one of the Japanese assistant deputy undersecretaries made an appointment with her to discuss scheduling a regular series of vacation charter flights directly into the new Denver International Airport, and the commercial attaché from the Japanese embassy in Washington requested a guided tour of military bases that were being decommissioned for civilian development. Precisely the sort of discussions that could lead to lucrative business investments for the state of Colorado.

In the old days, Dan's ability to fake his way to success would have driven her crazy. Tonight, she was too busy worrying about Matt to be anything other than appreciative. "Okay to leave?" he asked her quietly as the trade delegation prepared to move on to their official dinner with the mayor.

She nodded. "Yes, let's get out of here. Do you have a car?"

"No, I came by cab."

She drove them to the Cajun Kettle, one of her favorite restaurants that happened to be reasonably close to the governor's mansion. The chef was a native of New Orleans, and his menu was guaranteed to spice up the dullest evening. Not that Jess anticipated being bored. Boredom had never been one of the problems in her relationship with Dan. Almost everything else, but never boredom.

They ordered seafood, cooked with a traditional hot sauce of tomatoes and green peppers. The waiter opened their bottle of merlot, put a basket of bread on the table, then silently disappeared, his instincts apparently telling him that this was not a couple who wanted to indulge in chitchat.

Jess discovered that sitting across the table from Dan was bringing back a lot of memories she'd have preferred remain buried. Anxious to keep the time they spent together to a minimum, she cut straight to the point. "What's up with Matt?" she asked.

It seemed to her that Dan hesitated a split second before he answered. "He and Nancy have decided to put your grandfather's house up for sale. They say they're going to move to the suburbs. They have their hearts set on a four-bedroom colonial in Bay Village."

Jess rolled her eyes. "I've heard that story before. I'll believe it when I see Matt's signature on the sales contract."

"I guess he's serious this time. He and Nancy have signed on with a Realtor, they've trimmed the trees and painted all the walls off-white. There's a For Sale sign in the front yard." Dan cleared his throat. "They even spent one of their vacation weeks in the attic, cleaning through all the junk up there."

Dan shifted uncomfortably, as if he were reporting that Matt had been caught cheating on his income tax return. He swirled the wine in his glass, not drinking it. He cleared his throat again. "Your brother said there were trunks and boxes with stuff in them that dated back to the turn of the century."

"I can believe it," Jess said. "We used to play in the attic sometimes on rainy afternoons. Much more fun than the basement, which always smelled of mildew. There were trunks of old clothes up there, I remember. And broken-down oddments of furniture that must be old enough to qualify as antiques by now."

"That's what Matt told me. Most of the stuff went straight to the dump, of course. But Nancy's rescued a beautiful chest of drawers and some silk dresses that look ratty to me, but she says they're quite valuable."

"Nancy always was a whiz with a needle, so I guess she'd know." Jess watched as Dan took a hefty swallow of wine, his fingers crumbling a piece of bread he didn't seem to realize he was holding. What wasn't he telling her? Why, for heaven's sake, were they discussing her brother's efforts to clean up the attic in their old family home? She shivered, feeling a sudden chill. In her experience, Dan didn't find it difficult to deliver bad news. He'd looked less uncomfortable than this the night he told her he'd blown their rent money on a ticket to L.A.—on the chance that he would be allowed to audition for a part in a TV sitcom. He'd looked a *lot* less worried than this the memorable Sunday morning he strolled into their apartment and told her he'd slept with Shanna Ryan, because she might be able to get him a walk-on part in a new play opening somewhere off-off-Broadway.

Jess cut off the painful memories with the expertise she'd acquired during her three-year battle to cure her addiction to Dan Stratton. "You're making me nervous as hell," she said. "Stop trying to cushion the blow, Dan, and tell me what's bothering you. What's Matt found buried in the attic?" She smiled shakily, trying to calm her own fears by making a feeble joke. "Or wait, let me guess. He's come across a document proving our ancestors sneaked into the country on forged papers, so we're all illegal aliens."

Dan didn't smile. "Not quite," he said. "But you're on the right track. He *did* find some surprising documents up there among your grandfather's belongings." Dan opened the briefcase he'd been carrying—the first time she'd ever seen him carry such a symbol of corporate conformity—and took out two bundles of papers, pushing the thicker sheaf toward her. "Read these. Matt found them hidden among your grandfather's personal papers."

She took the bundle and quickly glanced through it. The waiter returned, but she only noticed their meals had arrived because she had to move the papers so he could find room for their plates. Dan seemed equally uninterested in his food. "Take your time," he said, pushing his plate to the side. "We have all night if need be."

Jess sorted through the pile of papers and photos Matt had found in the attic of the old Zajak house. They all concerned Elena and Rudolph Pazmany, her birth parents, the couple who'd died in a tragic car accident when she was four. Most of the documents were familiar, since the Zajaks had done their best to provide her with as much information as possible about her birth parents. At the time of the accident, Gene Zajak was already a widower, and too old to become an adoptive parent, but a couple of years later, his son and daughter-in-law had applied to adopt Jess. Frank and Barbara Zajak had been the most wonderful substitute parents any orphaned child could have wished for, and Jess loved them unreservedly and with deep gratitude, just as she loved her adoptive brothers, Matt and Todd.

Since no Pazmany relatives had been found, except cousins still trapped in Communist Hungary, the adoption had gone through quickly, with a minimum of fuss. When the adoption was finalized, the Zajaks made sure that Jess knew as much as possible about her "real" mother and father. Frank had gone to the Child Welfare Bureau and collected the Pazmanys' personal effects,

which the social workers had been holding ever since the
authorities in Queens, New York, cleaned out the apartment where the Pazmanys had been living before they died.

In addition to all the mementos from Queens, Grandpa
Gene had made a little scrapbook of clippings from the
Cleveland Plain Dealer, recounting the story of that cold,
wintry night when he'd found Jessica Marie huddled beneath the wrecked car containing the maimed and lifeless
bodies of her mother and father. Afraid of causing her
distress, he hadn't shown her the scrapbook until after she
graduated from college, but his tact had been unnecessary. Her birth parents were such shadowy figures in Jess's
mind that their death had almost no personal meaning.
She'd always enjoyed listening to Grandpa Gene's carefully sanitized version of how he found her hiding beneath the wheels of a car and brought her home to live with
his son and daughter-in-law. The fact that her birth parents died a horrible death had never seemed quite as real
or important as the fact that Grandpa Gene took her home
to Barbara and Frank, her new mother and father, and
that Matt and Todd became her very own brothers.

There were a couple of photos among the papers, both
of them familiar. One showed Elena and Rudolph Pazmany on their wedding day, outside city hall. Jess had
grown up with a copy of this photo, set in a silver frame,
standing on her bedside table. The other picture was a
faded color snapshot of herself in Elena Pazmany's arms.
Years ago, Grandpa Gene had paid to have the snapshot
restored and enlargements made. Jess had always liked the
picture. Baby Jessica slept peacefully, bundled in shawls,
one tiny hand poking out from the wrappings. Jess wished
that she could remember her birth mother, but she'd never
felt any sense of kinship with the woman in the photo, let
alone with the sleeping infant. Nevertheless, she'd always

taken comfort from the fact that mother Elena and baby Jessica looked as if they liked each other very much.

Jess turned the photo over and read the familiar inscription: *Jessica Marie Pazmany, age two weeks. Our beautiful little daughter!* She smiled softly, the words still retaining their power to tug at her heart. In some ways, the words had always been more meaningful to her than the picture, confirmation that Elena Pazmany had been a loving mother.

Putting the photos to one side, Jess shuffled through the remaining papers. A copy of Elena Pazmany's baptismal certificate, showing that her maiden name had been Korda. A copy of Rudolph Pazmany's immigration documents. Their wedding certificate. Her own birth certificate, showing she was born in New York Hospital at 9:35 p.m. on November 11, 1965, and that she'd weighed seven pounds seven ounces. There were also death certificates for Elena and Rudolph Pazmany, dated December 9, 1969.

It made Jess sad to think that she had never had the chance to know the people who had given her life, but the sadness was nothing new. She'd lived with the knowledge of her parents' death from earliest childhood, and the pain of her loss had been tempered because the entire Zajak family had showered her with so much love. Nowadays, she sometimes went for weeks at a stretch without remembering that, for the first few years of her life, she'd had a different set of parents. When people commented that she didn't look like anyone else in the Zajak family, she always felt a little jolt of shock at the reminder she was adopted.

"Thank you for showing me these," she said to Dan. "May I keep them? Actually, I think Grandpa Gene had already given me copies of almost everything that's here except the scrapbook with all the newspaper clippings and my parents' death certificates. I really appreciate that you took the time to give them to me personally, Dan, but Matt worries too much. There's nothing here to upset me.''

Dan continued to look alarmingly grim. ''There are another couple of things for you to see, Jess. Here. You need to take a look.'' He pushed the packet he'd been holding across the table.

The second packet was a manila envelope, addressed in a distinctive European script to Mr. Eugene Zajak, but it hadn't been mailed from overseas. The stamp was American and the postmark read Cleveland. Carefully, Jess pulled out the contents: a letter, tightly written on a single thin sheet of onionskin paper, a photo and a New York City Certificate of Death. She saw the name at the top of the death certificate. *Jessica Marie Pazmany.* Her mouth went dry, and she quickly turned the certificate over so that the name—her name—wasn't staring up at her. What did it mean? Who had died? She decided to deal with that later. Her hands shaking, she separated the photo from the letter and examined the picture with blank incomprehension.

The photo showed a couple with a young child, a little girl. Jess recognized Rudolph and Elena Pazmany at once, but she couldn't begin to guess the identity of the child pictured with them. The photo was typical of the holiday portraits Sears and other department stores had been taking for years. Against a background of Christmas baubles hanging from a branch of fake pine, the Pazmanys sat and smiled stiffly into the camera. On her lap, Elena Pazmany held a little girl, who couldn't have been more than two years old at the outside. She had hazel eyes and wispy, straight brown hair, fixed in two endearingly ridiculous braids, garnished with giant tartan ribbons. The child was wearing a scarlet velvet dress, white socks and shiny black patent-leather Mary Janes. The clothes Elena and Rudolph wore looked as if they might have seen better days. Everything the child had on was obviously brand, spanking new.

"But where am I in this photo?" Jess asked in bewilderment. She stared at the child seated on Elena Pazmany's lap and realized that, for no reason she could identify, she felt sick. "Have you looked at this photo?" she asked Dan, shoving it across the table. "Who is she? The kid in the photo, I mean. Oh, God—she must be my sister! Is that it? But she doesn't look anything like me! Are you telling me I had a sister I never knew about?" Hope and excitement flared briefly. "Is she alive and trying to find me? That would be so wonderful!"

"No, she's not alive." Dan looked at Jess, not at the picture. "Read the letter," he said, and took another gulp of wine.

It was easier to follow Dan's instructions than to think. Right now, Jess wasn't sure she wanted to think. She smoothed out the letter, which was dated September 19, 1980, and read it through twice before she even began to grasp what it meant.

Dear Lieutenant Zajak,
Do you remember me? I am Magda Mizensky and eleven years ago you came to my apartment to ask me many questions about Rudolph and Elena Pazmany, who were killed while they drive to visit me. As I told you, I have known Rudolph since he was young man, living in refugee camp with me in Vienna. He has kind and generous heart. Elena is also a good girl and she made Rudolph a good wife. I was sad like I was his mother when I went to the morgue and knew they were dead.

When you talked to me, you ask about Jessica, their little girl, my godchild. And now I must tell you why I write, because I am dying and my priest has warned me that God wants us to die with light hearts and clean souls. Many years ago, you asked me if Rudolph and Elena had a little daughter and I said yes. I say it because it is true. Rudolph and Elena had a daughter. At first I did not understand your questions, and so I agreed that the name of their child was Jessica Marie and that she was about four years old. What I said was true, and I did not mean to lie. Later, when I read the newspapers, I understood I have made a mistake. You believe Jessica Marie is still alive, but that cannot be. Jessica Marie was dead already seven months when you ask me those questions, and I knew that she was dead because I had cried with Rudolph on the phone when he told me of their loss. She died with leukemia in a hospital in New York but now I do not remember the name of that hospital.

You will ask why I did not come to you when I realize my mistake. Why did I not come and tell you that Jessica Marie Pazmany was dead months before there is accident which kills Rudolph and Elena? I can only explain you that I passed four years in Nazi prison camp, and four more years in prison camp run by the Communists who stole my country. After such a life, you learn never to give police answers to questions they do not ask. When you come to my apartment, you ask me if Rudolph and Elena have a daughter. You did not ask me if their daughter had died, and so I did not tell you that she had. Later, when I know you have identified another child as Jessica Marie, I do not correct your mistake. I was

afraid that you will punish me for having told you
wrong information the first time you ask.

I send you here the last picture that I have of Rudolph, his wife, Elena and my little goddaughter,
Jessica Marie Pazmany. Rudolph and Elena were
good people. I have not knowledge why they came to
Cleveland, but it was for important reasons, they told
me that on the phone, before their car was crashed. I
have not knowledge why they came here with a child
who was not their child. I do not know the name of
the child you found. I know only that she was not
Jessica Marie Pazmany and that I swear.

Signed,
Magda Mizensky

Jess finished reading the letter for the second time. The
smell of seafood soaked in Tabasco was suddenly overwhelming, and she pushed her plate violently away, afraid
she might be sick. Dan leaned across the table, cradling her
hands in his. She stared down at his thumb stroking her
knuckles, and she had the odd sensation that only this
small point of her flesh still belonged to her. The rest of her
body was gone, destroyed by the spidery strokes of Magda
Mizensky's pen.

"That must be Jessica Pazmany in the Christmas
photo," Jess said. Her voice came out thin with shock.
"The real Jessica Marie." She glanced furtively at the
photo, as if she had no right to intrude on the Pazmanys'
holiday cheer. "She's cute, isn't she?"

"Very cute," Dan said neutrally. "It's sad to think that
she died so soon after that photo was taken."

Jess picked up the old snapshot of Elena Pazmany
holding the swaddled infant, glancing from the baby to the
little girl in the Christmas portrait. The newborn didn't

look especially like the girl sitting on Elena Pazmany's lap.
But then, the swaddled infant didn't look anything like
Jess, either. Newborns simply looked like newborns.

Jess gently ran her forefinger over the familiar images of
mother and baby. "I always loved this picture, but that
baby isn't me, is it? It's the real Jessica Pazmany, not me."

"I expect so, although it's hard to tell with such a young
baby."

Jess ripped the photo clean down the middle, then stared
in horror at what her hands had done. "Oh my God, I
never meant to do that."

Dan quickly picked up the pieces of torn snapshot and
shoved them into his jacket pocket. "It's okay, Jess," he
said softly. "It's okay."

"Why didn't he tell me?" The words seemed ripped
from the depths of her soul. She poked savagely at Magda's letter. "It's dated 1980. Sixteen years ago. Thirteen
years before Grandpa Gene died. He had no right to keep
this information a secret from me all those years."

"No, he didn't," Dan agreed. "But you were fourteen,
remember, and a sophomore in high school when he got
this letter. You'd been part of the Zajak family for almost
eleven years. Are you sure you would have wanted to handle this sort of information at that point in your life?
Think about it. Teenagers have so much to worry about,
maybe he felt you couldn't deal with an identity crisis on
top of everything else. I'm sure your grandfather acted
with the best of intentions."

"He's not my grandfather," Jess said, her heart aching
with real physical pain. "I don't have the faintest idea who
my grandfather is."

"Of course you do," Dan said with unexpected brisk-
ness. "Barbara and Frank have been your parents for the
past twenty-six years. Gene Zajak was your grandfather,

and Matt and Todd are your brothers. Nothing's changed."

"Everything's changed," she said flatly. "Who am I? Where did I come from? Why was I in the Pazmanys' car? Why didn't my real birth parents step forward and claim me? Didn't they care that I was gone? Did some desperate single mom give me away to the Pazmanys as a replacement for Jessica Marie? Or did the Pazmanys go mad with grief when their own daughter died and kidnap me?"

"We don't have the answers to any of those questions yet," Dan said. "But we'll find them, Jess. Todd's a detective, he'll know how to set about finding answers—" He broke off. "What is it? What's wrong?"

"Jess. You called me Jess. But that isn't my name, is it?" She squinted sideways at the Christmas photo again, shamed by a surge of childish jealousy. "That's *her* name, and she's dead."

"That's not the way to look at things," Dan said. "You've been Jessica Marie for the past twenty-six years. I think you've earned the right to consider the name as much yours as hers. Hell, it's much more yours than hers after all this time."

Jess felt the stirring of old fears and forgotten memories. She shivered, chilled by a wave of long-suppressed dread. For the first time in years, she heard the scream of brakes, the crash of metal on metal, the smell of burning rubber and spilled fuel. With sudden startling clarity, she saw the unfamiliar face of a strange man peering down beneath the bumper of the car, intruding into her hiding place. Although she knew the face belonged to Grandpa Gene, she saw it with the terrified eyes of the child she had once been. Instinctively, inside the memory, she crawled away, hiding, protecting herself from discovery.

The vivid memory faded, but the tendrils of the past reached out, sending her a last frantic warning, yelling inside her head that she must never tell anyone the truth or something terrible would happen.

With savage anger, Jess pushed the warnings away. After all of these years, it was time to confront her past, to peel away the layers of forgetfulness she had so carefully bandaged over the aching wound of her fears. She looked up and stared straight into Dan's eyes.

"My name is Liliana," she said, the name tasting foreign on her tongue after so many years of silence. "I'm not Jessica Marie Pazmany, I'm Liliana."

Two

Liliana? Where in the world had that name sprung from? Shocked into silence, Dan stared across the table at the woman who had once been his wife. In the years since their divorce, he'd managed to convince himself that she couldn't possibly be as desirable as his memories of her. From his first glimpse of her at the governor's mansion tonight, he realized he'd been fooling himself. All night long, physical desire had been like a barbed steel thread winding its way through his other feelings, tightening around his lungs, making it difficult to breathe. Now, even desire collapsed under the weight of his astonishment.

He finally recovered his voice. "What do you mean, your name is Liliana? What are you talking about, Jess? You've never mentioned that name before."

She hunched into herself, looking small and fragile, and almost as bewildered as he felt. She glanced down at the papers still piled in front of her, but Dan was sure she didn't see them.

"I don't know what I meant. The name just came to me." Her voice was soft, husky with doubt. She poked aimlessly at the letter from Magda Mizensky, twisting it around their plates, as if seeing it sideways or upside down would make its contents easier to understand. "I had this sudden weird flash of memory, back to the night of the accident. I felt as though I was right there, under the car, smelling spilled gas, and hearing police sirens blaring.''

"You've never been able to recall any of your life from before the accident, have you?''

"Not until now.'' Jess stirred, her gaze shifting, but never managing to settle. "I was scared that night, really scared. But I'd never been on a plane before, so that may have been why. I remember we rode in a bus to the airport, and we sat right in the back, away from the other passengers. Ralph and Lena told me the police were looking for me. They made me promise I wouldn't tell anyone that my real name was Liliana. They told me we had to pretend I was their little girl, otherwise something bad would happen to me. Something awful. But I don't remember what.''

She'd called Rudolph Pazmany *Ralph,* Dan noticed, and she'd called Elena *Lena.* He decided not to mention that confusing detail to her, at least for the moment, in case he jolted her out of the flow of memories. He tightened his hand around hers, rubbing his thumb gently across her knuckles, offering comfort he knew she would never have accepted from him if shock hadn't left her too numb and battered to protest.

"Why do you think the Pazmanys told you to keep your real name secret, Jess? What bad thing was going to happen to you? Can you remember why you had to pretend to be their daughter?''

She finally stopped fiddling with the letter and looked up. Her unusually deep blue eyes were always striking, but tonight they appeared huge against the stark pallor of her cheeks. She was so beautiful it made his throat ache to look at her. "I was hiding from my daddy,'' she said. "We didn't want my daddy to find me. My daddy's mean.''

The hairs on the back of Dan's neck stood up at the sudden childish pipe of her voice. "Why didn't you want your father to find you, Jess? Why did you think he was mean? What had he done?"

She pursed her lips in a babyish pout, considering. Then she shook her head and her frightened, infantile expression was replaced by one of adult mystification. "I don't know," she said, dragging herself out of the clutches of the past with perceptible effort. "But it wasn't just Ralph and Lena who wanted to hide me from my father, I'm sure of that. I wanted to hide from him, too."

A custody battle, Dan thought. Maybe that's what this had been about. A routine custody battle that went tragically awry when the Pazmanys got killed. "What about your mother?" he asked. "What can you remember about her?"

Jess stared into the past, straining to catch at an elusive memory. "I don't remember anything about her," she said finally. "There's nothing there, just blankness."

Odd. If she could remember that her father was mean, surely she ought to remember something about her mother? "Can't you probe the blankness a little bit, Jess? There ought to be a couple of memories lurking in the back of your mind, now that you know where to look."

"But I don't know where to look. I don't really remember anything about my life before the day of the accident." She plucked at a loose thread in the hem of her table napkin. "Maybe the Pazmanys were trying to help me escape from abusive parents. If I can't remember my mother, and I remember wanting to hide from my father, my parents can't have been very nice people, can they? Perhaps that's why the Pazmanys taught me to lie about my name. If they rescued me from a bad home, naturally they wouldn't want my parents to find me."

"If they took you without permission, that's still kidnapping in the eyes of the law," he reminded her. "However rotten your birth parents might have been."

"Technically, I suppose, but I'm sure the Pazmanys were good people, Dan." She speared a shrimp with her fork, but didn't actually get it as far as her mouth. "They must have been good people. Whenever I get a memory flash about them, I feel all warm and...*cared for.*"

She sounded desolate at the prospect of abandoning her lifelong image of the Pazmanys as loving parents and solid, upstanding citizens. Her gaze kept flickering to the alien Jessica Marie in the Christmas photo, and Dan could see that she was close to tears. Knowing how much she hated to display emotional turmoil, he used the excuse of pouring them each another glass of wine to push the picture out of sight, under a folder. Her eyes drifted gratefully closed, and when she opened them again, she smiled at him with determined brightness.

He'd always hated those false smiles, calculated to insure that he kept his distance. He wished he had the right to lead her out of here, take her to the privacy of his hotel room and hold her in his arms until she cried out her bewilderment and sense of loss. Having the Pazmanys torn from their role as loving birth parents must be as wrenching as hearing that someone she loved had died. Unfortunately, he knew that if he put his arm anywhere near her, she was as likely to throw a punch at his jaw as to sob on his shoulder. When he'd screwed up his relationship with Jess, he'd screwed it up big-time.

He leaned across the table and spoke crisply, the way she always wanted him to. Jess was a great believer in shoving untidy emotions into neat, well-wrapped boxes. "You know, Jess, you probably shouldn't make too much of your snippets of memory, vivid as they may seem. You might want to consider finding a psychologist who has expertise in this area. A professional counselor would help you put your memories into perspective—"

Ignoring him as completely as if he hadn't spoken, he could see her gaze turn inward. "I remember I was sitting in the back of the car, and I had a pillow on my lap with a seat belt around it. After the crash, I remember unfastening my own seat belt and tumbling out into the freezing cold. I scooted under the car because I was terrified by the noise and it seemed safer under there. When Grandpa Gene told me to come out, I was scared...."

"Why was that? He had a friendly, lived-in sort of face. Weren't you glad to be rescued?"

"He said he was a policeman—"

"And that frightened you?"

"Yes, I think it did." She frowned. "I guess I was remembering that Ralph and Lena told me to keep away from policemen and not to tell anyone my name. I don't know why they'd said that, though."

"I can think of half a dozen reasons," Dan said, his voice very dry.

She didn't respond. Her fingers tapped nervously against Jessica Marie's death certificate. "Grandpa Gene was wearing a leather jacket, and there were snowflakes melting on his collar. They tickled my cheek when he picked me up. The tip of his nose was bright red and he smelled of cigarettes, the same cigarette smell as Uncle Ralph—"

She broke off with a small nervous laugh. "That's what I called him, you know. *Uncle Ralph.* Not Rudolph, or even Uncle Rudolph. *Uncle Ralph.* No wonder it always felt so strange to think of him as my father. Somewhere deep inside me, I knew he wasn't."

Little girls were taught to call older men *uncle* for all sorts of reasons, some benign, some not so benign, Dan reflected. "What did you call Elena?" he asked.

Jess thought for a moment. "Auntie Lena," she announced triumphantly. "I called her Auntie Lena."

Despite his reservations about the validity of her memories, Jess's smile was so glowing that Dan couldn't help smiling back. He knew she'd always been troubled by her inability to remember her past, although she'd never allowed him to see the extent of her worry, even in the early days of their relationship when she'd still trusted him, at least a little. Of course, her early trust had soon evaporated into scorn, and her tentative confidences had rapidly withered into silence. Jess had scant patience for a man who was failing in his chosen career, and even less patience for somebody who seemed to wallow in his own angst. She believed that brisk efficiency, coupled with a positive attitude, would take care of whatever problems fate hurled at you. If your heart broke, or your illusions shattered, she would expect you to wear a clean shirt and cheerful smile while you picked up the pieces. It was a very practical philosophy of life, but it meant that, while he'd wasted entire days drowning in a black funk of creative terror, Jess had been unable to see the ocean of self-doubt that incapacitated him. Oddly, after years of wishing his ex-wife would one day be forced to acknowledge the demons lurking beneath her well-lacquered surface, he now found himself hoping the letter from Magda Mizensky wasn't going to prove the weapon that would shatter her hard-won veneer of confidence.

Jess reached clumsily for her glass of water. "It's bizarre, isn't it? Yesterday—two hours ago—I was quite sure Elena and Rudolph Pazmany were my birth parents. Now

I remember clearly that I called them Uncle Ralph and Auntie Lena. Why couldn't I remember that before?''

"I think you know why," Dan said quietly. "If you'd allowed yourself to remember, then you'd have been forced to question everything your adoptive family taught you to believe about yourself.''

"But why would I want to believe a lie?''

"Because you were a bewildered little girl, with every reason to be confused about what was happening to you. The Zajaks took you in and showered you with love. It isn't surprising that it was much easier to suppress your own memories than to question the basis on which Barbara and Frank welcomed you into their family.''

Jess looked unconvinced, but before she could say anything, their waiter returned. He appeared taken aback by the sight of their full plates of food. "Is something wrong with your dinners, folks?'' he asked.

Dan shook his head. "No, nothing. I'm sorry, we just realized we weren't hungry, after all. Jess, is it all right if he clears everything away?''

"Yes, please." She turned to the waiter, seemingly in complete control of herself. She might be torn apart inside, Dan thought, but she already had her public image back in almost full working order. "I'm really sorry about wasting the food. I'm sure the meal was as delicious as always.''

"No problem.'' The waiter removed their loaded plates with determined courtesy. "How about dessert? There's always room for a piece of our Louisiana chocolate-mud pie.''

Jess kept her smile but didn't answer, confirming Dan's belief that her composure was about as solid as a marshmallow. "Perhaps some coffee," he suggested, and she flashed him a smile of genuine gratitude.

Dan nodded to the waiter. "Two regular coffees, please, with cream but no sugar."

"Yes, sir. Coming right up."

Jess made no comment on the fact that, without prompting, Dan had remembered how she liked her coffee. She was probably as anxious as he was to avoid any reference, however fleeting, that might set them spinning on a dangerous trip down memory lane. Their marital past was not a subject to be broached lightly. Even Uncle Ralph and Auntie Lena, parents-turned-possible-kidnappers, seemed relatively harmless by comparison.

Jess held the death certificate for Jessica Marie up to the light. "You know, something's just occurred to me. How do we know this is genuine?" She ran her fingers over the raised notary seal that supposedly guaranteed a certified copy of an official entry into state of New York records. "Maybe Grandpa Gene investigated Magda Mizensky's letter and discovered that her entire story was fraudulent. Maybe that's why he never said anything to me—"

"It's possible," Dan agreed. "Your parents almost decided to do some preliminary investigating before telling you about Magda's letter. I convinced them that you were entitled to know what she'd written, even if it turns out to be an old woman's crazy idea of a joke."

"You were right, thank you. I'd have been furious if they'd concealed this information. I'm having a hard enough time accepting that my grandfather kept this letter to himself all those years."

"He was only thinking of you, Jess. You know he always had your best interests at heart," he repeated.

"Yes, I do know that." She sighed. "For some reason, the entire Zajak tribe always wants to protect me. Despite massive evidence to the contrary, nobody in my family believes that I'm capable of taking care of myself. I don't understand why they have such a hard time recognizing that I have a steel spine and a cast-iron nervous system.''

The fact that she looked as if she belonged in a book of Victorian fairy tales might explain the Zajaks' determination to establish themselves as a permanent barricade between Jess and reality. Still, Dan had no intention of mentioning this. In keeping with her determination to fit right into the solid, salt-of-the-earth Zajak family, his ex-wife hated to be reminded of her ethereal appearance.

''Right now, all we can say about Magda's letter is that it might be a fraud. It's also possible she told nothing but the truth, and the death certificate's entirely genuine,'' he said. ''That's the whole point, Jess, isn't it? We need to stop speculating and start gathering some solid, hard facts. Our first rule ought to be *no leaping to conclusions*. We don't want to compound the mistakes that may have already occurred by making new ones of our own.'' He paused for a moment, then went on, ''What we know for sure is that Elena and Rudolph Pazmany died in a car crash and that you were found underneath the wheels of their wrecked car. That's it, Jess, we don't *know* anything else.''

''*Our* first rule? *We* don't know?'' Jess speared him with a gaze that was suddenly clear and sharply focused. ''I appreciate the tacit offer of help, Dan, but when did we decide that you would be involved in investigating my murky past? For that matter, who decided *anybody* was going to start inquiring into Magda Mizensky's claims? Certainly not me.''

''You're just going to *ignore* Magda's letter?'' Dan shook his head. ''Even for you, that's carrying willful blindness a bit far.''

She flushed angrily. ''That remark's so typical of you, Dan. My grandfather can keep this information hidden in his attic for thirteen years, and that earns nothing from you except a shrug of the shoulders. But when I say that I think it's too late to launch an investigation, you accuse me of refusing to face unpleasant facts. In my opinion, it's too late to start worrying about the truth or falsity of what Magda wrote. If I was wrongly identified, the mistake was made twenty-six years ago, and I've been Jessica Marie Zajak for most of my life. Does it really matter whether I was born Jessica Marie Pazmany, or Liliana Something, or even Unknown, fill in the blank?''

"It matters," Dan said, fighting a familiar surge of frustration at Jess's attitude. Under the guise of common sense and practicality, she hid painful emotions she was too scared to explore. Old demons from their marriage returned to snap at him. "I realize this news has been unwelcome, Jess, but that doesn't mean you can ignore it."

"Sure I can. It's stale news, with no significance in my current life."

"How do you know it's stale?" He spoke more curtly than he intended. "Suppose you have two loving birth parents who've spent years grieving for their lost daughter? If they exist, don't you owe it to them to be in touch? At least to let them know you're alive and well? And that's only one reason why you can't just walk away from this information as if you'd never been given it."

The color drained from Jessica's cheeks, leaving her skin a ghostly gray. She took another swallow of ice water, her teeth rattling against the glass, before she could answer him. He watched her as she pulled herself together and even managed to give a fairly convincing shrug. It was one of the things he'd always admired most about her—admired and simultaneously loathed—her incredible capacity to cope with the blows life hurled at her without any help, especially from him. Their marriage had been a wasteland of his inadequacy, made habitable only by her superachievements. Which, of course, had only made him feel more inadequate and more resentful of her accomplishments.

He shook off the dead weight of their past, determined to make her acknowledge her own needs, at least to herself. "For God's sake, don't hide from your feelings, Jess, not this time. You owe it to yourself to find out how much of Magda's letter is true, even if you don't owe it to anyone else."

Her smile broke for a moment, but she soon recaptured it, more sparkling and more obstinate than before. "I'll take your advice into consideration, Dan. And I want you to know that I sincerely appreciate your taking the time to bring me this information in person. You were absolutely right, I'd have hated to hear something like this over the phone from Matt or my parents. But now that you've shown me Magda's letter and held my hand while I came unglued, it's the end of your involvement. Thank you for being so understanding, and for taking the time to fly all the way out here."

His gaze narrowed. "I take it you're now through with coming unglued and plan to reconstitute yourself immediately into the standard Jessica Zajak model of self-assured efficiency?"

"There's a limit to how long it's reasonable to fret over something that's ancient history," she said with cool indifference to his sarcasm. "It's time to move on."

"I see. So the letter from Magda Mizensky is now going to be put in *your* attic, after spending years being hidden in Gene Zajak's. As far as you're concerned, there's no fact so unpleasant that it can't be ignored, right?"

"Something like that," she told him. "You know I'm a great believer in letting sleeping dogs lie unless there's a very good reason to wake them. You may remember it was one of the things you found most profoundly annoying about me.''

She sounded polite, almost friendly. Insults, of course, had never provoked her into the cleansing emotional outburst he craved, and nothing seemed to have changed in the years since their divorce. Dan watched as she drew in a slow, deep breath, smoothing away her irritation, reasserting her self-control. It took less than ten seconds for her to pound her recalcitrant emotions into subjection.

As soon as she had herself in hand, she gave him one of her very best fake smiles. ''As I said before, Dan, I sincerely appreciate your willingness to fly out here. And by the way, I'd be happy to reimburse you for the cost of your airfare to Denver. It was good of you to come chasing after me, I'd like to find some practical way to let you know how grateful I am.''

For a split second Dan was so angry he couldn't breathe. When he stopped shaking enough to think rationally, he realized he was furious chiefly because Jess had every right to assume he hovered on the verge of destitution and needed reimbursement for a five-hundred-dollar airline ticket. Fortunately, the coffee arrived before he could explode and make a total fool of himself by waving the banner of his post-divorce achievements in her face. He reminded himself that he didn't give a damn what she thought of him—he'd flown out to Denver strictly as a gesture of compassion. The fact that he still found her attractive meant only that he felt a physical urge to bed her. It didn't mean he wanted any sort of emotional involvement. Getting intimate with Jess was a bit like volunteering to cuddle a porcupine, and Dan had lost his taste for getting speared. These days he limited his cuddling to soft, silky kittens with their claws surgically removed.

By the time the waiter had finished arranging their coffee cups in front of them, Dan was once again capable of polite speech. Just barely. "Thanks for the offer, Jess, but I can afford to pay for my own airline ticket." He gulped his coffee, hoping to scald himself into silence.

For some reason, she wouldn't leave it alone. "Well, then, let me pick up the tab for dinner. Please, Dan. You shouldn't have to pay for food I didn't even eat."

He set his coffee cup in its saucer with exaggerated care. "I insist, Jess, this was my treat. Think of it as reimbursement for all the times I didn't come up with my share of the rent."

He should have quit while he was ahead. His words opened up a pit bordered by poisoned quicksand. They stared at each other, eyes haunted. Then they both jumped back from the brink. Jess reached blindly for her purse, rummaging for a tissue, and he pulled out his wallet, searching for one of his half-dozen credit cards, all of which were good for several thousand dollars. Oh, yes, Dan thought with bitter self-mockery. Now that he didn't have a wife to pay his bills, he managed to earn an annual income that was climbing briskly toward seven figures.

Jess was the first one to break the charged silence. "Will you at least let me drive you to your hotel? You might have to wait a long time for a cab at this time of night."

"Thanks, I'd appreciate a ride if it's not too much out of your way. I'm staying at the Brown Palace." Dan was stupidly, childishly glad to let her know he was staying at one of the city's oldest and most expensive hotels. Then he felt a flash of anger at himself for even caring what she thought.

In any event, Jess gave him no opportunity to boast. She didn't ask how he could afford a room at the Brown Palace, and she didn't blink when the waiter brought back his gold card with the charge for their meal approved—something that would have been close to a miracle during the years they were married. She simply gathered all the papers and pictures scattered over the table and tucked them into her briefcase, standing up to indicate when she was ready to leave. Dan followed, not even trying to make conversation. Meaningless platitudes were her thing, not his.

The night was surprisingly cool for late May, chilled by a wind sweeping in from the Rockies, carrying with it a hint of lingering high-country snow. As they walked to the parking lot, Jess shivered, juggling her purse and briefcase as she tried to button her jacket.

"Here, let me." Dan set down his briefcase and reached for the front of her jacket. When she pulled away, his hand brushed across the soft fullness of her breast. She froze into stillness, and the air around them vibrated with electric awareness, so that the sharp, shallow hiss of his own breath sounded obscenely loud in the quiet of the empty parking lot. In the amber glow of neon light, her eyes flashed with fire and her pale cheeks gleamed with smooth perfection, a poignant reminder of the golden warmth of her body.

Still, it would have been reasonably easy to pretend neither of them noticed anything amiss, to gloss over the fact that she was blushing and his breath wasn't quite steady. He knew damn well he should murmur an apology and walk on. Instead, he stood looking down at her for far too long, watching, almost abstractly, while his hand cupped the weight of her breast and his thumb brushed with deliberate provocation across her nipple.

Her lips parted and her eyes darkened. Otherwise she didn't move. Sensation flashed within him, something halfway between loathing and longing. Without any conscious decision, his head started to bend toward hers, the remembered taste of her kisses suddenly burning on his tongue.

She turned her head away, but she didn't step back. "Don't," she said, her voice strangled.

For a moment, he hovered on the brink of ignoring her protest and sweeping her into his arms. Then sanity returned. Like everything else in their marriage, sex had gone from spectacular to disastrous with the speed of light. At thirty-four, he was too old and much too jaded to gamble on a return to spectacular. Cataclysmically awful was far more likely.

"I'm sorry, Jess," he said, shoving the lapels of her jacket together and stepping away from her. "I guess it's too easy to fall into old habits when I'm near you."

"I hope not." She gathered her self-possession around her like a cloak, draping it across her shoulders, tugging its folds into prim-and-proper place. She gazed up at him with a controlled indifference that tore strips off his heart. He had a sudden, far-too-vivid memory of the last time he'd seen that expression. It had been on that hideous Sunday when he'd strolled into their tiny SoHo apartment, his stomach already burning with the acid of bitter regret, and announced with seeming casualness that he'd spent the night having sex with Shanna Ryan. Great, glorious, hot sex, the sort that Jess hadn't given him in months. The sex part had been true. The great and glorious part had been a desperate lie. God, who said he couldn't act? That little show had been the performance of a lifetime.

After Jess divorced him, it had taken him months to work out exactly why he'd chosen such a viciously hurtful method of bringing their marriage to an end. He hadn't yet managed to forgive himself for attempting to restore his sense of manhood by deliberately wounding Jess. Some nights, lying alone in the dark, he was afraid the stains of his marital failures would prove indelible.

The prospect of being shut up with his ex-wife in the confines of a Toyota Celica was suddenly unendurable. He held the door open for her. "I've decided to walk," he said. "I need the exercise."

She looked at him uncertainly. "It's very cold."

"I'll walk fast. We're only talking a mile or so. Good-bye, Jess, take care. It's been good seeing you again."

She smiled sadly. "You always were a lousy liar, Dan." She closed the car window and reversed quickly out of the parking lot, leaving him alone in the Colorado night.

When he realized he was staring at the emptiness of where Jess had so recently been, Dan turned impatiently, striding in the direction of Seventeenth Street. Yeah, he'd always been a lousy liar, especially where his feelings for Jess were concerned. But he was working hard on improving his capacity for self-deception. Any year now, he was going to convince himself he was happy as hell that she'd divorced him. Some time before his hundredth birthday, it was even possible he might decide that he didn't want to have sex with her ever again.

Dan, however, wasn't betting on it.

Three

Merton House Residential Care Facility, Durham, North Carolina
Friday, May 24, 1996

Dr. Edgar Foster, director-in-chief of Merton House, picked up the phone as soon as the orderly closed the door behind the stooped figure of Raymond Hill. He found the number for the clinic's kitchens and dialed, repressing a sigh. This morning's therapy session had not gone well. Raymond believed he was an android, with a computer modem in his brain that was linked directly to the voice of the Archangel Gabriel. Such proximity to angelic conversation usually left Raymond happy and benevolent, assured of God's personal attention. Today, however, Raymond had been miserable.

Ever since yesterday, the Archangel Gabriel had been full of wrath, infuriated by Raymond's failure to warn him that there would be no boiled eggs for breakfast. Unable to mollify the archangel with an offer of cornflakes, Raymond had spent the previous afternoon jumping on and off various pieces of furniture, trying to get back into Gabriel's good graces by learning to fly.

Things were no better this morning. The archangel still wanted boiled eggs, and he still wanted Raymond to learn to fly. Despite Ed's best efforts, the therapy session had gone from bad to worse. In midsession, Gabriel ordered Raymond to cleanse his body of poison by flying out the window into God's purifying fresh air. Ed had needed the help of two strong orderlies to prevent him.

Someone in the kitchen finally answered the phone and Ed requested that two soft-boiled eggs be immediately sent up to Raymond's room, one for Raymond and one for the Archangel Gabriel. After more than twenty-five years as a psychiatrist, he'd learned that it was sometimes smart to focus on the strictly practical, rather than the exotic trappings of a patient's delusions. If Raymond and Gabriel wanted eggs, Ed saw no reason why they shouldn't have them.

He hung up the phone, feeling a surge of familiar frustration at his inability to make Raymond's world come right, despite all the wonders of modern pharmacology. Raymond happened to be the twin brother of the famous TV newscaster, Chad Hill, and Ed always found it disheartening to see occasional flashes of the notorious Chad Hill charm thrusting its way through the wall of Raymond's psychotic fantasies.

Still, Ed had a full list of patients to see this morning. There was no point in allowing himself to dwell on Raymond's problems. He let his secretary know he was ready to see the next patient, then walked over to the office window, clearing his mind by admiring his view of the Merton House gardens. The North Carolina spring was already edging into summer: the tulip poplars were heavy with clean, rain-washed leaves, the magnolias were in full bloom and the sky was hazy with the promise of real heat by midafternoon. A perfect day to go sailing in his new catamaran.

Ed's gloom lifted at the prospect of a couple of hours on the water, alone with the sky, the sea and his boat. As the new director of Merton House, he'd spent far too much of the past month placating local dignitaries, answering stupid questions posed by government regulators and trying not to lose his temper with managers of health insurance companies who didn't know the difference between a paranoid schizophrenic and their own ass. He'd kept his temper through it all, and even managed to smile on rare occasions. Ed figured he'd earned a Friday afternoon off.

Two months ago, when he'd accepted the job at Merton House, he'd hovered on the edge of burnout. The loss of his wife to breast cancer had thrown him for a loop, leaving him drained of emotional stamina. After twenty years of working with juvenile offenders, the throwaway kids of urban society, Rosemary's death had left him with nothing more to give. He was exhausted from the constant battle to find funds, and he was resolved never again to get involved in the hopeless quest to solve the problems of a city that had outgrown its resources.

Merton House had turned out to be the haven he needed. Just being in a different state recharged his batteries. To his surprise, he'd discovered he thoroughly enjoyed being the director of an institution awash in money. Here at Merton House, he would never need to waste valuable time fund-raising. He relished the freedom from financial pressures. Astronomical fees assured that multiple physical, occupational and mental therapies were available on-site, everything from computers to crochet lessons. The residents of Merton House sure weren't neglected, Ed thought.

He turned back to his desk, checking his schedule. His next patient was Constance Howington Rodier, a 52-year-old suffering from severe depression, with intermittent psychotic hallucinations and seasonally induced panic attacks. He remembered her as a thin, mousy woman who looked every day of her age, with nothing much to say for herself. During their introductory session, she'd been so disphoric that Ed had been able to do little more than take note of her lethargy and generally blunted responses.

A buzz from his secretary and a tap at the door indicated that his patient had arrived. Constance Rodier shuffled into the room, her gaze vacant, her gait uncoordinated, her arms flapping as she walked. She stood, scuffing the toe of her slipper on the carpet, and waited for the nurse's aide to seat her in the armchair at the side of Ed's desk.

Constance dropped something on the floor, and the nurse's aide returned it to her with a cheery smile. It was a pair of glasses, Ed saw. The aide patted Constance on the shoulder. "Here you are, dear. Put them away in your pocket so's you don't lose them. That's right, dear. Tuck them deep down inside, or they'll fall out."

The attendant spoke in a slightly raised voice, as if her patient were either deaf or slow on the uptake. Even in an expensive institution like Merton House, with rigorous training programs for the staff, aides tended to treat all the residents as if they were mentally retarded. It was hard to convince them that psychosis and a high IQ could go together, at least until years of disconnection from reality began to take its toll.

Constance pulled the glasses out of her pocket again, and the aide shook her head. "Put them away, Constance, they're your reading glasses. You only need them for close work. Don't forget to bring these with you when Dr. Foster's finished, will you? You'll need them for your art class."

Constance looked up, her gray eyes sparking with the faintest hint of animation. "Is it Friday? Is Peggy coming?"

"Yes, Peggy's coming." The aide smiled, that special condescending smile the mentally healthy reserve for the mentally sick. "You'll like that, won't you, dear? You always have such a good time in sculpture class."

Constance hung her head, staring at the glasses' case in her lap. "Mmm."

The nurse's aide didn't seem at all surprised by Constance's lack of enthusiasm. She patted her on the shoulder again, and looked across at Ed. "I can come back and fetch her if you want, Dr. Foster, but she can get to the craft room by herself without any trouble, if that's all right with you."

Ed looked at Constance, who had finally returned the glasses to the breast pocket of her baggy sweater and seemed to be fully occupied with pulling a mustard-yellow thread out of the dull brown plaid of her skirt. She had apparently not noticed that spring had sprung and was still wearing a mismatched outfit drearily reminiscent of the chilliest days of February. Ed spoke gently, "Do you want Teresa to come back and walk with you to the craft room, Constance?"

Constance continued her self-appointed task of unraveling skirt threads. "I can go alone."

Despite the faint, apathetic slurring of the final syllables, her voice was low, husky and cultured. No real surprise in that. The annual fees for Merton House insured that only lunatics from the very best families were incarcerated there.

Ed nodded to the aide. "Thanks, Teresa, we probably won't need you. I'll page you if Constance changes her mind."

The door closed behind Teresa and silence hung over the room, interrupted only by the occasional scratch of Constance's fingernails against the tweed of her skirt. Ed leaned back in his chair. "I'm pleased to have this chance to chat with you again, Constance. How do you feel this morning?"

"Fine."

"That's good. Any problems sleeping or eating? Any nausea from the medication?"

She shook her head.

"Good. Is there something you'd like to talk to me about, Constance? If there's anything bothering you, I'd like to hear about it."

"No, there's nothing. I'm fine." She pulled a piece of thread from her skirt and carefully wound it into a small ball, absorbed in the simple task.

Ed went through the standard list of questions, attempting to gauge her mood, but they elicited little from her beyond monosyllables. None of the residents of Merton House felt comfortable making eye contact, but Constance seemed to have perfected the art of eye avoidance. After fifteen minutes of his one-sided conversation, she'd never once lifted her gaze from her lap. She'd also volunteered no information about herself, or her feelings, although she'd agreed, listlessly, that she'd heard no voices recently, didn't believe that anyone was out to get her and only "sometimes" felt suicidal.

"What are you going to make in art class this morning?" he asked her. "You're learning how to make clay models, aren't you? There's a note here from your craft instructor saying that you've done some very good work over the past few months."

She still didn't look up, but her voice took on a slightly firmer tone, a note of greater energy. "I like art class."

"And what exactly are you going to make this morning, Constance?"

"A chipmunk."

Whatever he'd expected her to reply, a chipmunk wasn't it. "Do you like chipmunks?" he asked.

"I like chipmunks. I like animals." She flicked the ball of thread onto the carpet and stared at it in morose fascination.

Two whole sentences, the most he'd gotten from her all morning. What's more, she'd volunteered that she liked both art class and animals. In contrast to the rest of their session, that was major self-revelation. Ed looked up from his notes. "Do you like animals better than people, Constance?"

"Of course." Her voice deepened when she added, "I'm crazy, not stupid."

Ed's hand jerked, leaving a blob of ballpoint ink on his desk blotter. He stared at Constance's hunched figure, but she was still picking at her skirt, her fingers plucking nervously.

He must have imagined the note of wry self-mockery he'd heard in her voice, Ed decided. If there was one thing he could almost guarantee about the chaotic inner world of the insane, it was that there was no room for irony in their disturbed psyches.

"Look at me, Constance," he ordered gently. He fully expected her to ignore him, but she lifted her head and shot him a long, jittery glance before dropping her head and rocking aimlessly back and forth in the chair.

Her eyes were huge, a startlingly lovely shade of gray-green, fringed by unusually long lashes. For a split second, Ed thought he'd seen rueful humor gleam somewhere in their depths before they lost focus and her habitual blurred gaze returned. He was surprised by the sharpness of his own disappointment when he saw her spark of momentary self-awareness disappear. Wanting to bring back the spark, he returned to the only subject that seemed to have provoked even a modicum of enthusiasm on her part.

"Why do you like animals better than people, Constance? Have people let you down when you needed their help?"

She shrugged. "No. I want to go now. It's time for my class and Peggy doesn't like me to be late."

Three sentences. It was the longest answer she'd ever given him, but he heard a note of real fear beneath the slurred and breathless response. "We need to chat for another few minutes," he said. "When did somebody let you down, Constance? What happened? What did they do?"

"I don't remember." The pace of her rocking increased. Ed set down his pen and leaned back in his chair. The nagging feeling that something wasn't quite right was growing stronger. Something about Constance's replies and her attitude wasn't hanging together.

"Everyone can remember some occasion when a friend or a family member let them down," he said. "It's a natural part of being human to make promises that we find out later we can't keep. Maybe your mother or father promised you a special treat that never happened. Maybe someone you loved didn't offer you help when you needed it. Maybe someone you trusted didn't live up to that trust...."

He stopped talking, but Constance didn't seem to feel any need to fill the ensuing silence by confiding some incident of betrayal from her past. She continued to rock back and forth, her chin resting on her chest, her arms wrapped protectively around her middle, a melancholy picture of self-containment and isolation. A picture-perfect portrayal, in fact, of the severely depressed patient.

She suddenly stopped rocking and sprang to her feet. She stumbled, righted herself and walked over to his desk, turning the clock around until she could see its face. "Look, it's ten fifty-five," she said. "Peggy will be here now. She'll be waiting for me. I need to go. We only have an hour of art class before I have to go to lunch."

Ed categorized her attitude as anxious rather than defiant, noticing that she made no move to leave the room, although there was nothing physically restraining her. No wonder the staff paid little attention to her, he reflected. After coping with thirty or forty variations of patients like Raymond who were trying to fly out the window to join hands with the Archangel Gabriel, it wasn't surprising that the aides and nurses were happy to ignore Constance. Except, dammit, he didn't believe she was anywhere near as quiet and docile as she appeared. Why couldn't he shake the uncomfortable feeling that he was being manipulated? That Constance Howington Rodier wasn't quite as far out of it as she seemed?

Ed always paid attention to his hunches, and he treated this one seriously. God knew, it wasn't only Hannibal Lecter who could play mind games with his doctors: many real-life psychotics were more than capable of leading their psychiatrists straight down the garden path. Cunning seemed to increase in direct proportion to desperation. However, there wasn't a single notation in Constance's file to indicate that she was anything other than a thoroughly apathetic depressive, the last sort of patient to indulge in mind games. And as for motive, why in hell would she want to create the illusion of being more removed from reality than she actually was? Of course, the question was absurd when posed in relation to someone who was certified insane.

Ed walked around his desk and sat on the corner of it, only inches away from his patient. She shrank back, recoiling from the closeness. He leaned forward, not allowing her the respite of evasion. "Constance, you can go to your sculpture class as soon as you answer a couple more questions. Do you know why you're here at Merton House?"

"I suffer from severe depression, with hallucinatory interludes, intermittent panic attacks and recurring suicidal impulses."

Nothing surprising in that admission. Contrary to popular belief, plenty of psychotic patients were aware of their own sickness and even took pleasure in reeling off the clinical symptoms. "Is that what other people say, Constance, or do you agree with the diagnosis?"

"Everyone is in agreement," she said, sounding bored.

"Including you?" Ed persisted.

"Yes," she said after a pause so small it was virtually imperceptible. "Including me."

"Why are you so depressed, Constance?"

"Because I suffer from severe depression, with hallucinatory interludes, intermittent panic attacks and recurring suicidal impulses."

Circular reasoning was one of the prime symptoms of an unhealthy pattern of thought. So why the hell did he, once again, get the feeling that Constance Rodier was playing with him? He spoke with deliberate harshness. "Merton House is a place for people who are mad. Are you mad, Constance?"

She was silent for a long time. "Yes," she said finally. "I'm mad. I belong here."

"How do you know you're mad?" Ed asked. "You told me earlier this morning that you don't hear voices, you don't have paranoid delusions, you don't think anyone's out to get you. So how did you figure out that you're mad and need to be locked up?"

This time she was silent for so long he was sure she wasn't going to answer him. She finally lifted her head and stared at him with such bleak self-loathing that he shivered. "I murdered my daughter and hid her body where nobody could find it. Now I can't even remember where I put her. Does that meet your definition of insanity, Dr. Foster? It sure as hell meets mine."

He said something in reply, but Constance didn't hear what it was. She dropped her head quickly, horrified by her own rashness. My God, she'd given herself away, she thought, trembling. This doctor wasn't like the others, despite his questions seeming as simplistic as those of any other psychiatrist she'd ever encountered. Even at their first meeting, ten days ago, she'd found herself wanting to respond to him. She'd fantasized about having a sensible conversation with him, an honest-to-God, rational discussion about the prospects for lasting peace in the Middle East, or the problem of beach erosion along the North Carolina shoreline. Anything, in fact, that was sane and normal. She'd resisted the temptation, but the danger remained. This doctor actually looked at her, not through her, and he listened to every nuance she allowed to creep into her voice.

She would have to be more careful from now on. Tonight, maybe she'd even take her medication. God knew that always left her feeling sufficiently zonked out that she didn't have to pretend to be viewing the world through a thick fog; she really was in a stupor. Until medication time, however, she would be doubly on guard. She schooled her features into the blank expression she'd perfected over years and years of practice, and allowed her gaze to drift into a haze of befuddlement.

She realized Dr. Foster was talking to her again. "Do the police know you killed your daughter?" he asked.

Of course they do. Why else do you think my family rushed to get me locked away in a maximum-security loony bin?

"The police?" Constance slurred the words, as if she couldn't quite remember who or what the police were. She found a new loose thread in her skirt and started to unravel it. "I don't know if they know," she muttered.

The thread pulled away, leaving a tiny hole, and she frowned, annoyed that it had snapped so soon. A soft, angry grunt escaped her throat, probably surprising her more than Dr. Foster. That was the trouble with adopting the quirks and mannerisms of her fellow inmates, Constance reflected wryly. After a quarter of a century, she was often no longer sure how much she was acting, and how much she was behaving in ways that had by now become ingrained habits. God help her, she actually found it soothing to pull threads from her clothing.

"Tell me about your daughter," Dr. Foster persisted. "What was her name?"

"Liliana." The name blurted out unbidden, the sound of it making her want to cry. She swallowed hard, her throat dry, her eyes feeling heavy with tears.

"Liliana? That's a beautiful name. I'd like to hear more about her." The doctor's voice was gently insistent. "Anything at all that you want to tell me. Was she pretty?"

Pretty? Liliana hadn't just been pretty, she was without doubt the most beautiful child Constance had ever seen.

And that wasn't just a mother's prejudice. Strangers had stopped her on the streets of Manhattan—*Manhattan* for heaven's sake!—to say how adorable her little girl was with her huge blue eyes and mop of white-gold curls. But she wasn't going to tell that to Dr. Foster. In fact, Constance couldn't understand why she'd been rash enough to mention her daughter, much less actually speak her name. She hadn't breathed a word about Liliana in years, and with good reason. Constance's memories of her life with Liliana were a secret treasure that she hoarded, images and flashes of recollection that she examined in solitude and strung together like pearls slipped onto the dreary, frayed string of her life in a maximum-security mental institution.

She was fairly sure all the long-term staff at Merton House knew the gory details of the famous case, even if the murder had occurred more than twenty-five years in the past. However, knowing and talking were two different things, and until Dr. Foster's arrival at the beginning of April, it had been years since anybody had discussed the events leading up to her incarceration. Keeping track of time was difficult in the surreal world of Merton House, but Constance doubted if anyone had asked about the specific details of her daughter's disappearance in at least a decade. Except Victor, of course. When Victor visited her each year, he always tormented her with reminders of the horrific crime she'd committed. And she always obliged him by succumbing to one of the terrifying flashbacks that induced nightmares, night sweats of awesome proportions and screaming fits of helpless, overwhelming terror.

Constance shuddered, dreading November and Victor's annual visit, even though it was still almost six months away.

Infuriatingly, Dr. Foster refused to accept her silence. "Did you love your daughter, Constance?"

Why wouldn't he stop asking questions? She decided to ignore him, realizing to her dismay that she was rocking back and forth in genuine agitation, clutching her arms around her waist as if to hold back the answers he wanted. *Act crazy long enough and eventually it's no longer a pretense.*

"Constance, did you love your daughter?"

It seemed there were still a few things she couldn't bear to lie about, and this was one of them. She closed her eyes, feeling the terrible sadness of her loss sweep over her. "Yes," she whispered. "I loved her."

"Then why did you kill her?" Dr. Foster asked.

"I don't know."

And, God help her, that was the stark, unvarnished truth. She'd killed her own daughter and she didn't know why, or even how she'd done it. Had it been to keep her safe from Victor? Could she ever have been demented enough to believe that death was the only way to keep Liliana safe?

"Constance, you're crying. Are you sorry that you killed your daughter?"

"Yes, damn you! Yes!" She sprang to her feet, running for the door. "I don't want to talk about it! I won't! I don't have to talk about it. I'm crazy, remember?"

For a second or two, she was profoundly grateful that she had been certified as insane, because that meant she was incapable of taking responsibility for her actions. Not for what she did now, or the terrible things she'd done in the past. That's what being crazy meant: she wasn't responsible for Liliana's death.

Blinded by tears, she couldn't find the door handle. She fumbled for it, desperate to get out of Dr. Foster's office.

She didn't hear him cross the room, but suddenly he was standing next to her, silently offering her a tissue. A tissue, not a shot of tranquilizer? His gaze was kind. And thoughtful, which was not a good sign. She dried her eyes, then blew her nose, turning to toss the crumpled tissue into the wastebasket at the side of the desk. She drew a shuddering breath, pulling a thick veil across the painful memories. Behind the veil, she gathered her strength, shutting out awareness of Dr. Foster. He was simply another faceless enemy, an intruder to be repelled.

"I want to go to my art class," she said woodenly.

"I have ten minutes before my next appointment, I'll walk with you," he said.

She scowled, letting the childish feeling of petulance flow over her, welcoming its protective cover. "I want to go by myself."

He held open the door, seemingly impervious to her churlishness. He fell into step with her as if she hadn't spoken. Short of staging an outburst, which would get her medicated and returned to her room, she had no choice but to let him accompany her.

"I haven't met Peggy yet," he said in a mild, conversational tone. "I'm gradually trying to get to know all the visiting instructors. Have you been working with Peggy for long?"

"Five months." She bit her lip. Was that a suspiciously specific response? She'd noticed that most of her fellow inmates had only an attenuated sense of the passage of time. Lucky them. Their days didn't pass with agonizing, stupefying slowness.

"Five months isn't very long," he said. "Did you just recently get interested in sculpture, or is Peggy a new teacher?"

"She's new." The mere thought of Peggy was cheering, even in her current edgy state. After the dear, doddery old craft instructor they'd had at Merton House for the previous six years, Peggy's arrival had been like a supernova exploding on the dark night sky of Constance's circumscribed universe. "Peggy's the best teacher I've ever had. She's really talented and very patient."

Constance knew she'd said too much as soon as she finished speaking. Worse, she'd allowed her voice to rise and fall in a totally normal rhythm. The heavily medicated residents of Merton House rarely managed to get their voices to follow the lilt of regular speech. The trouble was, Dr. Foster had shaken her up so badly that she seemed to have lost control of all her normal safeguards against self-betrayal.

She felt Dr. Foster's interested gaze rest on her, but he didn't say anything, which made Constance more nervous. Right now, everything about Dr. Foster was making her nervous. "This is the craft room," she mumbled.

She pushed open the padded doors without waiting for any response from the doctor, and breathed in the comforting smells of acrylic paint, paste, modeling clay and the raffia used for weaving projects. Through the multiple skylights the sun shone on a small group of women engaged, with varying degrees of concentration, in making woven place mats and misshapen hats.

Bernie Schulyer, dressed in a disposable surgical scrub suit and paper slippers, was in his favorite spot in front of an easel covered with a large sheet of poster board. He was painting eagerly, dabbing his brush into plastic cups of paint with swift energy, stepping back frequently to admire the effect. Peggy stood next to him, offering the occasional word of encouragement, suggesting minor improvements. She made no comment on the fact that

Bernie duplicated each brush stroke he made on the paper with another stroke of the same color on his own person. Some of the paint landed on his scrub suit, even more landed on his face, hands and hair.

Bernie's concentration broke when Constance came into the room. "Hi, Constance! I'm painting my father." His mouth tried to shape a smile but didn't quite make it.

"That's nice," she said, walking over to study Bernie's latest effort with genuine interest. Bernie always painted his father, with compelling results. Today Mr. Schulyer Sr. was a pale green blob, surrounded by various shades of darker green, decorated with a tracery of brown twiglike strokes. Mr. Schulyer tended to change color with the seasons, and today he was certainly reminiscent of spring. As always, however, the picture contained a hint of menace that left Constance mentally squirming.

Bernie added a gash of yellow to the upper left-hand corner of his portrait, circling his mouth thoughtfully with the brush as he studied the effect of this latest addition.

"Why did you paint your father's mouth yellow?" Dr. Foster asked.

Constance turned in surprise. She hadn't realized that he'd followed her across the room, and she was stunned by the question. In two years of watching Bernie paint, it had never occurred to her to connect his random slashes and blobs on the paper with the body part he painted the same color. As far as she knew, even Peggy hadn't made the connection.

Bernie's gaze flicked from the doctor to his painting. "Lies," he said finally, the brush circling his own mouth in a frenzy. "Yellow is for lies."

"Is it? I didn't know that. Thank you for explaining it to me. What does the green stomach mean, Bernie?"

Bernie shook his head, chewing on the end of his paint-brush, his powers of explication apparently exhausted. "His stomach is green," he said. "Green is for my father's stomach."

"It's a fascinating portrait," Dr. Foster said quietly. "Would you let me have it to hang in my office when it's finished?"

Bernie considered this request at length. "No," he said. "It's mine, not yours."

"All right. But I'd really like to have one of your pictures someday, Bernie. You do interesting work."

Bernie flashed another almost-smile. Dr. Foster inclined his head in a polite nod and walked over to the group of women weavers, leaving Bernie to stare at his portrait in perplexity, as if not quite sure what color he ought to add next, now that he'd had his work admired by the director.

Constance was relieved to see that Dr. Foster had no intention of staying at her side and watching her work. He sat down at the craft table and admired the various mats and hats, talking to the inmates and addressing the occasional question to the aide who was supervising the small group to make sure that squabbles over yarn didn't degenerate into fist fights or some other form of disturbance.

Peggy touched her lightly on the arm. "Hi, Constance, how are you doing? Are you ready to start work?"

"Ready." Constance dragged her gaze away from the craft table and smiled at Peggy, not bothering to conceal her pleasure. "You're sunburned," she said.

Peggy smiled. "I spent too long in the garden on Saturday," she said. "If all the tomato seedlings I've planted actually bear fruit, I'll be able to supply the entire county with tomatoes."

Constance chuckled. "Somehow, from what you've told me about your gardening skills, I don't think the local supermarkets need to worry."

Peggy sighed. "Too true. I have the world's brownest thumb. Anyway, let's get started." She unlocked the small, heavy-duty safe in the corner of the craft room and took out a knife while Constance opened the simple combination lock on the supply cupboard to retrieve everything she needed. Angling her chair to take advantage of the natural light, Constance sat down at the table, flexing her fingers as she considered the chipmunk family members she'd so far completed.

She'd idealized a half-remembered scene from her own childhood and created an old-fashioned tea party. Grandfather Chipmunk, dignified and somewhat portly, sat with his hands folded across his tweed vest. Grandma Chipmunk, elegant in a flowered frock, poured tea from a fat, round pot. A maid, in frilled apron, smiled as she handed around tiny cupcakes, and two little girl chipmunks giggled together, heads angled so that you could see they were whispering secrets to each other. For fun, Constance had included some of the Merton House regulars as guests. Two of the doctors were there, as well as Raymond Hill, whose chipmunk eyes were happily turned toward chipmunk heaven and—one assumed—an incoming message from the archangel.

Her original plan had never included a mother or father chipmunk, but last week Peggy had persuaded her to add a set of parents to the group. Constance was perfectly well aware that Peggy's request was motivated as much by therapeutic reasons as by artistic ones. Nevertheless, she'd agreed to make the mother and father chipmunks, fully intending to produce stock, stereotypical images.

Somehow, her fingers had refused to obey her. When she'd finished the mother, she'd produced a sleek, elegant creature with a supercilious smirk and cold eyes. Today she was planning to start work on the father chipmunk, and she had a suspicion her fingers would once again prove to have a will of their own.

The body was easy enough to shape—a sort of generic chipmunk, neither fat nor thin, neither tall nor short, his tail curled arrogantly upward. She made two or three attempts at the face, but the right expression eluded her, perhaps because she'd deliberately blotted out all memory of the parade of stepfathers who'd flitted through her adolescent years. For some reason, it suddenly seemed important to bring those long-stifled memories into focus, and she worked with a concentration that muted her surroundings. She delicately scraped away at the curve of the mouth, the slant of the eyes, the tilt of the nose, until she felt reasonably satisfied that she'd captured the essence of her multiple stepfathers—a self-satisfied chipmunk with a smarmy, insincere smile that barely masked his predatory, perverse sexuality.

Her head was aching by the time she'd finished, and she pushed her glasses back on her head, rubbing her eyes and blinking at what she'd created. It always took her a few moments to reorient herself when she'd finished a new piece.

"Who is he?" a voice asked quietly from behind her.

"My stepfathers," she answered absently, frowning because the position of the tail still wasn't quite right. The curl at the tip needed to be cocky, with a hint of underlying self-doubt, not arrogantly self-assured the way she'd made it.

"How many stepfathers did you have?"

"Only three that my mother married, but she changed lovers the way most women change panty hose. I lost count after a while, because they all looked the same. Behaved the same way, too."

"Did they all make sexual advances at you?" Dr. Foster asked.

On the brink of responding, Constance snapped out of her creative daze and registered just who it was asking the questions. She whirled in her chair, moving so fast that her arm swept the father chipmunk to the floor.

Dr. Foster made a small sound of distress and quickly bent to pick up the damaged model. "I'm sorry," he said, setting the piece back on the table where it sagged sideways with an air of drunken abandon. She realized they were staring straight into each other's eyes and she quickly dropped her gaze. Crazy people never made eye contact.

"You're very talented," he said. "Peggy told me that you're the most naturally gifted student she's ever had."

At any other time, Peggy's praise would have warmed her heart. Right now, Constance was too agitated to feel pleasure. Her habit of secrecy was so ingrained, so much part of her everyday existence, that she'd almost forgotten why it was so important. Conflicting emotions struggled for dominance: a strange longing to let down her guard and tell Dr. Foster everything, combined with a fierce anger that he could make her feel that way.

Anger won. She pounded her fist on the table, squashing the father chipmunk, turning him into nothing more revealing than a lump of modeling clay. Her hand knocked against the knife and she saw at once that the knife offered her an escape from the doctor's frightening questions.

She snatched the knife, turning in a single swift movement and pointing it straight at Dr. Foster's throat. "Go away," she said, focusing all her diffused rage exclusively on him. "Go away, or I'll kill you."

Around her, she was aware of the excited murmurs of the other residents. Violence, or the threat of violence, always resonated deep in the troubled psyches of Merton House inmates. Somewhere, far off to the side of her consciousness, she wondered despairingly if she was going to be allowed back into the craft room, or if this one desperate effort to save herself from questioning would get her barred from her major source of joy forever.

Dr. Foster wasn't responding the way he should have. He was supposed to back off at the mere sight of her knife, pressing the emergency-call button that would bring two powerful male orderlies to the room, restraints and shots of tranquilizer at the ready. Instead, he leaned forward, edging closer to the blade of the knife.

"That knife isn't sharp enough or big enough to kill me," he said, his voice soft. "And I think you're smart enough to recognize that, Constance."

From the corner of her eyes, she saw Peggy walking toward the table and Dr. Foster's impatient gesture sending away the instructor. Constance felt a giant wave of fury wash over her. He wasn't even scared of her. Didn't he realize that he damn well ought to be scared of her? She was a madwoman, a madwoman who'd murdered her own daughter.

She lunged toward the doctor, her hand stopping inches from his throat as she suddenly understood the terrible reality of what she was doing. Good God, she had spent twenty-six years expiating for the sin of killing her child. Was she going to add to her guilt by killing Dr. Foster?

Her body slumped, and the doctor caught her arm in a steely grip, but he didn't grab the knife or move her arm in any way. He just stared deep into her eyes, daring her to continue her attack. With a despairing cry, she opened her hand and let the knife fall to the floor. She heard the clatter of metal hitting rubber tile and sank back into the chair, collapsing onto the table, her head resting on her arms.

Dr. Foster put his arm around her shoulder. "If you're ready, Constance, I'll walk you back to your room," he said.

She stood up, shaking, nauseated by her own behavior. "Aren't you worried that I'll try to murder you en route?" she asked bitterly.

"No."

"Then you're crazy."

He actually smiled. "No," he said. "That's you."

Constance felt the weight of her entire failed lifetime pressing in on her. "Yes," she said. "I guess that's me."

Four

New York City
Wednesday, June 12, 1996

Juggling her purse and her briefcase, Jess slipped the key card into the lock of her hotel-room door and turned the handle quickly, before the little green light stopped flashing. Wrinkling her nose at the smell of stale air freshener, she kicked off her shoes and draped her suit jacket over the back of the room's only chair. Lord, she was exhausted! There was nothing like trying to pry information out of bored bureaucrats to make you feel as if you'd run a marathon.

She dropped her briefcase onto one of the room's two queen-size beds and herself onto the other. The bed frame squeaked and rolled her to the side, courtesy of the sagging springs. She shifted her weight to accommodate the bumps and hollows of the mattress, and tried not to listen as a fire truck and police car competed to see how much noise their sirens could make.

New York City, she thought wryly. Center of the universe, crown jewel of civilization. How could she have forgotten the multiple joys of visiting Manhattan on a budget of less than a hundred and fifty a day?

The phone rang. She decided to ignore it. Only her parents knew where she was staying, and she wasn't in the mood to talk to them, not just yet. Not until she'd come to terms with the fact that late this afternoon, one of the bored city bureaucrats had finally found the microfiche entry Jess had been looking for. According to the official records of the borough of Manhattan, three-year-old Jessica Marie Pazmany's death from leukemia had been registered with the authorities on the eighth of June, 1969. The notifying party had been William Loke, M.D., senior oncologist at New York Hospital.

Confirming that she'd officially been dead for more than a quarter of a century took some getting used to, Jess reflected. Not to mention the minor problem that since she obviously wasn't Jessica Marie Pazmany, who the hell was she?

The phone was still ringing. It seemed her annoying caller wasn't going to go away and leave her to brood in peace. On the sixth ring, she gave up and grabbed the phone. "Hello."

"Jess, it's Dan."

"Hello, Dan. Goodbye, Dan—"

"Don't hang up, Jess. I'm downstairs at the reception desk. I'd like to talk to you for a few minutes. Meet me in the lobby, would you?"

His voice sounded warm and subtly sensuous, and she steeled herself to resist. Her mood tonight was so unsettled, if she wasn't careful she could see herself doing and saying things she would later regret. "How did you know I was in New York?" she asked curtly.

"Your parents told me. They're worried about you, Jess. They asked me to give you a call, check in with you and see that everything was okay."

"They had no reason to do that." She stifled a surge of irritation at her parents' well-meaning interference. Typical midwesterners, they nursed an unshakable conviction that New York City was a sinkhole of vice and danger. No doubt they'd decided that even a feckless ex-husband was better protection than nobody at all. From Jess's point of view, they were disastrously wrong.

"You've done your duty, Dan. You can tell my parents you called, and I'm just fine. Reassure them I've had no violent encounters with drug-crazed addicts, or homeless hustlers—"

"Have dinner with me, Jess."

Her skin flushed with sudden heat. She gripped the phone, making sure none of the heat sounded in her voice. "Thank you, Dan, but I have a lot of paperwork I need to clear up tonight—"

"Christie's just back from six months in Europe. She's singing at El Greco's this week. I'll buy you *tiropitakia* and we can listen to her sing while we eat. Come on, Jess, that has to be a better deal than ordering an overcooked hamburger from room service, which I'll bet is what you were planning to do for dinner."

He was right about the hamburger, and El Greco's *was* a terrific restaurant. Christie, one of her ex-husband's limitless friends and acquaintances, was a folksinger with a hauntingly beautiful voice and a rich sense of humor. Jess enjoyed her company almost as much as her singing. The invitation was certainly tempting, but she didn't understand why her ex-husband seemed to be pursuing her, looking for excuses to spend time in her company. God knows, if *she'd* been desperate to get a divorce three years ago, *he'd* been frantic.

"You sound as if you really want to have dinner with me, Dan. Why?"

He hesitated for a moment. "The easy answer is because your parents asked me to look out for you and I'd like to oblige them."

"And the difficult answer?"

"I could say because we hurt each other so deeply when we were married that it's time to heal some of the wounds..."

"That sounds like a line from a very bad TV sitcom. At least be honest with me, Dan. God knows, brutal honesty used to be one of your more devastating characteristics. We had dinner in Denver less than three weeks ago and managed to snipe at each other with all our old vigor. Now you want to see me again. I need to know why you've developed this sudden urge to wine and dine me after years of total silence."

"I was silent for three years because I didn't know what to say. How many different ways could I apologize? But recently I've come to the conclusion that our marriage failed for a hell of a lot more reasons than the fact that I was an irresponsible bastard who screwed up big-time. We both contributed to the problems in our marriage, Jess."

She heard herself laugh, a harsh sound that contained no mirth. "I should have seen that one coming, shouldn't I? Why am I not surprised that you've now reached the comfortable conclusion that most of the problems in our marriage were actually mine? Sure they were, Dan. I was the bad guy and you were cruelly misunderstood. You sat around twiddling your thumbs and watched me work myself to the point of physical breakdown because I was such a bitch of a wife."

"Most of the problems in our marriage weren't yours," Dan said. "But some of them were. And I guess I'm hoping that circumstances might have changed enough in both our lives to give us the chance to see our relationship as it really was. We need to get our marriage into better perspective if we're ever going to be able to move on.''

Jess drew a shallow, nervous breath. ''Now it's my turn to be honest, Dan. You hurt me in more ways than I can begin to count, and I can't imagine many things I'd like to do less than to sit across a table from you and dissect the corpse of our marriage.''

''That's where we have our first problem,'' Dan said quietly. ''Our marriage isn't a corpse. It's still very much alive.''

''Sure it is,'' she replied with enough sarcasm to cover the panic stirring inside her. ''Those divorce decrees we signed were nothing but a trivial legal formality.''

''Yes, you're right, that's exactly what they were, a legal pretense that lacked reality for both of us. Divorce is supposed to free a couple from a failed marriage. Do you feel free, Jess?''

She wanted to say yes. God, she wanted to say yes! Her throat closed up, and her fingers tightened around the phone. This was like trying to accept Tim Macfadden's proposal, only worse. The words just wouldn't come.

The silence stretched until Dan finally broke it. ''You don't have to answer that question, Jess. Just agree to have dinner with me. Please.''

El Greco's was as noisy and crowded as Jess remembered. Carrying loaded platters that gave off wonderful steamy smells of eggplant, lemon and garlic, waiters moved with harried agility among the jam-packed tables. Otto, the owner, rushed up and greeted Dan with a hug reminiscent of Zorba the Greek at his most exuberant.

''You remember Jess?'' Dan said. ''We used to eat here when we were married.'' He grinned. ''On those rare occasions we could afford to eat out, that is.''

"Naturally I remember such a beautiful woman." Otto bowed over her hand, dark eyes gleaming. "How have you been keeping, *madame?* It is very good to see you again."

"It's good to be here," Jess said. Smooth, she thought in silent amusement. Very smooth. Otto obviously had the etiquette down pat for greeting ex-wives dining with their former husbands. No messing with Ms., Mrs. or Miss. No stumbling for the correct surname. Just a sophisticated, all-purpose *madame.*

The restaurateur wove a path for them to the only empty table in the place, a prime location between the window and the small raised dais where Christie would eventually sing. "Enjoy your evening together," he said, handing them leather-bound menus with a flourish. "And Mr. Stratton, congratulations on the new movie deal with Allied. I read about it last week. I'll look for you at the Oscars next year." He flashed a smile. "If you win, I'll tell the barman to name a drink in your honor." He sidestepped a group of guests preparing to leave and snapped his fingers to summon a waiter to their table.

Jess looked at Dan over the menu in openmouthed wonder. "A movie deal? What's Otto talking about? Have you landed a part in a movie? It must be the lead if it's in the papers. My God, Dan, that's terrific! Why didn't you tell me? We should celebrate!"

"I don't have a part in a movie."

She was surprised by the depth of her disappointment. Odd, she thought, that she still cared so much about Dan's career. "Oh, Lord, I'm sorry. I have a bad habit of leaping to conclusions."

Dan gave her a rueful smile. "Let's face it, Jess, I'm a god-awful actor. No director in his right mind would give me a decent part, let alone the lead."

"You aren't *that* bad." She tried to sound sincere.

He grinned. "You're right, I'm not bad, I'm terrible. In comparison, Tiny Tim is a major dramatic talent."

He smiled so cheerfully, she couldn't help smiling back. "Okay, Dan, I'll say it. You're a lousy actor. But if you don't have a part in a movie, what kind of a deal was Otto talking about?"

Dan—the original Mr. Cool—shifted in his chair, looking abashed. Sounding as though he was confessing an embarrassing secret, he mumbled his news. "One of my screenplays is going into production in Colorado next month. Last week, the money men announced they've signed Brad Pitt to play the lead."

Brad Pitt? Dumbfounded, Jess narrowly avoided dropping her menu into the butter. They were clearly talking about a big-time, huge-budget movie. She gulped. "You've written a screenplay? And sold it to a real Hollywood production company?"

His smile became wry. "Yeah, I sold it for real money to a real production company." He cleared his throat. "Actually, I've written two scripts and I'm working on my third. Allied Artists is going to produce all of them."

Jess's eyes widened. "I'm impressed. No, I'm awestruck. Tell me the story line for the script going into production."

"The hero's a washed-up former Olympic downhill skier whose ex-wife is murdered in the opening scene. Our hero immediately becomes the prime suspect in the murder. We have the requisite international conspiracy that threatens world peace, not to mention the requisite chase down the side of a mountain, and the requisite beautiful woman who may or may not be part of the international conspiracy. Naturally, our hero single-handedly preserves world peace, despite the fact that the bungling bureaucrats in the FBI and the CIA attempt to thwart his efforts at every turn."

"And he gets the girl in the end?"

"Of course, although not the one he starts out with. He gets the nice girl who's been his friend for years. I'm a sucker for happy endings."

"I'd say you have a surefire hit on your hands."

"Bite your tongue. The movie goblins are always lurking, waiting to snatch defeat from the jaws of box-office victory."

She laughed. "Let's see. You have Brad Pitt in the title role, the Colorado Rockies for background scenery and a script packed with action and romance. I'd say the goblins will have their work cut out turning this movie into a failure."

He hunched his shoulders, his anxiety not entirely feigned. "You have to remember I've just spent three years writing for the soaps, which means inventing a life-altering drama for every five minutes of airtime. I've gotten into the habit of imagining catastrophe looming around every corner."

Jess looked across the table at the man who'd once shared her bed, her heart and her life. She wondered why she hadn't noticed until this moment the subtle changes in him. Even in the depths of professional and personal failure, Dan had always exuded brash self-confidence. Success had transformed his cockiness into something quieter and much more potent. His magnetic charm was still there, but he no longer seemed to feel a compulsion to be the witty, scintillating, center of attention. Dan, she realized, was finally at peace with himself and the world. Ironically, his presence was more powerful because he'd learned to step back, out of the spotlight.

They didn't have their wine yet, so she picked up her glass of water and clinked it against his, smiling with genuine pleasure. Dan had a brilliant mind and a streak of creative talent a mile wide. She was delighted he'd found a way to express it, even though it wasn't as an actor. "Congratulations, Dan. I'm really happy for you. May you collect so many Oscars for best screenplay that you need a custom-made display cabinet to house them all. Two custom cabinets, in fact."

He grimaced. "Right now, I'd settle for not getting torn to shreds by every movie critic from coast to coast. I'm already discovering the truth of that old saw about the higher you climb, the bigger the crevice yawning at your feet."

"Feeling intimidated must be a novel experience for you," she said without malice. "Welcome to the club."

He threw her a puzzled look that she couldn't interpret, but the waiter came and she lost the chance to ask any more personal questions. They ordered spinach and cheese puff pastries, with salad on the side, and a bottle of ouzo to get them into the true Mediterranean spirit of the meal.

Jess realized she was hungry, not surprising since she'd forgotten to eat lunch. "How did you get started writing for the soaps?" she asked, nibbling on a breadstick.

"At the time it seemed like serendipity," Dan said. "Now I'm not so sure. These days, I often wonder why it took me so long to realize that writing was what I ought to be doing with my life."

"Why's that? Because writing's easy for you? Fun?"

He thought for a moment. "Not easy, and not always fun. Writing seems—natural. Acting always frustrated me because I never seemed able to get *inside* the character I was portraying. But when I write a screenplay, I experience exactly the sort of intimacy with the characters that I somehow never managed to achieve as an actor."

"So how did you get started? Write a script on spec and submit it to the producer?"

"No. I auditioned for a bit part in the soap *Night and Day* and actually got it. My role consisted of standing on a corner, underneath a street lamp, pretending to sell drugs to one of the lead characters. They hit a plot problem while they were taping my segment, and the director, producer and scriptwriters immediately exploded in a collective tantrum. They were all so busy screaming at each other, I had time to write up an alternative scene before they'd calmed down enough to notice I was still there. The producer liked my solution and kept me around for the rest of the week to work on that segment of the plot. Then they decided to extend the segment, and the producer asked me to write those scenes, too. Before you could say Jack Robinson, I was officially a full-time scriptwriter for the show. I only quit a couple of months ago when Allied Artists finally paid me enough money to convince me they were serious about picking up their options."

The waiter returned with their ouzo and brimming plates of Greek salad. While they ate, Dan entertained her with a story about Julia Roberts that sounded much too funny to be true, and described a meeting with Steven Spielberg that had left Dan stuttering with awe at the man's creative genius. Dan seemed caught up in his own stories, but she realized he'd simply been giving her a chance to eat something because, as soon as she finished her salad, he fell silent.

He set down his glass and leaned across the table toward her. "I guess that exhausts my supply of Hollywood gossip. I'm hardly on the inside track. Now it's your turn, Jess. Tell me what happened today. What did you find out about Jessica Marie?"

She was surprised at how much relief she felt at the prospect of sharing her news with him. "I discovered that the death certificate Magda Mizensky sent to my grandfather wasn't a fake," she said. "I saw the official ledger entry today. Jessica Marie Pazmany died on the eighth of June, 1969."

Dan exhaled sharply. "And you're sure you found the record of death for the right Jessica Marie? There's no chance of a mistake?"

She shook her head. "No mistakes. The parents are listed—Rudolph and Elena Pazmany, Elm Street, in Queens."

He covered her hand briefly with his. "I'm sorry, Jess. I know this isn't what you were hoping for."

She tried for a casual shrug and almost made it. "We both knew there was almost zero chance that the death certificate was fake. There was no reason for Magda Mizensky to lie."

"What are you going to do now?" Dan asked quietly.

"I'm not sure. Right after I confirmed that Jessica Marie had died, I went to Queens and tried to check out the neighborhood where the Pazmanys once lived. You know, find an old codger with a wonderful memory who'd lived there forever—"

"Any luck?"

"No, their apartment doesn't even exist anymore."

"There'll be other leads you can follow. The social workers who authorized your adoption must have investigated the Pazmanys' background. Their files must contain names of people you can track down."

"I don't know about that," Jess said. "The social workers must have done an incredibly sloppy job. Think about it, Dan. They didn't even realize Jessica Marie was dead!"

He frowned. "It's hard to imagine how they could avoid finding out something so important. You'd think the first neighbor they spoke to would have told them right off the bat that the Pazmanys' daughter was dead.''

"Unless, like Magda, the Pazmanys lived in an enclave of refugees like Magda who were all terrified of the police.''

"Every single one of them?" Dan shook his head. "That seems unlikely.''

"Then what do you suggest?" Jess sighed. "You know, when you first showed me Magda's letter, I was determined not to worry about it, but something you said that night forced me to change my mind.''

"What was that?''

"You said that maybe I had parents who were still looking for me. Now I keep imagining this sad couple, approaching retirement age, who have spent the past twenty-six years agonizing over what happened to their little girl. Which may be ridiculously sentimental, but it's still a compelling image. I've told myself that it's just as likely some teenage mom gave me to the Pazmanys and never spared me a second thought, but I wake up each morning and wonder if my mother's missing me." Jess tried to laugh. "Stupid, huh? But you planted the idea in my head and now I can't shake it loose.''

"Your feelings aren't in the least stupid. And since I'm the person who started you on this quest, I'd better see if I can't come up with some useful suggestions about how to pursue it. We never talked much about the Pazmanys when we were married. How much do you actually know about them?''

"In a nutshell, not much. In the past two weeks, Todd and I have checked every scrap of paper that exists in connection with my adoption. And the truth is we have amazingly little information about the Pazmanys. Rudolph was in a refugee camp in Vienna from 1956 to 1961, then he immigrated to the United States with Magda as his sponsor. Elena was an only child whose parents were dead at the time of my adoption. Rudolph was a carpenter. He'd just started work for a new company right before the accident. But it was a small family-owned firm that went out of business twenty years ago, which rules out personnel records at his place of employment. Elena was a qualified nurse, but she hadn't worked outside their home since I was born... I mean since Jessica Marie was born—"

Jess broke off, her voice catching. She found a tissue in her pocket and scrubbed fiercely at her eyes. "Damn, I'm sorry. I don't know what's the matter with me. I keep crying for no reason."

"It must be allergies," Dan said. "God knows, you've nothing else to be upset about. Hell, most people who find out they've been dead for twenty-six years invite their friends over to celebrate."

Jess hovered between tears and laughter. "You'd probably do just that."

"Maybe. We all deal with emotional pain in different ways. You bottle it up. I make jokes. If the pain's bad enough, it hangs around whatever you do."

"It's not being officially dead that bothers me," Jess said. "It's the fact that all my roots are hanging out with nowhere to plant themselves. I don't even have a birthday anymore, much less names to attach to my birth parents. I just feel so... displaced."

"Which is why it's important to get more information as quickly as we can." Dan sent her a teasing look. "Hell, for all we know, you may already be an old woman of thirty-one."

She gave a groan. "No, I've definitely decided I was younger than Jessica Marie. I'm still a fresh, young twenty-nine-year old."

"I'll have to throw a humdinger of a party when you turn thirty." Dan helped himself to a slice of crusty bread, but didn't eat it. "Have you considered hiring a private investigator, Jess? That's one of the good things about New York—there are bound to be at least a half-dozen firms here that specialize in tracing missing family members."

"I realize I'll probably end up hiring professional investigators. But I'd like to do some of the easy stuff myself. That way, finding out who I really am isn't going to cost me twice my annual salary in detective fees."

"You know who you are, Jess, but you do have a point about the cost of hiring a detective." Dan frowned. "Maybe you should check the hospital for Jessica Marie's medical records. The hospital must have taken some information about her parents when they admitted her, for billing reasons if for nothing else."

"I'd already decided the hospital where Jessica died was the next logical place to look. After I got back from Queens, that's where I went."

"But you didn't find anything useful?"

"I didn't even get to see her file. Medical records are only considered active for about seven years, so everything about Jessica Marie has been transferred from the active files to some microfilmed archival warehouse, and they won't let anyone except the patient or the next of kin view those records. Which means that I'm stymied, at least temporarily. I have to get a court order before they'll let me so much as peek at them, and heaven knows how long and complicated a process that will be. I guess tomorrow I'll try a different tack and search for the original report from the social worker who was assigned to find Pazmany relatives. Maybe there's more information in the departmental files than was extracted and sent to my parents."

"I wouldn't give up on the hospital if I were you. Why in the world would you need a court order to access Jessica Marie's medical records?"

She shot him an impatient glance, surprised at his question. "I just told you. The hospital will only release records to the patient or her next of kin. The patient's dead, and we don't know who her next of kin is, remember? That's my whole problem."

Dan shook his head. "You don't need judicial permission to access Jessica's files. The borough of Manhattan knows that Jessica Marie is dead, but nobody else does. In fact, the rest of the world knows quite well that she's alive. She's you. *You're* Jessica Marie Pazmany, at least officially. So if you want to check out Jessica Marie's medical records, you can. Find the appropriate office in New York Hospital, walk in and show them your birth certificate, your social security card, your passport, your driver's license and any other document they may demand. You've got 'em all. There's no way the hospital will be able to refuse you access to what appear to be your own medical records."

"But as soon as they start to look for my file, their records will show that I'm dead. Good grief, Dan, I'll get arrested for impersonating a dead person!"

"Jessie, my sweet, you can carry this obsession with being a law-abiding citizen too far, you know. Clerical staff are overworked and underpaid. The clerks won't care why you want to check out your medical records. They probably won't even notice that your file's lodged among those of the deceased. The clerks will just want proof that they followed official procedures before they handed the files over to you. That's all they're paid to do, nothing more."

Jess grimaced. "You make it sound easy, Dan, but with my luck these days, I'll get the only clerk in the hospital whose natural curiosity works overtime."

"If someone does happen to question your interest in the file, tell them it's come to your attention that your records contain incorrect information. Sound annoyed. Look angry. Mention the words *lawyer* and *lawsuit* several times. I'm willing to bet large sums of money this won't be the first time that a living patient's records have been misplaced among the dead."

Jess realized she was laughing. "Damn you, Dan. I should have known one dinner with you, and I'd be doing something outrageous within hours."

His gray-green eyes gleamed with faintly predatory amusement. "Jessie, my sweet, your definition of *outrageous* is in serious need of expansion. Stick around and I'd be happy to help you work on it."

"I'll just bet you would." Oddly, there was no rancor in her words, just amusement. She leaned back in her chair, aware that she was enjoying herself and refusing to get uptight about it. There was no law that said she couldn't enjoy Dan's company now that they were divorced. She was going to listen to Christie sing, eat *tiropitakia*, thereby consuming a week's supply of fat grams in one fell swoop, and enjoy her evening. Tomorrow would be time enough to start worrying again about who she was and why she'd been riding in that rental car with the Pazmanys twenty-six fateful years ago.

Dan held out the bottle of ouzo and offered her another glass. She shook her head and watched as he poured himself some. She'd always loved his hands, the shape of them, as well as the dexterity with which he performed everyday tasks. He glanced up and caught her eye. "What is it?" he asked.

She blinked, shaking off memories. "Nothing. Except maybe thank you for inviting me to have dinner with you tonight. I'm glad I came."

He held her gaze for several silent seconds. "You're welcome," he said finally. "I'm glad I invited you."

Five

"I need to see your driver's license, or some other form of photo ID." The clerk spoke without looking up.

"Yes, sure, I brought everything with me," Jess said.

The woman behind the tall Formica counter didn't respond except with an expression of bored resignation. Jess found her wallet and pulled out her driver's license and her social security card, her fingers not quite steady. She'd be an abject failure as a criminal, she decided. She'd have a heart attack, induced by sheer terror, long before she managed to commit any worthwhile crime. She laid out her IDs on the counter, resisting the urge to pour out a truncated version of her life history in support of her right to possess them.

"I have my passport, too, if you need it," she said.

"That won't be necessary." The clerk gave the driver's license a brief, sideways squint, then turned away to answer the phone. "I've seen all the identification I need," she said over her shoulder.

Jess gathered up her papers, shoving them back into her purse as if they were forgeries that wouldn't stand up to close inspection, rather than perfectly legal and legitimate documents. The clerk hung up the phone, wrote herself a note and returned to the counter. Jess smiled, trying not to look like an impostor intent on undermining the hospital's security systems.

Without a twitch of an answering smile, the clerk resumed checking off items on the printed form, squinting through her bifocals. "Reason for needing to access files?" she asked, pen hovering.

"I'm applying for a mortgage and I've discovered a problem with my credit rating." Jess tried for a casual laugh and instead produced a squeaky giggle. "Would you believe the credit agency reported that this hospital says I'm dead?"

"Are you?" the clerk asked.

Jess blinked, then gave a hesitant laugh. "You're joking, right?"

The clerk, Alma Schlunk, according to her name tag, reached toward a stack of preprinted cards sitting in a wire basket on the counter. "Sure I'm joking. A bundle of laughs, that's me." She shoved a card toward Jess, scribbling something in the top right-hand corner.

"Fill this out. Leave it next to the tray when you're done." Without a second glance, she went to her desk and began sorting a stack of files into four smaller piles.

Jess read through the card, which asked only for her name, a current address and the approximate date of the medical records being requested. Alma had already scrawled her initials against a line that instructed the clerk to inspect some sort of photo ID.

In a couple of minutes Jess had completed the card and returned it to the counter. Steadily stacking her files, Alma didn't look up or acknowledge her, so Jess sat down again on her plastic chair, where she could either stare at the walls, or read from a selection of pamphlets with cheery titles such as *Diabetes, the Silent Killer* or *The Prostate Gland and Male Menopause*. She should have remembered to bring a book. The criminal life, like a visit to the dentist, seemed to be composed of almost equal parts boredom and terror.

"Sorry to have kept you waiting," Alma said five minutes later, sounding marginally more friendly.

"That's all right. I can see you're very busy."

"Yeah, we're busy, all right." Alma sighed, wiping smudges of carbon off her fingers on a paper towel. "We were already understaffed, but the hospital brought in a team of consultants who recommended slashing expenses by getting rid of half the archival department. I wonder how long it'll take some genius in personnel to figure out that one person can't do the work of three?"

"If he has an MBA, at least a year. Otherwise, a couple of months should do it."

Alma laughed. She glanced through the card Jess had put next to the wire tray. "Okay, I'll just key this information into the computer and we should be able to locate your records in a few seconds."

She returned to her desk and typed briskly, then gave a little grunt of satisfaction. "Here you are. Pazmany, Jessica Marie. Admitted the tenth of February, 1969. And you're right. You're listed as dead since the eighth of June, 1969. Wonder how we managed that particular screwup? Be back in a moment. We keep this stuff in the room next door."

She returned a few minutes later, carrying a storage box of microfiche. "These are files for all the people leaving the hospital the same day you did," she said, tapping the container. She rifled through the contents and pulled out a fiche. "And you're here, just where you should be. Everything the New York Hospital ever knew about you is reduced to a few microdots on this fiche.''

''Great. I sure hope one of those dots explains why the records say I'm dead.''

''Yeah, I can understand why you might be wondering how that happened.'' Alma lifted a hinged section of the counter and gestured for Jess to accompany her to the microfilm viewer set into a carrel in a corner of the room. ''Let me show you how to work this machine. It can be temperamental.''

Jess sat down in front of the screen, and Alma slipped the microfiche into the scanner, explaining the simple operating system. ''I think that's everything you need to know,'' she said. ''Let's call up the first page of your records.''

Alma clicked on the viewing button and a printed page flashed onto the screen. *Welcome to New York Hospital,* Jess read. *Five Ways to Make Your Stay More Comfortable.* She quickly scanned the ensuing paragraphs and realized she was reading a leaflet containing information for patients being admitted to the hospital. She clicked on the button that enabled her to view the second page from her file and found herself staring at a set of instructions for the care of surgical wounds. The third page contained an invitation to contribute to the American Red Cross blood bank, and so on through half a dozen printed sheets of standard notices.

''I don't understand,'' Jess said. ''There's nothing here but general information about the hospital and its procedures. Is there another microfiche where my personal medical records are stored? None of this information is relevant to my case.''

Alma peered through her bifocals, squinting at the screen over Jess's shoulder. ''Weird,'' she said, clicking through all nine pages. "Wait a moment. Let me check a couple of other files from the same storage box. Maybe things in here somehow got mislabeled."

Jess gave up the chair in front of the screen and Alma inserted half a dozen microfiche in rapid succession, scanning each one. Jess could see that all the microfiche contained individual case histories, exactly as the labels promised.

"Well, that didn't help much, did it?" Alma swiveled on the chair, her fingers drumming the arm. "I've been here five years and I've seen most every screwup with the records you can imagine. But this is the first time I've ever seen a patient file with nothing in it but microfilmed copies of pamphlets." She turned back to the screen, reinserting the microfiche of Jessica Marie's file and fiddling with the controls of the viewer. After a minute or so, she shook her head. "I'm sorry, but there's not another word on this fiche beyond what you saw already."

"So if my case notes aren't on the microfiche, what happened to them?" Jess asked, surprised at the extent of her disappointment. She hadn't realized until this moment how much she'd hoped that answers to some of the questions raised by Magda's letter would be tucked away in Jessica Marie's hospital records.

Alma grimaced. "The original paperwork is all destroyed, that's for sure. After seven years, we don't keep the actual files anymore—the hospital can't afford the space to warehouse that much paper."

"So is that when the mistake happened? Someone destroyed the wrong parts of the file?"

"There's no way of knowing. The truth is, we have no system for finding out if your records are misfiled, lost or destroyed. I'm really sorry, but there's nothing more I can tell you."

"What are those numbers after my name—69-432247/bw?" Jess asked. "Does that mean anything, or is it just an archival file number?"

"It's your original patient ID," Alma said. "69 shows the year you were admitted. P is for pediatric. BW are the initials of the admitting physician. The rest is a billing code."

"Is there any chance you might have some information about me stored under that number? Separate from the medical history that would normally be in my file?"

Alma tapped her pen against her teeth. "I might be able to access the final status of your account," she said. "We do have the accounting department records on film."

"You do? That's great! What I need to find is an address—" Belatedly, Jess remembered that she was supposed to be checking the files because of a problem with her credit rating. "What I mean is any information from the accounting department records ought to be a big help to me in straightening out my problem with the mortgage company."

Alma didn't say anything for several seconds. Then she looked up. "Ms. Pazmany, let's stop talking nonsense, shall we? It's twenty-seven years since you were a patient in this hospital, and I'm willing to bet the family farm that nobody in this department has ever discussed your medical history or your financial behavior with any bank, lending institution or credit-rating service of any description. So while you may have all sorts of good reasons for wanting to examine your medical records, a credit check isn't one of them."

Jess felt her cheeks grow hot. "If you didn't believe my story, why did you agree to look for my file?"

Alma's gaze remained steady. "I believe people have a right to see their own medical records and they shouldn't have to explain why, except insofar as I need to protect the legal status of the hospital. In your particular case, we've followed procedures to the letter, and we turned up a computer entry that lists you as deceased, just as you claimed. Since you're alive, at least as far as I can tell, it doesn't surprise me at all that you want to find out why you and the hospital don't agree on this somewhat major issue. It also puzzles me that your file just happens to contain no useful information that might shed light on the situation. Fortunately, my job doesn't require me to speculate as to why this happened, or what it means in the greater scheme of things. I'm simply required to take steps to insure that any failures in our record-keeping systems are corrected. So if we're now agreed that I'm not a fool, and you're not dead, would you like me to see if I can find anything useful in the accounting department records?''

''Yes, I'd be extremely grateful.'' Jess drew a deep breath. ''Actually, Alma, what I'm really hoping to find is an address for my parents, or maybe something about the doctor who was in charge of my case.''

True to her word, Alma didn't inquire why Jess wanted this information. She sat down at her desk, clicked on her mouse, keyed in a few commands, then scribbled a series of numbers on a notepad. ''Accounting department records are kept in the back room on microfilm, organized by date. This may take a while.''

She was gone for less than five minutes. When she returned, she pushed a sheet of paper across the counter toward Jess.

''Here. This is a printout of everything that appears under your name in the accounting department records. For what it's worth, it shows that your bills were paid in full by the end of October 1969, and that the supervising doctor on your case was a man called Brook Weir.''

Jess took the paper, trying not to appear too eager. "Thank you very much, Alma, I really appreciate your help."

"Don't mention it." Alma would undoubtedly have said something more, but Jess was saved by the arrival of a harried-looking woman holding a baby in one arm and clutching a wriggling toddler in the other. For good measure, the phone rang again, and while Alma was answering it, Jess seized the chance to slip out of the room.

She hurried to the elevators, letting two come and go as she read the printout. In total, the page contained only four lines of text, but it was astonishing how much new information was packed into those four lines.

The header was brief and to the point: *Pazmany, Jessica Marie, deceased.* No surprise there, although Jess still felt a thrill of shock each time she saw written confirmation of Jessica Marie's death. The next entry showed that Jessica Marie's bill had been paid in full, and that her parents were the responsible billing party. Their address, though, was not the familiar one on Elm Street, but another one on Ninth Avenue, also in Queens.

The third entry revealed that the supervising physician was Dr. Brook Weir, with offices located at Park and Sixty-third in midtown Manhattan. Park and Sixty-third was one of the most expensive locations in the city. Jess was surprised that the Pazmanys had been able to afford the services of such a fashionable doctor. Even twenty-six years ago, only very successful specialists would have been able to afford to work in such a high-rent neighborhood. Perhaps Jessica Marie had been one of Dr. Weir's charity patients? Whatever their financial relationship had been, it was worth trying to find him and see if he still had records for the Pazmanys.

The final entry contained a pair of names that was entirely new to Jess: Mr. and Mrs. Wendell P. Grant, of Bartlett House, Old Cove Road, Hatterington, Long Island, were listed as coguarantors of the bill, along with the Pazmanys.

Jess gave a little whoop of excitement as she finished reading. Four lines of text and three new leads. This was just what she'd been hoping for—names to follow up, addresses to visit and people to track down who might be able to fill in the sketchy background of Rudolph and Elena's lives. She put the printout in her purse and pressed the call button for the elevator, seized with impatience.

She watched the flickering light mark the ascent of the elevator and tried to tell herself she was getting much too hopeful with almost no justification. She was searching for information about events a quarter of a century old. The doctor and the Grants were probably dead. Even if they were alive, the doctor—at best—was unlikely to remember anything beyond the medical details of Jessica Marie's case. As for the Grants, there was no guarantee they knew anything about how Jess came to be traveling in Rudolph and Elena's rental car the night of the crash.

Her efforts to be cool, calm and logical didn't succeed. Jess couldn't douse the hope that Mr. and Mrs. Wendell P. Grant would be able to provide her with solid information about her identity. She wasn't irrational enough to expect them to take one look at her and tell her who she was and where she'd come from, but Hatterington sounded as if it might be one of those small Long Island towns with a rich history. Exactly the sort of community that kept excellent records and made them readily available.

She would go to Long Island right away, Jess decided. Dan would be so pleased when she told him her trip to the hospital had opened up at least a minor window into the mystery of her past. Perhaps she should call him and see if he could make time to come to Hatterington with her. They could meet at Penn Station; he'd make the trip twice as much fun....

When Jess realized precisely where her thoughts were leading, she scowled so ferociously that she saw the nurse waiting next to her for the elevator cringe. Jess modified her expression and simultaneously hardened her heart. Dan might now be an employed person, with a successful career and a suddenly enhanced sense of fiscal responsibility, but he was still an adulterer, the man who had betrayed her in a myriad of big and little ways. Knowing how lightly he'd treated his marriage vows, she would have to be certifiably crazy to allow herself to be tempted by his seductive smile and laughing eyes. Thank God, her love life had not yet sunk to such a pathetic state that she could be beguiled by a couple of dinners and a few hours of interesting conversation. When she divorced Dan, she'd resolved that she would never again let him drag her down into the state of infatuated insanity where she'd languished for the first year and a half of their marriage. Nothing that had happened over the past couple of weeks was reason enough to break that promise to herself.

With her common sense more or less back in working order, Jess emerged from the revolving doors of the hospital onto the busy street. She set off to catch the bus for Penn Station and the Long Island Railroad. It was only ten-thirty—time enough for her to reach Hatterington, even if it turned out to be located at the far end of the island. The day was sunny and dry, perfect for doing touristy things. If she couldn't find any trace of Mr. and Mrs. Grant, maybe she'd indulge in a late lunch at a restaurant overlooking the water.

One way or another, Jess was anticipating an interesting afternoon.

"Morning, Teresa. Come in, Constance. Nice to see you again."

"Good morning, Doctor," the nurse's aide said. "Here you are, Constance, in you go. Doctor's waiting."

Ed closed his laptop computer and watched as his patient shuffled into the room. She sat down in her usual chair, hands drooping at her sides, head turned to avoid his gaze.

"Thanks, Teresa. I'll call you when Constance and I have finished our session. We'll be the usual forty-five minutes, I expect."

The aide hesitated. "She's been real uncooperative these past few days, Doctor. Are you sure you don't want me to put her in restraints? After all, she did try to kill you last week."

"That story's been exaggerated," Ed said. "Don't worry, Teresa. Constance and I will do fine together."

"If you say so." Teresa barely bothered to conceal her disapproval.

"Yes, I do say so. Thanks, Teresa, that'll be all for now."

Teresa turned on her heel, shooting him a fiery glance that suggested it would be entirely his own fault if she came back in an hour and found him spread-eagled across his desk with a knife in his back. And, of course, she'd be right. He *was* taking a risk, although not a very big one in his judgment. As far as he was concerned, the trade-off was worth it. Ed had long ago decided that the day he started medicating patients solely to make them less trouble would be the day he stopped practicing psychiatry.

"So how's everything been going this past week, Constance? Did you manage to get back to the craft room and finish that chipmunk you were working on?" He waited several seconds for her to reply, but she didn't speak. In fact, she gave no sign of having heard him ask the question.

"I know you heard what I said, Constance. Is there some special reason why you chose not to answer me?"

She remained as unresponsive as a lump of stone. Ed took off his reading glasses and examined the woman huddled in the chair on the other side of his desk. She looked more withdrawn and shrunken into herself than she had the week before. In deference to the climbing temperature, she was wearing a summer dress patterned with ugly purple flowers, but she'd teamed it with a pair of gray knee socks and a lightweight sweater in dingy beige. Ed wasn't much of a fashion guru, but he doubted if it would be possible to find a more dreary and unflattering combination of style and color. Depression usually led to an absence of sexual desire, combined with a complete lack of interest in physical appearance. Still, he found it incongruous that Constance could create such bright, witty and charming clay figurines when she couldn't manage to match her socks to her dress or her sweater.

"I read your case history over the weekend," he said, leaning back in his chair. "According to the notes in your file, your knife attack on me last week was completely outside your usual pattern of behavior. Usually you only get violent around the end of November. What happened, Constance? Why did you feel the need to attack me?"

She stared silently at her shoes.

He'd hoped to provoke her into responding, but obviously she wasn't that easily tricked into self-revelation. After twenty-five years of psychotherapy, Constance obviously knew how to protect herself from being caught off guard. "What is it about the end of November that upsets you, Constance? Is it something about the holidays? Thanksgiving? The approach of Christmas?"

The chair squeaked as Constance shifted in her seat, but she didn't answer him. "Perhaps it's not the holidays that bother you," Ed said. "Maybe it's the fact that the police believe your daughter was murdered right around the beginning of December. Is that what upsets you, Constance? When it gets to November, do you start thinking about your daughter and the person who killed her?"

"I killed her."

She spoke in a dull monotone, but at least he'd gotten a response. "Do you know why you killed her, Constance?"

Her hands gripped the arms of the chair. "I don't want to talk about it."

"Why not? Your daughter died a long time ago. Don't you think it's time to confront what happened?"

"It doesn't seem a long time ago to me." She spoke in a hoarse, painful whisper.

"Do you wish you hadn't killed your daughter, Constance?"

"Every day of my life."

"You need to come to terms with that remorse if you're ever going to feel well again. We need to talk about Liliana."

She sprang from her chair. "Don't do this to me! Don't keep pushing and prodding me! I don't want to talk about her!"

"It's really important for us to talk about her, Constance. I'm sure you didn't mean to kill your daughter, but somehow it happened. Why was that, Constance? What went wrong?" He paused for a moment. "Did your voices tell you to do it?"

She paced restlessly, the air around her vibrating with the force of her inner tension. "Sure," she said at last. "My voices told me to kill her."

Until now she'd denied that she had ever heard voices. Which was the lie? he wondered. "What else do your voices tell you, Constance? Can you hear them now?"

"Yes, I hear them all the time. They tell me that I'm a bad person." She shot a nervous half glance toward him. "They don't think much of you, either."

"You should tell them I only want what's best for you."

She hesitated. "They don't believe you."

"They should. So should you, Constance. Trust me, I'm here to help you."

Her only response was a flash of cynical disbelief so fleeting that he couldn't be sure he'd seen it. "Why don't you think you can trust me, Constance?"

She retreated back into silence. He watched as she paced, then stopped and stood in the middle of the room, as if the turmoil inside her was so great that she was paralyzed by it. She wrapped her arms around her waist and cocked her head to one side, looking exactly like Raymond listening to one of his messages from the Archangel Gabriel.

Too much like Raymond, Ed thought. She looked too damn much like the classic paranoid schizophrenic in the grip of a delusion. Was that why he couldn't put aside the conviction that she was acting? Mimicking the behavior of the sick people she saw every day? Or was he just reading a bunch of subtle signals and realizing that they didn't add up to a coherent whole?

"When did you first start hearing voices, Constance?" He spoke briskly since his offers of friendship seemed only to make her nervous.

"I don't know. A while ago."

It was time to let her know that he didn't believe her. "Looking back through your medical notes, I don't see any references to these voices, Constance. How often do they talk to you?"

"They're around all the time. Sometimes I ignore them."

"How do you manage to do that?"

"I tell them to go away. I think about other things."

The life of a schizophrenic patient was typically made unendurable by voices that kept up a running commentary on the patient's every action. Often, the voices yelled hideous abuse concerning the schizophrenic's sinfulness, stupidity and lack of worth. Ninety percent of the residents in Merton House reported hearing voices, and most of them invented elaborate schemes for holding the voices at bay. Ed would have staked his professional reputation on the fact that Constance wasn't one of the ninety percent.

He decided they weren't going to get anywhere unless he convinced Constance he couldn't be played for a sucker. "You know what, Constance? I don't believe you hear voices. I think you agreed with me that you heard voices telling you to kill your daughter just so that I'd stop asking you questions."

"That's not what I did. You're wrong. I did hear voices—I do."

"Then convince me. Tell me why the voices wanted you to kill your daughter."

"I don't remember!" She pounded her fist into the palm of her hand, her voice rising angrily. "Don't ask me about what happened to Liliana! I don't remember anything. Nothing at all. *Nothing!* I won't remember and you can't make me!"

At least he was finally getting an honest reaction from her. *Afraid to remember,* Ed wrote.

"All right, we won't talk about how Liliana died, at least not for today. But I'm very interested in learning more about her. Tell me about a happy day that you spent with her, Constance."

"No, I don't have to. I won't."

"Why not?"

Her breathing was jerky, her hands kneading in perpetual motion. "Remembering the happy days with Lili hurts as much as remembering the other stuff."

"Maybe that's because you never let yourself talk about her. Maybe it would hurt less if you shared some of your memories with me."

"Nothing in the entire world could make it hurt less."

Her voice echoed with so much grief that, for a surprising moment, Ed felt his detachment slip. He forced himself back to objectivity. "Consider it another way, Constance. Even if you're sure you've got nothing to gain, what have you got to lose by talking about her?"

She was staring at her damn shoes again. Ed controlled his frustration. "Look, Constance, talking to me couldn't make you feel worse, could it? So isn't there at least a small chance it might make you feel better? Why don't you risk telling me something about Liliana and then see how you feel afterward?"

Constance sat down in her chair and laced her fingers together. Then she turned her palms upward and linked her fingers the other way. "I wish you'd go back to California," she muttered.

Ed leaned forward. "I'm not going to go away, Constance. I'm going to be here for a long time, so you might as well get used to me."

"Dr. Grable never asked all these stupid questions."

"I have a different style from Dr. Grable's. In my opinion, this is the best way for me to help you get well—"

"You can't help me get well," she said quickly. "I'm mad. Psychotic. I need to stay here."

Frightened of being sane? Ed wrote. "Let's do a deal," he said. "I won't talk about helping you get better if you'll talk to me about Liliana. Just pick a day, a happy day when nothing special happened and the two of you had a good time together. That shouldn't be too difficult, should it?"

Constance got up and walked over to the window, staring out into the garden. She was silent for so long Ed had almost given up hope, when she started speaking. "We lived in Manhattan," she said without turning around. "The summer just before Liliana turned four was swelteringly hot, with oppressive humidity day after day. My grandparents kept inviting us to come and spend some time with them, to escape the city heat, but Victor didn't want me to go. He kept making excuses, saying we had engagements in the city. But eventually they called when Victor was in Washington and our housekeeper, Eva, was still with us then and I knew she'd never tell, so I agreed to spend the weekend with them." She stopped abruptly.

"Why didn't Victor want you to visit your grandparents without him being there?" he asked.

"I don't know." Constance blushed at the obvious lie. "Lili and I had a wonderful weekend," she continued hastily. "Three days, really, because we arrived on Friday at lunchtime and didn't leave until Monday morning. My grandparents' house is right next to the sea, and we played on the beach every day. Grandpa spent the whole of Saturday afternoon building a sand castle for Lili, and they had a great time, because he never got cross or impatient with her. He was the world's most gentle person, and she instinctively sensed that and responded to it. My grandmother sat on a wicker chaise longue underneath a giant awning and kept fanning herself with this enormous plaited straw fan. She looked like one of those eccentric dowagers who go native in some lost corner of the British empire.''

She stopped, her voice catching. ''I can't do this.''

''Yes, you can, Constance. Please go on. I'm really enjoying hearing about your stay with your grandparents. Where did they live? Somewhere fairly close to Manhattan?''

Constance traced a teardrop of condensation down the side of the window. ''They lived in Hatterington, out on Long Island,'' she said. ''When I was a little kid, I spent most of my summer vacations with them, and when I started high school, I lived with them all the time. Elena and I learned to swim together when she was ten and I was nine. We were always friends after that.''

Elena, Ed wrote, afraid to interrupt the hesitant flow of her story. *Who is she?*

''I'd always loved the water, and Lili did, too. She took after me in that, because Victor was secretly afraid of the sea, although he'd never admit it. Lili was in heaven that weekend—she splashed in and out of the water all day long. She could already do a kind of lopsided dog paddle before this weekend, but by Sunday afternoon, she'd learned to put her face into the water and do a kind of crawl. She was so pleased with herself, she kept splashing and giggling for hours at a stretch. I worried about her getting sunburned, because she was so fair-skinned, so we tried to persuade her to sit under Gran's awning and listen to a story. She wouldn't, of course."

"Did she get sunburned?" Ed prompted when the flow of reminiscence seemed about to dry up.

"Not really. She just turned pink. My grandmother bought her this little cotton sun hat with a pattern of strawberries and bumblebees all over it, and a toweling wrap to match. Lili didn't mind the wrap, but she hated the hat. She kept trying to take it off, and I kept putting it back on. Eventually she turned it into a game. She'd take off her hat and sit on it, and I had to tickle her tummy until she rolled over and I could grab the hat."

Constance's voice broke, and Ed heard the quick, harsh intake of her breath. "Why am I doing this?" she muttered, the question addressed to herself rather than to him. She whirled, eyes flashing, body rigid. Ed was astonished to realize that she must have once been a beautiful woman. "Damn you, Doctor! Why are you putting me through this? I won't remember her, *I won't!*" She leaned against the window, her body convulsed with dry, tearing sobs.

"Okay, I guess that's enough for today." Ed put his arm around her shoulder and led her back to the chair. "We won't talk about Liliana anymore, Constance, that's a promise. At least not for today. Let's talk about Victor instead."

Constance made a choking sound, somewhere between a laugh and a sob. "And that's supposed to be better?"

"I don't know," Ed said. "You tell me. Who is Victor?"

He already knew the answer to his question. He'd checked with the accounting department and discovered that Constance's bills were paid by Victor Rodier, her exhusband. Even for a resident of Merton House, all of whom tended to be well-connected, Mr. Rodier was a very impressive ex-husband to have. He was currently a federal judge on the influential Ninth Circuit, but that was small potatoes compared to the professional honors that lay ahead of him. The president of the United States had just announced his intention to appoint Mr. Rodier to an unexpected vacancy on the Supreme Court resulting from the death of Justice Williams.

Ed had read that the FBI was conducting standard background checks, and the media were scurrying to dig up dirt, but Victor Rodier's nomination was expected to sail through the Senate Judiciary Committee and to receive almost unanimous confirmation in the full Senate. The White House staff, not noted for its efficiency in finding candidates for public office, had picked a winner this time: a jurist who not only met with the approval of the American Bar Association, but also managed to soothe liberal consciences without mortally offending conservative principles. A miracle indeed.

Ed returned his attention to Constance, who was staring at the floor again, her burst of emotion conquered, her defensive armor back in place. She clearly didn't want to answer any questions about Victor Rodier, but he sensed that her resistance was far less entrenched than it had been in the case of her daughter. "Who is Victor?" he persisted. "Tell me about him."

She shrugged. "He's my husband. My ex-husband, I should say. The Honorable Victor Rodier, Esquire, attorney-at-law."

"I've heard of him, of course. He's a very distinguished and accomplished man."

Silence.

"Did you know that he's been nominated to fill the vacancy on the Supreme Court bench caused by the death of Justice Williams?"

"Yes, I knew. I read an article about his nomination in the papers last Sunday. Victor must be very happy."

If Ed hadn't been watching her so closely he'd have missed the tiny, downward twist of her mouth, as if she'd just tasted something rancid. What did Constance disapprove of? he wondered. Victor's nomination to the Supreme Court? Or did she resent the fact that this would make him happy?

"You sound angry, Constance. Why don't you like Victor?"

She looked straight at him, and he had the uncanny feeling that she was about to share with him something of extraordinary importance. Then her gaze lost focus and she stared past him. "I don't know what you mean, Dr. Foster. I never said that I don't like Victor. He's a wonderful man. Everyone knows that."

"But you're not everyone. Do *you* think he's wonderful?"

"Of course."

"Why is he wonderful, Constance?"

"He's been very good to me. He understands that I'm crazy, and he's forgiven me for... for what I did. How many men would be willing to do that? He pays my bills here, and visits me each year, just to make sure that I'm all right."

"Still? He visits you after all these years?" Ed was genuinely surprised. Paying bills was one thing. If you were rich, money was a commodity easily expended. Devoting time to visiting a hopelessly insane ex-wife was much more remarkable.

"Each and every year, right after Thanksgiving," Constance said. "He never misses. You wait until you see the basket of fruit and chocolates he brings for the nurses when he comes. They're all in love with him. And I believe he used to send your predecessor a case of vintage burgundy. A little token of esteem from a noted philanthropist. Sent in gratitude, you understand, for taking such good care of his poor, mad wife.''

''Ex-wife,'' Ed murmured, writing down *Thanksgiving* on his notepad. He circled the word. Victor Rodier visited at Thanksgiving, usually the only time of year Constance became violent. Coincidence? Or did the visits precipitate the violence? How in hell had this connection been missed? There was no notation anywhere in Constance's files linking the two events. But then, the notes in her file were almost criminally sparse. Even her original admissions records were missing and, so far, the clerk in archives hadn't been able to trace them.

''Your husband divorced you seventeen years ago, nine years after you were hospitalized. I wonder why he waited so long? Was he hoping you'd be cured, do you think, so that you could resume your marriage?''

She gave an impatient snort. ''No,'' she said. ''Victor wasn't waiting to resume our marriage.''

''Then why didn't he divorce you for nine years?''

''That's easy to explain,'' she said crisply. ''He was waiting for my grandparents to die so that he'd have control of my share of their money. He was smart to wait.''

''Why?''

''He got my money. Most people assumed my grandparents would cut me out of their will, but in the end, I inherited twenty-eight million dollars from them. All of which is now administered by Victor, on my behalf. I'd say his patience paid off handsomely, wouldn't you?''

Six

Long Island, N.Y.
Thursday, June 13, 1996

Jess was beginning to understand why detectives in the movies spent so much time complaining about their feet. After a mere two days of investigating the Pazmanys' murky past, she'd already reached the conclusion that the prime qualifications for a good investigator were comfortable shoes and dogged determination—in that order. Right now, her feet were in fair-to-middling shape; her determination wasn't holding up so well.

Hatterington turned out to be a town on the North Shore of Long Island, a couple of stops down the line from Oyster Bay and Sagamore Hill, the one-time home of President Theodore Roosevelt. She was the only passenger to disembark at the tiny Hatterington station, and the lone cabdriver waiting outside spoke just enough English to make it plain that he'd never heard of Bartlett House, or a couple called Mr. and Mrs. Wendell P. Grant. He did, however, provide the information that Old Cove Road covered a distance of more than ten miles, which put to rest Jess's vague plan of walking down a street full of quaint, turn-of-the-century houses, and knocking on doors until she came across the Grants, or someone who remembered them.

Jess had hoped to avoid another search through civic records, but there seemed to be no alternative if she was to discover anything about the Grants. Resisting the temptation offered by various coffeehouses and ice-cream parlors on Main Street, she walked to the center of town and found the courthouse on the east side of the square. A clerk in the tax assessor's office took only a couple of minutes to ascertain that there were eight estates located on Old Cove Road, all identified by lot numbers rather than by name or postal address. It took less than a minute more for the clerk to uncover that none of the eight properties was currently owned by anyone called Grant.

So what else had she been expecting? Jess thought resignedly. If records of the Pazmanys' past had been littered all over New York, presumably the social services people would have realized years ago that the child in the back of the Pazmanys' car was not, in fact, their daughter. At least Jess didn't have to invent excuses for asking the clerk to dig a little deeper into the history of Bartlett House. Property taxes were a matter of public record, and once she'd paid the token five-dollar search fee, the clerk expressed no curiosity about her wanting to know who had owned the property in 1969. He hunted through a huge, old-fashioned loose-leaf ledger and surfaced with the gratifying news that Wendell P. Grant and Olivia Naughton Grant had been the joint owners that year of lot number six on Old Cove Road, comprising twenty-seven acres of land, "together with dwelling, cottage, stables and other improvements."

"There's been no development on that street, so I can show you exactly where their property was...is...located," the clerk said, tearing a tourist map from a pad on the counter. He drew a line in purple ink from the symbol for the courthouse to a stretch of oceanfront road that touched the far western extremity of the town. "Here you are. I know this place. It's a beautiful house, must be a hundred years old at least. You can't see it very well from the road, but I like to sail, and you get a real good view of it when you're out on the water."

"Do you know who owns it now?"

"Not offhand, but I can look it up for you. Let's see, that's lot six, tax parcel number 527, on Old Cove..."

He hummed a Beatles tune off-key as he searched through the computer printout of the current year's tax assessments. "Here we go." He held a ruler against the line of computerized text so that he could read it accurately. "It's owned by a corporation, Ocean View Properties, Incorporated. For tax purposes, we have it valued at 3.9 million dollars, but that assessment's three years old. It's due to be revalued this year, and the taxes will go up, almost certainly."

"It's owned by a corporation?" Jess said, disappointed that her lead seemed to be unraveling. "You mean it's run as a hotel, or a resort, or something?" If so, it would scarcely be worth bothering to pay the place a visit. Her chances of finding an employee who'd remember the Grants would be close to zero. Quite apart from the fact that if Bartlett House and the surrounding land was valued at close to four million dollars today, it must have been worth a small fortune even in 1969. Which meant that, in all likelihood, the Grants had merely been philanthropists paying the bills for a sick child, not intimate, personal friends of the Pazmanys. Realistically, how would a nurse and a carpenter from Queens ever make the acquaintance of a couple living in a hundred-year-old mansion, on an estate tucked away in one of Long Island's most exclusive enclaves?

"It's not a hotel," the clerk said, shaking his head. "Officially speaking, it's a private residence."

"Then who actually lives there? Do you know?"

"I've no idea." He shrugged, closing the heavy ledger. "The people in this town tend to like their privacy, that's why most of them paid several millions dollars to move here. And the folks living on Old Cove Road sure don't mix and mingle with peons like me."

"But what does corporate ownership mean, precisely?"

"Could mean a lot of different things," he told her. "Ocean View might be the holding company for a Japanese investment partnership. Or it might be a front company for a Middle Eastern oil sheik—we've got several of those in town. Or it could be an American company headquartered in Manhattan, with a CEO who likes somewhere to spend his hot summer weekends. Happens all the time. The CEO buys a fancy house right on the beach, entertains clients there a few times a year, and writes off all the running costs to corporate expenses. If you're really interested in who owns the estate, you'll have to find out who's behind Ocean View Properties. If you drop in at the library, one of the librarians could tell you how to do that. You can't miss the library—it's right on South Street."

"Actually, it's the Grants I'm interested in, more than the house and the current owners."

"Then the historical society would be your best bet," the clerk said. "They collect photos and memorabilia on every house that was built before World War II, and on the families that lived in them, too. But it's staffed by volunteers and it's only open on the weekend."

"Maybe I'll come back tomorrow," Jess said, planning no such thing. Her earlier enthusiasm for finding the Grants was beginning to seem absurd, and rummaging through mementos of Bartlett House would provide no insights whatsoever into the doings of Elena and Rudolph Pazmany. She smiled at the clerk. "Thanks for your help, I appreciate it."

She walked down the courthouse steps into the bright afternoon sunshine, almost ready to call it quits and spend the remainder of the afternoon exploring Hatterington's generous supply of antique stores and gourmet-food shops. Main Street looked as if it provided a dozen different ways to blow your diet in three mouthfuls or less. An enticing prospect.

The cabby from the railroad station rescued her waistline. Loath to lose a paying fare on what was obviously a slow afternoon, he had driven over from the station and parked himself outside the courthouse, waiting for her. "You found the house you lookin' for, lady?"

"Yes, thank you—"

He sprang out of his seat and whipped open the rear door of his cab. "I take you there, lady. Take you back to train station afterward. You catch four-fifteen back to city. No more trains after four-fifteen until nine o'clock."

Ye Olde Ice Cream Shoppe was beckoning to her. But she'd come all this way, Jess decided, she might as well go look at Bartlett House. Maybe Mr. Ocean View Properties would be in residence and prove to be a mine of information about the Grants. Even if the place was empty, she would at least be able to tell herself that, by going there, she'd done all that was reasonable to track down one of her frail links to the Pazmanys. Which, she reminded herself, was why she'd made the trip to Long Island in the first place.

"Okay," she said, getting into the cab and handing the driver the map marked by the clerk. "That's where I want to go. Is it far?"

He glanced at the map. "Coupla miles. Maybe less. Get you back in time for four-fifteen train, no problem." The driver slammed the door and set off at breakneck speed, oblivious not only to the speed limit, but to the hazards posed by Hatterington's narrow, twisting roads, which clearly hadn't been reengineered since the horse was the town's major form of transportation. He squealed to a halt outside a set of padlocked iron gates, shaded by gnarled cherry trees, and waved in the direction of the winding gravel driveway.

"This your place. You walk to house. The gates are locked. I wait here for you." He got out of the car, leaned against the hood and lit up a cigarette.

Jess followed the cabby out of the car, not attempting to conceal her exasperation. "If the gates are locked, how am I supposed to get in and let people know I'm here?"

The cabby pointed to the beach, dimly visible through a grove of larch and pine. "That way. Walk across the beach." He puffed on his cigarette, looking very pleased with himself. Why shouldn't he? Jess thought morosely. His damn meter was still running.

She stared through the wrought-iron gates, trying to get some sense of whether or not anyone was home. The hum of a lawn mower persuaded her that they were, although with nine acres of grounds to maintain, presumably Mr. Ocean View Properties hired a service to cut his grass. She looked for a doorbell or an electronic intercom on the steel pillars supporting the gate, but there was neither, and rattling the wrought-iron bars produced no response from anyone. How the heck did the owners know when they had visitors? Jess could only suppose that guests didn't come calling at four-million-dollar estates without their cell phones.

The cabby was right: if she wanted to reach the house, she would have to go via the beach. Jess kissed a mental goodbye to her favorite linen slacks and clambered through the grove of trees, doing her best to avoid the prickly undergrowth. The view that greeted her when she emerged onto a narrow gravel path that marked the boundary between the beach and the Bartlett House property was almost worth the sacrifice of her slacks.

The beach was at least fifty feet wide. Dry sand was separated from smooth, wet sand by occasional rocks and an undulating line of seaweed that indicated the high-water mark of the last tide. With the pungent salt smell of the sea tickling her nostrils, Jess watched as a flock of sea gulls wheeled and dived, searching for dinner in amongst the damp fronds of seaweed or in little pools of seawater left in the rocks. She breathed deeply, dragging the moist, tangy air into her lungs, luxuriating in its freshness. The sound of waves lapping on the shore exerted an almost irresistible fascination, and for a second Jess was seized by a disconcerting flash of déjà vu. Before she could register precisely what it was about the scene that felt familiar, the sensation passed.

Perhaps the scene had evoked pleasant memories of her childhood. She could clearly remember the first time Grandpa Gene had taken her and the boys to his favorite fishing spot on the shore of Lake Erie, northeast of Cleveland. She couldn't have been more than six or seven at the time. That had been back in the bad old days, before the lake was cleaned up. The fish were still full of mercury and God-knows-what, and you couldn't eat anything you caught without jeopardizing your entire digestive system. So they'd thrown back the fish they'd caught—which suited Jess just fine—and cooked hot dogs over the grill. She'd been able to swim better than Todd or Matt, which didn't please them too much, and she'd beaten them in a couple of races to make sure they understood that girls were every bit as capable as boys. Then she'd left them to race each other to exhaustion while she cajoled Grandpa Gene into helping her build a sand castle, with turrets and battlements and a moat on which they'd sailed a little plastic boat. The boat had been a Cracker Jack toy, she remembered, a gift from Todd in one of his benevolent older-brother moods.

Thinking about the day brought a lump to her throat. Grandpa Gene had been such a wonderful person. He might have screwed up in not telling her about Magda's letter and Jessica Marie's death, but Jess didn't doubt for a single instant that he'd screwed up entirely out of concern for her.

She blinked and scuffed the toe of her sandal in the sandy path, putting the bittersweet memories of her grandfather aside. She'd always loved the water, but this beach struck her as especially beautiful. She could imagine how much fun a toddler would have playing in the sand, then running into the shallow water to cool off before scampering up to the house in search of lemonade and Popsicles. Funny, she could almost picture the family on the beach: grandmother and mother laughing indulgently while the grandfather helped his granddaughter build a giant sand castle. Making sand pies for the wall around the castle. Sneaking off her sun hat when her mother wasn't looking. Running down to the sea with her pail to bring back water to fill the moat... No, wait, Jess thought suddenly. That was what she'd done with Grandpa Gene at the lake, not here by the ocean.

Jess shook off the mental picture, which was simultaneously vivid and confused, and walked up the path leading to the house. Bartlett House was an 1880s-style frame-and-brick building, with sweeping verandas, an old-fashioned screened porch and a windowed turret that looked big enough to contain a large room. The view from the turret out to sea must be breathtaking, Jess realized, and she could easily understand why Mr. Ocean View Properties had wanted to own this place. She wouldn't mind owning it herself if she could ever come up with a spare four million dollars. She grinned at the thought.

The grounds between the back of the house and the beach were landscaped in a style Jess mentally described as tamed wilderness. The plantings were designed to look as if they might have appeared there by whim of nature, and every bush was trimmed to induce maximum foliage, the trees were lopped and cropped, and the earth weeded into submissive neatness. The yard workers had obviously been busy cutting back the ivy that grew over an arbor joining the house to the stables. A few fronds had been left dangling to validate the wild look, but giant wire baskets of clippings waited to be picked up and carted away.

She debated ringing the back doorbell, but that seemed too intimate a method of introducing herself to such an imposing household. She walked around to the front of the house and finally saw the tractor mower that was making all the noise. The driver was wearing protective earpieces to block the roar of the engine and appeared oblivious to everything except the row of grass in front of him. In the distance, down toward the gate, a couple of men were tending beds of impatiens and geraniums, the pinks, reds and mauves blending in a gorgeous splash of color.

The house itself was as well cared for as the grounds. Not only was the white paint fresh and the brick sandblasted, but the windowpanes sparkled and the stone steps looked as if they'd just been power-washed. To keep a seafront house looking this spic-and-span must require a fortune spent on professional maintenance, Jess thought. Bartlett House was certainly lovely, but the more Jess saw of it, the less likely it seemed that she would find anyone in this luxurious setting who had ever heard of an obscure immigrant family called Pazmany.

Still, she was here, she reasoned, so she might as well get on with her request. Her first ring at the doorbell wasn't answered. She tried again and eventually the door was opened by a thin, rather plain woman in her late fifties, with droopy jowls that reminded Jess of a beagle. She was wearing khaki twill shorts, knee socks and a collared knit shirt: the uniform of the preppy.

"Yes?" The woman looked bored and sounded extremely impatient.

"I'm sorry to bother you, but I wondered if it would be possible for me to have a word with anyone who might be familiar with the history of this house and the couple who used to own it."

The woman stared down her nose. "When you rang the bell, I assumed you were one of the yard workers."

Yard workers dared to ring the front doorbell? Brave guys. Jess fixed her polite smile firmly in place. "No, I'm not a yard worker. Before my marriage, my name was Jessica Marie Pazmany, and I was hoping to talk with a member of the family that owns this house—"

"How did you get in?" the woman asked, her gaze suddenly alert. She glared at Jess with an expression that suggested a bucket of fertilizer manure would have been more welcome.

Jess could feel her smile congealing into a grimace. "I walked across the beach—"

"The only access from the beach to this house crosses private property. You're trespassing."

"I'm sorry, I don't want to take up your time," she said, "but this is very important to me. I'm trying to find out about a couple who once owned this house. Their name was Grant. Mr. and Mrs. Wendell P. Grant and they were living here in 1969. Do you by any chance know where I can find them? I'm anxious to talk to them about a family called Pazmany. I was adopted when I was about four years old after an automobile accident, and I believe there might be some connection to the Grants—"

The woman's expression changed from disdain to anger. "Don't you people ever give up? Find someone else to harass with your stupid questions. Leave my husband alone or I'll call the police." She slammed the door.

Jess blinked, the sound of the slammed door reverberating in her ears. Obviously the woman had mistaken Jess for someone else, but who? A persistent door-to-door salesperson? A missionary for some obscure religious sect? She debated ringing the bell again and trying to give a better account of why she wanted to find the Grants. But when she attempted to come up with a reasonably short explanation, it sounded so absurd that she gave up.

Maybe she should make her way back to the center of town and see if the librarians had any collective memories that stretched far enough to include the Grants. Or maybe she should just return to Manhattan. She could always write a letter to Ocean View Properties, in care of the Bartlett House address, setting out who she was and why she was anxious to get in touch with the Grants. Although, in truth, she was beginning to wonder exactly what pertinent information she expected the Grants to provide. Even if she found them, even if they said they remembered Jessica Marie, so what? It was ridiculous to expect them to know about the unidentified child who had been traveling in the Pazmanys' car. The link was far too tenuous for it to be remembered twenty-six years later.

Jess was halfway down the gravel driveway before it dawned on her that the gate was still padlocked, and she would have to go back to the road the same way she'd come, via the beach. She stopped and turned abruptly, sufficiently absorbed in her own thoughts that she didn't notice an old man, who was standing by the bush he'd been clipping, until she bumped into him.

"Watch where you're going," he growled.

"Sorry," she apologized. "I wasn't paying attention."

"Too much of a hurry, that's your trouble. These days, everyone's always in a hurry." The man coughed a couple of times around his cigarette before going back to his clipping.

"The gardens here are very well cared for," Jess said, trying to make amends. "Are you in charge of them?"

"Have been for thirty years and more. Used to work here full-time, now I run a landscaping service. Nobody employs their own gardeners anymore."

Jess caught her breath. Good God, had she actually stumbled across an old family retainer she'd hoped to find? "Then you must have known the Grants," she said. "Mr. and Mrs. Wendell P. Grant. The people who used to live here in the late sixties."

He stubbed out his cigarette on a wet laurel leaf and tossed the butt into a wheelbarrow of garden trash. "Maybe I did. You a reporter?"

"No, I'm in public relations. I work for the state of Colorado, in their visitors' bureau."

He chopped furiously at the bush. "Visitors' bureau? So what do you do there?" He grunted. "If you ask me, all these government offices are just an excuse to waste tax-payers' money.''

Jess hung on to her temper. He certainly wasn't long on charm, she thought. But if he'd been working here for thirty years, the Grants must once have been his employers and it was worth expending some effort to persuade him to talk about them. ''For personal reasons, I'm really anxious to get in touch with either Mr. or Mrs. Grant,'' she said. ''I'd be very grateful if you could tell me where I might find them.''

''How grateful?'' the gardener asked, scratching his chin.

Belatedly, it dawned on Jess that the gardener was waiting to be bribed. So much for old family retainers chatting sentimentally about the past. She took a twenty-dollar bill from her purse and handed it to him. ''Here. Now can you remember where the Grants are?'' she asked.

He folded the bill and tucked it carefully into the pocket of his baggy denim coveralls. Then he jerked his finger over his shoulder, vaguely in the direction of town. ''They're in Raynham Hill,'' he said. ''Over in Frithport. You can't miss it.''

Jess barely repressed a flare of excitement. So the Grants had simply moved to another North Shore town. ''That's wonderful! Do you have an exact address for them?'' she asked.

''Don't need an address,'' he said. ''Just ask the man at the gate for directions.'' He turned his back on her and gave a lethal swipe to a protruding twig. ''Raynham Hill. Anybody in Frithport can direct you.''

''The Grants live in a gated community?'' Jess asked. ''I didn't know they had any developments like that in this part of Long Island.''

The gardener hacked out another cough, and Jess realized he was laughing. "Raynham Hill's the Quaker cemetery," he said. "Mr. and Mrs. Grant are both buried there. Have been for near about twenty years."

By the time she'd finished telling Dan the story of her wasted afternoon, Jess discovered she was laughing. She leaned back in her chair, sipped her wine and felt the frustrations of the day gradually fall away. She had no idea how he'd managed to talk her into having dinner with him for the second night in a row, but she was extraordinarily glad that she was here with him, and not alone in her hotel room, trying to decide if she should hang around in New York, or go back to Denver and hire an investigator.

She twirled the stem of her wineglass, watching the rich red burgundy tilt from side to side. "I don't know why I had it fixed in my mind that the Grants would still be alive," she said. "I didn't waste time tracking down Dr. Weir because I'd decided he'd either be dead or retired. Why didn't I assume the same thing about the Grants?"

"Because you love the North Shore of Long Island and were looking for an excuse to ride out there?" Dan suggested, taking the dessert menus from their hovering waiter. "We'll look at these in a minute," he told the man.

"Yes, sir." The waiter nodded deferentially and stepped away from their table.

Jess grinned. "You always did handle pushy waiters better than anyone else I know. I see you haven't lost your magic touch."

"At least with waiters," Dan agreed.

She felt a sudden flush of heat suffuse her cheeks at the memory of other areas in which his touch had once seemed magical to her, but he handed her a dessert menu without comment and she relaxed again. Nothing about Dan's behavior since she'd arrived in New York justified the way she responded to his most casual remarks with instant sexual awareness. Chill out, she admonished herself. She didn't want to make a fool of herself by reacting to innuendos that existed only in her imagination.

Dan poured the last of their wine. "I want to hear more about your encounter with the gardener," he said. "What did you say his name was?"

"Gus."

"Right. Did Gus tell you anything about the Grants except that they were dead?"

She wrinkled her nose. "Not much. Apparently they were both in their eighties when they died after brief illnesses. He said they were decent people, which, coming from him, was a compliment of the highest order. I asked him if he'd ever heard of a couple called Rudolph and Elena Pazmany and he said that he hadn't. I mentioned the name Jessica Marie, too, and that didn't seem to ring any bells."

"Mmm. If he didn't remember any of those names, that probably rules out my brilliant idea."

"Which was?"

"That one of the Pazmanys had worked for the Grants," he said. "If Rudolph had once been the estate handyman, for example, it would explain why the Grants took enough of an interest in Jessica Marie to pay for her medical bills."

"You're right, it would, but if Rudolph worked with him, surely Gus ought to remember his name?"

"Unless he's getting forgetful in his old age."

Jess shook her head. "Sharp as a barrel full of monkeys."

"What if Elena worked for the Grants before she was married?" Dan suggested. "In that case, Gus would only have known her maiden name, so Pazmany wouldn't mean anything to him."

"You're right. Damn! It never occurred to me to ask if he remembered a young woman called Elena Korda."

"Call back and ask tomorrow morning." Dan shot her a quizzical look. "Tell me you have a phone number for Gus..."

"Yes, I was at least efficient enough to get his card. I guess I will call, just to satisfy my own curiosity," she said. "Funnily, I think ol' Gus enjoyed reminiscing about the past once he got started. I had the impression he was on the brink of launching into a piece of juicy scandal when that prune of a woman from the house came out to speak to him. She was furious to find the two of us talking, and she told Gus that he should know better than to hobnob with reporters. I told her again that I wasn't a reporter. She repeated her threat about calling the police, and I decided that would be a very good moment to leave. I can't imagine why she has this hang-up about reporters. The woman seemed downright paranoid."

Dan shook his head. "She's probably just afflicted with old-money syndrome. Haven't you ever noticed that old money hires public-relations people to keep their names out of the media, while new money hires people to get their names in?" He grinned. "You'd think the two sets could work out some kind of a deal and cut out the middle-men."

Jess laughed. "But that would mean old and new money had to converse, and it'll be a cold day in hell before that happens. I'm sure this woman has never spoken voluntarily to a *nouveau riche* upstart in her life. She'd perfected that haughty down-the-nose squint you can do only if you've been intensively trained since birth."

Dan chuckled. Then his gaze locked with hers, and their laughter abruptly died. The sounds of the restaurant faded into silence and for a moment Jess was aware of nothing beyond the blood thrumming in her ears and the heat flaring in the pit of her stomach. Dan's eyes darkened and the skin over his cheekbones became tinged with sudden color. She wondered, almost abstractly, whether her own face betrayed sexual hunger with equal clarity.

It was Dan who looked away first. "Are you planning to track down Jessica's doctor tomorrow?" he asked, his voice only a little husky. "The state medical board must have a record of him, so he shouldn't be too hard to find."

"If he's alive." She took a sip of ice water, forcing herself to concentrate on what they were talking about and not that Dan, with his late-night shadow of beard, looked more sexy than any man had a right to. Okay, so he was overendowed with sexual charisma and her body was responding. So what? They both knew—God, how they knew!—that there was more to forging a successful relationship than a desire to tumble into bed. But she had to take another long swallow of water before she could continue.

"To be honest, Dan, I'm losing enthusiasm for this quest. It's too quixotic for somebody with my practical sort of nature. I don't want to turn out like those adoptees who spend their entire lives following up every clue and hint, however slight, that might lead them to their birth parents. Is it worth tracking down Dr. Weir? Even if he's alive and remembers Jessica Marie's case, what good does that do me? We end up confronting the same old problem—finding out about Jessica Marie isn't going to explain why the Pazmanys had me in the back seat of their car."

"Good point." Dan frowned. "Now that you've confirmed that Jessica Marie died and that the death certificate Magda sent your grandfather was genuine, her family history is irrelevant. The whole point is that you *weren't* the Pazmanys' child." He stopped for a moment before going on, "We need to stop obsessing about the Pazmanys and start looking in a different direction. You must have come into their care from somewhere. Where? The stork didn't bring you. They didn't find you under a cabbage. I think we should at least check into the possibility that there was another little girl, aged three or four, who went missing some time before you turned up in the back seat of the Pazmanys' rental car."

Jess felt her throat muscles constrict in visceral resistance to his suggestion. "What you're saying implies that the Pazmanys kidnapped me. We've discussed this before. I don't believe they did."

"Right at this moment, I'm not implying anything about the Pazmanys," Dan said. "I'm merely suggesting that we look through back issues of a few New York–area newspapers and see if there are any cases of little girls reported missing in the months between Jessica Marie's death and your arrival in Cleveland on the night of the ninth of December, 1969. At worst, we're going to waste a few hours scrolling through microfilm. At best, we might find reports of a child called Liliana who disappeared from her home right before you turned up in Cleveland."

She felt a little thrill of unease at the sound of Dan saying *Liliana*. And yet, she was the one who'd insisted that Liliana had once been her name, so her refusal to probe the possibility that she'd been the victim of a kidnapping was blatantly irrational. During the two years she'd been married to Dan, she'd never felt free to confess any of her inner doubts. Oddly, now that she wasn't married to him, it didn't seem necessary to keep up the pretense of total competence. Her inability to make their marriage a success relieved her of the obligation to appear perfect—what was the point of trying to fake something they both knew was a lie?

"The Pazmanys were my fantasy parents," she admitted. "Anytime the going got rough in my life, I would pretend that if the Pazmanys had survived the car crash, the three of us would have been the world's most idyllic family." She tried for a carefree laugh that cracked in the middle. "I get nervous when you suggest doing something that threatens to wreck my favorite fantasy."

"Maybe it's time for some major demolition work on that fantasy support system of yours," Dan said. "Sometimes, if you cling too hard to a dream, you forget there's a real world on your doorstep. Not quite as perfect as your dreamworld, perhaps, but a hell of a lot more interesting."

"It's not unusual for an adopted child to cope with the problems of adolescence by idealizing her birth family," Jess said, trying not to sound too defensive. "In every other way, I think most people would say I have a very down-to-earth view of the world."

"My God, Jess, you can't be serious," he said. "As far as I can tell, you've idealized every relationship in your life that's even marginally important to you. The Zajaks were more than content to buy into your dreams, but people like me, who prefer at least a gloss of reality to sugarcoat their fantasies, just get frozen out of your life."

"Is this one of your profound new insights into our marriage that you were talking about the other night?" Jess inquired hotly. "That I screw up relationships by idealizing them? For your information, I have excellent interpersonal relationships with my family, my colleagues. Everyone except you, in fact—"

"Sure you do. Why not? You not only idealize relationships, you work on the principle that you must never, in any circumstances, display your negative feelings to another human being. For most people, that means you're terrific to have around. For a man who would occasionally like a wife rather than a Barbie doll for company, the going can get tough."

Barbie doll? He was calling her a *Barbie doll!* Jess struggled to control a spurt of red-hot anger. "You, of course, prefer to spend your time with some cuddly sex kitten who waves her inadequacy in your face like a banner. Why, Dan? Is that because you can then go into your macho protective mode? Makes for great sex, I guess, when the little woman tosses all her burdens into your lap and allows you to take charge. *Lie back, baby, and Dan will help you forget all your problems.* Well, I'm sorry, but that's not the kind of wife I wanted to be. I'm a competent person and I'm not willing to pretend otherwise."

Jess realized that her voice was spiraling upward and that her hands were balled into fists on the table. She controlled the ridiculous urge to hit something, preferably Dan. Damn, why did she always let him provoke her into saying something she hadn't intended? And why the hell couldn't she keep sex out of their discussions?

Dan leaned across the table, eyes flashing, eyebrows drawn into a furious scowl. She could almost see the heated response forming on his lips. Suddenly his mouth twisted into an odd, self-mocking smile and he pulled back, looking at her with rueful amusement. "Hell, Jess, do you want to go to bed with me even half as much as I want to go to bed with you?"

She stopped herself a split second before saying yes. Oh, God, she'd never had a smidgen of resistance to that damn smile of his! Her steaming anger evaporated, metamorphosing into equally steaming desire. She didn't want to contemplate what would have happened next if they'd been alone, but she was honest enough to acknowledge—at least to herself—that it would have taken place horizontally and without clothes. Thank heaven they were in a restaurant.

She drew a deep breath. "I may want to go to bed with you, Dan, but anytime the urge gets overwhelming, I just remember Shanna Ryan and my desire cools off with gratifying speed."

Dan's gaze blanked for a moment. Then he looked at her, holding her gaze through sheer force of will. "Let me explain to you about Shanna Ryan—"

"No."

"Please, Jess, for both our sakes. It's past due."

She closed her eyes. "No. She . . . it . . . has no relevance to anything—"

"On the contrary, it has relevance to almost everything. The fact that I committed adultery with Shanna Ryan is an unhealed wound for both of us."

"Talk to your therapist," Jess said through clenched teeth. She thought she'd put enough distance between herself and her marriage to hear Dan say Shanna Ryan's name without reacting. But right now she was feeling sick, so obviously she'd been wrong. "As far as I'm concerned, *your* need to be unfaithful isn't something *we* need to discuss."

"Jess, hear me out. Give me five minutes and really listen to what I'm saying for once."

"Our marriage wasn't working. You found gratification somewhere else. End of explanation."

"You're not even close, Jess. By the time I met Shanna, I was desperate to end our marriage. But choosing Shanna Ryan as a weapon was an incredibly stupid thing to do. I hurt you in ways I never intended and I badly want to put things right."

"You can't. Accept that, and let's move on." Her mouth was so dry, her tongue felt as if it was sticking to the roof. "You hadn't slept with me for eight weeks, Dan, and then you strolled in and calmly announced that Shanna Ryan had just delivered the greatest night of sex you'd ever experienced."

"I was lying."

"You mean you didn't sleep with her?" Absurdly, Jess felt a tiny spark of hope.

"No, I slept with her. I mean that the sex wasn't wonderful."

Jess's hand shook as she reached for her glass of water. "What does the understanding ex-wife say at this point, Dan? Gee, I'm sorry? I hope it got better later?"

"There was no later. Shanna and I both knew from the beginning that this was strictly a one-night stand. She left to fly back to L.A. before I came home, and there sure as hell was nothing about our night together to bring her back to me for a repeat performance."

"And this is supposed to make me feel better about the way our marriage ended? We got divorced over a single night of lousy sex as opposed to getting divorced over a blistering, glorious affair?"

"Our divorce had almost nothing to do with sex, adulterous or otherwise. We got divorced because I was a self-obsessed failure, with just enough sense of self-preservation to know that I'd never find the guts to pull myself out of the morass with you hovering over me, stretching out your hand just far enough to prevent my head from sinking under."

Jess reached blindly for her purse, which was tangled somewhere in the legs of her chair. "Dan, I'm leaving. I don't want to hear this. I don't *need* to hear this—"

Dan took both her hands, holding them tight. "There's only one reason I slept with Shanna," he said. "I knew that committing adultery—having a flagrant, blatant affair—was the only way I'd ever convince you to divorce me. You were too loyal, Jess. You'd never have given up on me even though it was damn near killing you to stay in the marriage. Damn near killing both of us, in fact, although for different reasons."

She would have been wounded to the quick by the implications of what Dan was saying if she hadn't been numb with disbelief. How many more ways was he going to find to say that the failure of their marriage had been her fault? Thank God, she didn't have to sit and listen to him. That was the blissful release a divorce gave you: the freedom not to listen, not to feel hurt.

Jess tugged her hands out of his grip and pushed back her chair, stumbling to her feet. "I apologize one more time for my multiple failures, Dan. I was raised to believe that loyalty is a virtue. I'm sorry you found it such a pain in the ass."

She stormed through the dining room, completely indifferent to the stares of the other customers. She was vaguely aware of the maître d' speaking to her as she passed him. She had no idea if she replied. She escaped into the noisy, bustling haven of Eighty-fifth Street and stared blindly at the passing traffic. Oh, God, she'd forgotten what real rage felt like! Over the past three years she'd forgotten what it was like to seethe with so much aching, boiling fury that your skin felt too small and tight to contain your anger.

A cab drew to a halt at the curb and she stepped in before noticing Dan was right behind her. She tried to get out when she realized he intended to come with her, but he simply closed the door and directed the driver to take them to her hotel on Forty-second Street. Her rage exploded, but somehow she managed to keep it spuming and frothing inside, not spilling into the open where it would humiliate her. When she acknowledged that she was literally on the point of throwing punches at him, she sat on her hands. He was not going to reduce her to the ultimate indignity of physical violence.

"If you could try to stop looking like an early Christian martyr praying for deliverance from the barbarians I'd appreciate it," he said curtly. "My only purpose in getting into this cab was to see you safely back to your hotel. I have no intention of trying to give you any more explanations you don't want to hear."

Jess stared out of the window. "I appreciate that," she said. They traveled in silence for several blocks. By Fifty-seventh Street, her inevitable impulse to smooth things over got the better of her. "I apologize for leaving the restaurant so abruptly."

"Don't worry about it," he said. "On the New York scandal scale, that rated about a minus fifty."

"I shouldn't have accepted your invitation to dinner. Somehow, we always seem to set each other off. I guess we bring out each other's worst qualities."

"Possibly." Dan's voice was remote. "We're in luck, the traffic's amazingly light tonight."

"Yes. Well, thanks, Dan, for dinner and ... and everything. You've been a big help these past two days." Feeling calmer, Jess risked turning around and actually looking in Dan's direction. He made no effort to hold her gaze.

She cleared her throat. "I guess we won't be seeing each other again before I go back to Colorado."

"Probably not." Dan finally lifted his head, and his eyes met hers. The surge of primal recognition that passed between them shocked Jess's entire being into stillness.

"Damn!" Dan muttered under his breath. He put his hands on her shoulders. Slowly, in a silence broken only by the pounding of the blood in her own ears, he drew her toward him. "Since you're leaving, I guess we'd better say goodbye."

She struggled for air. "Goodbye," she whispered.

"Not that way." His head lowered and his mouth slanted across hers. "This way."

Jess resisted for all of half a second before melting into his arms. He kissed her with a passion that mirrored her own. He kissed her with a tenderness that brought back a hundred sweet, buried memories. Finally, just as the cab drew to a halt outside her hotel, he kissed her with a hunger that left her hot, trembling and achingly aroused.

Dimly, she was aware of the hotel doorman opening the cab door. She stumbled out onto the sidewalk, her mind blank as she watched Dan exit the taxi and pay the driver. He turned to her. Her stomach lurched. Was he assuming she'd invite him up to her room? What was she going to say to him? Yes or no?

Dan didn't escort her inside. He put his hands on her shoulders and slowly bent his head, but he didn't kiss her mouth. Instead, he dropped a fleeting kiss on her forehead and another one on the end of her nose.

"Goodbye, Jess," he said softly. "Have a safe trip home to Colorado." He touched her lightly on the cheek in a gesture that wasn't quite a caress. And then, not waiting for her to reply, he strode off briskly into the warm night.

Jess let out the breath she hadn't realized she was holding. She stared after him, her mouth open, her body jangling with unfulfilled desire. It was a damn good thing he hadn't expected her to say anything, she thought dazedly. Most of what she was thinking right now was definitely unrepeatable.

Seven

Merton House
Saturday, June 15, 1996

Lunatics, Constance had discovered, didn't cope well with families, and their families returned the compliment. Merton House inmates received few visitors, in part because of the hospital's remote location, but chiefly because normal people were intimidated by the prospect of making conversation with their crazy relatives. Parents, siblings and the rare spouse who risked the discomfort of a face-to-face encounter usually chose a Saturday afternoon, and always waited for dry weather. This enabled them to stroll through the gardens with the family lunatic, easing the stress of finding something to talk about. Flowers, trees and the weather could be counted on as more or less safe subjects, although there were pitfalls for the unwary even in these innocuous topics.

Constance recognized that a paranoid schizophrenic or a psychotic depressive was not the easiest person in the world to talk to, but she had long ago concluded that the tension generated during visiting hours revealed a great deal more about the nature of families than about the nature of lunatics. Merton House didn't accept violent sociopaths, with the result that many of the inmates were simply people too fragile and too sensitive to bear the burden of lies and deception that life in the real world demanded. Madness, she suspected, was not an inability to see the world as it was, but rather a cursed ability to see the world far too clearly.

Since her grandparents were dead and her mother hadn't bothered to keep in touch even when Constance was officially sane, she was faced with the trauma of outside visitors only once a year—in November, when Victor paid his annual duty call. The rest of the year she was free of the anxiety that tended to grip inmates after lunch on Saturdays.

Today was a Saturday, Constance knew, but it was only June, thank God, and she luxuriated in the knowledge that it was almost five months until she needed to feel worried. Seated by the window, she amused herself by imagining that the blast of air-conditioning was a cool summer breeze blowing in off the ocean, and that the heavy metal grilles covering the windows were storm shutters on the sturdy New England beach house where her grandparents had lived. Transforming steel bars into storm shutters required a stretch of the imagination, but Constance had learned to be really good at pretending.

The television was on, as always, the buzz of synthetic voices a comfortable antidote to the psychotic voices humming inside most inmates' heads. Constance didn't really hear the TV, any more than she registered the presence of the two nurse's aides whose duty it was to stop the patients from hurting themselves and each other. One of the blessings of familiar surroundings was that they eventually became invisible, however bizarre they might appear to outsiders.

The parakeets, which a therapist had decided would be a nonthreatening focus for the inmates' nurturing instincts, were more intrusive. They chirped and squawked in their expensive cage, prisoners within the Merton House prison. Constance cordially disliked the therapist in question, and had spent several engrossing hours trying to teach the birds to say, *Fuck you.* So far, she'd met with a signal lack of success; the parakeets' squawks remained as obstinately nonverbal as the day they'd arrived in the lounge. Constance realized she was beginning to develop a sneaking admiration for their stubborn refusal to cooperate, despite her blandishments.

Secure in the cocoon of her well-known environment, she paid no attention to the ripple of nervous movement, the bark of laughter from Olive, the squeaks from Bernie, the general uneasy stir that marked the arrival of a stranger in the lounge. Peggy had given her a supply of modeling clay—minus tools, of course—and Constance was working on another of her figurines. Not a cuddly chipmunk this time, but a red fox with a bushy tail, thick coat and sharp brown eyes. Dr. Foster's eyes, she'd acknowledged some time ago. Eyes that saw far too much and ruthlessly pursued their prey. No, *ruthless* wasn't the right word, Constance thought, adjusting the tilt of the fox's head, wishing she had a knife. Dr. Foster wasn't ruthless. *Relentless* was a better word. He'd scented a mystery where she was concerned, and he was determined to unravel it.

She pushed the fox to one side, frustrated by her lack of tools. There was only so much detail you could achieve with the broken handle of a plastic spoon. Would it matter if Dr. Foster realized she was feigning her symptoms? she wondered. What would he say if he knew that it was more than three years since she'd stopped taking most of her medication, unless it was forcibly injected by a member of staff? Even to pose the question made her stomach churn with a sickening mixture of terror and excitement.

Suppose he decided she was sane and that she no longer needed to be confined within the security of Merton House? Would that be so bad? Could she allow it to happen? When she'd finally come out of the fugue that followed Lili's death, Victor warned her that if she told people the truth about her daughter's disappearance, she would be arrested and tried on federal charges of murder and kidnapping. He assumed it was fear of the death penalty that kept her silent, or perhaps a desire to spare her grandparents the agony of a trial. In fact, as much as she loved her grandparents, her silence had never been because of them. She kept quiet because she knew she didn't deserve the release from suffering that execution would bring.

She no longer expected the police to be waiting to arrest her the moment she set foot outside the Merton House gates, but the police, the law and Victor's threats were almost incidental to her current dilemma. Some sins could only be expiated by a lifetime of punishment, and Constance accepted that twenty-six years of being confined in an asylum was nowhere near long enough to pay for the hideous crime of killing her own child. Because she'd been guilty of that unnatural act, she couldn't let Dr. Foster discover the truth about her mental state. She had no right to end her punishment.

Even now, after years of living with the knowledge of her own evil, it was still hard to accept that she'd committed such a terrible crime. Deep down inside, she harbored a stubborn conviction that she wasn't a bad person. Constance stared into the too-perceptive eyes of her fox, trying for the umpteenth time to reconcile Lili's murder with her belief—never quite lost—that she had truly loved Lili. She shook her head impatiently. Why was it so difficult to accept that she'd killed the person she loved most? Half the murderers in the world probably loved their victims. This stupid reluctance to process what she'd done was probably the best argument that could be produced in favor of her insanity. Twenty-six years and she still wasn't ready to admit the burden of her own guilt. If only she could remember what had happened after—

She cut off the useless wish before it was fully articulated in her mind. She stroked her hand along the rough clay of the fox's back. What did Dr. Foster really think of her? she wondered. Probably he didn't think of *her,* at all. Not as Constance Howington Rodier, at least. She was simply a patient with severe mental problems, and he was a conscientious doctor. A perceptive and intelligent doctor, who was nowhere near as easy to deceive as Dr. Grable. Grable's major concern had been his public image as the director of the nation's most luxurious mental health facility. He had wanted clean, docile and well-fed inmates. He hadn't been in the least interested in exploring their wounded psyches.

Dr. Foster's name was Edgar—the nurses had mentioned that. And one day she'd heard someone from the mayor's office call him Ed. She liked the name Ed. It seemed warm and friendly and unpretentious. She didn't want to think of him as Ed, though. Safer to remember, at all times, that he was a doctor, the director-in-chief of her prison, the final arbiter of her punishment.

"Hello, Constance, my dear. How are you feeling this afternoon?"

Constance froze. Her lungs contracted and refused to expand. Her fingers crooked into paralyzed claws over the fox's back. For a moment, she thought she was going to faint.

Victor was here.

If she'd been able to, she'd have run away. But she couldn't move. She stared blindly at the Formica surface of the table. If she didn't look up, if she didn't see him in front of her, maybe she'd realize his voice had just been a figment of her imagination, a flashback from her stormy past.

"Aren't you going to say hello to Mr. Rodier, Constance? He's come all the way here to see you, and when he's so busy, too." Teresa, the aide who was with Victor, put her arm around Constance's shoulders and tried to encourage her to sit up straight. She clucked her tongue against her teeth when Constance refused to raise her head.

"Goodness me, dear. What is the matter with you this afternoon? Not feeling too chipper?"

Constance usually tried to avoid Teresa, whose combination of false cheer and patronizing condescension set her teeth on edge. But right now, she gripped Teresa's hand as if it were a lifeline. Dear, good, tiresome Teresa. *Don't go. Don't leave me.*

"It isn't November," Constance mumbled. Her lips were so stiff that the words came out thick and disjointed. And nonsensical, of course, as far as Teresa was concerned.

"No, dear, it's June. Summertime." Teresa patted her shoulder comfortingly. "Isn't it kind of Mr. Rodier to come and see you? You remember Mr. Rodier, don't you, Constance? He's just been nominated by the president to fill the vacancy on the Supreme Court. Isn't that a wonderful honor?"

Constance made a strangled grunting noise. She hadn't meant to, and the sound reminded her of how thin the line was between the pretense of madness and the reality.

"Mr. Rodier was your husband. Do you remember that, dear?"

How in God's name did they expect her to forget?
Constance didn't answer Teresa. She was struggling to
draw breath and couldn't cope with finding words, as well.
Dammit, she wasn't prepared for this out-of-season meeting. She hadn't geared herself mentally to handle this. She
couldn't cope. She *wouldn't* cope. They couldn't make her
talk to him. They couldn't make her remember.

Terror restored her power of movement. She sprang to
her feet, so awkward and uncoordinated that she toppled
the small table which she'd been using as a workbench.

Victor's voice was kind, unbearably gentle. "Constance, my dear, calm down. Goodness, I certainly didn't
plan to agitate you like this."

She hugged herself tightly around the waist and fought
back the urge to scream and scream and scream.

"She's been doing so much better lately, too." Teresa
sounded genuinely regretful. "I'm real sorry, Your Honor.
Perhaps she'll perk up a bit once she gets used to the idea
that you're here. A lot of our patients get upset by any
change in their routine, you know? It's hard for them to
cope with change."

"I'm sure it is. What do you recommend, Nurse?
Should we take a little walk around the gardens, do you
think? Would the fresh air and the sight of all those beautiful flowers help to calm her down?"

"No." Constance forced the word out. She was shaking from head to toe and she spread her palms flat against
the wall to steady herself. "I won't go outside." Her refusal came out as a sullen, slurred mumble. Her fear of
what he always did to her was so consuming that speaking
normally was beyond her. In the gardens, he would find it
too easy to take her somewhere isolated, out of sight of the
staff.

"All right," Victor said, instantly soothing. He always appeared to offer her total understanding and complete support, which was why the staff never suspected him. "We'll stay inside if you'd prefer it, Constance. Don't worry, my dear, you're quite safe. I won't let anything or anyone hurt you."

Through a red mist of panic, she saw him turn to the aide. Constance couldn't move her head, but her eyes swiveled to follow his gaze. Teresa was smiling apologetically, as if Constance's bad behavior was her fault. "I'm so sorry she's like this. I do hope you won't have a wasted trip, Your Honor. This is such an honor for us, sir."

"On the contrary, the honor is mine. Important as I believe my job is, I'm sure that in some ways it's less demanding than the work you do. My ex-wife's illness has endured for so long that I've been given many opportunities to admire the dedication of the wonderful staff here at Merton House. It's heartwarming to know that there are still health professionals who are truly dedicated to alleviating the suffering of the patients in their care."

Teresa blushed with pleasure. "Thank you, Your Honor. We do try to make the residents as comfortable and happy as they can be."

"And a fine job you do of it. An excellent job." Victor switched his gaze to Constance, and his smile widened. She looked at his teeth, which were still white and straight. When she'd first met him, she'd fallen in love with his mouth. Or perhaps she'd fallen in love with his kisses. Victor had been the world's most expert kisser. At the memory of his mouth covering hers, she felt suffocated, on the verge of fainting again.

She was holding the wall, and she hoped nobody noticed her sway. Victor reached for her hand, then didn't actually take it. She wondered if he knew her flesh crawled at the prospect of his touch. Probably not. He was such a goddamn pompous ass that he would be incapable of envisioning his advances as unwelcome. She liked the thought of Victor as a pompous ass. She repeated the words under her breath, a mantra to keep herself from fainting. *Pompous ass. Pompou-sass. Pom-pus-ass.*

"Well, my dear, was that a hint of a smile that I saw just then?" Victor had always been uncomfortably observant. When she didn't reply, he continued smoothly, "I can see that you have a pretty new hairstyle. And you're wearing such a nice dress, too. It looks to me as if your nurse is quite right. You're feeling a little better these days."

Constance closed her eyes. If she didn't look at him, she didn't feel so weak. She eased her hands away from the wall, finger by finger, then swung around and grabbed the windowsill. With her back safely turned, she opened her eyes so that she could see out the window. Look at the trees, she told herself. There's a woodpecker. And on the branch over there, you can see a squirrel. Concentrate on the squirrel. Is it male or female? How the heck did you tell squirrel sexes apart?

She heard Victor sigh. "For a moment, I thought I saw a glimmer of recognition in her eyes. You know, Nurse, it's been years since she actually spoke to me."

"You never can tell, sir. You'd be surprised what they're taking in, even when they refuse to answer you. And Dr. Foster has seen enough improvement that he's cut her medications right back."

"Ah, yes, Dr. Foster. A man with innovative ideas, I believe. I wonder if you'd be kind enough to let the doctor know I'm here? One of my assistants called and made an appointment for me to meet with him at three-thirty."

"I know he's expecting you. I'll send for him right away."

"There's no rush, Nurse. This is strictly a courtesy call. I've been wanting to introduce myself to Dr. Foster ever since he took up his position here as director, and when the president had to cancel our luncheon today at the last minute, I realized the opportunity had finally presented itself. I'm due to have dinner with the governor in Greenville tonight, so you see, this was an easy stop on the way."

Teresa gave a little chuckle of admiration. "It doesn't sound like an easy stop to me, Your Honor. I sure do hope that Constance appreciates the efforts you've made to visit her today. I know everyone at Merton House is real grateful for the interest you take in our work."

"Thank you, it's my pleasure to offer what small assistance I can. Speaking of which, Nurse, could I trouble you for a drink to accompany this little box of cookies I've brought for Constance? Some iced tea, perhaps?"

"Certainly, I'll fetch it myself. I'll be right back."

Constance didn't look around, but she heard Teresa walk away, her rubber-soled shoes landing with solid thuds on the heavy linoleum of the lounge floor. She clamped her lips tightly together, fighting a renewed desire to scream. Then she wondered why she bothered. Eventually, panic would overwhelm her—that was inevitable. Victor always outwitted her in the end, and his presence invariably triggered hours of hideous, soul-destroying flashbacks: nightmare images of Liliana, her baby curls spread in a golden halo so that she looked like one of Raphael's cherubs, floating in a pool of blood.

Where was it written that she was obligated to endure such terrible memories? Constance asked herself despairingly. The sooner she allowed herself to lose control, the sooner the orderlies would run in with their blissful, mind-obliterating needles. It was one thing to punish herself. It was another thing to submit voluntarily to Victor's torture.

He came up and put his hands on her shoulders. She gagged. He tightened his grip, massaging his thumbs along her collarbone with tender concern. "My dear, you're simply one big bundle of nervous tension. Won't you sit down and talk to me for a few minutes? I've really been so encouraged by the reports I've received recently from Dr. Foster. He appears to have seen some very positive signs of improvement in your behavior."

Constance sat down in the chair opposite Victor, because that meant he would stop massaging her shoulders. Clever Victor. He'd always known exactly how to manipulate her into obeying his wishes. As she sat, she ducked her head and sneaked a glance at him from beneath lowered eyelids. A squinted half view was about as much of Victor as she could take at this moment.

His features had always been handsome, but his nose had seemed slightly too large when he was young. Now he'd grown into it, adding character to his face. His hair had turned silver over the past couple of years, and that, too, suited him better than the nondescript brown it had once been. Then, of course, there was his splendid mouth and shiny white teeth. No wonder the president had nominated him to the Supreme Court, Constance thought. Victor had not only spent his entire life preparing for the role, he looked as if he'd been born to wear those dignified black silk robes.

When he visited her in November, he always wore charcoal-gray suits, tailored by Oxford Clothiers of New York, teamed with shirts imported from Asher and Turnbull in London, and ties imported from Hermès in Paris—the recognizable perfect mix of patriotism and conservative sartorial flair. Today he'd come calling in tailored khaki slacks, a navy blue blazer and a paisley tie, the weekend summer uniform of the East Coast establishment. It must have been twenty years at least since she'd seen him wearing anything other than a dark business suit. Which reminded her that it must also be twenty years since she'd seen him at any time of year other than Thanksgiving.

A tiny spark of curiosity flashed briefly amid the black fog of her fear. What could possibly have brought Victor to see her now, when he was so busy getting his nomination approved, and when he was so much in the public eye? Maybe he just wanted to make sure that the skeleton in his family closet was hung out in the bright light of day. Victor was smart enough to realize that skeletons in the sun were comic—they had no power to frighten unless they were kept hidden in the dark.

Teresa bustled back, carrying a tray loaded with a plastic pitcher of iced tea, two frosted plastic glasses and two plastic plates. "Here you are, Your Honor, the tea's freshly made. There now, Constance, isn't this nice? You see, everything's going to be all right if you just take it steady."

Constance stretched out her hand to Teresa, her need greater than her embarrassment. "Don't go," she said. "Stay."

"I wish I could, dear. But it's the end of my shift. Look, Gina's over there, and Mary's just come on duty. You'll be fine." Teresa poured the tea and set the sweating glasses on paper napkins. "Well, goodbye, Your Honor. I'm so glad I met you. Now I'll be able to tell my kids I spoke to a justice of the Supreme Court! That's really something."

Victor shook her hand, smiling. "We mustn't jump the gun, Teresa. The Senate still has to hold confirmation hearings, then take a vote to confirm my nomination." Victor managed to look both charmingly modest and reassuringly self-confident at the same time, no mean feat.

"Public opinion can turn in a trice. You know what the media's like these days—they'd proclaim the pope was an atheist if it helped to increase their sales figures."

"You've got that right, Your Honor. Some of those journalists attack first and do their thinking afterward. Well, you can be sure they won't be hearing any gossip from us. Not that there's anything to tell them except how supportive you've been of Merton House."

When Teresa had left, Victor inserted straws among the clinking ice cubes and pushed one of the glasses of tea across the table to Constance. "Here, my dear. Would you care for one of the cookies I brought? I remembered shortbread was your favorite. It's a favorite of mine, too." He picked up a cookie and bit into it. "Mmm. It's delicious. Do try one, Constance. Really, my dear, I insist. You're much too thin, you know."

You need to lose weight, Constance. How many times had he told her that after Lili was born? She watched his hands, which were spread apart with seeming innocence. If he wanted her to eat one of the cookies, she'd resist with the last drop of her will. He couldn't get up and physically shove them down her throat.

"Constance? My dear, you're hurting my feelings. Please try one of these cookies, they're so delicious."

She shook her head, sucking desperately at the iced tea. Fright made the inside of her mouth so dry that she really needed to drink.

"Do you know, it must be nearly thirty years since I ate a cookie like this." Victor leaned back in his chair, his voice mellow. He sipped his tea. "Your grandmother used to order tins of Scottish shortbread from Fortnum and Mason, the gourmet grocery store in London, do you remember?"

"No." Her stomach was winding into a tight, hard knot of panic. He was starting to reminisce. Soon he'd say Lili's name. And then there would be the blinding flash of light, and the memories would begin. She could feel them stalking her, creeping up behind, lying in wait, biding their time to attack. She threw a quick, frightened glance over her shoulder, almost as if she expected to catch a glimpse of a memory waiting to pounce.

"What are you looking at, my dear?"

"Nothing."

"My dear Constance, this is progress indeed. Two coherent words out of you within the space of thirty seconds, and addressed directly to me. So you haven't completely lost the power of speech. I was beginning to wonder."

His lips, which circled the straw, swelled and pulsed until they became a throbbing, greedy red ellipse, about to swallow her up. His head expanded, his forehead widening until the sockets for his eyes became too big to hold his eyes in place. The sockets turned into dark, hollow tunnels, his eyes free-floating globules in the surrounding blackness. They were expanding, melting, dripping down in rivulets that consumed all the space around them.

Constance's thoughts dissolved into fuzziness while every physical sensation magnified to unbearable levels of intensity. The straw felt smoother, sleeker than anything she'd ever felt, the shard of ice clinking against her teeth was shockingly cold, the tweed surface of the chair so scratchy that it was agonizingly uncomfortable against the bare skin of her legs.

The black eye sockets closed in on her. The voracious red lips spoke, "Well, Constance, are you still dreaming about Liliana? Have you remembered yet what you did with her body after you killed her? Did you throw my poor little Liliana in the river, Constance? Or drop her over the side of your grandfather's boat? Poor Liliana, where is she? Don't you think she at least deserves a decent burial after all these years?''

Liliana. White brilliance exploded deep inside her head. But the explosion brought no light, only darkness, a living blackness so impenetrable that no breath could pass through. Constance sprang to her feet, clutching her throat, gasping for air. She heard the crash of the table falling. Lili ran toward her, arms outstretched, wearing the cute outfit dotted with strawberries that her great-grandmother had bought for her. The bumblebee flew off Lili's sun hat and flapped its giant wings in Constance's face. She beat at the wings with her hands, knowing that if she couldn't overcome the bee, Lili would die. The bee got bigger and bigger. She saw the giant stinger emerge from its abdomen, quivering in joyous anticipation of the death it was about to deliver.

Oh, God, dear God, please let me save her this time.

She heard the screams and knew that she was the person screaming. Somehow, she also knew that Lili's life depended on making the screams stop, but her lungs kept pushing and her throat seized on the gusts of air, bellowing out her terror.

The stinger was no longer protruding from the bee. Instead, Victor had sucked it up with his swollen red lips. He walked toward Lili, poisoned stinger pointed straight at her little girl's head.

No! She couldn't let him win again. Behind Victor, she saw a man she recognized. Ed. It was Ed! With an effort that made her heart threaten to burst, she forced the screams back down inside her.

"Help me," she begged him. "Ed, for God's sake, help me."

Eight

Ed strode across the room, reaching Constance before either of the aides. He grabbed her flailing arms, and she screamed again, flinching as though he'd inflicted physical pain. She cowered in a corner, huddled into a near-fetal position, and when he put his hand under her chin, forcing her to look up, her eyes were blank, focused on some horrible inner nightmare. Yet, for a desperate moment, he saw her struggle to become coherent. She fixed her eyes on his, holding his gaze for no more than a couple of seconds.

"Don't make me," she whispered thickly. "Ed... don't... make... me..." Her voice gurgled, then scaled into another scream.

Make her what? Ed shook his head in frustration. Damn, she'd really been trying to tell him something, not just babbling. And she'd called him by his name, he realized. Most psychotic patients barely saw their doctors as human, he thought, let alone as people with first names.

A handsome man in his late fifties, dressed like an escapee from a Noel Coward musical comedy, hovered anxiously at Ed's side. "Is she going to be all right, Doctor? One moment she was fine, the next minute she lunged for my jugular. And then this."

"She'll be all right."

"Then why is she screaming?"

"Because she's in pain. Acute mental pain." Ed glanced at the aide who was mopping up the iced tea Constance had spilled. "Mary, why don't you leave that for now and see if you can calm Bernie down? He's one of Constance's special friends, isn't he? He looks upset. Let's catch him before he gets really panicked."

As if on cue, Bernie started to keen anxiously, but the man at Ed's side barely glanced in the direction of the noise before turning back to Constance. "I thought she was supposed to be getting better." His distinguished features registered stern disapproval of the misinformation he'd been given. "This is worse than I've seen the poor woman in years. Good heavens, isn't there something you can give her to ease her distress? The way she's huddled against the wall like that, as if she's terrified of something—it's heartbreaking."

Ed waved away the two orderlies who'd come into the lounge at a run, hypodermics at the ready. "No, Aldo, hold off with the meds. Ramon, stay back. Let's see if we can get through this without tranquilizers. She isn't a danger to herself or anyone else at the moment."

The gentleman raised a disdainful eyebrow. "Are you sure that's a wise decision, Doctor? Can we be certain she won't harm herself?"

If he'd been more sure of the wisdom of his decision, Ed suspected the question wouldn't have bugged him so much. He spared ten seconds to register that he had no idea who this man was. Ed could be pretty supercilious himself when the occasion demanded, and this sucker was asking for it. He drew himself up, peered down his nose and put on his piss-off voice. "Should I know you? Is there some reason why you have a special interest in this patient?"

"I'm Victor Rodier and I assume you're Dr. Foster." He gave Ed a snooty stare, letting the full import of his famous name sink in. "Constance and I were married once, as you may have heard."

Victor Rodier. The judge. Jesus, he'd just insulted the Supreme Court nominee whose hobby seemed to be shoveling vast sums of money into the Merton House building fund.

Ed held out his hand. "Sorry, I should have recognized you, Judge, your picture has been on the front page of every newspaper recently. Congratulations on your nomination to the Supreme Court. And, yes, I'm sure it's a wise decision to limit the administration of potent tranquilizers. Your ex-wife has shown so much improvement over the last few weeks, I don't want her to slip too far back. I'm disappointed by this sudden relapse and I'd like to find out what caused it. If we medicate her, she won't be able to tell us anything."

Victor Rodier spoke dryly. "I wouldn't have thought meaningful communication was an option at this point, Doctor. With or without sedatives."

The guy had a point, Ed conceded silently. Constance looked out of touch with the world, floating in some unpleasant inner realm. God alone knew what psychotic demons held her in thrall. He knelt on the floor beside her. Swiftly, he ran his hands over her arms and down her body, checking for any obvious source of physical pain, double-checking that she hadn't managed to secrete a weapon. She wasn't physically injured, and she didn't have any weapons, but she recoiled from his touch as if every inch of her skin were intolerably sensitive. She waved her hands in front of her face in a circular sweeping motion, almost as though she were trying to wipe out some ghastly picture—clear to her but invisible to everyone else.

"Constance, what are you seeing?" Ed asked, keeping his voice low and speaking into her ear.

He was relieved that she seemed to hear and register the meaning of his question. Even more surprisingly, she made an effort to cooperate by answering him. "Hearing the light," she mumbled. "Scarlet blood...eating Lili."

During psychotic episodes, patients often experienced a blurring of the boundaries between the senses. Ed had seen it numerous times. Personification of inanimate objects was even more common. Walls that dissolved into suffocating blankets, chairs that became threatening monsters, an empty bowl that suddenly gushed blood—all were routine hallucinations. Routine from the point of view of the doctor, but Ed tried always to remember that, from the patient's point of view, the hallucinations were terrifyingly real. Patients could die from the physical stress of fighting against their delusions.

Constance pressed her palms against her eyes and leaned her forehead against the wall in a gesture of such abject despair that Ed winced in sympathy. Suddenly, she turned and clutched his arm. Her words were thick and garbled, and he had trouble making sense of them, but he thought she said, *"He makes the nightmares come."*

"Who makes the nightmares come, Constance?" he asked softly.

She didn't reply. Her eyes rolled up in her head, and she rocked back and forth, seemingly unaware of his presence. "Take her to the quiet room," he said to the orderlies. "But there's no need to restrain her. Just stay with her until I get there."

The orderlies looked nearly as disapproving as Victor Rodier, who was still hovering about six inches from Ed's shoulder. With a shrug that spoke louder than words, Aldo picked Constance up. She tried to struggle out of his arms, but Ramon stepped in to assist his partner, overpowering her attempts at resistance.

"Keep her as calm and quiet as you can until I get to the room," Ed instructed them. "I won't be more than five minutes."

Victor Rodier watched the orderlies carry his former wife out of the lounge, an inelegant sack slung between the two of them. His gaze was troubled and he soon turned away. Not surprisingly, he looked upset.

"I can see that this isn't a convenient time for us to talk," he said to Ed, his voice low and dispirited. He shook his head. "Every time I come to visit Constance, I nurture this foolish hope of seeing an improvement, and each time I'm disappointed."

"It's not easy to treat a depression as severe as Constance's, particularly when it's accompanied by episodes of intense psychotic delusion—"

"Doctor, please, there's no need to explain. I didn't intend to offer any criticism of you or your staff. Alas, I realize that her condition is incurable after so many years."

Ed hadn't realized that anyone outside of novels by Charles Dickens actually used the word *alas*. He reminded himself that people often sounded curt or pompous when they were worried. He tried to offer the judge what small comfort he could. "Mr. Rodier, I haven't been here long enough to give you an informed opinion about Constance, but you probably know that, statistically speaking, a depression of almost thirty years' duration is unlikely to cure itself. This latest outburst of violence and disassociation simply confirms that your former wife has serious mental health problems. However, I'm optimistic by nature and, despite today's setback, I don't want to give up hope. With the right doses of the right medications, and some intensive one-on-one therapy to prepare her for the transition, it's possible that your ex-wife might be capable of living in a less protected environment than Merton House, perhaps even a small group home.''

''Good heavens, you amaze me,'' Victor said.

''We can't move too quickly here, but I've seen Constance demonstrate periods of complete and sustained lucidity. For example, she is perfectly well aware that she was once your wife, and that you've recently been nominated to fill the vacant seat on the Supreme Court. She's doing impressive work in her occupational therapy classes, and her art teacher speaks highly of her capabilities. I've personally observed flashes of a sense of humor, a rare quality in a patient this severely depressed. At least for the time being, I'm going to work toward preparing Constance for release from Merton House.''

''I had no idea that we could ever hope for Constance's eventual release. What extraordinary news!''

Ed was immediately concerned that he'd sounded too upbeat. ''I'm sure you realize that we're talking about a very small window of opportunity—''

''Yes, of course, but after years without any hope this is certainly wonderful to hear.'' The judge shook his head. ''Although, Doctor, I confess it's hard to imagine that Constance would be safe in the outside world after witnessing her behavior this afternoon.''

''Think of this as a setback, not an example of her true abilities.''

''Excellent advice. I must try to follow it.'' Victor Rodier smiled, then his expression saddened. ''Constance was such a beautiful woman when I first met her, Doctor. Her hair had definite red highlights, you know, and it was curly. In the sun, she sometimes looked as if her face was surrounded by a halo of fire.'' He stopped and cleared his throat before he could continue, ''When I remember her as I once knew her, it's unbearably sad to think that we've reached the point where I'm excited to hear that she may, one day, be able to cope with living in a group home for the mentally impaired. What a tragic end to so much potential."

The judge reached for the immaculate white linen handkerchief tucked into the breast pocket of his blazer and turned away. The guy might look like a tailor's dummy, Ed thought, but he'd obviously been in love with Constance once upon a time. Damn! He needed to talk to Victor Rodier about Liliana, but he didn't dare leave Constance alone in the quiet room with the orderlies for more than a couple of minutes or they'd find an excuse to pump her full of tranquilizers. And he *really* didn't want to have that happen.

"Judge, here's a card with my beeper number," he said. "Or you can call here and they'll track me down—they always know where to reach me. I can imagine how busy your schedule must be at the moment, but I'll take a call from you at any time, day or night, provided I'm not with a patient. It would be very helpful in my treatment of Constance if I could hear from you firsthand about the origins of her illness."

The judge tucked his now-crumpled handkerchief into his hip pocket. "Her admissions records tell you the whole sad story, I'm sure."

Perhaps this wasn't the time to inform the man that Constance's admissions records were missing. Ed glided neatly past that issue. "If you are able to call, I'd be more than happy to fill you in on the details of Constance's case as I see them developing. The court has appointed you as her guardian, so there are no issues of confidentiality."

"I appreciate the offer, Doctor, and I shall certainly take advantage of it some time soon. In the meantime, to change the subject just a little, I would like to request that you get in touch with Adrienne Cooper at Bentz and Hentges. They're PR people, extremely reputable." Victor Rodier pulled a business card from the inside pocket of his blazer as they started to leave the lounge together.

"This is Adrienne's office address and phone number. She's the young woman who's handling the media for me during the nomination process. I'm sure both you and I are equally anxious to avoid giving irresponsible journalists any opportunity to exploit the sad situation in which my ex-wife finds herself. I've never made any secret of Constance's illness, or the tragic circumstances surrounding the death of my daughter, and I've gone on record many times about society's need to show compassion for the mentally sick. But there's always a television talk-show host or a supermarket tabloid scratching around the edges of the sewer looking for mud, and I would prefer not to have to read sensationalized accounts of the tragedy that ended my daughter's life. As you can imagine, it's not something I care to dwell on more than necessary. If possible, other than in connection with the work of the Liliana Rodier Foundation, I prefer not to see my daughter's name bandied about by the media."

He was *really* going to have to find out about Liliana, Ed reflected, taking the business card Victor held out. What the hell had happened to her? As for controlling the media, he was in complete agreement with the judge. There were plenty of honorable, hardworking journalists, but the fringe elements of the profession could behave with a sickening lack of responsibility, and it was always the most vulnerable people who ended up getting exploited.

"I'll call Ms. Cooper first thing on Monday morning," he said, pausing as he and Victor Rodier reached the point where the corridor leading to the intensive therapy rooms branched off from the main hallway. "I'll be glad to have her advice. There's nothing relevant to your appointment to the Supreme Court for anyone to uncover at Merton House, but—God knows—that's unlikely to stop some of the media scavengers from hunting."

"I try to remind myself that the occasional week or so of personal inconvenience is a very small price to pay for the protection provided to us all by the First Amendment." Rodier flashed him a wry smile. "Speaking strictly as a family man and not as a jurist, there have been moments over the past couple of weeks when I've viewed the glories of a free press through distinctly dark spectacles. My wife can't leave our house without tripping over some fellow with a camera. She's even getting harassed at our beach house on Long Island."

Ed shook the man's hand. "You have all my sympathy, Your Honor, but at least this should end once the Senate confirms your nomination."

The judge sighed. "Yes, that's what I tell myself. I understand the need to investigate my background, but I've discovered that understanding on an intellectual level doesn't make the process any easier to go through on a practical, day-to-day basis."

"I'm sure it must be very difficult," Ed said. "I acted as legal guardian for a couple of kids who were involved in a high-profile murder case back in California. Nothing like the circus you're going through, but it's tough to handle excessive media attention and keep your cool."

"Which, of course, is what the media ghouls are all waiting for. To see their appointed victim lose his cool." Rodier gave a wintry smile. "I am determined not to give them that satisfaction. Our public life is regrettably short on dignity these days."

Ed agreed wholeheartedly. "I have to turn right here, Judge, but you go straight on. Do you need me to call for an aide to see you out? The exit is at the end of this corridor, and to the left.''

"I can find my own way, thank you." Rodier held out his hand. "I'm very glad we had this chance to meet, Doctor. To be honest, I always felt that Dr. Grable was hardworking and well-meaning but perhaps not the most insightful of men." He gave a small conspiratorial smile. "And that was seriously indiscreet of me. I won't put you in the awkward position of having to respond to that inappropriate comment about your predecessor. Goodbye, Dr. Foster, I'll be in touch."

Ed picked up his pace as he hurried toward the quiet room. It was tragic about the Rodiers' daughter, he reflected, especially if Constance really had killed the child. If she had, the judge was one of the world's most noble characters, continuing to show concern and interest in the woman who had murdered his child. It was damned annoying to know so little about the circumstances surrounding Constance's original committal. Presumably it had been precipitated by the death of her daughter, but Ed would like to have seen what was written at the time.

The clerk responsible for the Merton House archives had been unable to find the missing admissions records despite an extensive search, and so far, she seemed to be having no success in prizing them out of Saint Jude's, either. Ed decided to call the director of Saint Jude's tomorrow and ask personally for a rush to be put on tracing Constance's file. Now that he knew the death of her daughter was a real event, and not a figment of her imagination, he needed to learn the precise circumstances of the girl's death. He couldn't effectively evaluate Constance's mental state if he didn't have an objective set of facts against which to check her stories.

He pressed in the electronic code that admitted him to the locked quiet room. He stepped silently across the gray, rubber-tiled floor, designed to muffle sound and provide easy cleanup. Devoid of furniture other than a bed equipped with full body restraints, and illuminated by neon strip lights hidden in tubing at the conjunction of the off-white walls and smooth ceiling, the purpose of the room was to provide surroundings free of as many external stimuli as possible. Depressing as he found the place, for a patient in the throes of a psychotic episode, the stark emptiness of the room was actually comforting. He hadn't sent Constance to the room as punishment for misbehaving, but in order to provide her with the environment most likely to calm her.

Constance was being watched over by Ramon. She'd been strapped to the bed, held immobilized by six separate, heavy-duty restraints. Ed controlled his irritation. "I said restraints weren't necessary, Ramon. Where's Aldo?"

"He had to go help with Bernie and Iris." Ramon jiggled his keys and Constance visibly cringed, but Ramon didn't seem to notice. "We had to restrain her, or medicate her, Doctor, and you'd said no shots. She was goin' wild. Tryin' to climb the walls. Look, her fingernails are bleeding."

Ed looked down at Constance's hands. Ramon was right. Her nails were bleeding. "Bring me some supplies so that I can take care of these," he said to the orderly. "Then go and help Aldo. I want to observe Constance for another few minutes, and I think she'll do better with as few people around as possible."

"Okay, Doctor." Ramon headed for the door, lips pursed in a silent whistle. He returned moments later with a plastic tray of sterile-pack first-aid supplies. "Here you go, Doctor."

"Thanks, I'll take care of her for now, Ramon."

"Sure thing, Doc." Ramon gave a mock salute and headed out. Ed had noticed before the man's indifference to the plight of the Merton House residents, and his health-care philosophy seemed to be *A comatose patient is a good patient*. Sometimes Ed wondered if Ramon realized that the inmates he guarded were sick people, not criminals.

Ed waited for the door to close behind Ramon before tearing open one of the sterile packs and starting work on Constance's hands. Her face was pale, her forehead beaded with sweat, but however violent her struggles had been earlier, she now lay limp and quiescent on the bed, indifferent to his ministrations, although the alcohol must have stung. Only the darting movement of her eyes indicated that she was awake. Ed knew that if she was still in the grip of a psychotic delusion, she was quite capable of hurling herself at him or the walls the minute he freed her. But her pulse had stabilized somewhat, and he decided to take the risk once he'd bandaged her badly torn finger-nails.

He put the sterile tray behind the sliding door that accessed the hall. Then he went back to the bed. "Constance, I'm going to remove the restraints." He spoke quietly, slowly and clearly. "Please don't do anything to hurt yourself."

A blink of her eyes was all the response he got. "Okay, Constance, do we have a deal that you're not going to hurt yourself?"

This time, she gave a small jerk of her head that seemed to be a nod of agreement. Encouraged by this sign of lucidity, Ed unbuckled the heavy padded strap at her waist, then moved on to her left wrist and right foot. She made no move to attack him. In fact, she didn't move at all. He stroked his hand lightly up and down her arm. She shook his hand away, but languidly, as if she didn't much care whether he touched her or not. Her bandaged fingertips caught her attention, and she held them up in front of her face, frowning as she stared at them.

Ed glanced at his watch. Three-thirty. In the lounge, less than fifteen minutes earlier, she'd reacted as if his fingers were sticks of fire, burning a path over her skin. Now, she didn't care if he touched her, hadn't even noticed that he'd bandaged her fingers. Interesting. He'd dealt with hundreds of kids messing around with drugs, and Constance's symptoms seemed more like someone strung out on acid than a woman in the throes of a psychotic delusion.

"Does your skin hurt, Constance?"

"No." Her reply sounded as if it had been dragged from some distant place.

"Did your skin hurt when I touched you before, when we were in the lounge?" he asked, freeing her from another restraint.

She pursed her lips and pressed her freed hand to her forehead as if focusing on his question required tremendous effort. "Skin hurt," she said vaguely, after a long pause. Was she agreeing that her skin had hurt? Or simply repeating his own words to him?

He unbuckled the final restraint on her right hand, alert for any violent move she might make. She didn't stir. "Why don't you sit up, Constance? Can you sit up?"

"Yes." She didn't move, apparently lost in contemplation of an invisible speck on the ceiling.

"Will you sit up? May I help you?" Giving her plenty of time to protest, Ed put his arm around her and gently pulled her into a sitting position. The bed was in the center of the room, so there was no wall for her to lean against. Wrapping her arms around her legs, Constance rested her chin on her knees and resumed her fixated stare at the blank walls.

Since the bed was the only piece of furniture in the room, Ed sat on the end near her feet. To prevent suicide attempts, there were no covers on the bed, so the temperature inside the room was kept relatively warm. Ed unfastened the top button of his shirt and loosened his tie. "Talk to me, Constance. Tell me what's going on. Why did you get upset back there in the lounge? Did seeing Victor make you unhappy?"

Constance flinched at Victor's name, but she finally turned to look straight at Ed. "Victor's a pom-pus-ass," she said thickly.

Ed resisted the temptation to express hearty agreement. "Victor cares about you," he said.

Constance tightened the grip of her arms around her legs. "No, he doesn't."

"He visits you. He came today, when he must be very busy. He's an important man, Constance, with a vitally important job, and yet he made time in his schedule to come and see you."

"He wants to hurt me."

"That's not true, Constance."

"I knew you wouldn't believe me." She let out a long, harsh sigh. A tear seeped from beneath her half-closed eyelid and spilled onto her cheek. "Help me, Ed. I can't stand it anymore. Make the pain go away."

He closed his hand around hers. "What's hurting you, Constance? What's making you feel so much pain?"

"The pictures inside my head," she said, her voice catching. "They're coming back. Pictures of Lili."

"Tell me about the pictures, Constance. What are you seeing?"

"My little baby." Her voice was thick with despair. "I can't save her. I never save her. Oh, God, I can't bear this! Why do I have to watch her die again?"

"Maybe this time you won't have to see her die. Tell me why you can't save her, Constance."

"Victor," she said after a long pause. "He's always there."

Did Victor Rodier truly share some responsibility for the death of their daughter, or was Constance simply demonstrating the extent of her paranoia? Ed had rarely felt more frustrated by his own lack of facts. Dammit, if he only knew what had really happened to Lili it would be so much easier to shape his questions appropriately. As it was, he could only respond to the cues Constance herself fed him.

"Maybe I can help you to escape from Victor," he suggested.

"Can't." Constance was becoming visibly agitated, slipping away from him. "Taking her to Elena's," she mumbled. "Elena will help me."

"That's a good idea," Ed said. "Can you tell me how Elena is going to help you?"

"Doesn't like Victor. She'll keep Lili safe." Constance's words were thick and slurred. Her breathing became irregular, her cheeks alternately flushing and turning pale.

"Oh, God, no!" She emitted a sudden, piercing scream, clawing at her face as if she wanted to rip away her own skin. "No, no! I didn't kill her, I didn't! I won't believe you! Where is she? Where's her body? *You* must have killed her, not me."

"Tell me how Lili died," Ed said, catching Constance's hands and pulling them away from her face. "I won't be angry, Constance. I won't blame you. How did she die, Constance? Was it an accident?"

She turned to him, kneeling on the bed in a position of desperate supplication. Blood from her torn fingernails had seeped onto her face and mingled with her tears. "It wasn't an accident. I didn't kill her. Elena took her away, I didn't kill her!" She was gasping and sobbing, writhing in an agony of grief. She threw herself against Ed's chest, not attacking him, but begging and pleading with frantic, manic energy. "Please, please, let me go to her. Let me find her! Oh, God, don't let him get to me before I find her! Let me find her first! You have to let me find her. She's only a baby, she needs me."

"You can go to her, Constance. I'm helping you to get better so that you'll be able to let Lili rest peacefully."

"No, he's stopping me." Her teeth started to chatter. She clutched Ed's hands. "I—didn't—kill—my baby. Oh, God, why won't anyone help me to find her? Grandma, I didn't kill her, you've got to believe me! Don't let them lock me away! Ah, God, no...."

Ed closed his arms around her shuddering body, patting her back as if he were soothing a child. "All right, Constance, stop worrying now. Lili is safe. It's all right. You have nothing to worry about. Calm down, now. Everything's okay."

She pulled away from him and hit his face with all the force of her hundred-pound weight. "You're lying to me! She isn't safe! Oh, God, Lili! I tried, I'm sorry. None of them will let me save you!"

In his twenty-five years of practicing psychiatry, Ed had rarely heard such total and complete desolation in a patient's voice. To hell with this. Enough of trying to find out what had set off this episode; Constance needed relief from the mental pain she was suffering. It seemed fairly clear that she associated the sight of her former husband with the tragic death of her daughter and that she reacted with a violent attack of mingled guilt and denial. Which would explain why she'd had this psychotic episode in June, when normally her attacks clustered around late November. It wasn't the date or time of year that was the precipitating factor. Constance's psychotic episodes were triggered by the sight of her ex-husband.

Ed was more than somewhat bothered that none of the psychiatrists working with Constance over the years had noticed the pattern. Or perhaps they had and simply considered it unimportant. Dr. Grable had written two full pages of notes when Constance once came down with pneumonia. Her annual psychotic episodes were summed up in a couple of terse sentences.

At least the connection to Judge Rodier's visits had now been established, albeit several years later than they should have been. When Constance calmed down from this latest episode, he would resume their therapy sessions and work with her toward the goal of teaching her to live with her grief. He would also inform Victor Rodier that he shouldn't pay any more visits until his ex-wife had learned to handle the guilt she felt in connection with her daughter's death. The judge was likely to be grateful for the excuse to get out of what was undoubtedly an onerous duty.

Ed pressed the electronic code that would bring back Ramon. Then he put his arm around Constance's thin shoulders and rocked her gently while she waited for the relief that medicated unconsciousness would bring. He stroked her limp, gray-threaded hair and tried to picture Constance as the vivacious, redheaded beauty Victor Rodier had described. His imagination wasn't up to the task.

The buzz of the electronic keypad told him that an orderly had arrived. Ed decided to administer a reasonably mild sedative, rather than the cocktail of Haldol and Ativan that were the powerhouse drugs for calming psychotic patients. Constance wasn't violent at the moment, and he simply wanted to give her the chance to rest.

She stirred in his arms, leaning against him with a degree of trust that surprised and touched him. Looking down at her, Ed wondered why he couldn't rid himself of the nagging feeling that he'd been handed a giant piece of a complex jigsaw puzzle—and that he'd just cleverly fitted it into entirely the wrong place.

Nine

Victor Rodier stepped into his chauffeur-driven Lincoln Town Car and nodded to the driver and the Secret Service agent who'd been assigned to guard him. There'd been the inevitable rash of death threats since his nomination, most of them meaningless. But, of course, it only took one crazy individual and one well-placed bullet to kill a man, so Victor didn't protest the twenty-four-hour security. Despite the inconvenience of having almost every move watched and accounted for, he found it rather gratifying that he'd finally reached a position of such national prominence that he played a starring role in the fantasy life of assorted kooks and weirdos. He leaned back against the soft suede of the seat and allowed himself to relax, just a little. Charming the governor, who was a stiff-necked Southerner of the old school, had been an exhausting business.

He spoke to the Secret Service agent. "This is going to be a late night for you, I'm afraid, Darren. How long a drive is it back to D.C.?"

"We estimate an arrival time of 0400 hours, Your Honor."

Victor glanced at his watch as they reached the end of the long driveway of the governor's mansion. Not quite ten o'clock, so his chauffeur was obviously planning to drive at a sedate fifty-five all the way back to Washington. He gave Darren a rueful smile. "I suppose it would be quite improper of me to suggest that the occasional burst of speed would be most welcome? I have a breakfast meeting with several journalists at seven-thirty tomorrow morning, and I was hoping against hope that I might manage to get a few hours' sleep in my own bed before I had to face their scrutiny."

Secret Service agents never smiled, but Darren permitted himself a faint relaxation in the stern line of his mouth. "I'll see that Ron gets the message, Your Honor. And if you'd like to try to sleep, I'll monitor any incoming calls for you."

"Thank you, Darren, I appreciate your help." Victor gave a sad shake of his head. "Really, my schedule is so full that I didn't have time to make this trip, but I was anxious to see my former wife again. I'd heard such promising reports about an improvement in the state of her . . . health."

Darren visibly hesitated. "I hope you found her well, Your Honor."

"Sadly, not as well as I'd expected." Victor sighed. "Mental illness is a tragic affliction, Darren. It can make monsters out of the most beautiful and gentle of people. People like my former wife."

"I'm sorry, Your Honor. I . . . er . . . I heard how you lost your daughter. It was a real tragedy."

"Yes, it certainly was. And the worst thing about losing a child is that there's some level at which the pain of that loss never goes away. It's still there, as raw and hurtful as the day the disaster happened. However, I try to remind myself that there's little point in brooding over the past, and that we mustn't get mired in our own unhappiness. The world is full of problems that we can solve if we set our minds to the task, so I'm sure the good Lord doesn't want us to dissipate our energies worrying about injustice and sorrow that only he knows how to cure."

"You've done more than most to help make the world a better place, Your Honor." Again, Darren hesitated to cross the boundary between professional duty and personal conversation. "My son was born with cancer of the spinal cord," he said finally. "They operated on him right away, and the surgery was a success, but when it came time for physical therapy and rehabilitation to help him learn to walk, the only place that would take him in was the Rodier Foundation. My wife and I often say that we don't know what we'd have done if it hadn't been for your foundation. We're real grateful to you, Your Honor."

Victor was always amazed at how often he met people whose lives had been affected in one way or another by the work of the foundation. Stories like Darren's always touched him when he realized that it was his efforts, and his vision, that had helped the foundation to function so successfully for more than a quarter century. He cleared his throat, but his voice was thick with emotion when he finally spoke. "You have no reason to thank me, Darren. In fact, I always feel a little guilty when people assume that I'm the generous benefactor behind the foundation. The money that supports the work of the foundation comes entirely from a trust fund that was established by Mr. and Mrs. Wendell P. Grant as a memorial to my daughter, Liliana. I'm a director of the foundation and the executor of Liliana's trust fund, but the money that established the foundation in the first place came from my wife's family. The Grants, you see, were Liliana's maternal great-grandparents."

Darren shifted uncomfortably, fingering his communicator, as if he felt the need to grasp a familiar object while venturing into the unfamiliar waters of personal conversation with a nominee to the Supreme Court. "You may not have put up the money, Your Honor, but we heard all about the work you do for the foundation when my son was in rehab. My wife and I, we can never thank you enough."

"If your son regained his health, that's more than enough reward."

"He's not only walking, Your Honor, he's playing soccer."

"Wonderful." Victor decided he was tired of being thanked. "Well, if I am not to appear entirely foolish at my breakfast meeting with the hounds of the press tomorrow morning, I had best try to snatch a few hours of sleep."

"Yes, Your Honor. I'll lower the lights, and close the privacy screens on the windows."

"Thank you." Victor took off his blazer and handed it to the Secret Service agent. "Perhaps you'd be good enough to hang that up for me." He adjusted the seat so that it reclined at a forty-five-degree angle and availed himself of the pillow and traveling blanket someone had thoughtfully provided. He unfastened the button at the neck of his shirt and loosened his tie slightly, but didn't take it off. A reputation for dignity was hard-won, and easily lost. In this day and age, you couldn't trust anybody's discretion, not even someone who seemed friendly, like Darren. Look at what had happened to the Clintons when a disgruntled bodyguard decided to blab about their private lives to the media. A smart pol like Bill Clinton should've known better. Never give your enemies a free shot.

Victor positioned his feet more comfortably on the footrest. He was grateful for the long, silent hours of darkness that stretched ahead of him. He would need every minute to decide what the hell he was going to do about the major fuckup in his life that seemed to be in imminent danger of occurring.

Not only was his cow of a wife showing signs of snapping out of her twenty-six years of bovine placidity, but Jessica Zajak had actually paid a visit to the old Grant house on Long Island. Thank God his current wife had happened to be staying there, he thought, or he might never have known about Jessica's visit. As it was, he'd conducted a swift follow-up and discovered that now—of all the fucking inconvenient times to choose!—Jessica Zajak was doing some in-depth research into her past.

He'd found out exactly what Jessica was up to by simply calling her adoptive parents, pretending to be a private detective Jessica had contacted. Naive folks that they were, in a few questions he'd elicited the information that she'd discovered some papers suggesting that she might not be Jessica Marie Pazmany, and that she'd rushed off to New York to investigate.

Victor couldn't imagine what papers she might have discovered, or how. God knows, he'd taken meticulous care to destroy everything, to close every loophole. Over the years, he'd never become lazy. He'd continued to monitor the situation, even when other—lesser—men would have felt sure they were off the hook and allowed the situation to slide. Like his annual visits to Constance, for example. Look how that had paid off, simply in terms of PR. Here he was, undergoing intensive media scrutiny, and because of the clever way he'd handled things, the fact that he had an ex-wife locked up in a mental institution was being played out in the press as one more example of the caring and humane attitude Victor Rodier would bring to his Supreme Court decisions.

After years of careful damage control, Jessica Zajak was not only an unexpected problem, she was a totally *undeserved* problem. He'd done nothing to warrant her surfacing at this crucial point in his career, he fumed silently. She'd had a perfectly happy childhood, dammit. Why the hell did she need to dig around in the past, inquiring about subjects that had no relevance, screwing things up for everyone? A less talented man might have felt some resentment. However, as he'd told Darren, life was too short to waste on worrying about cosmic injustice.

In contrast to ordinary people, with their fatal tendency to get distracted, Victor intended to remain focused. His task right now was to concentrate on making sure that nothing interfered with his successful appointment to the Supreme Court. Over the past twenty-six years, he'd learned how to work behind the scenes, moving slowly to cover his tracks, anticipating potential problems and taking care of them before they happened. Unfortunately, with the Senate Judiciary Committee hearings fast approaching, time was no longer on his side. Somehow, he'd screwed up in his interpretation of Dr. Edgar Foster's résumé, and instead of a burned-out has-been, he'd encouraged the Merton House board to hire a fire-eating reformer. In the normal course of events, he would simply have corrected his error by starting a slow, careful procedure to get the board to remove Dr. Foster, replacing him with a psychiatrist like Dr. Grable—a man much more interested in a cozy life than in his patients. Right now, time constraints made that desirable course of action impossible.

Victor prided himself on being a realist, with an almost unsurpassed capacity for coolheaded, logical analysis. It was one of the reasons he made such a wonderful judge. His passions were never involved, and he was able to administer the law in all its complex purity. He had the lowest rate of reversal on appeal of any judge in the history of the Ninth Circuit.

It was time to apply some of his abundant supply of cool rationality. What was a realistic assessment of his current situation? Victor smiled sourly into the darkness. Realistically, he was in deep shit.

Dr. Foster's presence at Merton House meant there was considerable risk of Constance regaining her faculties, although he shouldn't spend too much time worrying about his crazy ex-wife. She was still terrified of him, and he'd had no more trouble sending her off into cuckoo-land this visit than he had in the past. Security procedures at Merton House were deplorably lax. Perhaps he'd bring that to the attention of the board next time he attended one of their meetings. It always amused him to do things like that, provided he was sure he could work around any new regulations that came into effect.

Besides, even if Constance started to get obstreperous, he doubted if the old bag could remember anything that wouldn't be dismissed as delusional. So, given that the situation with Constance was unlikely to cause him anything more than inconvenience, Victor needed to make sure that the other end of the equation was taken care of.

And Jessica was that other end. Clearly she had to be silenced, and however much Victor mulled this over in his mind, he could think of only one way to guarantee her silence. Jessica needed to die. And what's more, she had to be disposed of quickly. Before she could do or say anything that might interfere with Victor's appointment with destiny. He hadn't spent the past twenty years planning his career path to the Supreme Court, only to have his dream fucked up at the last minute by a nobody like Jessica Zajak.

It would be unpleasant to kill Jessica. But he owed it to himself, Victor realized. Jessica's death was a sacrifice that couldn't be avoided. He was without question the most qualified person in the nation to become a justice of the Supreme Court. He couldn't allow loose ends from his past to deprive the people of the United States of a judge with such a keen legal mind and such a clever appreciation of the subtleties of the Constitution.

Fortunately, he had been preparing for the need to take action for several years now. He had already been provided with almost everything he would need to complete his task. During the eighties, when partisan strife began to turn all judicial confirmations into vicious battlegrounds, he'd understood how much at risk he was. During the lengthy—but somewhat sloppy—confirmation process before his appointment as Ninth Circuit judge, he'd worked out how he would silence Jessica Zajak if the need arose. Fortunately, during the course of those hearings, the need hadn't arisen and being a man of compassion, he'd simply put his plans on hold.

But now it was not only time to dust off his plans, it was clearly a matter of urgency to get this situation taken care of. Jessica Zajak was due to return to her office on Monday. He'd check to make sure that she was back in Denver, then he would set his plan in motion. By Monday, Jessica would be dead.

Poor woman, she was really too young to die. Victor felt sad.

She was relieved and delighted that Dan hadn't chosen to contact her, Jess decided, folding the last blouse into her suitcase and shutting the lid. Her desire to pick up the phone and call him was a natural response to him being linked in her mind to the revelation that she and Jessica

Marie Pazmany were two different people. The urge to speak with him was strong simply because she had news to share.

Tracking down Dr. Weir, the oncologist who'd treated Jessica Marie's leukemia, had been relatively easy, thanks to the records division of the state licensing bureau. Jess had first spoken with his office assistant, who'd informed her that Dr. Weir routinely destroyed even his micro-filmed records after twenty-five years, unless there were special circumstances, such as research implications. When Jess had requested a personal interview to show him some photographs that might jog his memory of Jessica Marie's case, the doctor had agreed, although he'd said that thirty years ago most children with leukemia died, and he tended to remember only the few rare kids who conquered the odds.

"That's how you cope with a specialty like mine," he said. "You train yourself to focus on the successes. And, thank God, we have a lot more of those today than we did back in the sixties and seventies. That's what keeps me plugging away, even on the bad days."

The doctor was leaving to attend a medical seminar in Chicago over the weekend, but he agreed to meet with Jess on Sunday evening at his office near Columbia University medical center. Jess debated whether it was worth wasting another two days in New York on such a slim hope of information, but in the end she decided that she might as well track down all the leads she could. She told herself— often—that her decision to stay had absolutely nothing to do with the possibility that Dan might call and invite her out again.

Dan, of course, didn't call, which was no more than she deserved, and Dr. Weir was able to provide almost no new insights. He turned out to be a still-handsome man in his fifties, with a rushed but friendly manner. She showed him a Christmas photo of Jessica Marie with her parents, and the doctor stared at it in silence for a couple of minutes.

"I do remember her," he said finally, his forehead wrinkling in concentration. "Her mother was a nurse. She was a remarkable woman. She knew the likely outcome of Jessica's illness, but she worked miracles to keep her daughter happy and as free of pain as possible. She calmed her child down before every treatment, and she was the one who finally had the courage to say enough when it was obvious that even the most advanced experimental procedures weren't going to work."

The doctor tugged thoughtfully at his mustache. "It's coming back to me now. Hungarian, you said her husband was? Yes, I seem to remember that he spoke with an accent." He cast a final glance at the Christmas photo. "She wasn't pretty, the mother, but she had a very nice face. I seem to recall that she had to be hospitalized for exhaustion after her little girl died."

"Would you say Elena Pazmany was sufficiently upset when her daughter died to do something crazy?" Jess asked. "Could she have gone completely off the rails, do you think, and done something that would otherwise have been out of character?"

"Define crazy, define upset," Dr. Weir said. Then he shook his head. "No, don't bother. Mrs. Pazmany struck me as one of the most well-balanced, caring mothers I ever dealt with. Based on my memory of her, such as it is, I'd say that it's extremely unlikely that her grief precipitated any form of mental illness. But, of course, I wasn't concerned with *her* mental state, only the physical condition of her daughter, so take these comments with a big pinch of salt."

"I will, but I appreciate your time and your help, Doctor. It's been astonishingly difficult to track down anyone who actually knew my parents."

"Well, good luck with your search." The doctor stood up and reached across the desk to shake her hand. "These aren't good memories, Ms. Zajak. You can understand why I prefer to file them away in a dark and dusty corner."

The weekend wasn't a total waste because she did manage to reach crusty old Gus, the landscaper out on Long Island. The effects of her twenty-dollar tip had clearly worn off, and he complained bitterly about being dragged away from a hockey game on ESPN. Afraid he would hang up on her, she asked him quickly if he remembered anyone called Elena Korda from his days of working with the Grants. Gus's first response had been a flat "no." She'd prompted his memory by suggesting Elena might have worked as a private nurse in the Grant household. Still nothing. The Grants, according to Gus, had never needed nursing care. Then, when Jess was on the brink of hanging up the phone, he'd remembered something.

"Never knew nobody called *Elena* Korda, but I knew an *Elisabeth* Korda once," Gus said. "She was one of those World War II refugees. She was a widow and she must've been working for the Grants twenty years at least by the time I started with 'em. She was their housekeeper, and they were real cut up when she died. She lived right in the house and they always treated her like she was a member of the family. Seem to recall she had a daughter. Mebbe she's this Elena woman you're looking for."

Elisabeth Korda had been the name of Elena's mother. Jess sighed at bumping into another literal dead end. By keeping those crucial documents in the attic for so many years, her adoptive grandfather had managed to make discovering the truth about her past almost impossible. Perhaps that had been his intention. The Zajaks were down-to-earth people who shared a belief that the here and now was a lot more important than what had happened in the past or might never happen in the future.

"When did Elisabeth Korda die?" Jess asked, wondering if it even mattered. Unless, perhaps, Elena's mother and daughter had died almost at the same time, driving Elena into a mental state where she was capable of kidnapping? "I guess it's a long time ago, and hard for you to remember."

"It's a long time ago, but I can tell you the very day she died." Gus sounded smug. "Same day they shot Robert Kennedy. That was a real bad year for dyin'. Martin Luther King was shot that year, too. Would've been the summer of '68, I guess. I remember it was real hot when they buried her. She wasn't an old woman, not a day over sixty, but she must've smoked three packs a day, and she got lung cancer."

Gus had been chain-smoking when Jess talked to him on the grounds of Bartlett House. Apparently, despite bemoaning Elisabeth's fate, he considered his own lungs immune from risk.

"She smoked those real strong cigarettes with a foreign name," Gus added. "Real funny smell, too. The cancer finished her off a few weeks after they diagnosed it. Come to think of it, I guess she had a grandkid as well as a daughter. They were both there at the funeral. I guess the daughter's husband was there, too." Gus sounded genuinely intrigued. "Funny how your memory plays tricks on you when you get older. I can picture the funeral home the day Elisabeth Korda was buried plainer than I can picture some places I visited a coupla months ago. So what do you think? This Elena woman you're looking for, she's Elisabeth's daughter, right? Why did you want to find her?''

"She was killed in a car crash when I was driving with her," Jess said, not knowing whether to feel relief or disappointment at uncovering such a mundane connection between the Grants and the Pazmanys. The Grants had obviously been both wealthy and generous, and there was nothing mysterious about their decision to pay some of the medical bills for their housekeeper's granddaughter. Unfortunately, having established the link between Elena and the Grants, Jess wasn't any closer to learning who she herself was, where she'd come from and why she'd been in the Pazmanys' car on that snowy night in December. Frustrated and restless, she'd thanked Gus and hung up.

After a night of stewing over her interview with Dr. Weir and Gus's news, she'd woken up with the oddest feeling that she teetered on the cliff-edge of discovery. She managed to rationalize away the feeling, but she still badly wanted to talk to Dan. At the very least, if she called him, she could share her confusion. She could also ask him to follow through on his offer to check the New York newspaper archives for any little girls reported missing in the weeks prior to Jess's arrival in Cleveland. The idea that she had two parents still alive, parents who had grieved for years over the disappearance of their daughter, was beginning to eat at her peace of mind.

But a night of insomnia didn't justify calling Dan. Surely to God she knew better than to trust her ex-husband as a source of emotional support or useful advice. The reason he seemed to offer a bulwark against the eroding framework of her life must be . . . Well, there had to be a reason, though she couldn't put her finger on it right now. Probably some weird psychological thing, connected to the fact that their marriage and divorce were the only major aspects of her life not tied up with Jessica Marie and the documents Grandpa Gene had hidden in his attic.

Jess smiled grimly as she put on her jacket in preparation for the flight home. Exploring the past was certainly causing some bizarre realignments of her mental furniture. Viewing her ex-husband as an anchor of stability in a sea of uncertainty was one of the strangest concepts her psyche had ever thrown up.

Suddenly, Jess realized she'd picked up the phone. She slammed the receiver back in its cradle. Enough, she told herself. Time to quit obsessing over her nonexistent relationship with Dan and check the bathroom to make sure she'd packed all her toilet articles. She looked down at the phone and realized she had the receiver in her hand again. When had she picked it up? Why had she picked it up? Not to call Dan. She would call her office in Denver, since she had absolutely no intention of calling her ex-husband.

She found her credit card, punched in the multiple codes and felt a surge of relief when her secretary answered on the first ring. It was only 8:00 a.m. in Colorado, but Marla always came in early, especially on a Monday.

Jess exchanged brief pleasantries with her assistant, agreeing that the weather was great and that there was no reason for her flight to be delayed.

"I'll come straight to the office from the airport," Jess said. "If you could have the pharmaceutical society files on my desk and waiting for me, Marla, I'd appreciate it. I need to get a proposal out to them by Tuesday evening at the latest, so I'll have to work on it at home tonight."

"Sure. And I'll get the standard brochures ready for the presentation package. That way, when you're ready with your proposal, the package will be all set to go."

"That would be a big help, thanks. Right now, I can't imagine what I was thinking, to take an entire week's vacation at this time of year."

"Maybe you thought you were entitled, since you haven't had a day off in six months?" Marla suggested.

Jess smiled. "Oh, right. I knew there must've been a reason."

She heard the sound of her assistant's chair rolling across the floor. "What's up?"

"Nothing exciting. The mayor's office has just this minute faxed over his schedule for next week. They say you requested it."

"I remember asking for it. I'm drawing a blank on why."

Marla laughed. "New York City sure must have been fun. It's not like you to forget anything, Jess."

True, she thought, but usually she didn't have business conversations in order to avoid thinking about how great it would be to crawl into bed with her ex-husband. Jess pulled herself together and spoke briskly, "New York City's just too noisy to allow coherent thought. But I remember now why I needed the mayor's schedule. The president of that German travel club, LuftWest, wants to meet with the mayor and discuss the problem he's been experiencing with transportation to the mountains in bad weather."

"And talking to the mayor is going to change the weather? Or miraculously expand the size of the Eisenhower tunnel?"

"Marla, the guy flies in seven and a half thousand German skiers per season, two chartered jumbo jets a week. If he wants to talk to the mayor, he gets to talk to the mayor. Let's arrange lunch or breakfast, or something. The mayor can look solemn and promise to talk to the state highway authorities about the need for more full-time crews to man the snowplows. Lord knows, they could use a few more road crews. The LuftWest president arrives in town late on Tuesday evening next week. He'll be in Colorado until Saturday. Beg and plead with the mayor's office to find an hour to make nice with the guy.''

"Okay. I'm making a note. I've faxed you most of the important stuff, Jess, but you have a stack of junk mail a mile high waiting for you."

"Anything look like interesting junk?"

"Nope, all boring except for one fancy gift-wrapped package. It's in one of those gold-foil bubble packs. Very fancy. Arrived by express courier half an hour ago. It's marked Personal."

A package marked Personal? Jess felt her pulse quicken. Undoubtedly from Dan, who was one of the world's best gift givers. So he hadn't ignored her since their dinner on Thursday, after all. "Is there a return address?" she asked, trying to sound cool.

"Yep. The Chocolatier, in Manhattan. Fifth Avenue. Embossed copper-foil return-address sticker on the gold bubble wrap. Looks real classy. The wrapping alone must have cost more than I can afford to spend on a gift."

Undoubtedly Dan. Nobody else was likely to be sending her chocolates from a boutique on Fifth Avenue. He'd probably chosen the white hazelnut truffles he knew she loved. "Go ahead and open the package," Jess said, hardening her heart. "And feel free to help yourself to the chocolates, Marla. I've been eating too many dinners in great restaurants these past few days, and I'm on a strict diet."

"What a deal! I'll save the card, so you know who to thank." Marla sighed happily. "You know me, I'm a regular chocaholic. I'm thinking about chocolate strawberry creams and drooling..."

"At breakfast time?"

"Honey, didn't you know that chocolate is nature's perfect breakfast food? Picture me searching for a knife to open the wrapping as we speak."

Jess chuckled. "Well, you enjoy the chocolates, Marla, and while you're munching, I'll think virtuous thoughts about my slender hips."

"Boss lady, you can be a real pain in the you-know-where sometimes."

"You must be referring to my butt—my slender, well-toned butt." Jess smiled, refusing to let herself speculate on what Dan might have written on the gift tag. Probably something cute and witty that would make her feel all warm and gooey inside. She'd have to insert some steel into her spine before she read his message. Two dinners, a couple of heated glances and a box of expensive bonbons wasn't going to make her forget the misery of her marriage.

"Is there anything else we should talk about?" she asked her secretary. "If not, I should leave to catch the airport shuttle. I'll be back in Denver by around three this afternoon—"

A huge crash reverberated through the phone, so loud that for a moment Jess was deafened. She switched the phone to her other ear, feeling her stomach knot with anxiety. What in the world was *that?* "Marla, what happened? Good grief, it sounded as if an entire wall of filing cabinets fell on top of you. Are you all right?"

Silence. Jess jiggled the phone rest. "Marla, answer me, for God's sake. What's happened? Are you okay? Talk to me, dammit! Marla!"

The phone line remained silent, then started to emit a busy signal. Mouth dry, sweat pooling in the small of her back, Jess redialed her office number. The phone returned a busy signal. She hung up and dialed the direct line to her boss's office. That was busy, too. Jess began to shiver, although her hands were sweating as she clutched the receiver.

She dialed the long-distance operator. "I want to place a call to my office in Denver. I think there's been some kind of accident. Will you check this number for me, please?"

She waited, her stomach cramping, until the operator came back on the line. "There seems to be a problem with that number, miss. It's showing technical problems. I'll report it out of service for you."

"No, wait! Don't hang up. Please, don't! I think something terrible's happened—"

"I'm sorry, but I can't help you, miss. There's no way for me to check on what's really happened at that location—"

"Then how can I find out what's wrong? I think my assistant may have been hurt. Badly hurt. I think maybe she fell ... tripped over something ... she could be unconscious ..."

"If you think someone needs medical assistance, I can connect you to the emergency-services number in Denver."

"Yes, yes. Do that, please."

"Connecting you now. Thank you for using AT&T."

A few clicks and a different female voice came on the line. "This is 911—Emergency."

For a moment Jess's mind went blank. How was she going to explain the problem? "I'm calling from New York," she said.

"This is the emergency line in Denver, Colorado. Please hang up and dial your local-emergency services number—"

"It's a Denver emergency I want to report. Don't cut me off! I was just talking to my office on the phone and I heard this terrible noise, like an explosion or something—"

"You heard an explosion?"

"Yes. At least I think maybe it was an explosion." Jess hadn't realized precisely what she'd been so terrified of until she said the word. "My assistant was opening a package addressed to me and then there was a huge bang and the phone went dead and I couldn't make her answer and I called my boss and he didn't answer and the phone company says there's a problem on the line but they can't check it out because they're not in Denver—"

"Slow down, miss. Let's take this one step at a time. Give me the address of your office here in Denver and we can take care of the problem."

"Fourteen Larimer Square. It's the Colorado Tourist and Convention Bureau. We're located on the ground floor of the Federated Insurance Building."

"Give me your name, please, caller, and a phone number where you can be reached."

"I'm Jessica Zajak. I'm the assistant director of the bureau. But I'm at a hotel in New York and I'm supposed to be leaving for the airport—"

"The phone number of your hotel, miss?"

Jess gulped, blinked and forced herself to focus on the numbers written on her phone dial. "It's area code 212, 555-8911."

"Thank you. Hold on a moment, please."

Jess was gripping the phone so tightly her fingers hurt. She wiped her sweating palm against her skirt and changed hands. The emergency operator came back on the line. "Are you there, Ms. Zajak?"

"Yes, what's happened? Something's terribly wrong, isn't it?"

"We have no reports directly from the site as yet. However, emergency vehicles have been dispatched to the scene. We had already received reports of an explosion at that location."

"Oh, God, no! Marla! I've got to get home and make sure she's okay."

"Don't hang up, Ms. Zajak. Sergeant Berini from our police department would like to talk with you."

"All right." Jess sat down on the bed, her legs shaking too much to hold her upright. Her hand was dripping sweat around the phone and she put the receiver in its cradle, staring at it blankly for several seconds before realizing that Sergeant Somebody couldn't talk to her because she'd hung up. She tried to decide what to do, but her brain couldn't seem to string ideas together in a logical order— or any order at all.

The phone started to ring. The police. She'd given them her number and they were calling back. But she realized that she'd already missed the shuttle bus to the airport and, if she didn't get into a cab soon, she'd miss her flight, too.

Unable to bear the thought of being stuck for another moment in her hotel room, thousands of miles away from whatever had happened in Denver, Jess grabbed her purse and suitcase and ran to the elevator, leaving the phone ringing unanswered in her room.

Ten

Denver
Monday, June 17, 1996

"I need to go to Larimer Square," Jess said to the cab-driver waiting outside Denver airport. "The Federated Insurance Building."

"Sorry, miss." The driver shook his head. "Don't know if they'll let us through. I was just in that area and the police have most of the access streets to Larimer Square blocked off. There's been an explosion and it's a real mess down there."

She'd known the news would be bad, but Jess felt a fresh shock of horror when she heard the worst confirmed. She moistened her dry lips, the aridity of the thin mountain air assaulting her after the humidity of New York City. "Is it... is it a very bad explosion?"

"Not real bad, I guess. Not like Oklahoma City or nothin', but I guess they're afraid of gas leaks in the area. That's what they're saying, anyway."

"My office is in the building where the bomb exploded," Jess said. "I need to find out what happened. Just take me as close as you can, and I'll walk the rest of the way."

"Okay, you're the boss." The driver picked up her suitcase and hefted it into the cab. "That's one heavy case you got there, miss. You're gonna have a hard time walking with this sucker, but I'll take you as close as I can."

"Fine." Jess got into the cab. She asked the question for which she was dreading the answer. "Do you know if anyone got hurt in the blast?"

"Couple of people, I guess." The driver started his meter, then checked his side mirror and edged out into the stream of traffic. If he drove a cab like that in New York, Jess thought wryly, he'd never get out of the airport.

The driver adjusted his dark glasses, squinting into the brilliant afternoon sun. "Sorry I can't tell you more. I've been kinda busy, not really listening, except to the traffic reports. I'll get one of the local all-news stations for you. Bet they'll have an update soon." He turned on his radio and fiddled with the dial for a moment. "Here you go. KIVA. They do more news than anyone else."

Jess watched empty fields flash by without really seeing them, listening as the radio broadcast scores from a seemingly unending list of sporting events. They were turning onto Interstate 25 before she heard the bulletin she'd been waiting for.

"This just in from the Denver police. Search of the debris following this morning's explosion in the offices of the Colorado Tourist and Convention Bureau has turned up preliminary evidence that the explosion was caused by the detonation of a device that may have been concealed in a letter or package mailed to an employee of the bureau. The gas company has finished its emergency inspection of the Larimer Square area and has completed temporary repairs to a pipe damaged in the explosion. Paramedics are reporting that one woman was killed, pronounced dead on arrival at Denver General, and there were three other people injured, one seriously enough to require hospitalization. We go now to our reporter on the scene. Anne, can you give us the latest word, please?''

''Yes, Gordon. The police have confirmed that the device that caused the explosion is relatively unsophisticated, a variation of something that was first used back in the 1920s by the Irish Republican Army. The damage is pretty much contained to the room where the explosion occurred, with minor damage to rooms in the surrounding area. I understand that the victim was Marla Harries, a five-year employee of the bureau. The name of the man who was hospitalized hasn't yet been released.''

''Do the police have any idea who sent the bomb, Anne? Any reason to suppose this is the work of right-wing paramilitary groups, for example?''

''We don't know, Gordon. At this stage, the police aren't ruling out any possibilities. However, the *Rocky Mountain News* reported that they've received a phone call from a man describing himself as a radical gay-rights activist, and he is claiming responsibility for the bombing. According to the *News,* the caller stated that he targeted the state's official tourist bureau because of what he terms the vicious, narrow-minded bigotry of Colorado's Proposition Two. He wants to punish the people of Colorado by attacking the state where it hurts most—in its tourist industry.''

''Frightening logic, Anne. Proposition Two, of course, is the amendment to the state constitution that limits gay rights. Listeners will remember this was approved by Colorado's voters during the 1992 elections, but it's been challenged in the courts ever since. Have the police commented on this report from the *News,* Anne?''

''No. And the police aren't saying whether they consider this a crank call or the genuine thing.''

"Well, thanks for the report, Anne. We'll get back to you later on this afternoon for the latest update on the casualties. Now, in political news from Washington..."

Jess rolled down the window and leaned out, swallowing gulps of air. After a couple of minutes, the nausea gripping her receded to the point where she no longer felt in danger of throwing up.

Dear God, Marla, please forgive me. But how could I know? She thought of Marla's son, who was due to enroll as a freshman at the University of Northern Colorado in the fall. What in the world would she say to him? How could she look Greg in the eye, knowing that she was the person who should have died? Instead, his mother had been killed, in the midst of joking and laughing about a box of chocolates. And all because of a crazy who was angry about a proposition that had almost no chance of becoming law.

"Did you know the woman who was killed, miss?"

Jess realized the cabdriver was talking to her. "Yes, I knew her." Her throat burned with unshed tears, and she swallowed twice before she could continue. "She was my assistant. A wonderful person, with a great sense of humor. Everyone liked her." When people died unexpectedly, Jess thought abstractedly, they always seemed to be called wonderful people. In Marla's case, it was true.

"That's too bad," the cabby said. "With the crazies they got roaming around out there these days, nobody's safe."

"She was going to be forty next month," Jess said. "She was dreading it. Said she'd put out a contract on anyone who threw her a surprise party." Suddenly, without warning, she was crying, sobbing uncontrollably because Marla would never have to face the trauma of her fortieth birthday.

"Look, miss, we're nearly there." The cabdriver seemed torn between embarrassment and an awkward desire to offer comfort. "The police have lifted the barricades that closed off the street. I can drive right up close to your building."

Jess found a tissue in her purse, blotted her eyes and blew her nose. When she paid the driver and offered him five dollars as a tip, he waved it away. "Nah, that's okay. Add a few bucks from me to your secretary's memorial fund." He put her bags down on the pavement and threw a dubious glance in the direction of her office building. A policeman stood guard at the entrance, which was sealed off by yellow plastic tape. "They're not going to let you inside," he said. "You want me to wait? Maybe you should go home, miss, and come back here tomorrow. It's probably not even safe inside the building yet."

"Thanks, but I'll be fine. I need to talk to the police anyway."

"Looks like you're gonna get to talk to a cop right now. He's headed in this direction. Well, I'll be off." The cabdriver hurried back to his car, obviously not a man who enjoyed the company of police officers.

"Can I help you, miss?" The cop eyed her bags with evident suspicion. Perhaps he suspected her of having another bomb in her suitcase, Jess thought with weary irritation.

"My name's Jessica Zajak. Marla Harries was my assistant." Jess fought back a fresh wave of tears. "I'm the person who called in to Emergency about the accident. From New York," she explained. "I just got back to Denver."

"Show me your driver's license, please."

Jess handed him her license and he examined it carefully before talking into his communicator. "I've got Jessica Zajak here, sir. She says she just flew into Denver from New York. Do you want to speak with her?''

"You bet I want to speak with her," came a voice over the speaker. "Send her in."

The cop clicked off his communicator and nodded to Jess. "If you'll come this way, Ms. Zajak, I'll let you through."

The tourist and convention bureau office space consisted of four back rooms, fronted by a reception area where visitors could walk in and pick up brochures and discuss their plans with one of the specially trained assistants. The first sight that greeted Jess as she entered the bureau was a gaping hole in the wall behind the reception counter where there had once been a giant poster of Aspen Mountain. The poster had been one of her favorites, a collage of forest green and dazzling white snow, with a lone bighorn sheep silhouetted against the brilliant winter sun. Until she saw the ugly jagged hole, Jess hadn't realized just what a lift that glimpse of blue sky and sunny mountain wilderness gave her spirits. She felt the tears building again in the back of her throat.

A tall, thin man stood up behind the impromptu desk he'd made for himself out of the table that normally was covered with glossy brochures. "Ms. Zajak? I'm Special Agent Will Ackroyd, with the CBI. I'm in charge of the investigation on this case."

Jess looked at his identification. "You're with the Colorado Bureau of Investigation?"

"Yes. We're working with the federal authorities, of course, but for now, our agency is coordinating the investigation."

She gave him back his badge. "I heard a radio report when I was driving in from the airport. They said that Marla...that Marla was dead on arrival at the hospital and that another man had been detained at the hospital. Who was it? Is he going to be all right? Is he going to make it?''

"The other victim was Gerald Sondheim," the detective said, discreetly activating a tape recorder. "He got a concussion when a filing cabinet fell over on him, but the hospital plans to release him tomorrow."

Weak with relief, Jess dropped into the nearest chair, scarcely noticing that it was still damp with the fire fighters' foam. "I can't believe Gerry was in here at eight in the morning."

"Mr. Sondheim told me it was unusual for him to be in the office at that hour. But the governor arranged an unexpected meeting, and your boss needed to do some preparatory work."

"Poor Gerry, what a day for him to come in early! But thank heavens his injury isn't worse. You're *sure* he's going to be all right?''

"The hospital says so."

"What about the other people who were hurt? Who was on duty at the front desk this morning?"

The detective shuffled through some notes. "Rosa Magrini," he said. "Fortunately, she was tidying the rack of brochures over by the door when the wall blew out. She was shocked and upset, but escaped injury, except for a few bruises. The other person who had to be hospitalized was Rick Vance, from the governor's office. He got a bad cut near his eye and the paramedics couldn't stop the bleeding. The good news is there's no actual damage to his eyesight. He's been released from the hospital already."

Jess winced. "So many people hurt! And can you imagine what would have happened if I'd asked Marla to keep the chocolates until I got back from New York? Suppose I'd opened that package in the middle of the afternoon? We often have as many as a dozen people in this front office at one time. Think how many of them might have been killed or injured!"

"We *have* been thinking," the detective said grimly. "Am I correct in assuming that Marla was killed while she was actually talking to you on a long-distance phone call, Ms. Zajak?"

"Yes. I was about to leave New York to catch my flight back to Denver and I was going through some of my mail with Marla. I asked her to open the package seconds before I heard the explosion."

"You asked her to open the package?"

"Yes, it was addressed to me," Jess said.

Agent Ackroyd appeared startled. "We'd assumed that the package Marla opened was either addressed to her, or to the office in general."

Jess frowned. "Well, of course, I couldn't see her, so I can't swear to precisely what she was opening. But a split second before the explosion occurred, we were talking about a package, addressed to me, that Marla assumed contained a box of chocolates."

"Mmm." The detective's expression became even grimmer. "This puts a slightly different twist on things. The fact is, Ms. Zajak, if this package was addressed to you, we have to assume that whoever sent it intended *you* to open it. And that means whoever sent it also intended *you* to die."

Jess's stomach churned. "You make it sound so personal."

"Maybe it was."

That possibility had been nagging at the back of her mind for the past several hours. Jess forced herself to confront the fear she'd been trying to ignore. "I can't believe someone was targeting me directly. Why in the world would anyone send a bomb to me?"

Ackroyd's mouth twisted into a grimace that could have been described as a bitter smile. "I was hoping you would tell me the answer to that question, Ms. Zajak. Why might somebody want to kill you? If I were you, I'd give that question some real hard thought."

The seat of the chair was suddenly too damp and uncomfortable to tolerate. Jess jumped up and paced, the sodden carpet squishing foam with each restless step. "I've no idea who might want to kill me. None. I'm not the sort of person to attract the attention of a madman who builds bombs in his basement. I'm not rich or powerful. I'm not a movie star. I haven't figured in any media stories recently. It makes no sense to think I'm a personal target for someone." She massaged her forehead, which did absolutely nothing for the headache starting to pound aggressively behind her temples. "It must be coincidence that the bomb was sent to me. It has to be. The guy who sent the bomb knew my name for some reason, so he mailed it to me."

The detective shrugged. "In my trade, you soon learn that it's dangerous to ignore the obvious. The package was mailed to you. Therefore the killer wants you dead. Seems like a real workable theory to me."

"But you're not listening to me!" Jess protested. "There isn't anyone who wants me dead!"

"Maybe you need to think harder and longer, Ms. Zajak. Why are you so sure there isn't anyone who might have a reason to try to kill you?"

"Because it's crazy. I lead a very dull life. There's *no* reason—"

"It doesn't have to be a reason you would consider rational. You're an exceptionally attractive woman, and that might have provoked jealousy on someone's part. Or you might have made yourself a dangerous enemy just in the course of your daily life.''

"Like I said, Agent Ackroyd, I don't exactly move in dangerous circles. The occasional hockey game with my brothers is about as close to a combat zone as I get.''

"You're deliberately misunderstanding. Anybody who gets angry enough can be dangerous. How about a neighbor who's mad about one of your pets trampling his flowers? Or maybe an ex-boyfriend who's angry that you turned him down?''

Jess thought about Tim Macfadden and tried to imagine him being sufficiently upset at her refusal to marry him that he would send her a letter bomb. The idea was so ridiculous that, in other circumstances, it would have made her smile. "I don't have any enemies,'' she said flatly. "Not lethal ones at any rate.''

"Everyone has a few people who don't like them, Ms. Zajak.''

"Of course, I realize that. I'm not some flake who believes all the world loves me. But there's a difference between people who don't like you and people who hate you enough to send a bomb through the mail.''

"Sure there is. But sometimes you can't tell which is which until after the bomb's been sent.''

Jess shivered. "No, Agent Ackroyd, you're not going to push me down that path. I won't start wondering if every person I've ever had a disagreement with is a psychopath. I'm not prepared to live my life that way. Besides, aren't you ignoring some other valid possibilities? I heard on the way into town from the airport that radical gay activists claimed responsibility for the bombing. God knows that makes no sense, but it makes a lot more sense than believing the woman downstairs sent me a bomb because my bathroom pipes burst and flooded her ceiling.''

"Did your pipes burst and flood your neighbor's ceiling?"

The guy was actually scribbling down a note. Jess sighed. "Yes, but the insurance company paid for everything to be repaired and Leslie's way too sensible to be nursing a grudge."

"Then why did you mention her?"

Jess tried to control her exasperation. "I mentioned Leslie *because* it would be crazy to suspect her."

"Then why pick on that incident and not another one?"

Was it because she'd always sensed an undertone of resentment beneath Leslie's superficially polite greetings? Jess wondered. No! Dammit, she wasn't going to start second-guessing her subconscious. "Leslie did not send me a letter bomb," she said through gritted teeth. "The idea's absurd."

She hated the way he kept taking notes about what she said, even though the tape recorder was whirring away, recording everything. "Could we get back to discussing the phone call to the newspaper, please?"

"We're investigating that now, but we can't assume someone's responsible for the attack just because they say they are. An incident like this sends kooks and fanatics of every variety rushing for their portable phones. Not to mention their fax machines and the Internet. Maybe this group that called the newspaper just feels the need to generate a bit of publicity for the cause of gay rights. Or maybe they're telling the truth and they decided to kill off a few public service employees to protest discrimination in Colorado. Rest assured, we're investigating that call as well as a half-dozen others. Including a coven of witches who say that they sent the bomb as a warning that excessive tourism in the Rocky Mountains is upsetting the spectral balance of the ether, whatever the hell that means." Ackroyd pinched the bridge of his nose, looking tired and discouraged.

Jess found it sickening that so many people were willing to piggyback a tragedy simply for the sake of publicizing their cause, but she was reluctant to abandon the idea that the bomb had been sent by some group or other of crazies. It was marginally less disturbing to think of herself as the unlucky victim of group insanity, rather than the prime target of an individual's focused hatred.

"Let's switch topics for a few minutes," the detective said, breaking into her disagreeable thoughts. "Let me make sure I have the facts straight. You were talking to your secretary when this explosion occurred. She was opening a package, you said, and then there was a loud noise, and the phone line went dead. Why was Marla Harries opening a package addressed to you? Did she routinely open your mail?"

"When I was out of the office, Marla would open any mail that didn't look personal. If she was in doubt, she'd set it to one side to wait for me."

"So this package appeared routine?" Ackroyd frowned. "But you said it looked like a box of chocolates. Is that a routine sort of gift to arrive at the office for you?"

"No. It was very much out of the ordinary. Quite apart from the fact that people don't usually send me gifts to the office, the way Marla described it, the package was eye-catching."

The detective's eyes gleamed. "Marla described the package to you?"

"Yes, it was a gold-foil bubble pack, with the return address on an embossed copper-foil label. Very distinctive, according to Marla."

"There was a return address?" Ackroyd looked up, startled. "Does that mean you remember where the package supposedly came from?"

"Yes." How tragically ironic it was that she'd suspected Dan of sending her the chocolates. She would never have asked Marla to describe the package in so much detail if she hadn't been worried that it came from him.

Jess shivered again as she registered how narrowly she'd escaped dying. She thought back, trying to recall everything Marla had told her. "The chocolates supposedly came from a swish boutique on Fifth Avenue in New York. It's called The Chocolatier, and I remember Marla said the package had been delivered early this morning—"

"She didn't say how it was delivered? By hand? FedEx? U.S. mail?"

"I'm sorry, I can't remember." In retrospect, Jess could see that her attention had been focused on all the wrong things during those crucial few moments of conversation with Marla. She'd been thinking about why Dan might have sent her the chocolates, not about how they'd been sent. "Looking back on our conversation, I have a vague impression that Marla implied the package was delivered after she arrived at work this morning. But I could be mistaken about that."

"We're already checking with all the courier services and with the post office, of course, but this information will be a big help. Thank you. You've given us a much better idea what we're looking for." Ackroyd appeared almost excited and even aimed a brief smile in Jess's direction. "Quite often, in situations like this, we're working blind because, when the letter bomb explodes, it destroys the evidence of how it was packaged. This description of yours gives us a flying head start."

Jess felt another chill ripple down her spine. "I'm usually the first person into the office," she said. "If I'd opened that package myself, you'd never even have known it was addressed to me, much less what it looked like."

"That's true. In the circumstances, we have more information than we could logically expect. Obviously, anything else you can remember is going to make the investigation that much easier for us."

"I've just remembered something," Jess said. "Marla told me the package was marked Personal. Personal to me." She clasped and unclasped her hands, then stuck them in the pockets of her linen jacket to hide their tremor. "I guess whoever sent that package really wanted to be sure I was the one who opened it."

"Yes, I'd say so." The detective's smile had long since faded. "You need to think again about anyone who might have reason to dislike you, Ms. Zajak. If this attack was aimed at you personally, and not at the tourist bureau, the person who sent that bomb isn't going to give up just because his or her first attempt failed. Before you go home, I'll give you a list of instructions on how to handle mail arriving at your home. You need to exercise extreme caution until we have the perpetrator in custody."

Jess drew in a shaky breath, torn between fear and denial. The situation was absurd. No way could she seriously believe there was a mad killer lurking in the shadows, plotting her death. On the other hand, how could she ignore the possibility? Agent Ackroyd wasn't joking: he expected her to make a neat checklist of friends and acquaintances who might be psychotic enough to mail her a bomb. But since none of her friends appeared psychotic, she'd have to suspect everybody or nobody—with the bonus of driving herself crazy in the process. How could she go through life afraid to open the monthly utility bill in case it exploded?

"I'll get back to you if I can think of any friends who might qualify as potentially deranged terrorist bombers," she said curtly.

"Thank you." The detective deliberately ignored her sarcasm. "I'm puzzled by something, Ms. Zajak. Is there some special reason why you would ask your secretary to open a package that was elaborately gift wrapped, addressed to you and marked Personal?"

Of course there was. She'd thought the package came from Dan. Jess wondered how in the world she was supposed to condense several minutes of neurotic, stream-of-consciousness brooding about her ex-husband into a crisp explanation that would satisfy a cop.

"I'm on a diet," she said at last, settling for the half-truth. "I have a sweet tooth and I'd been eating far too many rich desserts while I was in New York. I definitely didn't need to come home and start munching on chocolate truffles."

"And that's the only reason you told Marla to open the package?"

"Yes, basically. I didn't want the temptation waiting for me." Tears returned to her eyes as she remembered the friendly banter that had filled what turned out to be Marla's last moments on earth. "I told Marla to help herself to as many chocolates as she wanted, and while she was munching, I'd be feeling virtuous for sticking to my diet." Her hands balled into fists inside her pockets. "I t-told her she could admire my slender hips when I got back to the office."

"What was Marla's reply to that?"

Jess fumbled for a tissue and blew her nose fiercely. "She said I was a pain in the you-know-where."

"The ass?" Ackroyd suggested.

"Yes, that's what she meant. But she didn't say it. She wasn't in the least afraid to state her mind, but she never used foul language."

"Is that what Marla felt about you, Ms. Zajak? That you were a pain in the ass?"

Jess blinked, shocked out of her tears. "No, of course not! Well, not in the way you're implying."

"I wasn't implying anything, Ms. Zajak. You're jumping to conclusions. I was just trying to round out my understanding of why Marla was opening a booby-trapped package addressed to you."

"Well, then, you need to know that Marla and I were friends. Good friends. She was one of the best friends I have—had—in Denver."

"And she felt the same way about you?"

"Yes, I'm sure she did. We worked really well together, and we enjoyed a lot of the same things. We're both movie buffs—we went to the movies together almost every week. We had a standing date for Thursday nights." Jess stopped, then started over, her voice husky. "*Damn!* I still can't believe this happened! Marla was one of the world's good guys. Why do her family and friends have to go through this because some group of crazies gets off on terrorizing people?"

"I guess you don't expect me to answer that question." Ackroyd flexed his shoulders and Jess realized he looked every bit as weary and depressed as she felt. "All right, Ms. Zajak, let's start at the beginning again and work through. Tell me everything you can remember about your final conversation with Marla Harries."

"Again? But I just told you."

"I need to hear everything you said to each other. Right from the first hello." The detective put a new cassette into the tape recorder and pressed the record button. "Okay, let's go through this one more time. From the top, please, Ms. Zajak."

Eleven

Jess arrived home too emotionally drained to think, and too tired to feel anything much beyond a numb, aching regret. The uncluttered calm of her condo failed to work its usual soothing magic. The ivory walls looked stark instead of clean, the beige Berber carpet boringly functional. Her tropical fish were the only touch of color in an apartment too full of furniture chosen because it was neutral and multipurpose rather than because she really liked it. She sprinkled food into the fish tank and wished, with sudden intensity, that she had a dog. Marla had owned a dog, a giant boxer named Alfred the Great, with no brains, an excess of devotion for his mistress and a habit of plonking all of his ninety pounds on whatever pair of feet happened to be closest. What would happen to Alfred now? she wondered. Who would take care of him when Greg went off to college?

Jess felt chilled clear through to the bone. She took a hot bath, which did nothing to warm her up. Teeth chattering, she wrapped herself in a thick toweling bathrobe and curled up on the sofa, her toes tucked under an afghan, too apathetic to blow-dry the damp ends of her hair.

After twenty minutes of sitting motionless, staring at the blank screen of her television, engaged in the surreal task of wondering whether her neighbor Leslie might or might not be a psychotic maniac with a penchant for building bombs in her spare bedroom, Jess realized she was edging dangerously close to hysteria.

She choked back a gasp of laughter that verged on a sob. "Enough self-pity," she muttered, jumping off the sofa and tightening the belt of her robe. "Tomorrow you'll go visit Greg and tell him how sorry you are about his mother. But remember, you're not to blame for Marla's death. The person who sent the bomb is to blame. What's more, Leslie has *not* turned into a demented killer. She's still the same grouchy neighbor she was yesterday, before this happened. You are not—repeat *not*—going to drive yourself crazy wondering if *she's* crazy." Jess rubbed her aching forehead. "And while we're discussing crazy, it might be a smart idea to quit talking out loud in an empty room."

Determined to get a grip on herself, she wandered into the kitchen and let her gaze drift between the fridge and the stove, debating whether or not she had the energy to make herself a cup of tea. A stiff drink would suit her mood better, except that she had nothing alcoholic in the house. At this moment, she would have bargained with the devil for some of the wonderful thirty-year-old cognac Dan used to keep in their apartment, back in the beginning of their marriage. They would take a snifter to bed with them on days when life had seemed rougher than normal. They'd sip slowly, sharing the one glass, propped up against a stack of pillows, playing some game Dan would invent, and she would invariably lose. The forfeit for losing always involved being kissed in places and in ways that became progressively more erotic as the cognac disappeared. By the time the glass was empty, she was usually about ten seconds away from climax.

Sometimes she'd had to work hard at losing, Jess thought with the first twinge of humor she'd experienced since early morning. But for the punishment of having Dan kiss her, it was worth expending a little effort.

She sobered quickly. For the last six months of their marriage, there'd been no cognac, no cute marital games and not much sex. If Dan had walked into their apartment with a bottle of brandy, during those horrible final months before the divorce, she'd have accepted it with withering courtesy, while seething in silent fury about the phone bill that had to be paid, and the rent, and the utilities, and all the rest. She'd been right to take their financial responsibilities seriously, Jess reflected, but she sure had been a self-righteous pain in the ass, with her permanent air of semi-martyrdom and her long-suffering, die-away airs.

She set the box of tea bags on the counter, shocked by where her thoughts had led her. Although she'd always paid lip service to the idea that it took two people to make a marriage and two people to break it, in her heart of hearts, she'd considered herself blameless in the debacle that ended her marriage to Dan. It was disconcerting to view her behavior in a different, and far less flattering, light.

Still, there was no point in reassessing the precise reasons why her marriage had failed. Maybe Dan wasn't entirely at fault, as she'd always assumed, but however you might want to apportion blame between the two of them, she and Dan had worked a real number on their relationship. When you'd demolished something that thoroughly, there was no foundation for a new beginning. It was only in Greek legends that a brilliant firebird could spring forth from the ashes of past destruction.

Jess poured water into the kettle and set it on the stove. Stick to practicalities, she advised herself. Make some tea, mourn for Marla, plan how you can help Greg. Forget about Dan. Look what happened this morning because you couldn't stop obsessing about him. The wrong person opened the package because you were afraid of how you'd react if you found out your ex-husband had sent you a box of chocolates.

Jess scowled. Great! With almost no effort at all, she'd managed to bring the wheel of her guilt full cycle back to Marla and the bomb. Stomach knotted, she concentrated on the mundane task of opening a box of tea bags, putting one in a cup and emptying the rest into the decorative storage canister. The kettle whistled just as the phone rang. She poured boiling water into her cup and ignored the phone. After three rings, her brother Matt's voice sputtered into the answering machine, sounding as close to frantic as anyone in the Zajak family ever got. Jess's burden of guilt immediately tripled. Good grief, how could she possibly have forgotten to phone her family to reassure them that she was okay?

She grabbed the phone and spoke to Matt, Todd, her two sisters-in-law, her parents, the twins and even her niece, Kelly, who'd all gathered in her parents' home to wait for news of her. Kelly was sufficiently worried to abandon her blasé teenage indifference and sob noisily into the phone. Her mother, usually a placid harbor in troubled seas, couldn't seem to calm down and was unmoved by Jess's reminder that she'd told everyone she was spending the weekend in Manhattan, so her family should have realized she wasn't even in Denver at the time of the explosion.

"You changed your flight home once, why couldn't you have changed back again?" her mother demanded with irrefutable logic. "It was two hours before we could get anyone to tell us the name of the woman they were reporting dead in the explosion. And then they wouldn't confirm that nobody else was injured." In a small, reproachful voice, Barbara added, "You should have called home, Jess."

"I know." Guilt swelled and blossomed. "I'm sorry, Mom, really sorry. I was so fixated on getting to Denver and finding out about Marla that I forgot everything else. And by the time I finally got back to my apartment tonight, I was a zombie."

"We understand. I guess," Barbara said. "Well, anyway, that's all water under the bridge now and what's done is done. Thankfully, we can go to bed tonight knowing you're fine. Although it's terrible about Marla. She seemed like a real nice lady that time we went out to lunch last year. We went to that Italian place near your office, do you remember?"

"Yes, Mom, I remember." La Venezia had been one of Marla's favorite restaurants. They'd eaten there the day before Jess left for New York. Jess mashed her tea bag so hard with her spoon that it burst, sending tea leaves floating in her cup.

Her mother made a tsking noise. "These days, I don't even want to watch the news, it's always so depressing. It's a sorry old world, with the people who least deserve it carrying the heaviest loads. Still, I guess we have to keep plugging along, trying to find something good, even on the bad days. If we didn't have winter, spring wouldn't be half as welcome."

For once, Jess found her mother's determined optimism cloying. "I don't know, Mom. There's not much good to find in the fact that Marla got blown away by some lunatic who was willing to kill innocent people in order to deliver his crazy message."

"No, there isn't," Barbara agreed. "But Marla didn't die in vain, remember that. However hard it might be, we have to remember that there's a purpose to everything, Jess, even when we can't figure out the purpose right away."

"Yes, I guess so." She wanted to ask what the hell purpose there was to making Greg an orphan, but her mother had an unshakable conviction that God would right everything in the end, and Jess supposed she shouldn't impose her own bleak skepticism on Barbara's comforting faith.

Apparently sensing Jess's resistance, her mother changed the subject. She commented on the pleasant weather, reported that her apple tree looked set for a bumper crop and asked about the success of Jess's trip to New York.

"Did that detective manage to reach you, by the way?" Barbara asked.

"Which detective?" Jess asked. "Do you mean Will Ackroyd from the CBI?"

"What's the CBI?"

"Colorado Bureau of Investigation. It's like the FBI, except at the state level."

"No, dear, why would they be calling here? I mean the private investigator you hired. I wrote his name down somewhere. Here it is. Kupfer. From Kupfer and Associates in Brooklyn. His phone number is 555-7314. Area code 718. He called on Sunday morning and said he'd been trying to reach you in Denver, but you weren't home. He told me he had important information to pass on to you about the Pazmanys. He explained that everything he'd learned was confidential, so he couldn't leave a more detailed message. I didn't press him, of course, but I must admit I'm curious to hear what he's found out. Did he manage to get in touch with you?"

Jess started to say she hadn't hired any detectives, then decided not to give her mother anything new to worry about. Dan had suggested hiring an investigator to check newspaper reports of children who'd gone missing back in 1969. Probably he'd hired Mr. Kupfer without consulting her first—although it wasn't like him to be so high-handed.

A chill rippled down Jess's spine, puckering her skin with goose bumps. How odd that someone had been trying to locate her only hours before a bomb was delivered to her office. "We haven't reached each other as yet," she said, trying to keep the slight tremor out of her voice. "Did you tell him I was still in New York?"

"No, I told him you were in Denver, because that's where I thought you were."

Jess's chill intensified. Whoever had called her mother would have every reason to believe she'd returned to Denver. "But I'd already told Todd that I'd decided to stay in New York for another twenty-four hours. I called on Saturday, because I knew you'd be at church on Sunday morning. Todd said you and Dad were out bowling."

"And what in the world makes you suppose that Todd remembered to pass on your message?" Barbara asked, with unusual sarcasm. "He finally got around to mentioning that you'd phoned right before bedtime. Bedtime on Sunday, that is."

Head throbbing, Jess wondered if she ought to tell her mother that she hadn't hired any private investigator and that she had no idea who might have called Ohio in search of her. Better to wait until tomorrow and talk to Will Ackroyd first, she decided. There was no point in upsetting her mother for no reason, and the caller would most likely turn out to be an investigator hired by Dan.

"Sweetheart, are you sure you're going to be all right?" Barbara was often surprisingly insightful where her family was concerned, and Jess could hear the anxiety that lingered in her mother's voice, despite the cheerful flow of chatter. "Why don't you ask a friend to spend the night with you? When all's said and done, this isn't a good night for you to be alone."

Jess tried to pull herself out of the dumps and convince her mother that she was not only physically safe but also coping fine emotionally. In response to Barbara's urging, she promised that she wouldn't drive alone after dark until the bomber was caught. When her father came back on the phone, she reassured him that the police had set up an active security screen on all the bureau's incoming mail, and carefully concealed from him—and everyone else— that the booby-trapped package had been addressed specifically to her. Finally, after another round of goodbyes, she hung up.

The conversation with her family should have made her feel better. Perversely, by the time she was through telling everyone just how safe she was and that she didn't in the least mind being alone, Jess discovered that she'd talked herself into a major state of the jitters. She raced through the condo switching on every light she could find. When her intercom buzzed, indicating that someone was at the outside door, she nearly jumped out of her skin. Hands icy cold, she stared at the house phone, momentarily paralyzed by panic. Only the realization that it was more frightening not to know who was out there compelled her to unlock her hands from their death grip on the edge of the kitchen counter and pick up the phone.

"Yes?"

"It's Dan. Buzz me in, Jess."

"Dan." *Dan.* She closed her eyes and rested her forehead against the wall, weak with relief at the sound of his voice. *Thank God he'd come.* She knew he was the person she'd been longing to see.

"Jess, are you still there? What's going on? Let me in, dammit."

"Yes, yes, I will." She hung up the phone and pressed the button to release the outside locks. Heart thumping, she walked into her tiny vestibule and listened for the elevator. She heard the sound of a heavy door slamming and realized Dan had been too impatient to wait and had run up the stairs of the emergency exit. He pounded on the door of her apartment.

"Jess, open up. Let me in."

She drew back the bolts and he stepped inside, kicking the door shut behind him. He threw his garment bag to one side and pulled her into his arms, his movements rough and uncoordinated. His hands slid over her hips, drawing her up high and hard against him. Then his mouth came down on hers, kissing her with barely restrained violence.

Jess had spent the years since their divorce telling herself that Dan's kisses were just the same as any other man's. She'd lied. When his tongue thrust against hers, desire—instant and intense—coiled in the pit of her stomach. She knew that he hovered on the knife-edge of losing control, but far from being repelled, she responded eagerly to the dark passion of his kisses, reveling in the answering flare of her own need. The defenses she'd painstakingly constructed since their divorce were destroyed in seconds, revealing the full extent of her vulnerability. Not that she needed any confirmation of her susceptibility to Dan. Why else had she spent the last three years frantically avoiding any and all contact with him?

Heat scorched and sizzled through her veins, but it felt wonderful after the icy chill that had enveloped her all day. She clasped her hands at the back of Dan's neck, holding his lips hard against her own, returning kiss for kiss, fevered embrace for fevered embrace, until they finally broke apart, panting and gasping for air.

He framed her face, holding her head still, his breath fanning her cheeks. "My God, Jess, for three hours this afternoon, I thought you were dead."

"I stayed in New York over the weekend to talk with Dr. Weir. I wasn't in Denver when the bomb went off."

"I thought I'd never see you again. Never hold you again, never wake up to find you lying in my bed." His hands were shaking as he pushed open her robe and bent his head to trail kisses across her throat and breasts.

Jess closed her eyes, letting the spectacular sensations run riot. She wondered how in the world she'd managed to convince herself that she could live the rest of her life without Dan's lovemaking. God, she must have been suffering from a three-year bout of total insanity. She managed to unfasten two of his shirt buttons before giving up and ripping open the rest. She leaned close, breathing in the familiar smell of his skin, listening to the thud of his racing heart, feeling the heat inside her expand until her skin prickled and tingled with a thousand fiery pinpoints of desire.

"I really needed you to be here tonight," she said huskily. "Thank you for coming, Dan."

His grip on her shoulders tightened. "I didn't expect to find you alone."

"Then why did you come?"

"Because I hoped you might be alone, even though I didn't expect it."

She turned away, trailing her fingers along the framed poster of Vail's covered bridge that hung in her entrance. "I was waiting for you," she admitted in a small, low voice. "I kept waiting and hoping for you to come."

She heard Dan draw in a deep breath. "Jess, look at me."

She turned slowly within the circle of his arms and lifted her head until her gaze locked with his.

"You have to be honest with me for once, Jess—"

Indignation cooled her desire. "I'm always honest—"

"Let's not get into that right now. I want you, and tonight I guess I'm not willing to play the game by your rules. If you're looking for a friend—if you don't want to make love with me—this would be a real good moment to tell me to get the hell out of here." His mouth curved briefly into a wry smile. "Speak fast, Jess. For the next twenty seconds, if you tell me to leave, there's a slight chance I might go."

"Don't go. I want you to stay." Jess didn't stop to ask herself where those words came from or what they might imply for the future. For once, she wasn't interested in sensible, long-term plans. At this moment, all she cared about was the powerful support of Dan's arms holding her, and the wonderful, familiar strength of his body pressed close against hers.

"Thank God you didn't put my willpower to the test." Dan kissed her as he spoke, a torrid, openmouthed kiss that made her pulse throb and set her heart racing again.

"I'm not in the mood for tests tonight. Make me feel alive, Dan. Make me forget that I should have been at the office to open that damned package."

"Don't think about what happened today," he said. "Think about what's happening now. Think about the pleasure we're going to give each other." He untied the belt of her robe and pushed it from her shoulders. She let it fall to the floor, and when she felt it pool around her ankles, she kicked it aside.

Dan's breath expelled in a rough, choppy gasp. "You have the most beautiful body I've ever seen," he said hoarsely. "God, Jess, I swear you're even more desirable now than when we were married."

His husky voice was the most erotic sound she'd heard in three years. Jess would have sworn that she could feel her bones melting. The most amazing part of it was that, when Dan looked at her with that hungry gleam in his eyes, she actually felt beautiful and desirable and all those crazy things only he could make her believe about herself.

She unbuckled his belt and slid the zipper of his pants slowly downward. Silently, she caressed the pulsing hardness of his erection. She'd forgotten how good he felt cupped in her hand, forgotten how powerful she felt when his penis throbbed in response to her lightest touch.

He made a sound somewhere between a sigh and a groan. "Oh, Jess, how the hell did we survive three years without this?"

"I don't know." She closed her eyes. At this moment, she couldn't imagine living another three minutes without having Dan inside her, let alone another three years. The last lingering remnants of her common sense fled, sailing out the window on a cloud of sexual euphoria.

He bent her back over his arm, trailing his hand seductively down the front of her body, separating her thighs and teasing her into arousal. She shuddered as his fingers played over her, stroking her to the trembling edge of climax.

She was right on the brink when Dan spoke hoarsely, "Jess, this floor looks damned hard. We need to find your bedroom."

She hadn't even noticed they were still standing in the entrance to her condo and that she was crushed against the wall with Dan's knee thrust between her legs. Blinking dazedly, she turned and walked into the bedroom, sinking onto her bed and pulling Dan down next to her. She lay, cradled between his arms and the satin softness of her comforter, her entire body quivering in anticipation, her mind wiped blissfully clear of everything except desire.

He straddled her, bracing his arms on either side of her body. He looked down, his gray-green eyes glittering darkly, and his lips set in a hard, implacable line.

"What is it?" Jess asked.

"I was thinking that three years is a hell of a long time to wait," he said.

Too long? Or maybe nowhere near long enough. Jess didn't want to decide, didn't want her brain to spring back into action, posing awkward questions. Right now, she only wanted to feel. In answer, she pulled his mouth down to hers and simultaneously arched her hips off the bed, offering herself in a silent but explicit invitation.

For a second, Dan didn't move. Then he plunged into her, thrusting with fierce urgency, taking her on a swift, exhilarating ride to ecstasy. For a moment etched out of time, she soared high above the chasm of everyday reality. She climaxed a split second before he did, spinning off into the shimmering void where only Dan had ever managed to take her.

God, how she'd missed him.

Dear God, how she wished he'd never come back.

The distant hum of the filter in the fish tank sounded as loud as a jackhammer in the deathly quiet of the bedroom. Dan spoke first. "I have the doomed feeling that anything I say right now is going to precipitate disaster. Maybe you should speak first."

Jess thought of and discarded several replies. In the end, honesty seemed best. "I'm scared," she admitted.

Dan rolled onto his side, propping himself on one arm so that he could look at her. "Scared of what?" he asked. "The person who sent the bomb?"

Jess gave a tiny gasp of distraught laughter. "I'd forgotten about the bomb," she said.

Dan didn't quite smile. "I guess that's a compliment."

"Not really. I think it's part of the problem." She sighed. "When I'm with you, Dan, the whole world seems to shrink until there's nothing in it except the two of us."

"Makes for great sex," he suggested.

"But life is more than sex." Jess gave a rueful laugh. "Although ten minutes ago, you'd have had a hard time convincing me of that."

Dan's voice contained a note of surprise. "When we were married, you'd never have admitted that."

"What? That life is more than sex?"

"Hell, no, that comment was vintage Jess. But I never expected to hear you admit there are moments when sex can seem the most important thing in the entire universe."

At the start of their relationship, she and Dan had enjoyed such fabulous sex that Jess had never seen any need to discuss it. By the end of their marriage, if she'd mentioned sex at all, it was only to point out that a marriage needed more than sexual compatibility to make it work. By the time their divorce was finalized, she was so emotionally devastated she would have been quite happy to take a vow of lifelong celibacy. She'd dated Tim Macfadden for eleven long and boring months chiefly *because* her feelings for him weren't complicated by overwhelming sexual desire. Jess wondered if her decision not to accept Tim's proposal meant that she'd cured her knee-jerk habit of trying to mold her life into the diametric opposite of what it had been with Dan.

Still, she hesitated for a while before finally acknowledging the truth. "When we were married, I was naive. I assumed great sex was the easy part in any relationship. Now I know better. What we shared in the early days of our marriage was something special, and...wonderful. I've found out that I can't fall passionately in love with a man just because he's a nice, hardworking guy who treats me with respect. It's damned annoying, but that doesn't make it any less true."

Dan grimaced. "I guess now it's my turn to say something mature and thoughtful. Unfortunately, what I'm feeling is a strong urge to get the names of the men who've given you all these valuable lessons about sex and deliver each of them a crippling kick in the nuts."

Jess smiled. "You can step out of your macho-man mode, Dan. As far as I'm concerned, when we're talking sex, you're the undisputed, all-time champ. Nobody else comes close."

"Thank you for telling me that." Dan took her hand and brought it to his mouth. He kissed her knuckles, then turned her hand over, pressing a long, slow kiss into her palm. He was the only man Jess had ever met who could carry off the old-fashioned gesture and not look ridiculous while he did it. "I'm sorry I was such a lousy husband, Jess. That's an inadequate apology, I know, but I fell so damn deep in love with you that I kidded myself we could make it work, even though I should have been smart enough to know better. I wasn't ready to be married."

Her hand tightened around his. "I loved you, too, Dan." She swallowed over the sudden lump in her throat. "I guess that's why it hurt so much when everything started to come apart."

He pulled her close, cradling her head against his shoulder, speaking softly. "I never wanted to hurt you,

Jess. I'd have given almost anything in the world to avoid hurting you, in fact. But my life seemed to be heading at warp speed in a direction I didn't want to go, and eventually, I froze. Couldn't sleep, couldn't work, couldn't bear to watch you struggling to carry the double load, and yet I couldn't explain what was wrong." His mouth twisted into a self-mocking smile. "You're so efficient and practical, Jess. How the hell was I supposed to explain that I was paralyzed by the realization that I had no acting talent? That I had this creative monster eating away at my guts and no idea how to appease it?"

Efficient and practical? Yes, she thought, she was both of those things. She'd trained herself to fit right in with the rest of the Zajak family, shaping her personality to fit theirs, out of gratitude for the love they showered on her. And yet, a major part of her attraction to Dan had been that she'd known—right from their first extravagant, crazy date—that he shared none of her devotion to rules, regulations and common sense. Then, having married him, she'd spent most of their marriage trying to turn him into the man she'd known all along he wasn't.

"If you'd told me you were emotionally paralyzed," Jess admitted, "I'd have told you to snap out of it and get a real job."

"You *did* tell me to snap out of it and get a real job," Dan said. "I tried. I honest to God tried."

"You never told me you were looking for work—"

"I not only looked, I even got hired. I had half a dozen jobs, and got fired from all of them. You think I was about to tell you—professional competence personified—that I got fired from the Donut Hut for putting cheese filling in the chocolate doughnuts?"

"You got fired from the Donut Hut? That sleazy place on Washington Square?"

"Yeah, that's the one."

Jess giggled. "I can't believe you got fired from there! Good grief, that's quite an achievement, Dan."

"You're laughing now. At the time it wouldn't have struck you as even marginally amusing."

"No, you're right, it wouldn't." Jess sighed. "I guess my midwestern upbringing didn't equip me very well to cope with marriage to an aspiring Broadway actor."

"If I'd been an actor with talent, I might have been less of a pain to live with. What was driving me crazy was the realization that I couldn't act. My drama coach in college had convinced me I wanted to be an actor, so I couldn't understand what was happening to me. I'd go for an audition and mentally rewrite the script. I'd watch a movie on television and lie awake all night restructuring the plot. I'd get up in the morning, with the entire thing rewritten in my head, right down to lines of dialogue."

"I can't believe you didn't realize you wanted to be a scriptwriter."

"Can't you?" Dan laid his hand on the flat plane of her stomach and tickled her gently. "You, of all people, ought to understand how difficult it is to know what we really want out of life."

He'd made so many references to her capacity for self-deception, and Jess fought against the temptation to let this one slip by, just like all the others. "Would you care to elaborate on what you mean by that remark, Dan?"

He looked at her with an odd mixture of sympathy and cool assessment. "You're passionate, mercurial, intuitive, and you'd like nothing better than to run your own business. So what have you done with your life so far? You've ruthlessly controlled your passions, trained yourself never to listen to your instincts and forced yourself to work in one job after another where there's virtually no chance to develop your entrepreneurial skills—''

"You're wrong," Jess said tersely. "I have no desire whatsoever to run my own business. I need to feel financially secure far more than I need to be my own boss."

"That could be true," Dan agreed. "Maybe you have sublimated your entrepreneurial instincts. I guess it's not hard to understand why you might need security and a sense of order more than most people. If your entire world is turned topsy-turvy when you're a little kid, it's not surprising if you try to make sure that you eliminate as many risks from your life as possible."

"I suppose you think that's why our marriage ended so disastrously," Jess said. "You think I was afraid of taking the risk of loving you too much, so I set out to make sure you'd see how incompatible we were before we got in too deep."

"Is that what you think happened, Jess?"

"Stop repeating my own questions back at me like a damn psychiatrist," she said, sitting up in bed and hugging her arms around her knees, acutely uncomfortable with the direction their conversation had taken. "What can I say to convince you that I had a very happy childhood, with terrific parents who showered me with love?"

"We weren't talking about your childhood, Jess, we were talking about our marriage." He crooked his finger beneath her chin and gently tilted her head backward. "It's possible to have a wonderful loving family and still have problems fitting in. That doesn't mean Barbara and Frank failed, or that you aren't grateful to them for everything they did. I'm not adopted, my folks are great, and when I'm with them I sometimes still feel like an alien from outer space. We have plenty of conversations where you'd think we were trying to communicate via malfunctioning translation units."

She smiled at the image, relaxing a little. "I do feel defensive about being adopted," she admitted. "You probably can't imagine what it feels like to grow up in a huge, affectionate family where everything that comes to you instinctively and naturally is different from the people around you."

"Sure I can." He grinned. "That's what writers have, you know. Vivid imaginations." He kissed her with surprising tenderness. "Accepting that you're different from the Zajaks doesn't mean that you're disloyal, or that you don't love them as much as you should, Jess. It's just an acknowledgment of reality. That's one of the reasons I think it's so important for you to find out the truth about your past. If you can discover who your birth parents were, and what you were doing in Cleveland with the Pazmanys, I'm betting a lot of these inner conflicts you have about where you fit into the scheme of things will disappear like magic."

"Why would they?" Jess asked, taken aback by his suggestion. "Until a few weeks ago, I knew exactly who my birth parents were—Rudolph and Elena Pazmany. If I have all these inner conflicts that stem from confusion about my birth parents versus my adoptive family, why would they disappear just because I substitute the Smiths or the Johnsons for the Pazmanys?"

"Because, at some deeply submerged layer of your subconscious, I don't believe you ever accepted that the Pazmanys were your birth parents, or that you were the person your adoptive parents said you were. Why else would you have been able to pull up the memory that your real name is Liliana? You only needed to glance at those documents your grandfather had hidden in the attic and—almost instantly—a window to the past opened in your mind. Think what it must have been doing to your psyche if, deep down, you didn't accept what your new family was telling you about yourself and the Pazmanys. Think how many more windows you may have, Jess, just waiting to be opened.''

She felt a leap of emotion that was something between excitement and terror. Inundated with new ideas and insights, and needing time to sort them all out, she shifted the direction of their conversation. ''Speaking of the Pazmanys, my mother gave me some garbled message about a private investigator calling her, trying to reach me. Apparently, he had some important information about the Pazmanys.'' She racked her brains but couldn't come up with the name her mother had given her. ''Did you hire him?''

''I didn't hire a private investigator.'' Dan frowned. ''I did ask a friend of mine at the *New York Times* if he'd look through the archives for me and see if he could find any reports of a three- or four-year-old girl being kidnapped sometime before December 9, 1969. He called me yesterday morning to say that he'd checked January to June with no success, so I asked him to check July to December and get back to me. His name's Martin Kaiser. Does that sound familiar?''

Kaiser. Yes, the name did sound vaguely familiar. She was sure her mother had mentioned a name that began with a K. In all probability, this was the man who'd called her parents' home in Ohio, asking where she was. Who else could it have been? On the other hand, if he was a friend of Dan's, why had he been trying to reach her? ''If this Martin Kaiser had something new to report, why wouldn't he call you?'' she asked.

''Maybe he did,'' Dan said. ''I've been working nonstop on script revisions and I haven't checked my messages. When I got up today, I turned on the news and heard about the explosion at your office. To be honest, the guy could have called a dozen times, and I wouldn't know. I'll phone him first thing tomorrow and check out if he was trying to reach me.''

Jess's heart was pounding and her pulse racing. It was a strange feeling to reach thirty years of age and realize that you might be hovering on the very brink of finding out who you really were. "Perhaps Martin checked the index for July to December and wanted to let us know that he'd unearthed some information about a child who'd been kidnapped."

"Could be," Dan said, then shook his head. "Wait a minute, of course it can't be Martin who called your mother. I never mentioned you or your parents by name when I asked him to run this check. He owed me a couple of favors, so I just asked him to find out what he could and get back to me as soon as possible. Never said a word about who was involved, or why I needed the information. He doesn't even know your name, much less your phone number."

Jess tried without success to think back to precisely what her mother had said about the caller. Her mind wasn't a blank, but it was a useless whirligig of disconnected memory fragments, most of them meaningless. Frustrated, she decided that she was heartily sick of mysteries. She didn't want to worry about who'd called her parents, any more than she wanted to worry about why the package containing the bomb had been addressed specifically to her.

A chill rippled down her spine. Jess ignored it. Dammit, she wasn't going to start imagining that a demented killer was stalking her and had called her parents' home to check on her movements. There was nothing in the world about her character or the life she led that could possibly arouse the interest of a mad bomber. There was no reason to leap out of bed and call Agent Ackroyd to say that some man had called her parents' house. Her father was a cop, for heaven's sake. If there'd been anything even slightly suspicious about the caller, he'd have noticed.

"What is it?" Dan asked. "What did you just think of?"

"Nothing important," she said. "Dan, it's been a long day. Could we please talk about this tomorrow?"

He looked down at her. "Is there going to be a tomorrow for us, Jess?"

She didn't want to think about that, either. Tonight, she'd be more than happy if she could suspend herself in a pleasant, all-enveloping state of not-thinking. She slipped her foot between Dan's legs and put her arms around his waist, wriggling until she was pressed full-length against him. She felt the immediate and gratifying response of his body and gave a little sigh of relief and anticipation.

"Make love to me, Dan," she said softly.

"I love hearing you say that." His voice was gruff. "God, I missed having you in my bed, Jess."

"I missed you, too. Unbearably." She was shocked to realize the truth of her words, even more shocked at how easy it had been to say them.

He pushed her into the pillows and kissed her tenderly, bringing back a rush of sweet, long-buried memories. He made love to her with skillful passion, arousing her so completely she was almost able to forget that, while Dan was giving her such exquisite, soul-deep pleasure, somewhere out in the hot summer night there might be another man wondering why his carefully packaged bomb had killed the wrong woman.

Twelve

The Radisson Hotel, Washington, D.C.
Tuesday, June 18, 1996

The Senate Judiciary Committee hearings were scheduled to begin at ten o'clock next Monday morning, so Victor's PR team had arranged a press conference before to make sure that he went into the hearings on a renewed wave of positive media coverage. Victor had worked hard on his speech, but he wasn't feeling in top form as he delivered it, thanks to the infuriating failure of Jessica Marie Zajak to die as she was supposed to. His brilliantly crafted positions on abortion, the right of search and seizure, capital punishment, separation of church and state—all the great legal dilemmas of the day—came out sounding like a dry and morally timid stance rather than a generous embrace of the sensible political middle as he'd intended.

Fortunately, the Washington press corps was too full of its own importance to pay much attention to the occasional stumble in his presentation. His nomination process thus far had been so smooth as to have only limited news appeal. In fact, six days had gone by without a single mention of his name in either the *Washington Post* or the *New York Times*. That was highly reassuring in one way, Victor thought as he delivered his speech, but he did so love the thrill of opening the center pages of one of the nation's major newspapers and seeing his name leap out from a headline or editorial. Still, he could always look forward to Monday, when his statements before the judiciary committee would most likely be the lead story on the six o'clock news. Provided, of course, that the Bosnians or the Northern Irish didn't fuck things up for him and snatch all the limelight by deciding to blow up another batch of their fellow citizens.

With the official FBI investigations over, he could breathe a bit more easily. He'd told himself for weeks now that no amount of digging by the FBI would be able to unearth any scandal about him, chiefly because there was no scandal to unearth. Victor Bartlett Rodier was as pristine a citizen as his résumé suggested. Nobody was going to uncover any stupid blunders with unpaid taxes, hiring of illegal immigrants or embarrassing investments in slum property. Hell, no. Victor Rodier was Mr. Clean personified. Even his family life was picture-perfect, with two stepchildren who admired him and a wife who worshiped the ground he walked on. Not like Constance, who'd been a fly up his nose from the day he married her.

The second time around, he'd been a damn sight smarter about choosing his wife. The Grants had taken several annoyingly long years to die and leave him their money, and he'd used the time to refine his criteria for choosing a wife. Margaret Davenport, a wealthy widow five years older than Victor, had turned out to be the ideal spouse. Over the years, he'd actually become quite fond of her, although she'd grown to look more and more like one of the beagles she spent her spare time breeding. Still, she had several assets that Victor considered a great deal more appealing than mere beauty. Constance had been beautiful—stunningly beautiful—and where had that got him?

Nowhere, except up to his armpits in shit. Margaret, on the other hand, might be a dog to look at, but she was socially connected and sexually frigid, characteristics that more than compensated for good looks, as far as Victor was concerned. Poor old Maggie was so grateful to be treated with unfailing courtesy and friendliness that she went out of her way not to inquire if or when or who he was screwing.

Not that Margaret ever needed to worry about being humiliated by Victor's affairs. Ever since that disastrous fling during his marriage to Constance, Victor had handled his adultery with finesse. These days, he was smart enough to screw only those women who had much more to lose than he did if their liaisons became public. Women whose husbands were prominent members of the religious right had proved to be an especially fruitful field for Victor's sexual adventures. Every time the executive director of the American Family Values Coalition appeared on TV, Victor would chortle silently as he remembered the last time he'd seen the director's wife. Which happened to be on her knees, in front of Victor, delivering a quickie blow job, before taking off to join her husband at a rally condemning the loose morals of welfare mothers. Victor had appreciated the irony of the situation.

The net result of Victor's years of careful planning was that there were no skeletons in his closet that an investigator could find. None, that is, except Jessica Zajak. Jesus, he felt sick every time he thought about Jessica! He should have taken care of her years ago. Looking back, he could see now that his daughter should have been disposed of when she was still a kid. By the time she was twelve, all the old gossip had died down, Constance was safely locked up, the Grants were dead, and he would never have been connected to the death of an obscure orphan in

Cleveland. He should simply have made a quick trip to Cleveland, bopped her over the head and dumped her in the Cuyahoga River. Easier said than done, perhaps, but leaving her alive had definitely been a mistake. A big mistake.

Victor delivered the last few lines of his speech with a flourish. There was a polite murmur of laughter, then six or seven journalists spoke at once. He felt a burst of renewed confidence. *Yes,* this was good. He had their attention now.

Victor acknowledged Sam Donaldson first. It amused him to nod as if he couldn't quite remember the man's name. "Yes, Mr.... er... Mr.... you have a question?"

"Sam Donaldson, Your Honor, ABC News. The nomination process for you so far has been astonishingly smooth. Do you expect to encounter any difficulties with the committee hearings next Monday?"

Victor gave one of his modest smiles. "Over the past few weeks, I've been able to meet with each member of the Senate Judiciary Committee at least once. I'm pleased to say, Mr. Donaldson, that all the members of the committee have indicated that they see no reason so far why they would not be able to support my nomination."

"It's amazing that you've managed to satisfy senators with such diverse political opinions as Senator Brown from South Carolina and Senator Deeney from Massachusetts."

"I'm not sure that I *satisfied* either of them, Mr. Donaldson." Victor waited for the little ripple of laughter to die down. This was getting better and better. He was recovering from that badly delivered speech, returning to his usual masterful public form. He would forget about Jessica for now, and plan how to deal with her later. He gave Sam Donaldson a wintry smile. "I believe it would be more accurate to say that none of my judicial positions seems so offensive that any senator feels it incumbent upon himself to withhold approval of my appointment to the Supreme Court."

He was rather pleased with the pompous ring of his answer. People liked their judges to sound as if they'd swallowed a law dictionary. He gestured to Britt Hulme, who'd interviewed him last week over an elaborate five-course dinner. The guy was so right-wing in his views that he made Jesse Helms look moderate. You'd never know it, though, Victor thought, from listening to his on-air spots. Victor admired people who could control their convictions rather than letting their convictions control them. He gave Britt a warm smile. "Yes, Mr. Hulme. You have a question?"

"Thank you, Your Honor. There are several cases dealing with homosexual rights making their way toward the Supreme Court right now. These cases apparently precipitated the bombing of a state office building in Denver yesterday. You've never ruled in a case involving homosexual rights, Your Honor. How can the public expect you to view such cases?"

"On their individual legal merits," Victor said crisply. "Fortunately, our Constitution provides the same invaluable basis for cases involving homosexual rights as it does in any other. As a judge, if I strike a careful balance between our individual rights and our public duty, I believe I will produce judgments that are not only legally sound, but also in conformity with the moral values of the vast majority of American citizens."

"Unfortunately, not everyone shares your civilized views, Your Honor." The speaker was Myra Lyasson, the chief political correspondent for PBS. Undoubtedly a liberal do-gooder, Victor reflected. All those people over at

PBS were. Trust her to speak up without waiting to be called on.

She spoke quickly, so he couldn't ignore her. "The Denver bombing suggests that we have some radical groups who are getting impatient with this administration's failure to move forward on the gay rights agenda. What is your own opinion, sir, on such questions as whether or not states should allow gays to marry?"

His opinion was that they should have their perverted dicks cut off. Victor gave Myra his most beguiling smile. "The concept of group rights is really a new one, the product of this century, and especially the last thirty years or so. Consequently, we're still grappling as a nation with fundamental questions about what group rights truly mean. Is a person's sexual preference an appropriate basis on which to grant citizens special protection under the law? Or does this open up the concept of group rights in a way which is ultimately too expansive for our society?"

"I would like to hear your answer to those interesting questions, Your Honor."

I just bet you would, you pushy broad. Victor adjusted his features into the reverent expression that he'd found worked well when mentioning the Constitution. "One of the major strengths of our law is the way in which ancient principles, tested by time, can be construed so that they take account of new situations. From a constitutional point of view, I personally don't believe that it's helpful for us to speak in terms of gay rights as group rights. It would, perhaps, be less divisive to our nation if we attempted to address this difficult issue more in terms of the existing laws concerning property and freedom of religion, because this is where the true crux of the problem lies. I'll give you an example of what I mean. If you are a homosexual who has lived for thirty years with the same partner, should you have the right to pass on property to your partner without paying an inheritance tax? A husband and wife have that privilege, so shouldn't two loyal and devoted homosexual lovers have the same privilege? On the other hand, to cite a problem coming from a different perspective, if you're a devout, conservative Christian, should you be required to rent an apartment to a homosexual couple whose behavior contravenes everything you personally believe in?''

He flashed Myra another smile, looking straight at her, as if they were the only two people in the room. He'd found that even sophisticated journalists were surprisingly susceptible to the suggestion that they were somehow on an inside track with people in the public spotlight. "You can see that many of the questions raised by this catch-all phrase of 'gay rights' are very complex and touch on such profound issues as our individual liberties, freedom of religion and property rights. And I'm quite sure you don't expect me to deliver a twenty-second verdict on any of those profound issues this afternoon.''

Another gratifying round of laughter. And for all their vaunted expertise, no one called him on the fact that he hadn't actually said a damn thing about his views on gays. The very idea of two limp-wristed queers wanting to get the government's seal of approval when they set up housekeeping made him sick to his stomach. Not that he'd ever express such feelings. Victor was always amazed by the number of smart men who destroyed their own careers because of an inability to keep their lips buttoned. Victor was prepared to wait until he made it onto the Supreme Court bench before he lobbed any of his judicial hand grenades. Just wait till his appointment was signed and sealed in stone, he thought—people were going to get some major surprises. Court appointees had life tenure, and once he was safely ensconced, one thing was sure: he wasn't going to be the wishy-washy moderate people expected.

His scorn for the gay life-style was part of the reason he'd chosen to call the *Rocky Mountain News* pretending to be the leader of one of the radical gay rights splinter groups. Let the queers and queens of the world get the blame for killing that employee at the tourist bureau. They fucking deserved it, even if they hadn't actually mailed the package.

He frowned, annoyed with himself for letting his thoughts drift back to the failed bombing. Focus, he warned himself. Stay focused. Don't allow yourself to worry about Jessica. Not until you're alone.

Victor answered a few more questions, provoked a few more polite and sympathetic laughs, then exited to his waiting limo, graciously accepting the compliments of his staffers and PR flacks. Thank God he'd survived yet another ordeal on the road to confirmation. And, in the end, he'd survived it with his usual impeccable grace and style.

Now all he needed to do was come up with a workable plan for silencing Jessica Marie Zajak, and the Supreme Court of the United States would finally have itself a justice worthy of the position. The sacrifice of one insignificant woman was small potatoes when you stacked it up against the benefits he would bring to the country once he was seated on the bench of the highest court in the land.

Supreme Court Justice Victor Rodier. God, what a beautiful sound that had!

Thirteen

Merton House
Tuesday, June 18, 1996

"Come in."

Constance drew herself up, patting her new short hair-style self-consciously. She was terrified at the prospect of what she was about to do, and yet she felt light and strangely free, as if the burden of guilt and sadness she'd carried for twenty-six years had already lifted from her shoulders. The events surrounding Victor's last visit had shown her that she trusted Ed Foster in a way she had trusted nobody else since Ralph and Lena died. With his help, she'd fought her way to accepting that it was finally time to confront the painful reality of Liliana's death. There was relief in that realization, and even a subdued happiness. Shoulders squared, head held high, she opened the door to Dr. Foster's office and stepped inside.

He was reading a fax and only gave her a cursory glance. "Yes?"

"I've come for our therapy session, Dr. Foster."

He did a double take at the sound of her voice, eyes widening in gratifying astonishment. "Constance! Come in. Goodness, for a moment, I didn't recognize you. You look great! Fabulous!"

"Th-th—" She swallowed convulsively. "Thank you."

"Your new hairstyle's terrific! And your dress is lovely, too. What's that color called?"

"Antique rose."

His smile bolstered her fragile self-confidence. "It suits you. You should wear it more often."

"Thank you," she repeated, grateful to him for reassuring her that she didn't look ridiculous, like stringy old mutton dressed up as frolicsome lamb. But old habits died hard, she discovered, and she had to control the urge to pluck nervously at the front seam of her dress when she answered him. She walked over to her usual chair—frightened at how hard it was to remember not to shuffle—and sat down, crossing her legs neatly at the ankles and forcing herself to maintain eye contact with him.

His expression remained kind, shrewd and genuinely appreciative of her improved appearance. There was nothing to be scared of, but after years and years of avoiding people's gaze, Constance found it threatening in the extreme to sustain eye contact for more than a couple of seconds. Panic bubbled inside her as she realized she could barely meet this most elementary test of normal behavior. How in the world was she to persuade him she was sane, when she couldn't even look him in the eye? She gripped the arms of the chair, pushing the panic down, refusing to let it take over.

Dr. Foster closed the folder he'd been working on. "I don't have to ask how you're feeling this morning, Constance. Obviously you're feeling great."

"Er...yes, thank you. Pretty good."

"What would you like us to talk about today, Constance?"

In her mind she'd rehearsed a short, eloquent speech outlining the three major reasons why she'd decided to trust him and ask for his assistance in gaining her release from Merton House. But her tongue wasn't accustomed to making its way around logical, articulate speeches, and what she actually said was, "You have to help me, Doctor. I've decided I don't want to be mad anymore."

She flushed miserably, frustrated by her inadequate attempt at communication, but Dr. Foster didn't laugh or mock her with platitudes.

"I think that's a very wise decision," he said, getting up from behind the desk and walking around to pull up a chair so that they were sitting opposite each other, almost as if they were friends enjoying a regular conversation. He leaned forward, hands clasped loosely in his lap, inviting her confidence. "Tell me why you reached this important decision, Constance."

"I've decided it's safe to trust you." She fell silent, her fears rushing back. Was she right to trust him? What would happen if he didn't believe her?

Nothing, she reminded herself. *There's nothing he can do that's any worse than what you've already been through.* Except take away hope. The frail flower of hope that had never quite died, despite twenty-six years of withering in the absence of sun and fresh air.

"I'm honored to know that you trust me," Ed said, sounding as if he meant it. "Are you ready to tell me why you decided to be mad in the first place, Constance?"

Put like that, she suddenly wasn't so sure. "It's a long and complicated story. I don't expect you have time to listen. Maybe we should arrange another day—"

"I'll make time. This is important for both of us." Ed depressed the button on his intercom. "Elaine? Reschedule my eleven o'clock meeting with Doug Larusse, please. Hold all calls for the time being. I don't want any interruptions—"

"What about emergencies?"

Ed smiled tightly. "I only want to hear about emergencies that involve fire trucks and/or police squad cars. Okay?"

"Okay, but it's going to be very difficult to reschedule your meetings, Doctor—"

"I know, but do it anyway. That's why you're such a great assistant, Elaine. You can work these miracles for me." Ed cut off the intercom, precluding any more discussion. "Okay, Constance. Now you can tell me your story, and I have the rest of the morning to listen."

Where to begin? Constance rubbed nervously at her forehead. Oh, God, this had all seemed so much easier in the quiet seclusion of her room. First, she'd planned to give a concise explanation of how she came to be sent to Saint Jude's. Then a rational explanation of why she'd encouraged everyone to believe she was insane. Finally, a reasoned but persuasive indictment of Victor Rodier. Now she couldn't even find the words to start her story. Perhaps she really *was* mad. Perhaps that was why she couldn't weave her way through the maze of her past and find the appropriate place to begin.

"I can't tell you," she blurted out. "The right words are inside my head but they won't come out."

Ed took her hand, rubbing his thumbs in a soothing rhythm over her knuckles. "It's okay, Constance. Relax and the words will come. Do you want me to ask some questions to help get you started?"

She shook her head and stared down at his hands, wrapped around hers in therapeutic reassurance. She wondered how long it had been since anyone had given her a hug out of friendship or genuine affection. Half a lifetime, at least. The reminder of how many arid years she'd wasted, locked away from the normal pleasures of life, made her angry enough to spark an adrenaline surge that set the words flowing.

"I want to explain to you why I agreed to stay locked up in here, even though I'm not really crazy, but I'm discovering that it's difficult to behave like a normal person after twenty-six years of living in a mental institution. It scares me sometimes that I'm not always as much in control of my actions as I want to be. I shuffle instead of walking briskly, I've acquired all sorts of nervous tics and habits. I'm beginning to wonder how long a person can play the role of a madwoman before pretense becomes reality."

"That probably depends on the reason why you started the pretense in the first place," Ed said. "Maybe you should explain that to me."

"At first, it was simply apathy," Constance said. "After Liliana died, there was nothing left that seemed worth living for, so I couldn't see any reason to fight what everyone was saying about me. Later on, when I realized that Victor might be telling the truth about Liliana, I wanted to punish myself in the worst way I could think of."

"What truth was Victor telling you about your daughter, Constance?"

"You know already." Constance felt her breath squeeze out in short, choppy gasps. "Victor told me that I'd killed Liliana in a drug-induced frenzy. That I'd murdered my own child. Once I believed that, staying locked up with a bunch of lunatics in a maximum-security mental hospital like Saint Jude's seemed pretty much what I deserved, so I decided not to fight the system anymore. I wanted to be punished."

"What's happened to change your mind?" Ed asked. "Do you think you've been punished enough?"

"Not exactly. I've never had a clear memory of what happened when Liliana disappeared, and I've decided it's time to find out how much I really do remember. But mostly, I'm fighting back because of Victor's nomination to the Supreme Court. These past few weeks, I've realized that allowing people to believe I'm mad is a way of giving up, of letting Victor win. Fighting him is hard, and without Liliana to make me strong, I couldn't see any point in keeping up the struggle. Now I have a reason to fight again. If there's one thing I know for sure, it's that Victor isn't the right man to become a Supreme Court justice. And I'm probably the only person in the world who has the power to stop his nomination."

"It must be a good feeling to have that much power over Victor."

Constance gave a short laugh. "It's a terrifying feeling," she said. "I would never find the courage to keep fighting if it didn't all seem tangled up with what happened to Liliana."

"Do you still believe you killed your own daughter?" Ed asked.

Even though she'd accepted weeks ago that he was much more perceptive than any other psychiatrists she'd dealt with, Constance hadn't expected him to home in so quickly on the dilemma at the heart of her decision. "I don't know anymore if I killed Liliana," she admitted. "Victor claims I killed her when I was high on LSD. I have nightmares about seeing Lili dead, with blood dripping from her body. But I have no idea what the nightmares mean. The boundaries between dreams and reality can get pretty blurred when you're flying high on an acid trip."

"Did you do other drugs apart from LSD?"

"I never did any drugs. Not intentionally." She realized she was clutching crumpled fistfuls of her skirt, and she hastily opened her hands. She hesitated, then decided that, since she was trusting him with so many secrets, she might as well go for broke.

"About three years ago, I gradually stopped taking all the medications that were prescribed by the doctors here. Every week or so, I'd eliminate one more pill. I was afraid to stop them all at once, in case I went into a brain seizure or something. And then, a few months ago, it reached the point where I wasn't taking any medication at all, unless it was injected. Since I stopped taking the drugs, I've started to remember all sorts of things that the medication had kept suppressed."

She had succeeded in stunning him into silence. He stared at her, face blank with shock. "You're not taking any medication at all?" he said finally.

"No, none."

He put on his glasses, then took them off again. Constance felt a thrill of victory at having so completely confounded him. "How did you manage to deceive the nurses?" he asked. "Dammit, Constance, they're supposed to watch each patient take their prescribed medications."

"But, of course, they don't," she told him. "Actually, it was fairly easy to get away with not taking the pills. I've always been a cooperative patient, so they had no reason to keep a close check on me. This institution's no different from any other. If you want to beat the system, you have to be the easiest person to manage, the one who never causes trouble. I'd keep the pill in my mouth till the nurses weren't looking, then I'd shove it down the arm of a chair, or I'd wrap it in a Kleenex and drop it into the pocket of my sweater until I could flush it down the toilet. Nothing very clever, but I didn't have to be clever. I'm just boring

Constance Howington, who always does what she's told and never makes a fuss.''

"You're not in the least boring, Constance, and obviously, you don't always do what you're told." Ed pulled a file from the stack on his desk and read through it. "You've weaned yourself from some pretty potent medications.''

"Yes, it was sometimes difficult to flush away so many pills.''

"What happened when you stopped taking them? How did you feel?''

"More energetic," she said. "Physically more coordinated. It was much easier to think coherently, and I began to develop a real interest in the outside world. I could read the newspaper again without getting confused. I could watch a movie on TV and not lose track of the plot. Peggy realized that I was bored and restless, so she took me under her wing and gave me books to read about sculpture and helped me with my modeling. Of course, the more I knew about what was going on in the outside world, the more difficult it became to behave like the other patients, but I needed to keep up the pretense, otherwise the nurses would start to get suspicious and then they'd make me take all the medication again.''

"An interesting dilemma," Ed said dryly.

"One of many. Strangely enough, as my head began to straighten out, I found myself thinking more about the past, not less. And the more I thought, the more I began to wonder. . . .''

Ed waited, then prompted her quietly. "What did you begin to wonder, Constance?''

She answered in a rush. "I began to think that maybe I hadn't killed Liliana.''

"If you didn't kill her, what do you think happened to her?" Ed asked mildly. "She disappeared, didn't she? If you didn't kill her, why hasn't anyone found her?"

"Because she's dead. I realize that."

"Then how did she die? Was it an accident?"

"No." Constance drew in a deep breath. "I think Victor must have killed her."

There, she'd said it, made the terrifying accusation, and the world still seemed to be spinning on its usual axis. Constance pulled a tissue from her pocket and wiped her sweaty palms. She'd expected at least a clap of thunder, or a drumroll from stage left. Or maybe Victor materializing in a puff of smoke, threatening dire retribution.

Ed was silent for a moment or two. "Everything always seems to come back to Victor," he said finally. "If we're ever going to untangle this mess, perhaps you should go back to the beginning and tell me how you came to marry Victor."

"That's easy to explain," she said. "I fell in love with him. I was young, if that's a valid excuse for being stupid."

"How young were you when you met him?"

"Eighteen. I'd just graduated from high school. We got married in the fall, right before my nineteenth birthday."

"Eighteen is young," Ed said with an encouraging smile. "We're all allowed to make mistakes at that age, and most of us manage to make some humdingers. You have to stop beating yourself up for behaving like a human being, Constance."

"Other people live down their mistakes, but mine seem to have had consequences that echo forever."

"Have you ever stopped to consider that you can cut off an echo quite easily? All you have to do is insert a sound break in the correct position. Confront the full reality of your past mistakes, Constance, and I'm willing to bet those mistakes will stop haunting you. Try telling me about your relationship with Victor, and we'll see if we can't bring the past to a close. How did you meet him? Let's start there.''

Constance struggled to order her thoughts. If she couldn't explain how she'd come to marry Victor, how in the world could she hope to make Ed understand what had happened later, after she was married? Steeling herself, Constance reached into the pool of memories that had been off-limits for years.

''When I was a teenager, I lived with my grandparents, out on Long Island in a town called Hatterington, in an area that's known as the Gold Coast—''

''I'm familiar with the area.''

''Then you know that it's a rather unique mixture of new wealth and old money, although when I was a teenager, it was much more old money than new. Victor's family had once owned a big estate in Hatterington, but his father had lost most of the family inheritance through bad investments, and they'd been forced to sell. Even though Victor didn't have a house there anymore, he often caught the train out from Manhattan and spent the weekend with his cousins. Nobody seemed to care much that he couldn't really pay his own way on the social circuit. He was intelligent, handsome, athletic, charming—he got invited everywhere.''

''Does this mean you knew him for a long time before you married him?''

''I only knew him by name, but not in person. We actually met for the first time at the annual hunt ball, which I'd attended under protest because I disapproved of hunting. Victor managed to convince me that he agreed with every impassioned word I had to say on the subject, and I totally neglected to notice that his wholehearted support of my position didn't extend one inch beyond our private discussions. We spent the whole evening together, dancing and talking and reorganizing the politics of the world. Very youthful and intense. He kissed me on the veranda of the country club on the stroke of midnight, and I think I fell in love with him right then."

"So far, it sounds like a fairy-tale romance. How long did it take before the two of you were engaged?"

"Three months," she said. "If Victor had asked me sooner, I'd have said yes. He was my fantasy lover come to life. Not only handsome and smart, but because of his family's financial situation, he was also hardworking and far more mature than any of the other men I'd dated. He'd made his way through Princeton and Harvard Law School on scholarships, and he won every academic honor you can think of."

"A talented man," Ed commented.

"That's an understatement. When he started dating me, I was the envy of all my friends. Well, all of them except Elena Korda. She never trusted him, which showed amazingly good judgment on her part. She dropped a couple of fairly broad hints that he wasn't quite as perfect as he seemed, which I naturally ignored. Recently, I've begun to wonder if her lack of trust stemmed from the fact that Victor had made a pass at her, and Elena was too loyal to tell me."

"Who was Elena?"

"She was the daughter of my grandparents' housekeeper—and my best friend. We lived in the same house and we went to the same school, although she was a year ahead of me. Being thrown into such close contact, it was inevitable that we'd either love each other or hate each other. We decided to be soul mates. Her father had died fighting against the Russians when they took over the

Hungarian government after World War II, and my father had died fighting in Korea, so in some ways we had a lot in common." Constance smiled. "Although, I'd say Elena was roughly a thousand percent more mature than I was."

"Why would you expect Victor to make a pass at her?"

"At the time, of course, I *didn't* expect him to make a pass at her. But looking back, I can see that Victor had a lord-of-the-manor attitude toward women and sex. He was the handsome aristocrat and Elena was the humble serving wench, so I wouldn't be at all surprised if he just assumed she'd be delighted to succumb to his advances."

"Wouldn't it have been rather risky to seduce the best friend of the woman he was hoping to marry?"

Constance shook her head. "I'm sure it never crossed Victor's mind that I would have an intimate friendship with the daughter of my grandparents' housekeeper. Not that it would have stopped him from seducing her. In fact, it would probably have increased the pleasure he took in the seduction."

"Why do you think that?"

"Because Victor has always loved flirting with danger, and it would have amused him to seduce Elena and see if he could get away with it."

"That's a risky attitude for a poor man with ambitions. Damn risky."

"Yes, it is, isn't it? But I don't think Victor's ever lost the need to walk on the edge of the precipice. In his own unique way, Victor's a gambler."

Ed looked doubtful. "He may well be a gambler, but he's held several very prestigious positions. Don't you think his political opponents, or the media, would have found out long before now if he'd gone around seducing every woman who happened to be his social inferior?"

"But he hasn't done that," Constance explained. "I think his attitude toward sexual conquest changed quite rapidly. By the time we'd been married for a year or two, Victor wasn't interested in seducing *the peasants*. He wanted the thrill of seducing sophisticated women who were the wives of successful, socially prominent men. Raising the stakes for each seduction, and not getting caught, was one of the ways Victor reassured himself that he was smarter than other people."

"You're very eloquent in your descriptions of Victor's character."

"I've had twenty-six years to think about him," Constance said, with only a trace of bitterness. "Being locked away from the world leaves plenty of time for reflection, even when you spend weeks at a time too medicated to think."

"How long did it take before you began to detect some hints that Victor might not be the perfect husband?"

"Longer than it should have. Long enough to give birth to Liliana. He manipulated me quite successfully for almost two years."

"Why do you think he succeeded in manipulating you?"

"I had a rather strange childhood," Constance told him. "And I was confused about how a normal marriage felt from the inside."

"I remember you told me your mother married several times."

"Yes, my father was an air force colonel who died in Korea when I was seven. My grandparents always insisted that my mother really loved my dad, and after he died in a prisoner-of-war camp, she went to pieces. I don't remember my father very well—I wish I did. I only remember that after he died, my mother took me to live in San Francisco, where, from my childish perspective, her major purpose in life seemed to be introducing horrible new 'daddies' into our home. By the time I was fifteen, she'd already been married and divorced three times and I'd lost count of how many lovers—not to mention stepbrothers and stepsisters—had flitted in and out of our house.

"The day before I agreed to marry Victor, Mother had arrived in Long Island with an especially poisonous lover in tow. She always seemed to select the same disastrous type of man, the sort who screamed gigolo to everyone except her. Or maybe she just *liked* the gigolo type. God knows, she kept her lovers on a tight rein, and they had to beg for every penny of pocket money. She was super-rich, you see, because there was money in my father's family, as well as my mother's, so her wealth was first a lure, and then something she turned into a powerful weapon. Not surprisingly, the men in her life resented being bludgeoned into submission, and they often tried to get back at her by flaunting their affairs in her face. A couple of them decided that their revenge would be sweeter if they had their little flings with me."

Ed made a small, sympathetic sound, and Constance looked up, feeling her cheeks grow hot with remembered anger. "I kept running away, but my mother wasn't willing to admit that her lovers were causing the problems, so she would explain away my actions by telling the authorities I was unstable, dabbling in drugs. It wasn't true—seeing my mother and her lovers tripping out was enough to convince me I never wanted to get caught in that scene—but it was one of the things Victor used against me when Liliana disappeared. When he told the police and the doctors that he'd been trying to cure me of a terrible drug habit, they believed him. I had an official record of drug abuse, you see."

"Yes, I can see how that might be a problem."

"Actually, I think it was the final nail in my coffin, which is sort of ironic when you think of it. My mother lies about me, and my husband uses her lies to persuade everyone he's telling the truth. Anyway, I finally ran away for good when I was fifteen, because my mother's husband-of-the-month kept trying to seduce me. And, fortunately, this time I ran straight to my grandparents, who took me in, believed every word I said and generally provided a safe haven for the next few years."

Ed's expression had become grim. "Did you ever have counseling to help you deal with the sexual abuse?"

She smiled wryly. "My grandparents weren't that liberated, Dr. Foster. There was a limit to how much dirty linen they were prepared to wash in public."

"A doctor's office is hardly *in public*."

"Hatterington being the sort of town it is, everyone would have known I was visiting the local shrink. In my grandparents' view, lots of love and plenty of New England common sense was a much better cure than wasting time chattering on a psychiatrist's couch. To be honest, I think they were probably right. I wasn't all that scarred by my various stepfathers, because I always ran away before they could really hurt me."

Ed looked at her steadily. "Running away from your problems can be a dangerous habit to fall into, wouldn't you agree, Constance?"

She was pulled up short by his sudden insight into her own behavior. She was fifty-two years old, and she had never before realized the extent to which she'd always coped with her difficulties by running away from them. She let Ed see her surprise. "I never understood that about myself before. Even when I married Victor, really I was running away."

"But you said that you were happy living with your grandparents. If you married Victor as a form of escape, do you know what you were running from?"

She grimaced. "The usual teenage things. My mother, going to college, growing up, tackling life outside the safe circle of friends my grandparents had provided for me. Victor seemed to represent the ultimate in security, with just enough sex appeal to be exciting."

"You found Victor sexually exciting?"

"He was the ideal lover for me at that time," Constance said simply. "He was an accomplished flirt, he kissed elegantly and he never pushed me beyond the point I wanted to go. He could easily have seduced me, but he didn't, which made me all the more besotted. By the time we left for our honeymoon, I'm sure I was a lot more anxious to get into bed with him than he was to have sex with me. Very clever of him, of course. And when we finally did make love, he was so restrained there was nothing threatening about it. It was all sweet kisses and missionary discretion."

"He sounds like a very considerate husband."

"Victor was desperate for money," she said. "Not because he wanted to live extravagantly, but because he remembered what it had been like in the days when his family was rich, and he wanted to regain the power that money brings with it. When he found out how much money I was likely to inherit, and how much annual income my trust funds generated, he set out to present himself to me as the man of my dreams. He succeeded." She sighed. "I'd had a pretty chaotic adolescence, but I don't believe that's why he fooled me so easily. I think he's a brilliant actor, with the actor's capacity for portraying an emotion that he may not even totally understand. Victor didn't just deceive me, he deceived everyone else, too. The day of our wedding, my grandmother took me aside and told me I'd made a wise choice. My grandfather bought us a penthouse co-op on Park Avenue as a wedding gift, and said I'd just married an honorable man who was destined to go right to the top of his profession."

Constance spread her fingers over her knees. "Grandpa was half-right, I guess. Victor sure has reached the pinnacle of his profession, hasn't he?"

"If last night's news coverage is anything to go by, I would say so," Ed agreed. "Victor Rodier is the closest thing to a shoo-in that the Supreme Court has seen in twenty years."

"And it'll be a disaster for America if his nomination is confirmed," Constance said. "That's why I decided the time has come for me to face the past. I want you to take the information I'm going to give you, Doctor, and find a way to present it to the Senate committee—see if you can't get Victor's nomination derailed. God knows, there are enough muckraking journalists eager for a story. If we give them a thread to pull, maybe they'll unravel the whole sticky web Victor's spent a lifetime spinning."

She became aware of a change in Ed's silence, and she stopped abruptly. When she saw his carefully controlled expression, she pulled away from him, smiling with harsh self-mockery.

"Oh, my," she said. "How dense of me not to have understood sooner. You've been humoring me, haven't you? Prodding me along with those super-bland questions and encouraging smiles. Allowing me to ramble on about Victor, all the while thinking that this hatred directed toward him is simply a new and more interesting form of my old paranoid delusions. Poor mad Constance who's just come out of a major psychotic episode and is now firmly—but insanely—convinced that her ex-husband is a conniving rattlesnake who would lie, cheat, steal, and maybe even kill in order to further his own monumental ambitions.''

Ed spoke with infuriating gentleness, confirming her worst fears. ''Constance, I have no trouble at all believing that Victor treated you badly. I'm willing to believe that he's done some things in the past that may be less than entirely honorable. But let's not get hung up on whether or not he's the best candidate for a vacancy on the Supreme Court. That's not really for us to decide, is it? Why don't we concentrate on your personal relationship with him and leave the senators to reach whatever conclusion seems right on the public issues?''

Constance sprang to her feet, frustration bringing back her old clumsiness. Her body once again seemed all giant feet and flapping hands. ''Don't you see how you're playing his game?'' she demanded. Too loudly. She recognized at once that her voice was too loud and forced herself to lower the pitch. ''Don't let Victor deceive you, too, Doctor. I'm inside Merton House, so I must be crazy. He's been nominated to the Supreme Court, so he must be honorable. What's wrong with this picture? Well, what's wrong is that I'm only in here because Victor schemed and lied and manipulated to get me confined here. I—am—not—crazy. I'm not!''

Her voice was rising again and Ed had on his most soothing expression. Constance wanted to scream with disappointment or cry at his betrayal. Whatever she did, however she struggled, Victor was going to win. For three years, she'd suffered through the hell of weaning herself from all those medications so that she could reclaim her memories, but conquering her drug dependence hadn't been enough. Even Ed didn't believe her accusations, and she'd thought he was becoming her friend. Once again

Victor was going to win. How long did she have to go on paying for the crime of marrying the wrong man?

She felt the buildup of impotent rage that had no outlet. Overcome by the oppressive need to lash out, to rail against the injustice of fate, she swept her arm across Ed's desk, sending books and papers crashing to the floor. Her anger crested and she swung around looking for something else to destroy. Right on the brink of disaster, a tiny voice hauled her back.

Constance leaned against the desk, gripping the edge as if it were a lifeline. Dammit, she wouldn't allow herself to fall into the self-defeating patterns of the past. She wasn't going to give up this time. She would keep talking until Ed finally *had* to start listening.

Shaking, but under control again, she levered herself away from the desk, sat down in her chair and met Ed's gaze head-on. "Listen to me, Dr. Foster. I'll say it one more time. *I am not mad.* I am not delusional. Maybe I'm a bit socially maladjusted, but hey, that happens after twenty-six years of living with lunatics. When I tell you that Victor Rodier is a monster, I have as firm a grasp on reality as you do. What's more, I'm going to do my damnedest to prove that to you."

His gaze went silently, but expressively, to the scattered books and papers.

Constance winced and got to her feet. "Okay, that was a minor setback on my road to fully operational sanity. I'll pick them up." She hastily gathered an armful of medical journals and returned them to his desk.

"Leave them, Constance." He smiled with maddening kindness. "I'll deal with the mess later. I need to make sure that the papers get back inside the correct files."

"I'm sorry," she said, meaning it this time. "I didn't intend to cause you extra work." She sat down again, wondering bleakly how she could convince him she was sane when she'd just given him a first-rate excuse to doubt everything she said. "Dr. Foster, please try to see things from my point of view. Suppose you somehow got locked away in a facility for severely delusional psychotics. Suppose you had a case-history file full of medical notes, signed by reputable psychiatrists, saying that you were a paranoid depressive who had periodic delusions of being wrongly incarcerated. How would you set about convincing the doctors examining you that you were perfectly sane? That your enemy in the outside world was conspiring to see that you were kept locked up?"

"I'd have a very difficult time of it," Ed acknowledged quietly. "Constance, that's why the legal process for authorizing a person to be confined against their will is so complex. We have to be sure we don't make mistakes. You must accept that it's not likely a mistake has been made in your own case."

"Thirty years ago, there were almost no safeguards," she said. "Can you remember that far back, Doctor? Don't you remember how easy it was to get people confined back in the sixties?"

"That's very true, but there's the review process that safeguards—"

She snorted. "Don't make me laugh, Doctor. Ever sat in on a Merton House review panel? Once you're in here, once the mistake's been made, the typical inmate has no chance of correcting it. The more I claim conspiracy, the more you're going to believe I'm crazy."

"Constance, look at me, because I certainly believe you are more than sane enough to understand what I'm going to say now."

She complied, although it was painful to see the mixture of kindness and patient tolerance in his face. With a tiny spurt of shock, she realized that what she really wanted to see in his eyes was admiration—male admiration for an attractive female.

Oh, great, she thought disgustedly. Now I'm dropping into the ultimate cliché: the scrawny, old mental patient who falls in love with her strong, handsome psychiatrist. She flushed at the silliness of her own feelings, but a spark of newly discovered courage kept her gaze locked with his.

"I'm going to be honest with you," Ed said. "If I based my judgment of your mental health on my observations of your daily behavior, or on the conversations we've had during our therapy sessions, I would be much more inclined to accept your version of the facts. But Constance, there's no denying the fact that four days ago you were in the grip of a powerful psychotic delusion. At times, you were physically violent. At one point, you were virtually catatonic—"

Was there any purpose at all, she wondered, in trying to convince him of the truth? "Four days ago, I'd been drugged," she said wearily. "I suspect with LSD, but, of course, I can't be sure."

"Drugged!" Ed's gaze narrowed. "Are you accusing the staff here of dosing you with an illicit drug?"

"No," she said dryly. "I'm accusing Victor Rodier of dosing me with an illicit drug."

Ed got up and turned abruptly away, saying nothing. Constance shrugged, trying to tell herself that she didn't care. Of course, he didn't believe her. She'd rolled the dice, gambled and lost. Had she ever really anticipated anything else?

"It's all right, Doctor." Slowly, she pushed herself out of the chair, limbs feeling weighted and heavy. "I see now that it was expecting too much to march in here, announce that I've been feigning half my symptoms for the past several years and expect you to agree right away that I'm a sane person with good reasons for what I've done." She walked to the door, her body feeling aching and weary. "Let's forget this conversation, shall we? Have a good day, Doctor."

"Wait." Ed's voice called her back.

She paused inside the door without directly acknowledging him.

Ed spoke quickly. "If you're accusing your husband of administering LSD, you must have some inkling as to how he administered it. How do you think he did it, Constance? How did he even get the drug past the search area in the reception hall?"

She turned and sent him a mocking glance. "Come on, Doctor. Are you telling me that the orderlies in the reception area conducted a thorough body search of my ex-husband? *The Honorable Judge Victor Rodier?* The president's nominee to the Supreme Court of the United States? The guy could have walked in here with a nuclear missile tucked under his arm and nobody would have questioned him. As for a tiny vial of LSD... Please, don't make me laugh. I'm not in the mood."

He surprised her by agreeing. "You're right," he conceded. "I'm sure the orderlies didn't search Judge Rodier properly—probably not at all. But since you're so suspicious of him, how did he persuade you to take it? He only saw you in the patients' lounge, surrounded by other people. Are you trying to tell me that he opened your mouth, forced apart your teeth and shoved LSD down your throat?"

"He had no need to do anything so dramatic. He brought a fancy box of imported shortbread cookies with him and kept urging me to eat one. I refused. The sprinkles of sugar across the top of the cookies looked to me like the ideal spot to drop a little acid." She smiled with bitter irony. "I always underestimate Victor. Of course, he expected me to refuse the cookies, that's why he kept pressing me to take one. He used the old magician's trick—focus the audience's attention on a bright red herring, so that you can pull off the trick using an inconspicuous fillet of sole."

"You're claiming he focused your attention on the cookies and slipped a dose of LSD to you another way. But if the drug wasn't in the cookies, then where was it? How did he persuade you to take it?"

"Why, Doctor, if I didn't know better, I'd think you were treating my accusation seriously."

"Maybe I am," Ed said. "Take a chance, Constance. Tell me how you think he slipped you the drug."

She was so tempted not to tell him, not to raise her hopes one more time, only to have them dashed. She stared at him in bleak silence, her mocking sarcasm entirely deserting her.

"Constance, please." His voice was low and urgent, and for the first time, it didn't quite sound like a doctor's voice. "I can't help you if you don't give me the ammunition."

She wouldn't expect him to believe her, she decided. That way she wouldn't be hurt when he dismissed her accusations. "I don't know exactly how he did it, of course, but I'm guessing he put the stuff in my glass of iced tea. Teresa brought the tea, so I wasn't really paying attention to it, although I thought I was watching his hands closely enough to be sure he hadn't messed with it. But I was so nervous about the cookies, and about what he was saying to me—"

"What was he saying to you?"

"I don't recall exactly. The usual taunts about Liliana. Where had I buried her body, that sort of thing."

"Go on. Tell me how you think he got the drug into the iced tea. Was it in a jug? Did he pour it out?"

"No, Teresa brought the jug and poured it into two plastic glasses. After I recovered, I thought back over everything I could remember about the time I spent with Victor. I remember he pushed one of the glasses across the table toward me, and I'm almost sure he put a straw into the glass. I think the LSD may have been stored inside the straw. That way, with the first sip of tea, I swallowed the LSD right along with it."

"My God, Constance, with all the other medications you're supposed to be taking, Victor ought to be afraid of killing you."

"Well, he's been doing this for years, so I guess he only gives me a very small amount, otherwise you're right. I'd either be dead, or have totally fried brains. But Victor knows perfectly well that once you've taken LSD, especially if you had a bad reaction, it only takes a minuscule amount to bring on powerful, nightmarish flashbacks. So I guess Victor administers minuscule doses. Anyway, like I told you, he's a gambler. He's willing to take the risk that I won't die. Or if I do, that there won't be an autopsy. Or if there's an autopsy, that they won't find the LSD. Or if they find the LSD, that they won't associate it with the Honorable Judge Victor Rodier. I'd say he's working with pretty good odds, wouldn't you?"

"No, I'd say his risk of discovery has to be enormous. Suppose you refused to drink the iced tea? How would he get rid of it?"

"Easily. I'm crazy, remember? I lose control at the slightest provocation. He'd knock the tea onto the floor and pretend I did it. That's more or less what happened last week. When the hallucinations started, I jumped up, my hands whirring like windmills. The table we were sitting at went over with a bang, spilling the tea and scattering ice cubes. At the time, I thought I'd knocked over the table, but maybe I hadn't. Maybe Victor knocked it over. If *I'm* not sure what happened, despite sitting right across the table from him, nobody else would suspect him, even for a second."

Constance gave a sardonic smile. "You do see the beauty of his plan, don't you, Doctor? Victor probably picked up the straws, crumpled them and helpfully deposited them in the nearest trash can. Meanwhile, the orderlies were mopping away any evidence of LSD in the iced tea before he'd even left the building."

Ed looked at her thoughtfully. His expression had reverted to careful neutrality and, once again, revealed no clue as to whether he believed what she was saying. "You're confined to a hospital for the hopelessly insane. You've been here for more than twenty-five years. If Judge Rodier dislikes you, he doesn't have to see you. Nobody would think less of him if he stopped visiting you. What possible reason could there be for Judge Rodier to go to such extraordinary lengths to slip you an annual dose of LSD?"

"For years, I assumed it was simply to torment me, to punish me for having killed his daughter. Now I'm beginning to realize that, to take so many risks, Victor must have a more pressing purpose than tormenting me. I think he wants to make sure that everyone at Merton House is given a regular reminder that I'm crazy. That way, if I suddenly get the urge to start making strange accusations about my ex-husband, nobody's going to listen to me."

"You're suggesting that Judge Rodier is capable of visiting you every year, for twenty-six years, on the off chance that you might make some defamatory remarks about his character?"

"He's been planning his appointment to the Supreme Court since the day he passed the New York bar exam," Constance said. "I'd say a day trip to North Carolina once a year is a small price to pay for making sure I don't accuse him of murdering Liliana. Or if I accuse him, that no one is going to listen."

"Let's be completely honest with each other, Constance, or we're not going to get anywhere. First, I'll acknowledge that the symptoms you exhibited earlier this week are at least as consistent with a bad reaction to LSD as they are with violent psychosis. I'll even admit that a couple of your symptoms aroused my curiosity. However, in exchange, I want you to admit that it's quite a leap to move from acknowledging that you might have ingested LSD, to accepting that Judge Rodier—one of our nation's most respected jurists and a noted philanthropist—is the person who administered the drug."

"Believe it, Doctor."

"Wait, let me finish. I've realized for weeks now that you've been faking some of your symptoms, but I have to tell you, Constance, feigning madness for twenty-six years is a damn good way to convince any psychiatrist that you're only borderline rational. And, to put it bluntly, walking into my office to announce that—quote—you've decided to stop being mad is not the sort of statement to inspire confidence in the state of your mental health."

To her own surprise, Constance laughed. Not a bitter gasp, or a crazy guffaw, but a quiet little laugh of genuine amusement. "I can see your point, Doctor. But now listen to me, and see if you can understand my point. You're the person who's most responsible for the changes in me. You listened, you cared, you genuinely tried to reach me. And you did. I've finally found the courage to do what you've been urging me to do. I'm going to confront my past. And I want you to listen while I do. All I ask of you is that you listen with an open mind.''

He looked at her steadily, with cool assessment. Then he smiled and her heart gave a tiny leap of hope.

"All right," he said. "Tell me what happened when you and Victor were married, Constance. Tell me all about it, and I'll listen with an open mind.''

Fourteen

Late Summer, 1969

By their first wedding anniversary, Constance already knew that marrying Victor had been a mistake—that she'd been in love with the idea of love, not with Victor himself. But since she had no intention of repeating her mother's pattern of changing husbands and lovers with the passing seasons, she clung to the fiction that her marriage was a happy one. The discovery that she was pregnant made the pretense feel real, especially since Victor seemed gratified by the idea of impending fatherhood and reined in the cruelty of his vicious tongue.

Constance turned out to be one of those rare and lucky women who breezed through pregnancy, and Lili was an easy baby to manage, perhaps because she was so robust. Very few women in the sixties nursed their babies but, persuaded by her friend Elena, Constance overruled Victor's objections and insisted on breast-feeding Lili. Victor made no secret of the fact that he found the process disgusting, more suitable for barnyard animals than for humans. He didn't speak to her for a week after an important cocktail party when her overfull breasts leaked milk and stained the silk bodice of her dress. When he finally spoke again, it was to order her to cease and desist her peasant-like obsession. Reluctantly, Constance had submitted to his orders.

Through it all, Lili had thrived, and although Constance sometimes wished Victor would show more interest in his daughter, caring for their baby left her happier and more fulfilled than she'd ever been in her life. Wildly in love with Liliana, she paid Victor so little attention that it took her several months to notice that her husband deeply resented the way he'd been shoved to the periphery of her life.

Guiltily aware that she'd allowed motherhood to consume her, Constance resolved to pay Victor more attention, to listen appreciatively when he talked about the cases he was arguing in court and to make a greater effort to sparkle at the endless round of social events he considered so important to his career.

Her resolutions were sincere, but her efforts weren't very successful. At some level, she knew she was using Lili as an excuse to avoid facing the problems in her relationship with Victor. Unfortunately, her sporadic efforts to behave like a dutiful wife merely highlighted the fact that her heart wasn't in it. She really didn't *like* Victor very much. In one of their increasingly frequent and ugly arguments, Victor accused her of having used him as a stud: he'd given her Lili, and now she had no further use for him. With a fatal flare of temper, Constance had told him he had no reason to complain: he'd been well paid for his services.

Afterward, she'd been ashamed of herself. She hated that she'd behaved just like her mother—that she'd used her wealth as a weapon to wound Victor's pride. She did her best to make amends, but the seeds of financial conflict had been sown. Victor was living on her money, and they both knew it. The humiliating truth had been exposed and refused to be decently reburied.

By the time Lili celebrated her fourth birthday, in August of 1969, their marriage was in big trouble. Constance hadn't known how much trouble, though, until the night of the Lamberts' dinner party in late September. If she could say there was a single moment when the whole hideous nightmare of Lili's death began, that moment would have to be the Lamberts' party.

Chuck Lambert was the managing partner of the law firm where Victor worked. His first wife had died in a sailing accident, and Chuck had recently remarried. His second wife, Daphne, was twenty years younger than Chuck, a beautiful woman and a gracious, friendly hostess. Constance rather liked Daphne, although she was intimidated by her sophistication. At twenty-four, Constance still felt gauche in the company of Victor's business acquaintances.

The meal that night had been delicious, and Constance had enjoyed herself. She'd even drunk a couple of glasses of red wine, which might have been a mistake. Red wine didn't always agree with her, and the combined smell of perfume and cigar smoke was beginning to seem overpowering. Thank God the French doors to the balcony stood ajar, she thought, sitting in the living room after the meal.

Constance yawned, wondering how long it would be before Victor was ready to go. Since it was the home of his boss, she couldn't just make an excuse and leave. She owed Victor that much loyalty, she supposed, even if she did think of divorce more and more often these days. Young associates in a prestigious law firm couldn't afford to offend the senior managing partner, and Victor had told her it was especially important for both of them to make a good impression on tonight's guest of honor.

The guest in question was the senior senator from Idaho, a Goldwater Republican who was the ranking minority member on the Senate Judiciary Committee. A distinguished jurist, Victor had told her. In Constance's opinion, he was also a lecherous old fart. He'd already pinched her bottom twice before they even sat down to dinner, and with the meal over, she was taking care to keep out of reach of his roving fingers.

She sat in a high-backed Queen Anne chair off to the side and admired the competence with which Daphne was dispensing liqueurs and coffee from a trolley brought in by a white-gloved butler. Daphne carried an after-dinner drink to her husband. She rested her hand for a moment on Chuck's shoulder and dropped a fleeting kiss on the top of his bald head. Chuck flashed her a quick, proud smile of thanks before returning to his conversation with a visiting British barrister. Constance felt a pang of envy. She wished she and Victor could share an intimate little moment of affection like that. She glanced around the room, trying to find Victor, but she couldn't see him. He was probably closeted in the library, discussing politics or some point of law with one of the other guests. Constance knew better than to go in search of him. Her husband didn't appreciate having his business conversations interrupted.

The party showed no signs of breaking up. Three of the partners' wives were discussing menu options for a charity ball they were planning. A banker from Boston was expounding on the amazing fact that the U.S. economy was such a successful growth engine that the nation could afford to pay, not only for the war in Vietnam, but also for President Lyndon Johnson's War on Poverty, without placing any drain on the national budget. Irritated by his smugness, Constance remarked that a quick walk through Harlem or the South Bronx might suggest that the War on

Poverty had so far met with no more success than the war in Vietnam. The banker patiently explained why she had misinterpreted what she'd seen, and why she had no understanding at all of events in Southeast Asia.

The discussion turned from the politics of poverty, to the space program, to baseball and finally back again to Vietnam. These days, it was impossible to attend a dinner party without having a discussion about Vietnam. Constance opposed American involvement in a war that seemed to her unwinnable. However, she knew her antiwar views would be highly unpopular among this conservative crowd, and she allowed her thoughts to drift, making no attempt to contribute to a debate that was rapidly becoming heated.

She hoped Lili wasn't having a disturbed night. The poor sweetie was just getting over a cold, and she'd been running a slight temperature all day. Constance wasn't really worried about her, though. She had every faith in Eva, their housekeeper, who was an absolute treasure, and a devoted fan of Lili's. Eva was one of Elisabeth Korda's refugee friends, and she'd been with Victor and Constance since the first week of their marriage. Even if Lili woke up, she would be quite happy to let Eva console the child.

Damn! While she'd been daydreaming about Lili, the revolting old senator had moved from his seat on the other side of the hearth and was now standing right next to her, peering down the neckline of her dress. He was so engrossed in the view that his glass of Scotch was in danger of spilling over her shoulders. Judging by his slurred voice and the sweat beads popping out on his forehead, Constance decided it was touch and go whether he would pass out before he stopped drinking.

''Excuse me, please.'' She got up, not attempting to be subtle. The senator, caught off balance, almost fell over.

He extended a wobbly hand. "Don' go, li'l lady—"

"I must." She smiled. "I have to find the ladies' room." She squeezed between chattering groups and made it out onto the balcony before the senator could sufficiently gather his drunken wits to protest that the guest bathrooms were both located in the opposite direction.

What a ghastly man! She hated the way so many important men thought that their position entitled them to paw and maul any young woman unlucky enough to cross their path. Constance walked into the shadows of the balcony and leaned against the balustrade, ignoring the little groups of guests who'd come outside to take advantage of the warm night. She gulped down lungfuls of air that smelled of leaves, wishing her head would stop aching. She was shaking, she realized. Mr.-Old-Fart-Senator-From-Idaho was bringing back unpleasant memories of her stepfathers. Lord, she hated elderly men with straying hands!

Some sixth sense alerted her, and she turned just in time to see the senator lumbering out from the drawing room. Damn and double damn! If she wasn't careful, she'd get trapped out here behind one of the potted pine trees. She hurriedly scanned the balcony for any other open doors, but they were all closed.

She simply wasn't willing to be fondled by the senator, even if he was the guest of honor. Damn her red hair and big breasts. Some men seemed to have trouble realizing that she wasn't a second Rita Hayworth, but rather a boringly domesticated mother with almost zero sexual expertise and an old-fashioned belief in honoring her marriage vows.

She dodged behind two ladies complaining about Bloomingdale's policy of charging for delivery, and hurried around the corner of the balcony. Unfortunately, this side of the penthouse didn't seem to present any better getaway than the other. Constance had almost given up, when she finally discovered a sliding door that stood open a crack. Thank goodness! Once safely inside, she'd search for Victor and stick like glue to his side. To hell with not interrupting his important business discussions. Tonight, she really needed her husband's protection.

She opened the glass doors and slipped inside, finding her escape route blocked by a double layer of voile curtains and cretonne drapes. Heavy footsteps warned her that the senator was getting much too near. With the obstinacy of the very drunk, he'd blundered around the corner and was now lurching along the balcony.

Constance disentangled herself from the layers of curtain and stepped into the room. Too late, she realized that the room wasn't empty. The light shining in from outside cast a spotlight on her hostess, the impeccably elegant Daphne Lambert, who at this moment looked anything but elegant. She was pressed against the wall, eyes closed, designer gown rucked up to her waist, being vigorously and enthusiastically banged by a man whose trousers hung around his ankles and whose back was turned toward the balcony.

Constance started to tremble. She made a jerky, involuntary movement, and her hand knocked against a tallboy, betraying her presence. Daphne's eyes flew open. She saw Constance and gave a little shriek of horror. Her hand went to her throat, resting on her three strands of perfectly matched pearls. Probably a wedding present from Chuck, Constance thought with shocked irrelevance.

"Oh, my God!" Daphne gasped.

The man who'd been screwing Mrs. Chuck Lambert scrambled to pull up his trousers. He didn't turn around, but he didn't need to for Constance to recognize him. It was Victor. Her husband.

Constance fought against a wave of nausea. If Victor was discovered having sex with the managing partner's wife, his career would be over. Chuck would lose a wife he obviously loved and Constance would be humiliated. The senator from Idaho was about two seconds away from stumbling onto the scene. In a lightning-fast decision, she stepped out onto the balcony, closing the door behind her.

"There y'are, li'l lady." The senator gave her a beaming smile. "Caught ya!"

Constance discovered that she couldn't speak.

"Let's go back inside. It's gettin' shilly...cold...out here." The senator careened toward the sliding door.

Constance stepped in front of him and brought her spiked heel down square in the middle of his instep. She felt a vicious satisfaction when he howled with pain.

"Goodness me, whatever is the matter?" The senator's wife—a thin, gray-haired woman with a reedy voice and an air of permanent anxiety—rounded the corner and looked accusingly at Constance.

"I believe your husband has hurt his foot." Constance was in no mood to be conciliatory to anyone, especially not a woman who looked set to blame the victim for her husband's marauding hands. "Perhaps you should take him home before there's permanent damage. Excuse me, please."

Somehow, she got back to the drawing room without calling attention to herself. She hid in the bathroom for twenty minutes, too numb to know exactly what she was feeling. By the time she emerged from her sanctuary, the party was breaking up. Victor, looking the picture of innocent dignity, was laughing at one of Chuck's jokes.

Daphne, hair perfectly coiffed, designer gown once again smoothed over her slender hips, was graciously assisting the hobbling senator out to the elevator, while his wife followed behind, mousy and resigned. Constance lurked in a corner, hovering between rage, betrayal and a bewildering feeling of inadequacy. Victor and Daphne looked so self-assured! Was she the only person who felt utterly bowled over by the events of the evening?

The cab ride home with Victor was notable for the stony silence that prevailed for the entire length of the journey. Victor seemed to feel no need to speak, and Constance had so much hurt and anger stewing inside her that she didn't know where to start.

Arriving back in their own apartment, all her repressed outrage exploded. ''How could you do something so despicable?'' she demanded, throwing her evening purse onto the hall console and storming into their bedroom. She ripped off her gossamer-fine mohair evening wrap and tossed it vaguely in the direction of her closet. ''How could you betray my trust and Chuck's, too? I feel physically sick when I think about what I found you doing with Daphne tonight!''

Victor removed his cuff links and slipped off his tie. ''You're making a mountain out of a molehill,'' he said, his mouth pinched. ''Chuck can barely get it up these days, and Daphne's a young woman with a healthy sexual appetite. That's all there is to it.''

''That's *all?* You're having sex with your boss's wife—in his own bedroom, for God's sake!—and I walk in on the pair of you . . . and you call that a *molehill?*''

Victor took off his jacket and dropped it into the hamper with his other clothes waiting to be picked up by the dry cleaners. ''You're the only person who saw us, Constance. No harm's been done. God knows, you've made it perfectly plain that you'd prefer me not to bother you with my sexual demands—"

"I haven't!" she protested vehemently. Perhaps a little too vehemently because she knew there was a grain of truth to his accusation. "Just because I'm sometimes tired from taking care of Lili doesn't mean that I'm rejecting you!"

He paused in the entrance to his walk-in closet. "How long is it since we last had sex, Constance?"

"I don't know. A week—"

"Or three," he said bitterly. "Or maybe it's even four. No wonder I found Daphne attractive. And she takes care of herself, too, so that a man can actually enjoy looking at her body. Not like you, Constance. You're at least ten pounds overweight, and you have been ever since Liliana was born."

"You keep saying that, but my doctor says I shouldn't lose any more weight, that I'm too thin already—" Constance pulled herself up short. "Wait, this is crazy! We're not talking about me, Victor. We're talking about *you*. You and Daphne Lambert. Quite apart from the blow to our marriage, have you thought about the insane risk you took tonight? Suppose it hadn't been me who found you? The door to the balcony wasn't locked. It wasn't even shut, for God's sake, and the senator from Idaho was only a couple of steps behind me. What if he'd found you, instead of me? All hell would have broken loose. Chuck Lambert wouldn't just have fired you. He'd have made sure you never worked anywhere in this city again. And I can't say I'd blame him."

Victor didn't answer her. He walked into the bathroom where he stepped into the shower and turned the water on full blast. She followed him into the bathroom. "That's it?" she demanded, turning off the water, almost incoherent with rage. "You're just going to walk away from this and carry on as if nothing had happened?"

"Nothing *has* happened," he said, wrapping himself in a towel. Then he smiled, his expression cruel and openly contemptuous. "Nothing that hasn't happened a dozen times before, that is. And with women who fuck a hell of a lot better than you or Daphne."

She flushed bright scarlet, shocked at his crude language. The full implication of his words took a second or two to penetrate, but when she realized what he was admitting, tears pricked at the corner of her eyes. He'd had multiple affairs before this fling with Daphne Lambert, and he was as good as telling her that he would continue to have many more such affairs in the future. She had married Victor knowing almost nothing about his character, and she still didn't fully grasp what made him tick. But she understood him well enough to know that it wasn't only in his career that he needed the challenge of conquest and the thrill of taking risks. In his personal relationships, as well, he craved the twin sensations of conquest and domination.

Constance faced the truth squarely for the first time. Victor had committed adultery, but she had stopped loving him years ago. She no longer liked Victor—could never live happily with him—but he was Lili's father, and the only sexual partner she'd ever had. It hurt to think that their marriage had been brought to an end in such an ugly and sordid way, and she cried for the death of her naive fantasy.

She stumbled back into the bedroom, searching in her chest of drawers for a clean nightgown. She pulled out something pink and silky and headed for the door. Victor barred her way.

"Where are you going?" he demanded.

"To one of the guest rooms. I can't sleep in here with you. Not anymore."

For answer, he locked their bedroom door and pocketed the key. "Eva's too damned nosy, as it is. She's not going to find you sleeping in the guest bedroom and start asking questions about subjects that don't concern her. Our marriage is nobody's business but our own."

Shocks were piling on top of each other in rapid succession. Constance was finding it difficult to think. "Our marriage?" she said. "After tonight, surely to God you don't think we have a marriage?"

"Tonight has got nothing to do with us or our marriage." His tone of voice suggested that he was explaining something elementary.

"From my point of view, it's got everything to do with us," she said. "I have no intention of sleeping with you, Victor. For God's sake, you've just admitted that you've had dozens of affairs!"

He walked over to the bed, wound his watch and set it on the nightstand. He didn't speak.

Constance gritted her teeth. "Give me the key," she said. "Let me out of here. For heaven's sake, Victor, don't be so childish. I haven't checked on Lili. She was running a fever, and I need to make sure that she's all right."

"Lili will survive a few more hours without you hovering over her. Behave yourself tonight, and I'll unlock the door first thing tomorrow morning." Victor turned back the covers. "Get in, Constance, I have an early start tomorrow."

"I'm not sleeping with you. No way." She ran to the door and started to pound on the heavy wooden panels. "Eva! Eva! I'm loc—"

He grabbed her from behind, clamping his hand over her mouth. "Stop screaming, and I'll let you go. Scream again, and I'll put a gag on you."

It was crazy, she thought, but she was actually beginning to feel frightened of him. Her own husband. She let herself go limp in his arms and he slowly released his hand from her mouth. "That's better. Now come to bed."

Tight-lipped, she walked over to the bed and pulled off the satin coverlet. She let it drop onto the floor and added a pillow. "I'll sleep here."

"Like hell you will." Victor snatched her arms, holding them behind her back to prevent her lying down. "You're my wife and you'll sleep in my bed."

An image of Daphne Lambert squashed between the wall and Victor's body flashed into Constance's mind, and she almost gagged at the thought of lying next to him. "There's no way in hell you're getting me into bed with you, Victor. Not tonight. Not ever again."

"You'll do what you're told," he snarled.

"I won't. You can't make me sleep with you."

She shouldn't have threatened him. She knew that, the moment the words were out of her mouth.

"Don't challenge me, Constance. I don't like to be challenged." He punched her in the ribs with such brutal force that she doubled over, gagging and retching, gasping for breath. While she was still off balance, he knocked her onto the bed, flat on her back. In one swift, athletic move, he grabbed her hands and held them over her head. At the same time, he straddled her body, pinning her down, holding her immobilized against the mattress.

Through a haze of pain, Constance registered the incredible fact that Victor was not only aroused, but that he intended to have sex with her. "Don't," she pleaded. "Victor, don't do this, please. If you do, it'll be rape."

Blood rushed into his face, turning it dark red. "You're my wife. A husband can't rape his wife, it's a legal impossibility."

He thrust into her. She screamed with pain, but he grabbed a pillow and held it over her face. For a moment, she thought she might suffocate before he was through with her, but he was so aroused that it was less than a minute before he'd finished. He removed the pillow from her face and shoved it across the bed. Panting, eyes gleaming with an odd sort of triumph, he looked down at her. "You're more fun when you don't want it," he said. "Remember that, next time you decide to refuse me."

He rolled off her, stood up, stretched and walked around the foot of the bed to his side. He sat down on the edge of the mattress, just as he always did, and carefully set the alarm for seven-thirty. Then he switched off the bedside light and lay down.

"Good night, Constance."

She remained stubbornly mute, and for a moment she could feel the tension radiating from him again. Then, in the near-darkness, she saw him shrug. He turned from his side to his stomach and back again. Within five minutes, he was asleep. As far as Constance could tell, while she lay awake, he slept peacefully for six and a half hours, stirring only when the alarm went off promptly at seven-thirty.

Sparing her no more than a brief glance, Victor got out of bed, pulled on his robe, unlocked the door and stalked silently from the room. He returned a few minutes later with a sleepy-eyed Lili in his arms. Constance warned herself not to be swayed by this apparent attempt to patch things up between them.

Victor set their daughter in the bed, and she jumped around happily, full of four-year-old energy, showing not the slightest sign of last night's fever. "Mommy!" Lili gave a final big bounce that threw her into Constance's arms. "Mommy, let's go to Grandma's house. I want to go swimming!"

Constance pushed a mop of white-gold curls out of Lili's eyes. "It's too late in the year to go swimming, sweetie. Maybe we can go to see Grandma on the weekend. Today we have some other things to do."

Lili pouted. "I like it at Grandma's house better."

"I know you do, sweetie. But we can't go today. Have you had breakfast yet?"

"Not yet. Eva's making pancakes." Lili jumped off the bed and held out her hand. "I'm hungry. Are you hungry, Mommy? Let's eat breakfast."

"Okay, I'm coming. Wait while I find my slippers." Constance tied the sash of her robe, some of the hurt of the past night dissipating under the soothing balm of Lili's smiles. Lili's hand, hot and a bit sticky, tugged impatiently at hers.

"Constance." Victor's voice halted her at the doorway to the bedroom.

She swung around, reluctant to acknowledge him. "Yes?"

"Don't make any rash moves," he said softly, and she realized how off the mark she'd been in assuming Victor wanted to repair the previous night's bad behavior. "Don't think about consulting a divorce lawyer, Constance, because if you do, I'll make sure that you never see Lili again."

She drew in a sharp breath. "This isn't the time or the place to discuss our future—"

"It's as good a place as any. Understand this, Constance. I'm perfectly satisfied with our marriage, and I've no desire to end it. If you try to divorce me, I'll sue for custody of Lili.''

She might not be a brilliant lawyer like Victor, but Constance knew that mothers were awarded custody of the children in virtually every divorce case. "That's an empty threat,'' she said, her hand unconsciously tightening around Lili's. "The court is never going to award custody of a little girl to her father.''

Victor directed a look at her that sent chills racing down her spine. "Don't try to fight me on this, Constance, because you're not going to win. The courts won't give you custody of Lili if they decide you're an unfit mother.''

Constance was unnerved by Victor's cool self-assurance. He was accustomed to finding his way around the tangled legal system, and he knew how to cover all the angles. Could he possibly make good on his threat? Impossible, she decided. She tilted her chin defiantly. In choosing to make Lili a weapon between the two of them, Victor had made a major mistake. "No court in the world would ever accept that I'm a bad mother,'' she said. "Everyone who knows me also knows that Lili's the most important person in my life.''

Victor's eyes flickered. "I'm advising you for your own good, Constance. Don't try to fight me. Trust me, you won't win.'' Without a backward glance, he walked into the bathroom, closing the door quietly—confidently—behind him.

Fifteen

Denver
Tuesday, June 18, 1996

Dan had brewed a pot of coffee and found the orange juice by the time Jess finished showering and came into the kitchen. She eyed him warily. The morning after the night before didn't seem any easier to cope with just because the man facing you across the breakfast table was your ex-husband. She edged sideways into one of the kitchen chairs. "Hi."

"Hi. Mmm, you smell wonderful." He handed her a mug of steaming coffee, black but not too strong, the way she liked it first thing in the morning. He poured juice over clinking ice cubes and pushed that toward her, too.

"It's my shampoo." She took a sip of juice. "Sorry I slept so late."

"It's only nine-thirty." Dan grinned. "Besides, we had a tiring night."

She blushed and buried her nose in her coffee mug. In the bright light of morning it was a tad embarrassing to recall the enthusiastic lack of inhibition with which she'd responded to Dan's sexual overtures. "Were you planning to go back to New York today?"

He sat down opposite her. "Not unless you're planning to throw me out."

She looked at him. "No, I'd... like you to stay around for a while. After what happened yesterday, I'd appreciate the company."

"I'll call the studio and let them know where I am. Is it okay if I give them your phone number?"

"Yes, that's fine."

He reached across the table and slowly closed his hand around hers. "It feels good to be spending time with you, Jess. I've missed you like hell, and not just in my bed."

She looked at his fingers entwined with hers and felt a surge of emotion so intense that for a moment she couldn't speak. Seeing him across the breakfast table made it easy to understand why she'd spent the past three years ruthlessly excising every memory of him. But now Dan was back in her life, and the barriers she'd erected weren't strong enough to protect her from the truth of her own feelings.

"I've missed you, too," she said. She shot him a mischievous glance. "Especially in my bed."

Dan's mouth twisted into a wry smile. "I'm thirty-five years old, and I work in a business where I meet some of the most glamorous women in the world." His voice was husky. "You're the only woman who can turn me on with a casual remark like that."

Jess's gaze turned wistful. "We had some wonderful times together, didn't we, Dan?"

"Yes. Before I totally screwed everything up."

"You screwed up, but so did I." She drew in a shaky breath. "Although I didn't deserve Shanna Ryan." The acknowledgment that she shared some of the blame for the failure of their marriage was like a giant crack opening up the Arctic ice of her resentment, freeing her from captivity of her own bitterness.

"I'd ask you to forgive me for what happened with Shanna, except I know what I did was unforgivable." Dan's hands tightened around hers in a grip that was almost painful. "I've spent the past three years wondering how the hell I came to do something so goddamn stupid. The answers I've come up with never begin to justify what happened."

"You already explained that you were desperate to end our marriage."

"Yeah, well, I achieved my goal, didn't I? The marriage sure came to a swift end. I guess my only excuse for being so damn stupid is that it's a hell of a lot easier to be wise after the event. Those last few weeks we were together, my supply of basic sense must have been running real low."

"We both needed the chance to step away from each other and finish growing up," Jess said. "Our relationship was so intense, neither of us knew how to handle our feelings."

"God, Jess, I still don't know if I've learned how to handle my feelings for you." His voice deepened. "I can't describe to you what it was like yesterday to hear that a woman had been killed by a bomb blast and to spend hours not knowing if it was you. I think I went slightly insane. Sometimes, having a vivid imagination can be a curse."

She shuddered at the reminder of yesterday's terrible events. "I'll have to go and see Greg this afternoon, although I can't think what I'm going to say to him—"

"Who's Greg?"

"Marla's son. He's just graduated from high school, and his father lives out in California somewhere. I hope to

God his father will start playing a more active role in Greg's life now that this has happened. With his mother killed, the poor kid's going to be so alone...."

Jess felt tears clog her throat, and she reached for a napkin to blow her nose. "Damn! What happened to Marla is so unfair! The package wasn't even meant for—" She stopped abruptly, knowing that Dan would be all over her if he found out that she had been the intended target of the bomb. He'd be nagging her to post security guards at each corner of her bed and never to leave the house without a retinue of bomb-sniffing dogs. And that would just be the beginning.

"Okay, Jess, what are you deciding not to tell me?"

"Oh, it's nothing. Nothing important."

"You always were a hopeless liar, and you don't seem to have improved one bit since our divorce."

"Some people might consider that a plus," she said.

"You weren't talking about cosmic injustice just now, when you said it was unfair that Marla died. You started to say that the package containing the bomb wasn't even sent to Marla. Who was it sent to, Jess?"

She sighed. "Well, if you must know, it seems possible that it was sent to me. Gift wrapped in gold foil." Her voice sounded thin and scared even to her own ears. "Somehow, that makes it more horrible. That there's a fanatic out there crazy enough to send me a gift-wrapped package of death."

Dan's face turned white. Silently, he gathered her into his arms, rocking back and forth as he comforted her. "What are the police doing to protect you?" he asked, his voice grim.

"Dan, you can't assume I'm still in danger, just because the bomb was addressed to me—"

"No, of course not." Dan didn't attempt to moderate his sarcasm. "That would be a real crazy leap in judgment. Jess, for God's sake, get real. You've been threatened, and you need to take the threat seriously. And so do the police."

"I *do* take the threat seriously, but the police assured me that people who send bombs through the mail almost never target the same person twice."

"I'd sure like to hear that the CBI isn't relying on an 'almost never' statistic to protect you."

"No, they're taking all sorts of precautions. They've made arrangements for my personal mail to be screened before it comes anywhere near my mailbox, and Ackroyd—he's the agent in charge of this case—is checking to see if there are any groups that have a special dislike for a woman in my sort of job."

"You're telling me there are hate groups opposed to *travel agents?*" Dan demanded.

"I know it sounds incredible, but the FBI has a listing for fanatics who hate women and government bureaucracy enough to target me. There seems to be a lot of hate going around these days."

"So how does the CBI explain that these crazies sent the bomb to you and not to Marla?" Dan asked. "She fits the profile as well as you."

"Not quite, apparently. I'm the assistant director of the bureau, so I'm much more visible than Marla. My name appears on the bureau's letterhead, and I go to a lot of official functions where people can see me doing my job. But for the moment, Ackroyd's leaning toward the view that I wasn't the target at all and it was sheer bad luck the package was addressed to me."

Dan stroked her hair back from her forehead, framing her face with his hands. "The CBI are the experts, and I ought to stop second-guessing their judgment. But somehow, it's real difficult for me to accept that your name got chosen at random.''

"Dan, don't you see? I *have* to assume my name was on that package by chance. If I start believing there's some crazy individual out there, plotting to kill me, then *I'll* go crazy. I can't live my life in a state of permanent semi-terror.''

''Of course you can't.'' Dan let out a ragged breath. ''I'm sorry, Jess. It's just that spending most of yesterday afternoon wondering if you were dead or alive made me confront my feelings for you, and I'm doing a lousy job of dealing with the aftermath.'' He looked down at her, his expression hard to read, despite the bright sunlight streaming in through the kitchen window. ''Jess, do you remember the night I asked you to marry me?''

The scene flashed in front of her inner eye, poignantly vivid. They'd gone to their favorite French bistro in the Village, and she'd ordered the house specialty, chocolate torte, for dessert. The waiter had brought her portion cut into the shape of a heart. Lying next to the cake had been a gardenia blossom, with a diamond and emerald engagement ring nestled around the stamen of the flower. ''How could I forget? The entire restaurant applauded when I said yes.''

Dan didn't answer her smile. He met her gaze, his eyes dark and uncertain. ''This time there's no diamond ring and no fancy, romantic dinner, but I can promise you I understand exactly what I'm asking, which is more than I did before.'' His voice thickened. ''I love you, and I want to spend the rest of my life with you. I want you to be the mother of my children, the person I grow old with. Will you marry me, Jess?''

It ought to be difficult to answer him, she thought. She was a sensible, practical woman. With their record of failure, shouldn't she at least insist on spelling out ground rules for renewing their relationship? Suggest counseling? Taking things steady? A long period of friendship without commitment? After the terrible hurts they'd inflicted on each other in the past, why did it seem so easy to cradle his hand against her cheek and turn to press a kiss into his palm? Somehow, yesterday's bomb blast seemed to have blown away her anger. She saw her bitter resentment for what it had been: her way of refusing to accept any blame for the failure of their marriage.

She looked up at him, flooded with the wonderful, exhilarating feeling that she'd finally come home. She reached up to touch her fingers to his cheek. "I love you, too, Dan. Yes, I'll marry you."

For about five seconds, Dan remained stock-still, his expression blank. Then he let out a whoop. He hauled her into his arms and kissed her feverishly, with a passion that was achingly familiar, and a sensitivity that was entirely new. "God, Jess, this time we'll make it work, I swear."

She'd thought that she would never be able to feel closer to Dan than she had in the early days of their marriage, when they moved into their tiny SoHo apartment and set up their home. She realized now that their relationship was deeper and richer for having survived the pain of betrayal and the strain of separation. She was prepared for the rush of emotion, but she was surprised by the force of sheer sexual desire that swept through her as they kissed. Suddenly she was laughing, feeling the sort of uninhibited joy that had been alien to her for three long and arid years. She walked backward into the bedroom, unzipping her shorts as she walked. She felt sexy, provocative, teasing—all the things she hadn't allowed herself to be for far too long.

And Dan was following her, shedding his jeans, T-shirt and sneakers between kisses.

They collapsed onto the rumpled bed, laughing and panting, struggling out of their last few items of clothing. Jess's happiness was more intense because the shadow of yesterday's bombing still lurked in the dark periphery of her awareness. Her eyes met Dan's, and their laughter died as suddenly as it had come. His gaze roamed over her body, gratifyingly hungry, gratifyingly aroused. "God, Jess, you are truly the most beautiful woman I've ever seen. I do love you."

Her breath caught on a tiny sigh of pleasure. "Bet you say that to all your women."

"No," he said. "Only to you. Only you, Jess."

It was noon before they made it out of bed again. Newly showered and dressed, they made their way back into the kitchen. Dan ground coffee beans while Jess defrosted bagels and put them into the toaster.

"Jess, we need to talk." Dan set the coffee machine to perk and leaned against the counter. "With everything going on between the two of us, some important stuff got shunted to one side. I learned something amazing just now while you were in the shower. Remember that journalist friend of mine? The one who works for the *New York Times?*"

"Do you mean Somebody Kupfer? The one you mentioned last night?"

"Not Kupfer, Kaiser. Martin Kaiser. Remember I said I'd give him a call today and see if he'd been trying to reach me?"

"Mmm..." Jess wiggled the bagel, both sides of which were firmly stuck in the toaster.

"I called him a few minutes ago." Dan leaned across her and lifted out the bagel.

Jess scowled. "How did you do that?"

"I picked up the phone—"

"No, how did you get the bagel out of the toaster?"

"I refrained from yanking at it. It's a piece of dough, Jess, not an alligator you have to wrestle to the ground."

"Huh, it's amazing how the tone of your conversation alters now that I've been dumb enough to agree to marry you."

"Jess?" He turned quickly, saw that she was smiling, and let out a quick breath. He crooked his finger under her chin and tilted her face upward. "Jess, we're going to get married soon, aren't we?"

"Yes, I think we are. I don't want to wait, do you?"

"Never been more unwilling to wait in my life. As soon as we can get the paperwork in order, let's do it." He kissed her softly. "Now that we have that settled, could you please pass the cream cheese?"

She laughed, for no reason and every reason, and slid the tub across the counter. "Here, help yourself. What do you think of the bagels? They're not quite New York–deli standard, but they're pretty good, aren't they?"

He slathered cream cheese across his bagel and bit into it hungrily. "They're great. Although broiled shoe leather would taste pretty good right now. Look, let's eat this at the table, shall we?" Dan picked up the plate of bagels and Jess followed, carrying the coffee mugs.

"We have to focus here for a few moments," he said, sitting down at the table in front of her balcony. "Martin Kaiser gave me some astonishing information just now and we need to talk about it."

"Dan, stop it. You're looking solemn enough to make me nervous."

"I didn't mean to worry you. But the fact is, Jess, I believe we may have discovered who your parents are."

The muscles in Jess's stomach cramped violently. She put down the remnants of her bagel. "Martin found something in the newspaper archives." It was a statement, not a question.

"Yes. Remember I asked him to check for any children who went missing prior to December 9, 1969? He found a few references to missing children scattered through the archives, but none of them were girls under five, and none of them had names remotely like Liliana."

The blood was drumming so loudly in her ears that Jess had trouble following the precise sense of what Dan was saying. "So why is this important?"

"Martin pointed out this morning that there was quite a famous case of a little girl who went missing in December, 1969, but the first reports about her disappearance didn't appear in the paper until the twelfth, three days after you'd already been rescued from the car wreck in Cleveland."

"Then this child can't have anything to do with me."

"We should have realized that in kidnapping cases, the police don't necessarily release the details to the press right away. If there's a chance that the victim's life will be put at risk, the authorities simply conceal information. Sometimes there's a total news blackout. I'm guessing that's why there were no reports about you until you'd been missing for a while."

Jess let out a nervous breath. "Dan, if Martin found out something about my parents, you'd better tell me what it is. Stop trying to cushion the blow. However bad it is, it can't be more horrible than what I'm imagining right this minute. Were they both ax murderers or something?"

"Far from it. It turns out that last week Martin was helping to prepare an article about Judge Victor Rodier for the Sunday magazine supplement, and he came across an entire file of information about the Liliana Rodier Foundation."

Jess licked her bone-dry lips. "Liliana Rodier? There's a foundation called by that name?"

Dan nodded. "It's privately funded, in large part by Judge Rodier himself, so it's small and nowhere near as famous as Ronald McDonald House, or the Make-A-Wish Foundation, but from what Martin told me, it's greatly respected in the medical world. It's done some wonderful work for kids suffering from terminal illness." He looked at her intently. "Judge Victor Rodier founded the institute in memory of his missing daughter, Liliana Elizabeth Rodier. Liliana disappeared in December, 1969, and was never found."

Liliana Elizabeth Rodier.

Jess whispered the name over and over inside her head. *Liliana Elizabeth Rodier.* The name filled her with a sense of completion, bestowing a wholeness that she'd never recognized was lacking until the hollow hidden deep inside her core filled with the certainty of having found her true identity at last.

Liliana Elizabeth Rodier. As clearly as she knew the name was hers, she heard her mother calling out to her. *Lili, where are you? Lili, sweetie pie, hold Mommy's hand while we cross the road.* Her mother's voice was light and pretty and full of warmth. Hearing it again, even inside the privacy of her own head, Jess realized that she'd cut off all memory of her mother because it was simply too painful to remember.

Jess felt Dan's thumbs brush against her cheeks, and she realized she was crying. He spoke quietly, "We shouldn't build too much on this, Jess, but it's a place for us to start. There will be lots of gaps to fill in before everything finally gets resolved, but it would be a huge coincidence if Liliana Rodier disappeared from Manhattan in December and you turned up in Cleveland the same month, a different missing child who just happened to be the same age and have the same name."

She forced herself to be calm. "Coincidences do happen."

"There's another twist to this I haven't told you yet. Liliana's great-grandparents were an extremely wealthy couple called Mr. and Mrs. Wendell P. Grant."

Her head jerked up. "The people who paid for Jessica Marie's medical treatment?"

"The very same. And the people who employed Elena Pazmany's mother. So there's the link we've been searching for."

Jess's calm collapsed. "Are you suggesting this proves that the Pazmanys kidnapped me?"

"No, but I'm suggesting that all these facts taken together make it extremely likely that you're the long-lost Liliana Rodier. We've found out where you came from, Jess."

She didn't know where to put her hands, so she knotted them together and shoved them into her lap. "If I'm Liliana Rodier, where's my mother? Does she have any more children?" She stared at Dan. "Oh, my God, imagine if I have a bunch of younger brothers and sisters."

"I don't know about your mother, or brothers and sisters, but if you're really Liliana Rodier, you have a father who's about to become a Supreme Court justice," Dan said. He gave her an encouraging smile. "I guess that's impressive enough to begin with."

The distinguished-looking gentleman she'd seen interviewed on television by a slew of reporters might be her father? Jess tried to summon a picture of him from her past, but all she could remember was Ralph and Lena telling her they had to hide from Daddy. Jess decided to concentrate on the present. Her father was about to become a justice of the Supreme Court. Matt and Todd would never stop teasing her when she told them the news.

She started to laugh, then sobered abruptly at the sight of Dan's worried gaze. "Don't worry, I'm not hysterical. The whole situation suddenly struck me as irresistibly comic, that's all."

"It's a lot to take in, I know that, but we have to decide where we're going from here. Martin senses he's hovering on the verge of a major story. I'm assuming that the last thing you want is to have your reunion with your parents played out in front of the media, so I'm doing my best to keep him off the scent. But I figured we needed information badly enough to take a few risks, so I took the liberty of giving Martin your fax number. I didn't tell him your name, but I asked him to fax me as much information as he could about Liliana Rodier and the circumstances of her disappearance."

"My parents think I'm dead?" Jess shook her head. "Of course they do. That was a dumb question."

"I guess as the years went by, your parents had no choice but to assume you'd been abducted and murdered. Martin mentioned that Liliana Rodier was declared legally dead in 1976. Judge Rodier applied to the probate court to be allowed to use the funds in Liliana's trust to start the foundation. You were declared missing and presumed dead at the same time."

Jess gave a shaky laugh. "Jessica Marie is really dead, but everyone thinks she's alive. And now you're telling me that everyone thinks Liliana Rodier is dead, but I'm really alive.'' She rubbed her forehead. "You'll understand if I find this a bit overwhelming.''

"Brace yourself, honey. I'm not going to lie and say this is gonna be easy. The Rodiers may or may not be willing to accept your story at face value. Even if they're willing, the courts aren't likely to be so agreeable. At a minimum, you're going to be asked a hell of a lot of pushy questions, and Judge Rodier will probably insist on DNA testing. And we'd better pray you can get *that* done before the media gets wind of the story.''

"Why would the media care? This is old news—''

Dan stared at her. "You're joking, right? The long-lost daughter of a Supreme Court nominee turns up a quarter of a century after everyone accepts that she's dead, and you can't see why that's newsworthy?''

She nodded reluctantly. "I guess so. . . .''

"I'd better be up-front with you, Jess. My line of work doesn't help any with this situation. If the publicity people at Allied get wind of your story, they'll make damned sure it's played to the hilt. We've *really* got to take care how we handle this.''

Jess winced at the prospect of being reunited with her birth parents under the glare of a dozen or so roving Minicams. "We can't decide what to do until we know more about Liliana's disappearance,'' she said.

"Martin's fax may have arrived by now. I haven't checked.''

Jess pushed back from the table before he'd finished speaking, and ran into the spare bedroom, which she used as a home office. "There's a huge long fax waiting,'' she said, staring at the pile of shiny pages with hypnotized fascination. "It must be from Martin.''

"Then I guess we'd better read what he's sent us," Dan said as he followed her into the room.

She was grateful to him for downplaying his own excitement in an effort to keep her balanced. Not that his determined calm was having the slightest effect on the tumultuous state of her feelings. She snatched the pages out of the fax machine, sat at her desk and read so fast that she'd gone through half a dozen sheets before she realized that she hadn't grasped a single word she'd read.

Dan had been picking up each page as she tossed it aside. His expression remained so carefully blank that Jess was worried. "What is it?" she demanded.

He looked at her inquiringly. "Didn't you read this stuff?"

"I couldn't take anything in," she admitted ruefully. "My brain blanked out."

He handed her a long, densely written article. "Read it slowly, Jess. It explains everything far better than I could."

Rodier Child Still Missing.

Jess stared at the headline and at the accompanying picture. It was a studio portrait of a chubby-cheeked girl, with a mop of curls that gave her an old-fashioned, Shirley Temple sort of cuteness. The blurred fax made it impossible to see any details of the child's features, except that she had big eyes and seemed to be smiling.

Was she looking at a photo of herself? Jess had no idea. She felt no sense of kinship with the photo, but then, for years she'd grown up trying to convince herself that she felt connected to the photographed baby in a bundle of white shawls carried in Elena Pazmany's arms. Perhaps she'd simply grown wary of feeling emotion for pieces of paper.

She started to read the newspaper article again, this time forcing herself to go slowly enough to understand.

Authorities have so far been unsuccessful in their attempts to trace the whereabouts of Liliana Rodier, daughter of Mr. and Mrs. Victor Rodier. Mrs. Victor Rodier, the former Constance Elizabeth Howington, is the granddaughter of Mr. and Mrs. Wendell P. Grant of Hatterington, Long Island, and the daughter of Mrs. Hillary Howington Nussbein, of San Francisco.

In view of the family's vast wealth, it was at first assumed that Liliana had been kidnapped. However, the FBI confirmed today that no ransom demand has been received by any member of the family, and fears are growing that little Liliana may have been the victim of foul play.

Hundreds of calls offering help and information have been made to the FBI offices in New York, but so far these tips from the public have produced no results. The FBI is expanding its search outside the New York area, but local police are beginning to concentrate their efforts on known pedophiles. Detective Yarrow issued a statement on behalf of the police today saying that the "chances of finding Liliana Rodier alive seem to be diminishing with the passing of each day."

Victor Rodier has increased the reward he is offering for the safe return of his daughter to ten thousand dollars. Mrs. Rodier, meanwhile, is said to be on the verge of a nervous breakdown. She is under the care of her doctor and heavily sedated.

According to statements given to the FBI by the Rodiers' housekeeper, Mrs. Rodier is the last person known to have seen Liliana alive. Mr. Rodier, in a statement to the press yesterday evening, insisted that his wife is grief-stricken by the disappearance of her daughter and completely unable to provide the authorities with any clue as to what might have happened to Liliana.

Jess finished reading and looked up to find Dan watching her. For a moment, neither of them spoke. Jess finally broke the silence that was becoming prolonged enough to be awkward. "Did you get the same impression I did?" she asked. "It's almost as if they suspect my mother of being responsible for my disappearance."

"That seems to have been the theory the police were working on," Dan agreed. He held out another fax. "You should read this article, Jess. It's dated the fifteenth of January, 1970. It seems your mother was institutionalized soon after you disappeared."

"Institutionalized?"

"Committed to a mental hospital," Dan said. "Here, see for yourself."

Her stomach was churning, but Jess took the fax and read it with close attention.

Mrs. Rodier Confined To Saint Jude's Residential Care Facility In Upstate New York

After more than three weeks of intensive searching, the FBI today announced that there seemed now to be only a slight chance of finding Liliana Rodier alive. No trace of the little heiress has been uncovered in the past month, and authorities have begun to focus their attention on the precise events surrounding her disappearance.

Constance Howington Rodier has been under sedation ever since her daughter disappeared, and her doctor today issued a statement saying that, acting on the advice of two consulting psychiatrists, Mrs. Rodier has been committed to Saint Jude's, a private maximum-security hospital for the mentally ill, located near Rochester.

Detective Yarrow, of the New York City police, questioned Mrs. Rodier extensively prior to her commitment, and has been able to elicit from her no information other than the basic facts, which have never been in dispute: namely that Mrs. Rodier left her Park Avenue apartment on December 7, 1969, with Liliana in her charge, and that she took her daughter to a place where she believed the child would be "safe." Mrs. Rodier insists that her daughter was alive when she left her in this place of safety. She has, however, refused to say where this safe place is, claiming that her daughter's life is at risk from unspecified "enemies" and that she herself is being systematically poisoned by illegal drugs slipped into her food.

Detective Yarrow conceded that his department believes that Liliana is dead, but until her body is found, and in the absence of any hard forensic evidence to prove that a murder has taken place, the district attorney is unwilling to press formal charges. Detective Yarrow further conceded that the D.A.'s office had concluded that Mrs. Rodier, if charged with the murder of her daughter, might well be declared mentally incompetent to stand trial.

Mr. Rodier issued a brief statement saying that he believed his wife was now in the right place to receive the help she needed.

Reached at her villa in San Francisco, Mrs. Hillary Nussbein, mother to Mrs. Rodier, expressed her sorrow at the turn of events, but admitted that Constance had always been a problem child, having run away from home on at least two occasions, and having repeatedly experimented with illegal drugs.

Mr. and Mrs. Wendell P. Grant issued a statement through Raynes and Bruton, the family lawyers, saying that they still hoped for the return of their much-loved great-granddaughter. They made no comment on the possible involvement of their granddaughter in Liliana's disappearance.

It took Jess a full minute before she was able to speak. "They locked her away," she said. "That poor woman! She got tried and convicted of murdering her child without benefit of a lawyer, a judge or a jury."

"And the real irony is that there never was a murder victim in the first place," Dan said. "I'm guessing that the missing Liliana Rodier was safely tucked away in Cleveland when that article was written."

"Being spoiled and petted by Barbara and Frank. Not to mention Grandpa Gene." Jess cut off a gasp that was half sob, half laughter. "My mother took me to the Pazmanys' house for some reason, and they took me to Cleveland. Then they died before they could tell anyone where I was."

"That seems about the size of it."

"My God, Dan, how in the world are we going to straighten out this mess?"

"First, I guess we should approach Judge Rodier." Dan frowned. "Although we probably shouldn't do that right away. Isn't he just about to start his hearings in front of the Senate Judicial Committee?"

"I've lost track," Jess told him. "But I must admit I'm a bit leery of confronting a soon-to-be justice of the Supreme Court and blithely announcing that—maybe—I'm his long-lost daughter. So would he please take a blood test so that we could find out for sure.''

Dan gave a wry laugh. ''When you put it that way, it doesn't seem likely that we'd get past his clerks and aides, does it? Maybe we should try to approach Constance Rodier first. Although you have to realize that it could be a depressing encounter. If she was confined to a mental institution, she may not be a very stable person.''

''If she's my mother, I want to see her, whatever shape she's in. And if she isn't my mother... Well, I guess we'll have to face that problem when we get there. First of all, we have to find out where Constance Rodier is living these days. Or if she's even alive, come to that.''

''She's alive, and I know where she's living.'' Dan gestured to the sheaf of faxes. ''Judge Rodier gave an in-depth interview to the *Washington Post* a few days ago, and Martin sent us a copy along with everything else.'' Dan rifled through the slippery sheets of fax paper and finally found what he was looking for.

''Here it is. Judge Rodier is very eloquent on the subject of mental illness, and full of praise for the people who care for his ex-wife and other 'unhappy victims' like her. Constance Rodier is currently living at a place called Merton House, a residential-care facility in North Carolina.''

Jess realized that her palms were sweating and her heart pounding. Her lungs seemed to have forgotten how to expand and contract. ''Let's call directory inquiries and see if we can find a phone number for Merton House,'' she said. ''I'd like to talk to Constance Rodier's doctor as soon as possible.''

Sixteen

November, 1969

Constance couldn't believe what she was hearing. Her grandfather sat at his desk, in the walnut-paneled study that had been familiar to her since childhood, but she felt disoriented, as if she were the only human being left in a world taken over by aliens.

"But, Grandpa, you don't understand! Victor's taken control of all my money. I tried to access my trust-fund account and I couldn't. Don't you care? That's our family's money, my father's money, and he's taking it!"

"He hasn't taken control of the capital, my dear. He's simply helping to administer the income from your various trusts, and I assure you he's doing that extremely well."

"How do you know he's doing it very well?"

"Because I've seen the records," her grandfather explained patiently.

"What about the housekeeping? The grocery bills? There isn't enough money in my personal account to meet this month's bills!"

"That isn't really a problem, is it, my dear? You know Victor wants to pay those expenses directly out of his own income. He likes to feel that he's contributing as best he can to the cost of running your household." Her grandfather smiled. "Consider his feelings, Constance. A man needs to feel he's the breadwinner in his own home. Just be grateful that your husband takes his responsibilities seriously and doesn't rely on your family's money for his expenses."

"But the trust fund is my money," she said stubbornly.

Her grandfather took off his glasses and looked at her solemnly. "You're still a very young woman, Constance. You have a sweet little daughter to care for, and that takes up your time, just as it should. Victor explained to us that you had a bit of difficulty handling your trust-fund accounts, and that a rather unsavory stockbroker persuaded you to invest half a million dollars in a high-risk venture that ended up losing every cent you invested—"

"But Victor was the one who persuaded me to do that—"

Her grandfather shook his head. "Constance, your husband has kept me informed of how he's dealing with your financial affairs every step of the way. When you bought those shares in Ramco, he told me that you'd done it in flat contradiction to his own advice."

"But he was telling me to buy the shares at the same time he was telling you the opposite!"

"You must have misunderstood his advice, dear. He presents the accounts to me on a monthly basis, and has done since the first month you were married. I must have seen twenty or thirty documents that you've signed since your marriage, and each one authorized Victor to take charge of another aspect of your affairs—"

"But I didn't read what I was signing," Constance said, immediately realizing what a disastrous admission that was.

Wendell Grant frowned. "It pains me to hear that, Constance, after all the advice I tried to give you. *Always read the fine print.* I must have drummed that into your head a hundred times. All I can say, my dear, is that you were careless and we should be extremely grateful that your husband is such a responsible man. He's made back every penny you lost in that disastrous stock gamble, and he's even added a little to your net worth. His handling of your finances is impeccable."

"I bet it is," Constance said, absorbing the bitter knowledge that Victor had once again outsmarted her. In an abstract way, she could even admire his little deal with the Ramco shares. She had only herself to blame for the mess she was in. With a supreme indifference to money that could only come to someone who'd been born to great wealth, she'd paid no attention to the way Victor had gathered all the reins of her financial life into his hands while insinuating himself into her grandfather's good graces. Now she was reaping the frightening consequences of her own neglect. She should have known that her husband was way too clever to have pillaged her trust fund without covering his ass. But Victor not only had his rear end elegantly draped, he'd managed to convince her grandparents that he was an honorable, hardworking husband trying as best he could to cope with a flighty and immature wife.

A shiver of fear ran down Constance's spine. She'd made this trip to Hatterington today planning to tell her grandparents that she wanted to divorce Victor. Were they going to be on her side? Since that night several weeks ago when she'd caught her husband having sex with Daphne Lambert, each new day had brought a fresh discovery of just how clever he was. Her plans had been stymied on every front. But it wasn't until this afternoon that she'd realized his ruthlessness was even more impressive than his cleverness.

Over the past four years, pride had kept her silent on the subject of her marriage, but clearly, the time had come to swallow her pride and tell her grandparents exactly why she needed to divorce Victor. Fortunately, she knew her trust funds had been set up in such a way that her grandfather retained ultimate control, so once she'd explained the truth, he would be able to take the necessary steps to remove Victor and return the income to her.

She got up and paced nervously around the room, wondering how to present her situation without shocking her grandfather too much. He was a gentleman of the old school, and she would only embarrass both of them if she accused her husband of raping her.

"Grandpa, I want to divorce Victor," she blurted out.

Her grandfather's gaze fixed on her sadly. "Constance, my dear, this isn't sensible. He's a good man, and he's destined to go far in his career. Why, only the other day, Chuck Lambert was telling me that Victor's the most brilliant, industrious associate they've had in their firm for the last decade."

Frustration made her reckless. "And did Chuck Lambert happen to mention that Victor is also having an affair with his wife?"

"With Daphne? You think Victor's having an affair with Daphne Lambert?" Her grandfather sounded totally incredulous. Which wasn't altogether surprising, Constance thought despairingly. She'd have been skeptical, too, if she hadn't caught them in the act.

"Yes, with the sainted Daphne."

"My dear, you're allowing your imagination—"

"It's not my imagination. I saw them together. Victor was actually having sex with her at one of Chuck's parties."

"At a party? Where Daphne was the hostess?" Her grandfather shook his head, his cheeks flushed scarlet with embarrassment. "I don't know what you saw, but you certainly misinterpreted it. Even if I could believe your husband was capable of doing something so dishonorable as to seduce the wife of his managing partner, he's certainly much too savvy to do anything so suicidally stupid."

Her grandfather sighed, then got up to put his arm comfortingly around her shoulders. "Constance, my dear, Victor confided to your grandmother and me that you've been having a difficult time recently. He explained that you'd been trying to lose weight and that you got addicted to those nasty diet pills. Really, sweetheart, you're already too thin. You shouldn't let those ridiculous fashion magazines make you think otherwise. No man wants his wife to look like Twiggy."

"Except Victor," she muttered.

Her grandfather ignored her. "I realize you've been having problems with your nerves, and that the doctor had to prescribe something to help you sleep. But you have to trust my judgment, Constance. You're very vulnerable where drugs are concerned, and it's the chemical imbalance in your body that's making you feel this way about Victor, not the facts of the situation." He patted her arm. "Now I want you to promise me that you're not going to do anything rash about a divorce until you're feeling like your old self again."

Constance was angry, mostly with herself. Her grandparents were good people—perceptive people. If she couldn't persuade them of Victor's duplicity, who would she be able to persuade? "Grandpa, listen to me. You have to believe that I'm not strung out on sleeping pills, or diet pills, or anything else for that matter. The simple truth is that Victor doesn't love me, or Lili. He just wants to have control of my money, so that he can live the way he wants to live. He's using me—and he's manipulating you—to make sure that he doesn't lose the prize of our family's wealth now that he's won it."

Her grandfather raised a disbelieving eyebrow. "I think you can trust me to have sufficient experience of the world not to be easily manipulated, Constance."

"You may have experience of the world, Grandpa, but you suffer from one major disadvantage when you're dealing with Victor—you're an honorable man, and he isn't. Victor's a master of deception. He wants my money, and he's willing to do almost anything to get it."

"Constance, enough of this. Your husband works sixty hours a week. He's carrying a heavier caseload than any other associate in his firm. He doesn't have time to pursue a lavish life-style, even if he wanted to. And he doesn't need your money—the salary he earns more than covers everything he spends on himself."

"Except for the penthouse apartment on Park Avenue, the housekeeper, the cleaning service, the Mercedes we keep garaged on First Avenue at a cost of a hundred dollars a month. Not to mention the gourmet catering service that delivers dinner—"

"But Victor doesn't have those luxuries for himself, Constance. Why does he order dinner from a catering service? Only so that you won't need to cook. As for the car, he has that for you and Lili. How often does Victor drive anywhere? Once a month, perhaps? Not more—"

"He doesn't need to drive it. He just needs to know the car is there, his to command. The Mercedes is a power trip for him, not a transportation device."

"I've observed Victor for five years now, and I've seen with my own eyes that he's a man of simple tastes and moderate habits." Her grandfather gave her a worried hug. "Constance, I love you very much and I want only what's best for you. It would break my heart to see you follow the same disastrous path as your mother. Stick with Victor, my dear. Work on your marriage. And stop this self-defeating belief that people are only interested in you because of your money. Look at your mother's wasted life, and tell yourself that you're not going to repeat her destructive pattern."

"Divorcing Victor has got nothing to do with my mother. I'm not in the least like my mother."

"I know you're not." Her grandfather looked down at her, his eyes misty. "Have faith in yourself, Constance. Believe me when I say that Victor doesn't care about your money. Lord knows, I've met enough of your mother's fortune hunters to be able to recognize the breed at a glance." He pulled her close and kissed her forehead. "Now, dearest, take that sweetheart daughter of yours home and resolve that you're going to work things out with her father. Promise me, Constance. For Lili's sake, as well as your own."

She'd promised, of course. But for the first time in her life, Constance had no intention of honoring the promise she made to her grandfather. The tiring drive home provided plenty of scope for berating herself for past failures, but she was coming up short on plans for insuring that she retained custody of Lili.

She left the Mercedes at the garage and took a cab back to their apartment. In the elevator, inspiration struck.

Elena would help. The Pazmanys might not have much experience with trust funds and custody battles, but they had the best supply of common sense around. Even more important, they'd never managed to hide that they didn't like Victor.

Constance let herself and Lili into the apartment and walked toward the kitchen, calling to the housekeeper as she went. "I'm home, Eva."

Lili hopped over the marble tiles of the hallway. "No stepping on the cracks, Mommy, or else the tiger will eat you up."

"Okay." Constance went up on her toes and crept from one marble square to the next. Three steps on, she deliberately trod on the grouting.

"Oops, you missed. Now the tiger's going to eat you." Lili giggled, but her blue eyes were very wide, and there was a tiny hint of fear in her gaze. She was such an imaginative child and Constance marveled at how she could get totally caught up in the games she invented.

"I hear the tiger coming," Constance whispered.

"Oh, no!" Lili's mouth formed a circle of delicious terror.

Constance smiled, offering reassurance before Lili's game really scared her. "Or maybe it's just Eva coming to say hi. Yep, I guess this time we scared off the tiger."

"It's not Eva," Lili said. "It's another lady."

Constance straightened. She'd forgotten she was still standing on tiptoe, and swayed for a moment before recovering her balance. She turned and saw a middle-aged woman, brown hair scraped back into a bun, wearing a blue gingham coverall, her hands folded primly in front of her. To say that the woman didn't look friendly would have been a major understatement.

"Who are you?" Constance demanded, ill at ease even though the woman hardly seemed dangerous.

"Good evening, Mrs. Rodier. I'm Maureen O'Leary." She stopped, as if no further explanation were necessary.

"Should I know you?" Constance asked, thinking the soft Irish name was wasted on a woman who looked like the matron in charge of a reform school.

"I'm your new housekeeper, Mrs. Rodier." Maureen O'Leary shot a faintly disapproving glance in Lili's direction. "Would you like me to take the little girl and give her a bath?"

Constance felt Lili's hand tighten around hers. Absurdly, she actually felt guilty that Lili looked a bit disheveled after a windy fall day by the sea. "Thank you, but I'm afraid there's been some mistake, Mrs. O'Leary. You did say that was your name?"

"Yes, ma'am."

"Well, I didn't hire a new housekeeper. Where's Eva? Why didn't she call me when you arrived? She must have known I hadn't hired you."

A note of wariness entered Mrs. O'Leary's voice. "I was given to understand that you'd fired your previous housekeeper, Mrs. Rodier. She wasn't here when I arrived to take up my duties."

"Fired her? Fired Eva?" Constance stared at the woman. "What are you talking about? Eva was here when I left this morning. We agreed last night that she'd cook chicken potpie for Lili's supper—"

Lili tugged at her hand. "Mommy, where's Eva?" she asked in a small voice. "We don't know this lady, do we?"

"We sure don't." Constance, however, had a damn good idea where she'd sprung from. She bit her tongue to refrain from yelling at Mrs. O'Leary, who had probably done nothing to deserve it. "Did my husband hire you?"

Mrs. O'Leary was definitely beginning to look wary. "Well, I understood that you'd called the employment agency, Mrs. Rodier. But it was Mr. Rodier who interviewed me—"

"When? When did he interview you?"

"Yesterday morning—"

"Well, Constance, I see that you've met Mrs. O'Leary, our splendid new housekeeper." Victor emerged from his office and strode down the corridor, beaming as if he were presiding over a reunion between devoted, long-parted friends.

Constance had no intention of participating in Victor's charade. "Where's Eva?" she demanded. "What have you done with her?"

"Done with her? What an odd way of phrasing your question, my dear." Victor gave a small chuckle and exchanged a conspiratorial glance with Maureen O'Leary.

Constance spoke through clenched teeth. "I'll rephrase my question. Where is Eva, Victor?"

"Well, now, my dear, surely you remember that you got rather annoyed with Eva last week and told her she was to be out of the house by nine this morning—"

"I did no such thing. If you fired her, Victor, you can damn well un-fire her. Where did she go? To her son's home in Brooklyn? I want her back immediately." Constance turned to the silent Mrs. O'Leary, rage bestowing an odd, icy sort of calm.

"Mrs. O'Leary, I'm sorry that the situation here has been misrepresented to you. If you'll tell me what salary was agreed between you and my husband, I'll give you two weeks' wages in lieu of notice, and I'll call the employment agency tomorrow and explain that there's been a mistake—"

"There's been no mistake," Victor said. "Whether you remember the incident or not, Constance, you fired Eva last week, and she left this morning to catch a plane for California. She's gone to stay with her sister in California and I've hired Maureen as her replacement. Maureen is aware of the special circumstances in our household, and she feels that her experience as a practical nurse makes her well qualified to cope."

"What special circumstances? What the hell are you talking about, Victor? Why in the world would we need a nurse?"

He looked at her reprovingly. "Constance, please. Watch your language. No profanities in front of the child."

Lili clung to her mother's knees. "Mommy, I want Eva. Where is she? Has she gone?" Lili started to cry.

Swiftly, before Constance could react, Victor squatted so that he was eye level with his daughter. "Sugar-pie, no tears. You know how upset Daddy gets when you cry." He pulled out a snowy-white handkerchief and mopped at her eyes, turning her sobs to uncertain chuckles when he tickled beneath her chin. "I think Mrs. O'Leary has made a hot dog for your supper. Why don't you go with her into the kitchen while your mother and I have a little chat about some grown-up things?"

"Mommy?" Lili looked to Constance for permission.

"It's all right, sweetheart. We'll talk to Eva tomorrow and get her back as soon as we can. You go and eat your supper now."

Maureen O'Leary pinched her lips, but she held out her hand and spoke to Lili with perfect friendliness. "Come along then, dear. Let's see if I fixed your hot dog the way you like it."

"With ketchup," Lili said. She gave a tentative little skip as she tucked her hand into Mrs. O'Leary's. Lili's life was so full of love that she assumed everyone in the world was her best friend. "Do you like ketchup? I like ketchup. Eva likes ketchup, too."

"I prefer mustard on my hot dog," Mrs. O'Leary said. "But ketchup is good with French fries."

Constance waited until their voices faded completely before swinging around to confront her husband. "Would you be good enough to tell me what that ridiculous piece of playacting was all about? What the hell did you hope to achieve by pretending I'd fired Eva?"

"I was teaching you your place," he said coolly.

"By firing my housekeeper and then lying about it?" Constance was determined not to let Victor see how upset she was by his high-handed behavior. "Other than punishing your daughter, I've no idea what you expect to achieve."

"Perhaps I'm hoping you'll learn that I'm no longer willing to follow around behind you, cleaning up your messes." Victor spoke curtly. "You fired Eva once too often, and this time I decided I was tired of begging and pleading with her to overlook your foul temper and your violent mood swings. I decided just to let her go. I paid her enough money that she was willing to leave without causing a fuss. I certainly didn't want her to run to your grandparents carrying outrageous stories."

Constance felt the whole surface of her skin start to prickle. "What are you talking about, Victor? I've never said a cross word to Eva in my life. She's an absolute treasure."

"I'm not going to stand here arguing with you, Constance. I've learned that attempting to make you see reason is a waste of my valuable time. Maureen O'Leary understands that you haven't been well recently, and that you have days when you can't manage to get out of bed—"

Constance was suddenly ice-cold with fear. "The only day I didn't get out of bed in the past two years is the day after you raped me. And that's because when Lili and I had finished breakfast, you locked me in the bedroom and told Eva I didn't want to be disturbed."

"If that's the fantasy you want to believe tonight, Constance, then so be it. Until you're willing to get yourself the professional help you need, I guess Lili and I will just cope with your moods as best we can. You're my wife and Lili's mother, and what you need to remember is that we love you. We understand that you really can't help these lies you tell all the time."

Constance barely managed to refrain from lunging at his face and clawing his eyes out. "You conniving, deceitful son of a bitch! My God, I hate you! You sent Eva away because you couldn't convince her to look the other way when you mistreated me. My grandparents have known her for years, and if she told them you'd locked me in my bedroom, they'd believe her. You were afraid of her, so you fired her, you bastard!"

"Eva was a good woman, Constance. Let's not drag her into these paranoid delusions of yours."

"I don't have paranoid delusions." Her voice cracked and trembled with the force of her anger. "Don't think you're going to get away with this, Victor, because I won't let you. No way, no how. You picked the wrong woman to try this trick on."

"What trick, my dear? Oh, Mrs. O'Leary, I didn't hear you come back. Has my daughter finished her supper already?"

"She's eating it now." The woman eyed Constance with outright disapproval. What had she overheard? Constance wondered. Probably the edifying moment when she'd called Victor a lying son of a bitch right after he'd said how much he loved her. "The reason I came back, Mr. Rodier, is that Lili has some spots behind her ears. It looks to me as if she might be coming down with chicken pox. I did hear there was a lot of it going around right now."

Much later, when Constance had all the time in the world to look back and wonder about might-have-beens, she did ask herself if Victor could have imprisoned her so successfully if it hadn't been for Lili's chicken pox. Sometimes she thought the answer might be no, but most of the time she felt certain that if her daughter had not gotten sick, he would have found some other circumstance to twist to his advantage.

Lili came down with a relatively mild case of chicken pox. It kept her bed-bound for two days, itching for two more, and housebound for another week while the spots scabbed over and finally disappeared. Constance, preoccupied with taking care of Lili, as well as trying to track down Eva, avoid losing her temper with the rigid Mrs. O'Leary and advance her plans for divorcing Victor, never gave a thought to the possibility that she might catch the disease from her daughter. When she woke up one morning in a cold sweat, with a blinding headache, she couldn't imagine what was wrong.

Victor soon enlightened her. "Your face is covered with chicken pox," he said, lip curling in distaste. "I'll see that the doctor comes to check you over."

"I can go to him. Doctors don't make house calls anymore."

"You're not well enough to leave the apartment. I'll speak to Dr. Armon personally and make sure he understands that. Ah, Mrs. O'Leary," Victor said as the woman appeared in their bedroom doorway, "as you can see, my poor wife has succumbed to the chicken pox. Perhaps you could help move her things into one of the guest bedrooms until she's well again? She needs to be able to sleep undisturbed."

"Yes, sir. I'll see to it right away."

"Mrs. Rodier also seems to be running a fever, so I'm going to ask Dr. Armon to stop by and see her. She shouldn't go out. And perhaps you'd better keep Lili away from her. It's exhausting to have a small child bouncing all over you when you don't feel well."

"Yes, of course, Mr. Rodier. Don't worry. I'll take good care of your wife."

"I'm sure you will, Mrs. O'Leary. You've only been with us a short time, but I already know it was a lucky day for me when I was able to persuade you to come and join our family."

"Thank you, Mr. Rodier. I enjoy working for you, and Lili's a sweet child."

Constance closed her eyes, feeling too sick to watch the housekeeper preen and simper for her husband. It was amazing that other women never seemed to sense the deadly coldness at the heart of him. But it had taken her almost four years of marriage to get the full measure of the man, and she was still learning the depths of his deceit. Perhaps, she thought wearily, she shouldn't blame Mrs. O'Leary for being dazzled after two weeks.

The housekeeper, in fact, proved quite a kindly nurse and Constance needed all the kindness she could get. The chicken pox, which had barely bothered Lili, nearly did Constance in. Her head pounded sickeningly if she tried to lift it from the pillow, and when she stood up, she felt weak, nauseated and dizzy. And the spots! She had spots up her nose, on the edge of her eyelids, on the soles of her feet and inside her belly button. Nothing seemed to ease the itching, and if she did manage to drift off to sleep, she would soon wake up and find herself staring at bloody fingers that she'd used to scratch one of the spots raw.

For a week, it took every scrap of energy to get out of bed when she needed to go to the bathroom. If Mrs. O'Leary hadn't patiently spooned cream of wheat down her throat and brought her glasses of ginger ale, she would have gone for days without eating or drinking. Constance was even grateful to Victor for coming home early one day and driving Lili to Hatterington. She had to admit that Lili required a higher-octane energy than she could find.

The morning finally came when Constance woke up and felt like a human being again. She could hardly wait to get out of bed to take a shower, although she was so weak after days of vomiting and semistarvation that she had to hold on to the furniture to make it from the bed to bath.

The shower was worth the effort. Feeling like a new woman, she dragged herself back into the bedroom and examined the meager supply of clothing that had been transferred to the guest bedroom. Two robes, a pair of slippers and some underwear. She was tying the belt on one of the robes when the housekeeper came into the room.

"Mrs. Rodier! It's nice to see you up and about." Mrs. O'Leary put down a tray that held a bowl of cream of wheat and the usual glass of ginger ale. "You've had a shower. You must be feeling better."

"Much better, thank you." In reality, Constance was already paying the price for her burst of activity and felt like a wrung-out dishrag.

"Why don't you eat your cream of wheat while it's hot?" the housekeeper suggested. "You need to rebuild your strength."

Constance grimaced. "Cream of wheat reminds me of how terrible I felt these past few days. Would you be offended if I skipped the cereal today?"

"Well, you need to eat."

"What I really fancy is a piece of crisp toast."

"I could make that. And would you like a cup of tea to go with it, maybe?"

"Tea sounds heavenly."

Mrs. O'Leary actually smiled. "Tea and toast coming right up, Mrs. Rodier."

After breakfast, Constance slept most of the day, waking only to appease her suddenly ravenous appetite. Mrs. O'Leary's bedside manner was brisk to the point of gruffness, but her hands were gentle. By early evening, fortified by several cups of weak tea and more toast, Constance was feeling robust enough to sit with the housekeeper in the kitchen while they shared a dinner of chicken noodle soup and homemade biscuits. It would be too much to say that Mrs. O'Leary had a sense of humor, Constance decided, but it no longer seemed impossible to imagine getting along with her until Eva could be found. After all, it wasn't Mrs. O'Leary's fault that Victor had hired her under false pretenses.

Her husband still wasn't home when she went back to bed at eight o'clock, but Constance was delighted to avoid him. With returning strength, she was starting to plot divorce strategies again, and she had no desire whatever to see Victor. She decided that, by the weekend, she'd be fit enough to drive to Hatterington and pick up Lili. After that, she'd visit Elena and Ralph and get their advice. Between the three of them, they'd be able to come up with a plan. After all, this was 1969, not the Dark Ages. Even a husband like Victor couldn't keep her chained to a marriage she was determined to end.

On that somewhat cheerful thought, Constance fell into the deepest, most peaceful sleep she'd enjoyed in more than a week.

She awoke to the sound of voices outside her bedroom door. Victor and Maureen O'Leary. The bedside clock showed that it was ten-thirty.

"Now that my wife's up and about again, you'll have to start watching her very closely," Victor said.

"I understand, Mr. Rodier." The housekeeper hesitated. "Although she didn't seem edgy today. Not as if she was looking for a drink or anything. To tell you the truth, she seemed real normal, anxious to see her little girl again, and real polite to me."

"My wife is a victim, Mrs. O'Leary, not a monster. Of course she was anxious to see Lili. She loves her daughter, and she's always tried hard to be a good mother. As I explained to you in our initial interview, Mrs. Rodier will have brief periods when she seems to cope quite well without alcohol or drugs. Then she'll relapse. Remember the first day you came here, and you'll understand what we're up against. You saw how she reacted to your presence. Denial, refusal to accept responsibility for her own behavior—"

"And she was drunk, I realized that right off," the housekeeper said. "She hid it well, but I'm used to looking for the signs. I caught her off guard, and when she turned around to speak to me, she tottered so bad on those high heels of hers, I thought she was going to fall."

"Very perceptive of you, Mrs. O'Leary. Make sure you watch her closely tomorrow. On no account let her out of the house, whatever excuse she dreams up. You know how many of those pills we destroyed when we searched the house. Once she discovers that her secret stash is gone, she'll be desperate to get a new prescription. We mustn't let her succeed. I'm confident if we can just keep her off those cursed diet pills for a couple of months, the problem will solve itself.''

"You can count on me, Mr. Rodier. Good night, I'll see you at six-thirty tomorrow morning."

"Good night, Mrs. O'Leary. And thanks again for everything."

Constance heard the soft, rubber-soled thud of Mrs. O'Leary's steps moving away. Stunned into momentary paralysis, she didn't move or speak when Victor walked quietly into her bedroom and crossed over to the bed.

She realized how important it was not to let him know what she'd overheard. She kept her eyes closed and tried to breathe regularly. When she felt her eyelids flicker, she deliberately made a sleepy, snuffling noise and turned onto her side, burying her face in the pillow.

Victor stood watching her for at least five agonizing minutes. God knows what he was thinking. Probably plotting new and better ways to convince everyone she was a drug-addicted lush, Constance thought bitterly. She'd never detected any particular affection for Lili in him, and she couldn't quite understand why he was concocting such an elaborate plan simply to insure that he got custody of their daughter. Or did he really think that he could use the threat of losing Lili to prevent her from seeking a divorce?

She puzzled over that for a long time after Victor had left her room, locking the door behind him. He'd already convinced her grandparents that she was irresponsible and irrational. He was working hard to persuade Mrs. O'Leary that nothing she said could be trusted. If she went into a divorce court and claimed that he'd been committing adultery with Daphne Lambert and multitudes of other women, she would have a hard time getting anyone to believe her, especially since Daphne Lambert had so much to lose by admitting to the affair. Daphne wanted to remain Mrs. Charles Lambert, leader of the New York social scene, main beneficiary of Chuck's will. She wasn't about to blow everything she'd worked for by confessing that she'd allowed herself to be seduced in her own husband's bedroom.

Constance tossed and turned, sleep stubbornly elusive. Something was missing in her understanding of what was going on. However cleverly he schemed, ultimately Victor must realize that his machinations only made it more certain that she would divorce him. Maybe he would gain custody of Lili, maybe he would succeed in ruining Constance's reputation, but his ultimate goal—control of her multimillion-dollar trust fund—would surely elude him. He might get an allowance of a few thousand dollars a year for Lili's education, but that would be nothing compared to what he would be losing. So why wasn't he falling over himself to effect a reconciliation?

Her bedroom was taking on the subtle gray hues of dawn when the answer came to her. Of course. Why had it taken her so long to understand? Victor didn't intend to divorce her. He intended to kill her.

Seventeen

December, 1969

Maureen O'Leary took her assignment as guard dog seriously, and it was three days before Constance could escape the housekeeper's vigilance. Given the severity of her bout with chicken pox, Constance actually felt quite well, but she didn't let either Victor or Mrs. O'Leary know that. Instead, she exaggerated her few remaining symptoms, complaining constantly of fatigue. To a certain extent, her ploy worked. Seeing that she was docile but no longer in need of constant nursing, Victor arranged for Liliana to be brought home from Hatterington over the weekend, and Mrs. O'Leary gradually relaxed her guard.

On Friday afternoon, as usual, Constance said that she was feeling sleepy and needed to lie down. She'd heard Victor mention the night before that the parquet floors in the living room were due to get their quarterly clean and polish, so she bided her time until the housekeeper was occupied at the other end of the penthouse, supervising the work crew. With the hum of floor polishers drowning out betraying sounds of her activity, Constance figured she would have somewhere between ten and fifteen minutes to get out of the apartment.

She had her escape plan all worked out. She drew the drapes tightly closed, tucked a pillow under the bedcovers and rearranged her bedside lamp so that it blocked the view from the doorway. The resulting scene wouldn't have fooled Victor for a second. Constance could only hope Mrs. O'Leary would be less perceptive.

It seemed ridiculous to be afraid of the doormen in her own apartment building, but Constance wasn't going to make the mistake of underestimating her husband ever again. Who knew what crazy story he might have fabricated to make sure they didn't let her outside? She'd already discovered that Victor had been through her purse and removed her money, her checkbook and her charge cards for Saks and Bloomingdale's, but she hoped there would be enough loose change in Lili's piggy bank to buy a few subway tokens. Praying that the workmen wouldn't turn off their machines right as a door or floorboard creaked, she crept into her daughter's nursery, shoes in hand, grabbed the piggy bank, then ran back into the kitchen.

Mrs. O'Leary, thank God, was still occupied with warning the cleaning crew not to bang their equipment into the furniture. Constance slipped out the back door and headed for the service stairs. Her luck held. The stairs were deserted, and, eight minutes after Mrs. O'Leary first let the cleaners into the apartment, Constance emerged triumphant onto Sixty-third Street. Ducking out of sight of the doormen, she hunched inside her jacket and walked quickly toward the Lexington Avenue subway, inhaling gulps of chilly December air that tasted like nectar after three weeks of being imprisoned in the apartment.

She wished she could drive out to Hatterington, reclaim Lili and escape to a safe haven where Victor wouldn't be able to find them until the divorce was finalized. A sim-

ple-sounding goal, but impossible to achieve. Her grandparents would call Victor within seconds of her leaving
their house with Lili. She needed to bide her time until Lili
came home to the apartment tomorrow. Even then, escape wasn't going to be easy.

Constance had concluded that her father's younger
brother would be the most likely person to help her. Uncle
David had always been fond of her, and he lived in Cleveland, a town where Victor had no contacts. What's more,
David Howington was a corporate lawyer for one of the
nation's largest oil companies, and was distinguished
enough not to be intimidated by Victor's impressive legal
credentials. She knew her uncle traveled a lot on business,
but Constance had no intention of calling him to find out
his upcoming travel schedule. She was learning to be wary
of signaling her plans in any way that Victor could get wind
of. She *almost* trusted her uncle David, but she couldn't
take the risk that he might call her grandparents—or Victor—to check out her story.

Hurrying into the subway station, Constance counted
the money from Lili's piggy bank. Five dollars and sixty-
seven cents. Enough to buy a one-way ticket to Hatterington. It had been almost a week since she last saw Lili, the
longest they'd ever been separated. Constance resisted the
urge to ride out to her grandparents' home and demand
that they hand over Lili. Better to stick to her original plan.
Leave her grandparents entirely out of the escape loop. Go
to Elena's, and beg for help.

It took her less than thirty minutes to reach Elena's
neighborhood in Queens. There were no subway delays,
the rain had stopped, and Elena was home. Constance
hadn't realized how close she was to the breaking point
until Elena opened the door, wrapped her in a warm hug—
and Constance burst into tears.

"My God, Connie, what is it?" Elena tossed Constance's jacket over a hook and took her straight into the kitchen. "I'd like to lie and say you're looking great, but the fact is, you look like hell."

"It's been a rough few weeks. I had chicken pox among other things."

"Oh, no! That's always so much worse when you get it as an adult. How's Lili? Did she have it, too?"

"Yes, but she's fine. She's been staying with my grandparents for the past few days." Constance wiped her eyes and tried to smile. "It's good to see you, Lena."

"You, too, honey. Sit down before you fall down. You look really frazzled."

Constance sat at the kitchen table. "I feel a lot better now I'm here with you."

Elena set a pot of coffee on the stove. "I tried to call you a dozen times, but I could never get past Victor and that dragon lady he's hired as a housekeeper."

"You know about her?"

"Yes. I got this incredible letter from Eva out in California. She wrote that Victor fired her, but he gave her so much money to leave without making a fuss that she'll never have to work again. She says he personally drove her to the airport and put her on the plane and that she never had a chance to say goodbye to you."

"Let me have Eva's address, will you? I need to write to her."

"Sure." Elena searched in a drawer and pulled out an envelope. "Here, you can read her letter. The address is inside." She brought coffee and cream to the table and took two ceramic mugs from the cupboard. "Now, tell me what's going on. Everything."

Constance wrapped her hands around her coffee mug. "*Everything* might take us a couple of days."

"Then give me the condensed version."

"I need help, Lena. I badly need help."

"Anything Ralph and I can do, we will. You did so much for us when Jessica Marie was sick, we owe you big-time. So tell me what the problem is."

Constance drew in a shaky breath. "I think Victor's trying to kill me."

At least Elena didn't laugh or ask her if she'd gone crazy. She stirred her coffee, then added more cream and stirred again. "Why would Victor want to kill you?" she asked at last.

"For my money," Constance said.

"I don't understand how killing you makes Victor rich. All your money's tied up in a family trust and surely, with you dead, the trust would go to Liliana?"

"In theory that's true. But Victor would be Lili's sole living guardian, so he could spend the money almost any way he wanted."

"But presumably under strict supervision. Would that be worth killing you for?"

Constance shivered. "I notice you don't dispute the fact that Victor's capable of committing murder. You're just questioning why he would bother."

Elena was silent for a long time. "I guess it's okay for me to say this now, but I've never trusted Victor. On the other hand, that doesn't mean I accept that he's planning murder. I still don't see how your death would benefit him."

"I'd call having access to four or five million dollars in Lili's trust fund a pretty big benefit."

"Why? He already has access to that same four or five million through you."

Constance frowned, trying to find the words to make Elena understand. "Victor isn't greedy in the usual sense.

He doesn't want to go out and buy a luxury yacht, or keep a string of racehorses, or fly around the world in a private plane. But he wants to have the *power* to do those things if he chooses, without reference to me. He hates the fact that I have more money than him. Does that make any sense at all?''

"Sort of. But from Victor's point of view, wouldn't it be easier to do a deal with you? Why run the risk of murder?" Elena shook her head bemusedly. "Lord almighty, Connie, listen to what I just said. Okay, Victor is a world-class creep and I've never trusted him, but this conversation is nuts! We're talking about regular people here, living in the real world. This isn't the movies. Respectable lawyers don't plot the death of their wives. If Victor wants money from you, all he has to do is offer you a quickie divorce in exchange for a payoff."

"You mean, I pay him a million bucks, and he agrees not to contest the divorce?"

"Yes, something like that."

Constance got up and paced around the cozy kitchen. "On the face of it, you're right. Which is why I keep asking myself why I'm so sure he's planning to kill me."

"And what answer did you come up with?"

"I've decided that he's scared of me. Victor has this public image that he's desperate to maintain, and I'm the person who can blow the whistle and expose him. If Victor lets me divorce him, he's afraid that I'll tell people about his affairs. and if I name names, and quote dates, then his brilliant career will be over."

Elena shot her a quizzical glance. "Do you really have the lowdown on him?"

"Yes. Victor lost his temper with me a couple of times and said things I'm sure he regretted later. I've not only caught him committing adultery with his boss's wife, I've been thinking back, remembering little incidents, putting them into a fresh perspective. I bet I could tell you the names of at least half a dozen married women that Victor's seduced in the past four years."

Elena pulled a face. "I'd have thought that was more of a problem for the women he seduced than for Victor. What about the infamous double standard? If two married people have an affair, the woman's a whore, but the man's a stud."

"The fact that he's committed adultery wouldn't be a problem for Victor if he'd seduced clerks and shop assistants. He runs with a high-powered crowd, and I don't suppose his sophisticated lawyer friends give a damn whether or not he's faithful to me. But they sure don't expect him to seduce *their* wives. And they sure as hell don't want the reputation of the firm sullied by a public revelation that Victor's been screwing the wives of his clients. That's the ultimate no-no, like a doctor having sex with his patient. The bottom line is that Victor knows I could ruin him, and he's not going to let that happen."

"Even if I accept that Victor wants to kill you, how's he going to do it?" Elena asked. "It's not that easy to commit murder and get away with it."

"He's laid a lot of the groundwork already," Constance said. "He's gotten rid of Eva, he's convinced our new housekeeper that I'm a drug addict and he's keeping me locked up in the apartment, away from my friends. I think he's going to arrange for me to fall when I'm supposedly drunk. Or perhaps he'll push me out the window and tell everyone I threw myself over the ledge when I was high on acid—"

"My God," Elena said. "You're serious, aren't you? You're really serious. You think your husband wants to kill you."

"Yes," Constance said quietly. "I'm nearly certain of it."

"Shouldn't you go to the police?"

Constance almost laughed. "Victor would probably like me to do that. He's managed to convince my own grandparents that I'm borderline crazy. Can you imagine what he'd say to the police?"

"Do you want to stay here?" Elena offered. "You shouldn't be in the apartment with him, Connie."

"I can't leave Victor until Lili comes home from my grandparents'. If I stayed here tonight, Victor might claim I'd abandoned him and Lili. And Mrs. O'Leary would back him up."

"So what are you going to do?"

"I'm going to take Lili to my uncle David's house and ask for his help. He's my father's brother and he's a corporate lawyer. Not the sort of man to be bullied, even by Victor. But I may need somewhere to stay with Lili, just for a couple of days, until I can make arrangements to fly to Cleveland. If I could stay with you, Lena . . ."

"Of course you can," Elena said at once. "Or come to our new apartment if you can't get away until after next week. We're moving. Let me give you the address and the directions on how to get there. Here, I have it all written down."

Constance studied the sheet of paper in silence for a long while. "Okay, I have the directions memorized. I don't want to write anything down."

Elena's expression became grim. "You don't want Victor to know where we're living."

"No, I really don't. I don't think he'd hurt you, Elena, or I wouldn't have asked you to help. It's just that I don't want him to have even the slightest clue as to where Lili and I have gone."

"I understand."

"And you'd better not call me at my apartment. Mrs. O'Leary reports every incoming call to Victor and we don't want to remind him you and Ralph exist."

Elena's face paled. "Connie, this is beyond a joke. Can't you fire her? It's dreadful to be spied on like that."

Constance shrugged. "Victor might replace her with somebody worse. Mrs. O'Leary isn't a bad sort, she's just been duped. Victor has her convinced that I'm either a drunk or a drug addict, or possibly both. She thinks she's protecting me from my own worst self if she tells him who's called and what they said. Victor has her conned into believing all my incoming calls are from drug dealers or friends who sit around with me shooting heroin."

Elena shook her head. "Connie, are you sure you should go back there?"

"No, I'm not sure," she admitted. "But until I can walk out of that apartment with Lili, I can't walk out."

Elena gave her a final hug. "Ralph and I will be waiting for you," she said. "Remember, any time, night or day, you can come to us."

"Thanks, Elena. You and Ralph are the greatest."

Chilly dusk had changed to bitingly cold night by the time Constance got home. She'd braced herself to face Victor's wrath, but she wasn't prepared for the hatred with which he greeted her as she walked into the living room.

"Where the hell have you been?" He threw down the file he'd been reading and strode over to grab her, his manner so menacing that she stepped back from the force of his anger.

She was ashamed of her fear, and she lifted her chin defiantly. "I went for a walk."

He stripped off her jacket and tossed it aside, dragging her over to the fireplace where fake logs glowed with electric fervor. He pushed up the sleeve of her sweater and felt the bare skin of her arm. "You're freezing cold. You've probably given yourself pneumonia."

She shivered, but it was from revulsion at his touch, not from the cold. "I'm tired. I'd like to go to bed. Let go of my arm, Victor."

"Certainly, my dear." The sudden softness of his voice chilled her far more effectively than the December wind. Instead of loosening, his grip on her arm tightened and she felt a sharp, painful prick in her upper arm.

"What are you doing?" The jolt of fear she felt was immediate and intense. When she realized that he'd injected her with something, she felt the blood drain from her face. "Have you poisoned me, Victor?"

"Don't talk rubbish," he said, pulling down the sleeve of her sweater and picking up the glass of scotch he'd been drinking when she came in. "You're crazy as well as drunk." Before she could think, much less move, he shoved the glass between her lips, pouring the liquor down her throat.

She spat it out and wrenched free of his arms, coughing and spluttering. "You're the one who's mad!" she said in a choking voice. "Victor, I honest to God think you've gone totally insane." She turned to push past him, but her legs couldn't seem to obey the command to walk. She tottered forward, her sense of space so distorted that she careened into a side table, sending the lamp crashing to the floor.

Victor's face loomed over her, his obscenely huge teeth protruding from a mouth that was waiting to devour her. A nightmarish image of Little Red Riding Hood flashed into her mind. Her tongue struggled to give shape to the words inside her head. "Don' tush me," she moaned. "Go 'way, big bad wolf."

Victor leaned closer. She screamed.

Through a blur of dancing colors, she saw Mrs. O'Leary come running into the living room. "My word, whatever is going on?"

"My wife's finally come home," Victor said. His voice sounded tired and defeated.

"Oh, my goodness! Is she . . . all right?"

"I'm afraid not. She's been drinking. I dreaded having this happen again. Could you help me get her into bed, Mrs. O'Leary?"

"Yes, Mr. Rodier. Oh, my heavens, she reeks of liquor."

"Yes, I'm afraid she really tied one on this time."

Constance pushed feebly at the arms coming at her from all sides. "Haven't bin drinkin'," she protested. "Drugged. . . ."

"Dear Lord, is she saying she's taken drugs?"

Constance's thoughts seemed to rise and fall like the swell of ocean waves. She wanted to tell Mrs. O'Leary something, but she'd already forgotten what. Victor had injected her with some sort of drug. That was it. She had to speak now, make the housekeeper understand.

Her mouth opened. She heard herself make a gurgling sound. She closed her eyes.

Ed decided he couldn't allow Constance to talk any longer. Her voice was becoming hoarse, and she was visibly approaching the point of physical and mental exhaustion. Somewhere in the middle of her extraordinary story he realized that he'd stopped listening to her as a doctor dealing with a delusional patient and had started listening to her with horrified fascination. He wanted to hear the end of her story, to find out how Liliana had died and Constance had ended up in a maximum-security mental hospital. But first, she needed some time to relax. He poured her a glass of ice water and walked over to her side. Holding out the glass, he put his arm around her shoulders.

"Here, Constance, drink this. Your throat sounds sore from talking."

She took the glass but avoided his eyes. "You don't believe me, do you? Why would you, anyway? It's a fantastic story."

He heard the weight of grief behind her question, the dull, resigned acceptance that nobody would ever accept her version of events. For a split second, Ed hesitated. Was he really ready to put his ass on the line and fight to get the world to acknowledge that Constance Rodier wasn't insane, and that the Honorable Judge Victor Rodier had almost certainly treated her with criminal violence? *That* sure wasn't going to be an easy story to sell to the public or to the Merton House board of directors. He considered hedging his bets. He could hide behind one of the soothing platitudes of his profession, neither accepting nor denying the truth of her story until he'd investigated further. Then he realized that, after twenty-six years of mental torture, Constance deserved something better from him than cautious ass-covering.

"I believe you," he said.

Obviously startled, her head jerked up. She looked at him and he could tell that she saw he was telling the truth— he really believed her. Ed felt as if he were watching the scene in the *Wizard of Oz* where Dorothy opens the door and steps out of the black-and-white world of Kansas into the Technicolor magic of the Land of Oz. Constance was transformed before his eyes. Slowly, carefully, as if she'd almost forgotten how, she shaped her mouth into a radiant smile. "You don't think I'm crazy," she said.

"No, I don't think you're crazy." Ed found her smile captivating. He had trouble looking away, but this session had already spilled over into the lunch hour. He had less than five minutes to get himself to the boardroom, where he was supposed to be eating lunch with two of the doctors on staff and a research team from the University of North Carolina.

He took her hand and cradled it between his own, a sympathetic gesture he'd used a hundred times with his patients, male as well as female, young and old alike. But his feelings on this occasion were different, oddly personal, as if Constance were a friend he wanted to comfort. Disconcerted, he dropped her hand and went to his desk, depressing the intercom. "Elaine? Let Doctors Brady and Green know I'm on my way, will you?"

"Yes, Doctor. You have seven urgent phone messages."

"I'll get to them right after lunch." Ed disconnected and turned back to Constance. "I'm already late for a meeting," he said. "Any minute now, Elaine is going to fire me."

Constance smiled again, still having the same strange effect on him. Ed blinked and cleared his throat. "I'm going to order a sandwich for you to eat in your room, Constance. I don't think you should have to brave the dining room today. Then I'd like you to spend the afternoon in the garden. It's a beautiful day, and the humidity isn't too high. Walk around a little, take a snooze if you feel like it and try to relax. Then we'll talk again."

"Next week?" she asked. "We'll talk next week?"

"No, tonight. You've waited twenty-six years to get somebody to listen to you, Constance. I guess that's long enough. Come to my office right after dinner, and we'll spend however much time it takes to get to the end of this story."

She turned her head away. "Thank you." Her voice was muffled. "I'm really grateful to you, Ed ... Doctor."

It saddened him to think that she should be so grateful to him when he had done nothing except listen with an open mind while she talked. He crossed to her side and crooked his finger under her chin, tilting her head to look at her. He brushed his fingers across her eyelids and felt the wetness of her tears on his skin. His throat felt suddenly tight. He suspected there had been far too many tears in Constance's life, and not nearly enough laughter. "Walk with me as far as the lobby," he said, opening the door to his office.

When they came out into the little reception area where Elaine worked, she stood up, stepped around her desk and physically barred his passage. "Here are your phone messages," she said. "I think you'd better call the mayor before he goes into cardiac arrest."

Ed took the sheaf of messages. "I'm working on it, okay? I'll get to all these before five, that's a promise." He turned and strode so fast along the corridors that Constance had to run to catch up with him.

"I don't think Elaine approves of me," she said.

"Don't worry. Elaine doesn't approve of me, either."

She laughed. "Do you think she practices that disapproving squint over her glasses in front of a mirror."

"No, I'm sure it's a natural talent." He stopped at the point where their paths diverged. "Take care, Constance. I'll see you tonight."

"Yes." Her voice was husky. She turned quickly and walked away.

Ed realized he was staring at her retreating back. He shook his head impatiently, and continued toward the boardroom, shuffling through his phone messages as he walked. The mayor's office had called twice. Dr. Fellini from U. Penn wanted to talk about his preliminary research findings concerning the effects of sleep deprivation on his chimpanzees. Jessica Marie Zajak had called three times in three hours. She left no message except to say that she needed to speak urgently with the medical director of Merton House in connection with one of his patients.

Ed paused with his hand on the boardroom door. What an odd coincidence, he thought. Constance told him just this morning about the tragic death of Jessica Marie Pazmany, and minutes later somebody called Jessica Marie wants to talk to him.

He pushed open the door and greeted the people waiting for him. The kitchens at Merton House would have done credit to the finest of country clubs, and the lunch spread out at one end of the boardroom table was perfect for a hot summer's day. Ed helped himself absentmindedly to strawberries and a smattering of finger sandwiches.

He tried to listen as the residents and the university researchers made some important comments about the need for reliable, controlled studies of the effects of experimental drugs on mental-health patients. During a pause in the discussion, Dr. Green turned to him. "What do you think, Ed? Do you think the results from Howard's study of prisoners on death row can be applied to a more general population?"

"Where's area code 303?" Ed asked. "Isn't that in Colorado?"

Silence fell around the table. Dr. Brady cleared his throat. "I believe it's the area code for Denver, Ed. My brother lives there."

Denver. Jessica Marie Zajak had called him from Denver. She hadn't said which patient she wanted to talk to him about, and she couldn't possibly have anything to do with Constance. According to Constance, Jessica Marie Pazmany had been dead for years. He looked up and realized that four pairs of eyes were watching him.

"Excuse me, will you please?" He pushed back his chair. "I have to make an urgent phone call. But please do carry on with your discussion. I'll be back in a minute."

The phone offering the best hope of privacy stood on a table at the far end of the room. The discussion around the boardroom table resumed, stilted at first, then gaining momentum. He dialed Jessica Marie Zajak's number and realized that his pulse was racing in a manner that was altogether ridiculous on any rational grounds.

A man answered the phone. "Hello."

"This is Dr. Edgar Foster of Merton House. I'm looking for somebody called Jessica Marie Zajak."

Did he imagine the sudden increase in tension at the other end of the phone? Hell, of course he imagined it. His behavior over the past five minutes had been slightly nuttier than that of the average Merton House inmate.

"Hold on a moment, please, Doctor. I'll get Jess for you."

A female voice came onto the phone. "Dr. Foster?"

"Yes."

"Doctor, you don't know me, but my name is Jessica Zajak. Are you the doctor who's in charge of patient care at Merton House? I'm sorry if I'm pestering the wrong person, but we've had a really difficult time finding out who I should call."

"I'm the medical director here. If you'll tell me what information you need, I'll try to direct your call to the appropriate person."

"This is very awkward for me, Doctor. I need to talk to you urgently about one of your patients. But it's so difficult to explain the situation that I'd much prefer to speak with you in person, if that's possible."

"Which patient do you want to see me about, Ms. Zajak? Is he or she a relative?"

There was a long pause. "This is a very complicated situation, Doctor. I know I keep saying that, but it's almost impossible to give you a capsule version of my problem over the phone. The patient I want to talk to you about is called Constance Rodier. Do you know her personally?"

Ed tried to absorb what she said: she wanted to talk to him about Constance, and her name was Jessica Marie. Afraid of making an utter fool of himself, Ed spoke with exaggerated care. "Yes, Ms. Zajak. I know Mrs. Rodier."

"Is she—" Jessica Marie's breath caught audibly. "Is she able to recognize people? D-does she understand when people ask her questions?"

"I'm sorry, Ms. Zajak. You must realize that I can't give out patient information."

"No, of course, you can't. Forgive me, I'm not thinking straight. Dr. Foster, I really need to see you. I know you have no reason to believe me, but I assure you, this is important. You're on East Coast time, and we're two hours behind you here, but we've checked with the airlines already and if we leave from Denver tomorrow morning, we can catch a flight to Washington, D.C., and then get a connection that would have us in Durham late in the afternoon. If we pick up a rental car at the airport, we could arrive at Merton House around six or seven tomorrow evening. Is there any chance that you'd be willing to see us at such short notice?''

Ed knew he was being totally idiotic, but he had to ask the question anyway. ''Ms. Zajak, before we discuss my schedule for tomorrow night, could you tell me if you're married? And if you are, what was your maiden name?''

''Zajak *is* my maiden name.''

Ed relaxed his white-knuckle grip on the phone. What else had he expected her to say? It was ridiculous to keep pressing the issue, but somehow he couldn't leave it alone. ''I have one more question for you, Ms. Zajak. Do you by any chance know a family called Pazmany? Rudolph and Elena Pazmany, to be precise.'' He waited for her to say no. Christ almighty, of course she was going to say no.

''I know them,'' she said. After a tiny pause, she added, ''Until six weeks ago, I thought they were my parents.''

Ed used his sleeve to wipe the sweat from his forehead. ''I'm going to hang up now, Ms. Zajak, because I have several people waiting to speak with me. But I agree with you that it's very important for us to meet. I'll look forward to seeing you. I believe we'll have a lot to talk about.''

Eighteen

Constance looked younger and prettier every time he saw her, Ed thought. Tonight there was an attractive glow of color in her cheeks and a soft sheen to her newly washed hair. She was reed-slim and less than average height, but in the moss-green dress she'd chosen to wear, she appeared petite and feminine rather than thin. His wife had always teased him that she could put on orange eyeliner and blue lipstick and he wouldn't notice anything amiss, but he noticed tonight that Constance had miraculously recovered all those mysterious female skills that enable women to look eminently desirable.

Ed pulled up short at the word *desirable*, then realized it was the right one. Constance looked so attractive tonight that he needed to remind himself that she was his patient and there were strict professional guidelines as to how he could behave toward her. Incredible to think back a few short weeks to the pathetic and seemingly psychotic woman he'd met when he first came to Merton House.

"Would you like some coffee?" he asked, gesturing to the two small armchairs he'd arranged in a corner of the room, away from the formality of his desk.

"No, thank you. I had two cups at dinnertime." Constance sat down, arranging her skirt rather awkwardly around her knees. She clasped her hands in her lap and looked as if she was trying hard to find something to say. He realized this after-hours visit to his office might be the closest she'd come in years to anything even approximating a social visit, and he was struck anew by how normal she'd managed to keep herself for a woman surrounded by the isolating walls of a mental hospital.

Ed set his mug of black coffee on the low table, and smiled at her. Not merely a professional smile, but a warm smile of admiration for her courage in surviving years of incarceration with her soul more or less intact. "Constance, this is a difficult situation for both of us. I want you to know that everything you've told me will remain absolutely confidential until you decide otherwise. But I also want you to know that, as far as I'm concerned, tonight I'm not just listening to you as your doctor, I'm listening to you as your friend."

"Thank you." She looked away, biting her bottom lip. "Friends have been in short supply in my life, Doctor, which makes me doubly grateful for your friendship."

"Tonight isn't going to be easy for you," he warned. "When you tell me what happened to your daughter, I imagine you'll be confronting some powerful demons."

"I know." For a moment, all the color drained out of her face, leaving her cheeks gaunt and pale. Then she shook her hair out of her eyes and squared her shoulders, visibly bracing herself.

"All right, then, let's get started." Ed gave her hand a quick squeeze. "When you got back from the Pazmanys' apartment, Victor injected you with some drug that made you act drunk and uncoordinated. What happened next?"

"My grandparents brought Lili back the next day, as they'd agreed." She plunged into her story as if afraid to take any more time to stop and consider. "Victor did his usual brilliant job of pretending to shield my problems from them while all the time cleverly conveying the impression that I spent most of my days in a drug-induced haze. My grandmother suggested sending me to a drug rehab center, which was the last thing Victor wanted, of course, so he quickly backtracked and said he'd take care of me with Mrs. O'Leary's help."

"Did you try to convince your grandparents that you weren't addicted to drugs? Or to alcohol?"

Constance shook her head. "I'd already decided that the smartest thing to do was to keep my mouth shut tight and wait for the chance to escape to Elena's with Lili." She gave a wry grimace. "I guess you'd say that's another example of how I always try to solve my problems by running away from them, but I still don't see what alternatives I had. I assumed that once we were at my uncle David's house, out of Victor's clutches, it would be fairly easy to convince people that I was a good mother, who wasn't hooked on diet pills, or alcohol, or anything else."

"Running away isn't *always* the wrong choice," Ed said. "If you meet a bear in the forest, it's a lot smarter to climb a tree than try to tame the bear."

"And Victor has such very long, sharp claws." She smiled, then quickly sobered. "Anyway, for good or ill, I'd given up trying to convince people Victor was lying. I was determined to make a run for it. Getting myself and Lili out of the apartment wasn't easy, but eventually I succeeded."

"How?"

A hint of mischief sparkled in her eyes. "I locked Mrs. O'Leary in the closet Victor had decided to use as his wine cellar. It was the only room in the apartment with an old-fashioned key lock that you could turn from the outside. Since I was supposed to be an alcoholic with no access to the wine, there seemed a certain poetic justice to locking her in there. Then I barricaded the door with furniture, just to be on the safe side. It was snowing, and bitterly cold, so I bundled Lili into her snowsuit, grabbed my coat and made a dash for Elena's apartment. We made it without anyone having the faintest idea where we'd gone."

"So what happened? What went wrong?"

"Money," Constance said succinctly. "Or rather, the lack thereof."

"Money?" Whatever Ed had expected to hear, money wasn't it.

She smiled with bitter self-disdain. "Yes, in my wonderful planning, I'd forgotten all about the minor problem of money. If you've always had lots of it, you honestly don't think very much about money. My grandparents tried to teach me about thrift and consideration for the less fortunate, but the lessons weren't grounded in my everyday reality. With a background like mine, it was easy to forget I needed money for the plane tickets to Cleveland. I knew Elena and Ralph had struggled to pay Jessie's medical bills, but I'd just blithely assumed their financial problems were over—" She broke off. "No, that's not right. The truth is that I didn't even consider how I was going to pay for my tickets. I simply assumed that Elena and Ralph would lend me the money and I'd pay them back the minute I got to uncle David's house."

"But they weren't willing to lend you the money?"

She looked shocked at the suggestion. "Oh, no! They were willing—more than willing. It was only when we were all having dinner that I realized they *couldn't* lend me the money because they didn't have it. They'd just put down the security deposit on the new apartment and paid the first month's rent. They'd paid off the last of Jessie's medical bills. They didn't have two hundred dollars in the bank, let alone the thousand dollars I'd intended to borrow. We spent all night discussing how to raise the money for my plane fare. We kept debating whether or not we could trust my uncle David to send the money without telling Victor I'd called and asked for a loan. In the end, we decided that calling David was too risky."

"So what did you do?" Ed asked.

"I had at least three thousand dollars in my personal checking account, but the trouble was, I couldn't access the money because Victor had taken away my checkbook. Eventually, Ralph pointed out that I could cash a counter check at the bank, provided I had identification. So we agreed that first thing the next morning, I'd go to the bank and try to cash a counter check. Then I'd come back to pick up Lili and go straight from the Pazmanys' apartment to the airport. I planned to buy our tickets at the airport and take the next flight out to Cleveland."

"Sounds like a workable plan," Ed said.

"We all thought so, and it might have worked with any other man except Victor. But then, with any other man I wouldn't have needed the plan in the first place." Constance got up. "Ed, I don't know if I can do this anymore. My stomach is in knots, my hands are shaking and I feel as if someone is squeezing all the air out of my lungs."

Ed came and stood behind her, gently turning her around. "I'm here to help, Constance. You've done great, so far. Can you hold it all together just a little bit longer?"

"I don't know." She looked up at him, her beautiful eyes bright with unshed tears. "It *hurts*, Ed."

He felt his breath catch in his throat, and he stepped back, afraid to stay too close. "Constance, believe me when I promise that you'll feel better when you've told me your story. And don't forget why you're putting yourself through this. Not only for your own sake, but because you want the world to know the truth about Victor Rodier. I agree with you that he shouldn't be appointed to the Supreme Court, but I can't just go to one of the senators on the judiciary committee and make vague accusations that Victor Rodier is a nasty man. If we're going to derail his appointment, I'm going to need hard facts."

"I'm not sure I can give you hard facts." Constance drew in a shuddering breath, but to his relief he saw that she had herself under control again. "In the end, it comes down to my word against his, and who do you think will be believed? Would *you* believe me rather than Victor if you were a senator?"

"Maybe." Ed took her hands. "Let's get down and dirty about this, Constance. You have a lot at stake here. Victor destroyed your life to protect his own ambitions. You've spent more than a quarter of a century locked up in a mental institution, and he's spent the same time living a life of luxury—on your money. Hell, Constance, isn't it worth a queasy stomach while you rake through difficult memories if you can get a taste of revenge?"

She laughed, albeit somewhat shakily. "When you put it like that—you're right."

Ed smiled. "Attagirl. Now, let's get back to basics. Just let the memories flow. What happened when you and Lili arrived at the Pazmanys'?"

"We had a fun evening, considering the circumstances. I slept on the couch in the living room and had a better night than I'd had in months, just knowing we were nearly free of Victor. We all got up early the next morning. Ralph left for work. I helped Lili get dressed, which took forever because she insisted on doing everything herself, including fastening each button on her sweater and tying her own shoelaces.''

Her voice shook, and she fell silent, her expression becoming haunted. Ed took her hands, chafing them gently. "You didn't take Lili to the bank with you?" he prompted.

"No. I kissed Lili goodbye. She put her arms around my neck and hugged me. She said that she loved me." Constance's voice cracked again. She blinked rapidly several times before she finally managed to resume speaking. "I told her to be a good girl and do what Auntie Lena asked her. And that... that was the last time I remember seeing her."

Ed fought the almost overwhelming urge to take Constance into his arms and hug her. The trouble was, he didn't know anymore where the dividing line between man and doctor lay, and he couldn't trust himself to keep the embrace strictly therapeutic. When he spoke, it was a struggle to maintain a sympathetic but professionally impersonal tone. "If that's the last memory you have of your daughter, it means you don't remember being with her when she died."

"No, I don't remember how she died, or what happened to her body." Constance appeared brittle with strain. "I have these nightmarish visions of Liliana drowning in a pool of her own blood and of me being powerless to rescue her, but I don't know what I did to her, or even if I was the person who did—whatever happened."

"Your other memories are so clear, Constance. Why do you think these last memories are so muddled?"

"I've realized that the reason I couldn't remember what happened to Lili was because Victor drugged me. Whatever happened, whether it was Victor who killed her or me, I do know that I was absolutely and totally out of my head when it happened."

"Obviously you and Lili never made your flight to Cleveland."

"No, I never even made it out of the bank. I wrote the cashier's check at the counter, and the clerk was all helpful smiles. There was no problem in cashing the check, he told me, since I had my driver's license with me. But because I wanted a thousand dollars in cash, I'd just need to step into the manager's office and sign another couple of forms. When I got to the manager's office, I was told he was with another client, so I'd have to wait 'a little while.' I hung around for ten minutes or so, and finally the manager showed up, and he was even more smiling and friendly than the original clerk. I was nervous—I didn't altogether trust them—but I had no choice. A bank is sort of like a church. It's not a place where you feel free to protest the rules and regulations, but it sure seemed to be taking them a heck of a long time to type up a couple of forms."

"Did you get your money in the end?"

"No." She shrugged, her gaze bleak. "You can guess what was going on, of course. When Victor discovered I was gone, he knew I'd need cash before I could get out of the city, so he'd called and alerted the bank manager that I was mentally unstable and showing a dangerous tendency to drug addiction. He told the bank manager that he was frantic to get me home again before I did myself a major injury. When I came into the bank trying to collect a thousand dollars in cash, the clerk assumed I was in the midst of a drug-purchasing binge and that, by refusing to pay me, he was saving me from my worst self."

"Didn't you protest what the bank manager had done? In this day and age, his actions would be considered illegal. He had no right to refuse you access to your own account.''

''Wives didn't have the same legal protection from their husbands back in the sixties.'' Constance gave a grim smile. ''Anyway, you can bet Victor would have had all the legal angles safely covered. After all, that's his specialty. Naturally I fought and protested about going home with him. And the more frantically I protested, the more I confirmed the manager's opinion that I was as hysterical and unbalanced as Victor claimed. There Victor stood in his three-piece charcoal-gray suit and button-down oxford shirt, and I was yelling that he wanted to kill me. You can imagine how convincing that sounded. Victor had actually brought his secretary with him to help—quote—restrain me, and when we got home, he started haranguing me in front of his secretary and the housekeeper. Where was Lili? What had I done with her? Was she safe? Had I harmed his precious little girl?''

Constance spread her hands palms upward in her lap. ''I wouldn't tell him where I'd taken Lili,'' she said simply. ''I just kept saying that I'd hidden her somewhere and that he was never going to find her. It drove him wild that I could defy him like that. His anger was—frightening.''

Ed poured a glass of ice water and handed it to her, watching as she drank. ''Why didn't he think to call the Pazmanys? After all, Elena was your best friend. Wasn't she the first person he should have thought of?''

''Yes, but Victor didn't know that. He had no idea I still met with her regularly. Elena was the daughter of my grandparents' deceased housekeeper, and as far as he was concerned, that made her a nonperson. Actually, I don't think he really cared where Liliana was. She was just an excuse to rant and rage at me in front of his secretary and Mrs. O'Leary.''

"Didn't he love his daughter at all?"

Constance thought for a moment. "I don't know the answer to that. I'm not sure if Victor is even capable of feeling love, except as a reflection of his own needs. Of course, you have to understand that Victor didn't really think Liliana was in any danger, so there was no reason for him to worry. He assumed—correctly—that I'd hidden her with friends so that I could start divorce proceedings in relative safety, away from his control. Victor's purpose that day had nothing to do with Lili. He was simply determined to convince everyone I was crazy. Which he probably considered was a more civilized way to handle the problem of silencing me than having me killed, his other option."

Ed filled his coffee mug again and paced around the room before coming back to her side. "Constance, everything you've told me makes perfect sense—up to a point. What I don't understand is how we get from there to here. On the seventh of December, we left Lili safely playing with a good friend of yours in an apartment in Queens. On the eleventh of January, you were committed in an advanced state of psychosis to Saint Jude's maximum-security mental hospital in Rochester, New York. What in hell happened between those two dates? Not only to you, but especially to Lili?"

"I don't know," she said sadly. "It's not a very satisfactory answer to such an important question, is it? Victor drugged me to make outsiders believe I was crazy, but because of the drugs I couldn't think straight. So I clung to this obsessive, drug-induced belief that the only way to keep Lili safe was to refuse to tell anyone where she was. I don't think Victor intended any harm toward Lili, but he'd worked himself into a lose-lose situation. If he kept me drugged, he couldn't find Lili. And if he stopped drugging me, I could tell everyone what he'd done. Victor didn't like his choices, but it was more important to keep me silent than to find our daughter. Obviously, though, he couldn't just ignore the fact that his child was missing. When days went by and I wouldn't talk, and nobody came forward to say that I'd left Lili with them, my grandparents insisted that Victor call in the police and launch a full-scale kidnapping investigation. He was forced to agree.''

''You've no idea what drugs Victor used on you, I suppose?''

''I've always thought he must have given me the occasional whack of LSD, alternating with Valium to keep me sedated.''

''How did he get away with drugging you so heavily? Why didn't your grandparents protest?''

''Everyone assumed I was on the verge of mental breakdown because Lili had disappeared. The Valium my husband gave me was prescribed by his doctor. But illegal or prescription, the result is that the entire period, from when Victor picked me up at the bank to the day I got committed to Saint Jude's, is a dark haze pierced by brief flashes of awareness and recurring nightmares about Lili dying. Or maybe they weren't all nightmares. On one occasion, they apparently found me in a sweat suit and slippers, wandering around the subway. God only knows how I escaped that time, because I sure don't. Maybe I really *did* kill Lili while I was on the loose. My grandparents told me I'd confessed to them that I killed Lili to save her from Victor, which sounds like the sort of whacko thing a crazy woman might say.''

Her mouth wavered in a heartbreaking attempt to smile. ''Do you want to change your mind about declaring me sane, Doctor? Are you beginning to wonder if the real truth is that I'm blocking out the memory of how I killed my daughter because it's too horrific for me to remember?"

"That's always a possibility," Ed said. "Although what you might have done years ago under the influence of powerful, mind-altering drugs has got nothing to do with whether or not you're sane today. You also need to remember that one of the most potent effects of LSD is the way it chemically alters the brain to break down the barriers between fantasy and reality. If you ingested LSD and then started to fixate on the idea that Lili was dead, you would have recurring flashbacks that might be appallingly vivid—and there'd be no way for you to determine whether you were flashing back to an LSD fantasy or a real event."

"And if Victor slipped me another dose of LSD every year when he visited me—"

"If you have one bad trip on LSD, you're likely to have the same type of bad trip every time you ingest it. You'd remember the same events, play out the same dreadful scenario in your mind each and every time."

"I really do hate him," she said quietly.

"Speaking as your psychiatrist, that seems an appropriate response. Speaking as your friend, I'd say it was a serious understatement."

She gave him a tiny smile. "Thank you for that."

"You're welcome. But could we come back to a slightly different subject? I want to know what the Pazmanys were doing while this massive commotion was going on. Okay, I understand why you didn't tell anybody that Lili was staying with them, but that doesn't explain the Pazmanys' silence. Why didn't Ralph and Elena come forward and say to the police, 'Hey, stop your investigation. We have the kid you're searching for right here.'"

"Because they were dead," Constance said.

"What?" Ed barked. He kept thinking that Constance wouldn't be able to spring any more surprises, and he kept being proved wrong. He lowered his voice. "The Pazmanys *died*? When? How?"

"They died in a car crash a couple of days after I took Lili to them. That's all I know."

Ed realized that his thoughts were racing ahead, leaping back and darting sideways, making it hard for him to concentrate on the answers to his own questions. Had Victor arranged for the Pazmanys to be killed? But that would have to mean he knew all along where Constance had hidden his daughter, and that made no sense. Ed kept thinking of the woman who'd called him earlier in the day. Jessica Marie. A woman who'd said that, until a few weeks ago, she'd believed Rudolph and Elena Pazmany were her parents. And now she wanted to talk to him about Constance Rodier. You didn't need to be Sherlock Holmes, he thought, to deduce that this young woman wouldn't be flying from Colorado to North Carolina at a moment's notice unless she had some weighty matters on her mind.

"Who told you that the Pazmanys died?" he asked. "Not Victor, presumably, since he scarcely remembered they existed."

"Neighbors told me. Well, not exactly neighbors. The people who moved into their apartment."

"How did you meet these people? Did they come visit you in the hospital?"

Constance laughed. "Come on, Dr. Foster. Even your so-called friends don't come and visit you in a mental hospital, much less strangers. No, I found out about Ralph and Elena because I went to their apartment in Queens."

"But I thought you were locked up in Saint Jude's."

"I was. But once I was admitted to the hospital, I started to get better. Not surprising, really, because there was nobody shoving LSD and Valium down my throat any longer. There was even a young doctor there who decided I wasn't crazy and shouldn't be in the hospital at all. He got me assigned to a minimum-security section of the hospital while the bigwigs argued over my case and whether it was safe to release me. When my head finally cleared, I was absolutely horrified to realize how much time had passed with me either zonked out or hallucinating, but I knew Elena and Ralph must have been taking good care of Lili, and I figured it was just a case of getting myself to Queens and taking her back. I even revived my old plan of taking Lili to my uncle's home in Cleveland.''

"So it doesn't seem to have occurred to you at this point that your daughter was dead?"

Constance frowned. "Well, no, I guess not. That's odd, isn't it?"

"Yes, it is, if you were present when she was killed." *If she was killed,* he almost added, then bit his tongue. "But go on. How did you get to Queens?"

"After the past few months of living with Victor, escaping was getting to be my specialty. I made it out of Saint Jude's hidden under a pile of dirty bed linen in a laundry van. Not a very original escape plan—I'd watched the same scene a hundred times in the movies—but it worked. I had no money, of course, and it took two days on the road before I managed to hitch rides all the way from Rochester to Queens. I went straight to Elm Street to talk to the Pazmanys." Constance stopped.

Ed leaned forward, tension making his voice hoarse. "Go on."

"They weren't there," she said. "There were strangers living in their apartment. A young couple who'd just moved in. They were very kind, considering what I must have looked like after two days on the road." Tears overflowed onto her cheeks, and continued unchecked, as if she could allow herself to cry for Elena and Ralph, but not for the loss of her own child. "They told me the Pazmanys had been killed in a car crash in Ohio back in the early part of December."

"What about Lili? Did they say if Lili had been with them?"

"Of course, that was the first question I asked. What about Lili? They said they didn't know anything about a little girl. They only knew the Pazmanys had died in a car crash." Constance wiped away her tears and spoke tonelessly, "It was the first week of February when I went back to Queens, and the Pazmanys had been dead for almost two months by then. And all that time, nobody had found Lili, or seen a trace of her. It was a terrible shock. I guess I wasn't as strong as I thought. I passed out right on the street in front of the Pazmanys' apartment building, and when I woke up again, I was in an ambulance, being taken to the local hospital emergency room. I hadn't eaten much for the previous two days, what with being on the road and everything, so I guess I was in a somewhat pathetic state. Anyway, half an hour later, Victor was making arrangements for me to be transferred back to Saint Jude's. I never bothered to escape again. What was the point? Lili was dead. Ralph and Elena were dead. My grandparents thought I was a murderer. My mother never even came to visit from California." Constance tried to shrug. "I guess it didn't seem to make much difference where I was. On balance, Saint Jude's was better than living with Victor."

Ed felt that he'd been doing a pretty fair job so far of not allowing wishful thinking to influence his judgments, but he couldn't maintain his neutral pose any longer.

"Constance, for God's sake, don't you realize what you've just told me? Think about it for a moment! You're sure you left Lili alive and well with the Pazmanys. A few days later, the Pazmanys are in Ohio. What possible reason would the Pazmanys have to travel to Ohio, early in December, right after you asked them to take care of Liliana? There's only one reason I can think of."

"What's that?" Her question was scarcely more than a whisper.

"They were taking Lili to your uncle's house in Cleveland. Doesn't that make perfect sense? When you didn't come back to claim Lili, Elena and Ralph must have realized that you were in Victor's clutches again. Somehow, they took Lili to Cleveland. Because of a tragic accident, they never made it to your uncle David's house. And he didn't know they were coming, of course, so he had no reason to be worried when they didn't arrive."

Constance looked up, an expression of hope slowly dawning on her face. "You mean, maybe I didn't kill Lili? That all those hideous nightmares have no basis in anything except the LSD?"

"From what you've told me, I'd say that there's almost no chance that you killed your daughter."

Constance's whole body seemed to spasm. She slumped in her chair, face hidden behind her hands. When she finally looked at him again, her face was ravaged by grief. "Oh, God, Ed! How terrible to feel such overwhelming relief because Lili may have been killed in a hideous car accident that took the life of my two dearest friends. What a horrible, perverted cause for rejoicing. But I can't help it. Knowing that Lili didn't die at my hands would make life seem bearable again."

For a second, Ed considered suggesting that Lili might not have died at all, but he quickly rejected the idea. Constance wasn't mad, but there were limits to how much emotional turmoil even the sturdiest of people could survive. He had no right to plant seeds of hope that he might have to cut down the moment they took root.

He tucked her hand into the crook of his arm. "I think this has been a long and emotionally tiring day for you. Let me walk you back to your room and see you settled for the night."

"I don't want sedatives," she said quickly. "I've had enough medication shoved at me to last two lifetimes."

"All right, no sedatives, but try to get some rest, Constance. Don't let your mind run over and over what we've been talking about. And that's doctor's orders."

"Yes, Doctor." She smiled. "I'll try to be a good patient."

"This weekend, I was thinking I might sign you out of the hospital for a few hours and invite you to have brunch at my house. And that's got nothing to do with being your doctor. I'd just like your company."

She stared at him in blank, stupefied silence. "Sign me out?" she said hoarsely. "You mean, go outside the Merton House grounds?"

"Yes, why not? I'd like to talk to you some more, discuss your plans for the future, and I thought Sunday brunch at my house would be a good time to do that. I make a pretty mean pancake, or so my wife always used to tell me."

Constance cleared her throat. She started to speak, then stopped and tried again. "I haven't been outside the walls of Merton House for fifteen years," she said. "I'd love to come to your house, Ed. Thank you."

Ed felt a surge of powerful rage on her behalf, more powerful, perhaps, because she'd forgotten that she was entitled to be angry at what had happened to her. He thought of all she'd missed during so many years of unnecessary confinement, and his rage solidified into a cold, hard desire for vengeance. He prided himself on being a live-and-let-live kind of guy, but the fury he felt toward Victor Rodier was beyond the range of his previous experience. Victor had spent his whole life in a ruthless march to power, not caring who got trampled in the process, and somehow Ed was going to find a way to stop the son of a bitch from achieving his goal of appointment to the Supreme Court. A relatively minor punishment, all things considered, but richly deserved.

Constance touched him on the arm. "You're looking ferocious," she said. "You don't have to invite me to your house if you'd rather not, Ed."

He glanced down at her upturned face. Her cheeks were pink, her nose was slightly shiny and she'd lost most of her lipstick. "I definitely want you to come to brunch," he said. "In fact, my weekend will be ruined if you refuse." He suddenly realized that he wasn't entirely joking.

"Then it's a date," she said, and the pink of her cheeks immediately turned several shades darker.

Ed grinned. "You're right," he said. "It's definitely a date. Now all we have to hope is that I don't burn the pancakes."

Nineteen

Jess had never actually been inside a mental hospital, but she'd seen plenty in movies and was prepared for the worst. When she and Dan walked into the cheerful, flower-filled reception area at Merton House, she wondered if they'd come to the right place.

Far from being policed by sinister Amazon nurses in white lab coats, the only human being in sight was a young man, casually dressed, seated behind a counter that looked like the reception area in a fancy hotel. "Can I help you folks?" he asked.

Jess was slightly disoriented by the contrast between her expectations and reality, and Dan answered on their behalf, "We're here to see the director, Dr. Foster. He's expecting us. I'm Dan Stratton and this is Jessica Zajak."

"Thank you, Mr. Stratton, I'll let the director know you and Ms. Zajak are here. Would you like to take a seat on the couch over there? You'll find a good selection of this month's magazines on the coffee table."

Jess and Dan retreated to the sofa. "I guess we needn't have worried that we were going to find ourselves fighting to rescue Constance from the gulag," Dan said.

"Have you noticed this place has the sort of reverent atmosphere only vast amounts of money can buy?" Jess murmured.

"Sure I noticed. Next time I need somewhere quiet to write, maybe I could get myself checked in for a week or two."

Jess shivered. "Don't joke about it, Dan. It's creepy in here."

The receptionist called them back to the counter. "Dr. Foster is going to join you in the reception lounge right away. If you would just step through the metal detector, which is built into the archway immediately behind you, I'll unlock the door to the lounge for you."

Jess and Dan exchanged wide-eyed glances but obediently walked through the metal detector into the reception lounge. The door clicked shut behind them. "This is *definitely* creepy," Jess said. "Why in the world do they need to lock up visitors, for heaven's sake?"

A voice spoke behind her. "We're not really locking up our visitors, Ms. Zajak. It's more a case of making sure that our residents can't get out of the hospital by way of the visitors' lounge."

Jess swung around and saw an athletically built man, slightly above average height, with a tanned, weather-beaten face and a remarkably nice smile. As the man caught full sight of her, his smile faded and his hand—held out ready to shake hers—dropped back to his side. He stared at her in shocked silence.

"Is something wrong?" Jess asked. From the corner of her eye, she saw that Dan was already edging toward one of the telephones. Was this Dr. Foster, she wondered anxiously, or had they encountered one of the crazy inmates?

The man must have noticed their silent communication. He recovered his composure, grinned and held out his hand again. "Sometimes it's tough to tell the guards from the residents, isn't it? But I'm Edgar Foster, the director of Merton House, and you must be Dan Stratton and—Jessica. I've been looking forward to meeting you."

The hesitation before Ed Foster said her name was almost imperceptible, but Jess picked up on it all the same. She suddenly realized there was a simple explanation for the doctor's odd reaction to her. She eyed him speculatively. "Doctor, Dan and I have spent the entire journey down here trying to come up with a coherent, logical explanation of why we asked to see you so urgently. We decided that we needed to explain the entire background to you and work up gradually to our grand finale, otherwise you'd dismiss us as kooks or scam artists and send us packing. I'm going to say to hell with coherence and logic and go with a hunch. You were shocked when you saw me a moment ago. Was that because..." She drew in a deep breath. "Was that because you thought I looked like Constance Rodier?"

The silence in the lounge grew heavy. Finally, the doctor let out a sigh. "You're about four inches taller, a few pounds heavier, twenty years younger and your nose is different. But your eyes and your mouth...when you smiled..." He ran his hand through his hair, clearly at a loss for words. "Well, the likeness is uncanny."

"Even if we're mother and daughter? Likenesses are strong in some families." Jess was shaking and Dan put his arm around her waist to support her.

Dr. Foster tapped a pen against the back of a chair. "Constance Rodier's daughter was officially declared dead many years ago."

"But I'm alive," Jess said softly. "And I believe she's my mother."

There was another long pause before the doctor replied, "Constance Rodier's daughter would be a very wealthy woman."

Jess flushed hotly. "Maybe you've spent too long working with rich and crazy patients, Doctor. Outside these walls, there are lots of people who don't consider money the most important thing in the world. I don't give a damn about the Rodier money. I just want to let my mother know I'm alive, and see firsthand that she's okay and... and well cared for."

"She's in a mental institution, Ms. Zajak. What does okay mean in those circumstances? This institution is full of sick people."

"I realize that. I just want the chance to tell her I'm alive and healthy, and that my adoptive family are wonderful people, who did a great job of raising me and making me feel loved. And if she isn't alert enough to understand that, well, after all these years, I guess it would be nice just to sit and hold her hand for a while."

Ed Foster didn't say anything. Dan took the briefcase she was holding and placed it on a nearby table. "Doctor, let's sit down and discuss this reasonably," he said. "I guess it's your job to be suspicious. Jess, show him your adoption papers and Jessica Marie's birth certificate, and let's try to explain to him—"

The doctor interrupted without even looking at him. "Why were you adopted, Ms. Zajak? When did it happen? How did it happen?"

"I was in a car crash when I was just four years old," Jess said. "The people driving the car were killed—"

"What were their names?" the doctor demanded. "What was the date of the crash?"

"Rudolph and Elena Pazmany. The accident happened in Cleveland, Ohio, on the ninth of December, 1969. I was

pulled out from under the wheels of their car by a policeman, and his family eventually adopted me."

The doctor sat down, his body going slack. "So that's
what happened," he murmured. "You were identified as
the Pazmanys' daughter. They thought you were Jessica
Marie."

"Yes."

"How was that possible?" he asked, shaking his head.
"Their daughter was dead.... She'd been dead for
months...."

"It's a long story," Dan said.

The doctor gave a bark of laughter. "Funny, somebody
else said that to me only yesterday morning. This seems to
be my week for long stories. Why don't you tell me
yours?"

More than an hour went by before Jess finished explaining to the doctor about Magda Mizensky's letter,
Grandpa Gene's secret cache of documents, the sudden
recollection that her real name was Liliana, her unsuccessful search for someone who'd known the Pazmanys,
her visit to Bartlett House in Hatterington and finally the
clippings from the *New York Times* that told the story of
Liliana Rodier's disappearance and presumed death. The
doctor didn't comment much, beyond asking for clarifi-
cation or posing the occasional question. Jess supposed
that he had an obligation to protect vulnerable, mentally
ill patients from people who might otherwise prey on their
weaknesses, but she found his attitude frustrating. What
would happen if he refused to let her see Constance?
Would she have to get a court order? *Could* she get a court
order? The only way to prove beyond question that Constance was her birth mother was by means of a blood test,
which Dr. Foster might be able to block.

"I don't know why I was in the Pazmanys' car that night," she said, closing the last of her files. "I guess Dan's right. The most logical explanation is that Ralph and Lena kidnapped me, and then they got killed before they could demand a ransom from my parents. I'm having trouble accepting that explanation because I can't shake the feeling that I'd known the Pazmanys for a long time and trusted them completely."

"Maybe this is one occasion when you should trust your instincts," the doctor said, and he actually smiled at her. "I happen to know that Constance and Elena were close friends."

"They were? I'm really pleased to hear that." Jess couldn't resist shooting Dan a triumphant, told-you-so glance. "Dr. Foster, I know this is short notice, but I would very much like to meet my mother some time tomorrow if that's possible."

"Where are you staying tonight?" the doctor asked.

"We didn't make reservations anywhere," Dan said. "But we saw plenty of motels as we were driving in from the airport. We shouldn't have any difficulty finding a room."

"If you like, you could stay with me," the doctor said. "My house is only a couple of miles from here and I have a guest room ready and waiting."

"That's very kind of you," Jess said. "But we couldn't possibly put you to so much trouble—"

"No trouble," the doctor said, rising to his feet. "That's all settled, then. Would you wait here for a minute, please? I'll be right back."

He left the room without giving them a chance to answer. "Damn!" Jess said. "Why do I get the feeling that he's invited us to stay so that he can keep an eye on us? Did you notice that he didn't answer my question? Is he going to let me see my mother or not?''

"I think he will, when he decides Constance is ready for the meeting. And you have to face the fact that may not be tomorrow, Jess.''

"I feel as if we've been separated for so long, I can't bear to miss another day.''

"I know. But I think he's a smart guy and a compassionate doctor, and if he tells you to wait, I'm betting it would be in your mother's best interests to obey his wishes. You were so busy telling your story that you probably didn't notice how carefully crafted all his question were. I'd guess that Dr. Foster knew quite a lot of what you were going to say before you said it.''

"How could that possibly be?''

"There's only one reason I can think of. Constance must be aware of at least some parts of your story. I got the impression that your mother might have left you in the Pazmanys' care for some reason, and Dr. Foster knows why.''

"Then why did all his reactions seem so...I don't know...so noncommittal?''

"You have to remember Constance is his patient. Any discussions she may have had with him are confidential. He wasn't at liberty to fill in the gaps in your story with information Constance has given him.''

"I guess so.'' Jess paced the room. "I'm exhausted, but I'm so full of nervous energy I'll explode if he doesn't come back soon. Where's he gone? What's he doing?''

"I went to fetch someone who'd like to meet you,'' Dr. Foster said, stepping back into the lounge. He turned toward the door, extending his hand. "Constance, why don't you come in and join us?''

The world seemed to freeze around Jess. Her gaze fixed on the doorway behind the doctor, and her peripheral vision faded so that the room, the doctor and even Dan blurred into invisibility. A petite, fragile-looking woman stepped hesitantly into the lounge.

Dimly, Jess heard the doctor's voice speak out of the enveloping fog. "Constance, this young woman is your daughter, Liliana Elizabeth. Ms. Zajak, this is your mother, Constance Howington."

For an endless moment—an hour, a second, a lifetime—Jess couldn't move. Then her mother spoke. "Lili?" she whispered. Her hand reached out blindly and clutched the doctor's arm for support. "Lili, oh, my God, it's you! You're alive! Ed said you were here.... I can't believe it."

The sound of her mother's voice broke the spell that held Jess frozen. She felt hot tears pour down her face at the same instant she started forward. She ran straight into her mother's outstretched arms, tears and laughter all jumbled together in a gush of wild emotion.

For a long time, Jess just wanted to hold and be held. After a while, she realized that Dan and the doctor were urging her to sit down. Afraid of overexerting her mother—after all, it was late, and this was a hospital—Jess led the way to a set of chairs grouped around an occasional table.

Shyly, Constance reached out and stroked Jess's cheek. "You always were a beautiful baby, but you grew up to be even more beautiful," she said.

Jess took the tissue Dan was offering and wiped her eyes. "Dr. Foster says I look just like you."

Constance laughed, but she blushed with pleasure. "Then we'd better send him straight out to be tested for new glasses." Her hand crept along the sofa cushion and linked with Jess's. "I want to hear everything about you," she said. "Where you grew up, where you went to school, what your hobbies are. Do you like to swim? You used to love swimming and riding your tricycle. And peanut butter and banana sandwiches. That was your favorite meal—"

"It still is," Dan said. "Although she'll settle for champagne and strawberries if she absolutely has to."

Constance smiled. "You must be Lili's husband," she said, reaching out to shake his hand. "Ed told me she was married. I'm so happy for you, Jess."

"Well, he's sort of my husband," Jess said. "He was my husband, and then he was my ex-husband—"

"And now I'm going to be her husband again," Dan said. "And this time, I promise to get it right."

Constance looked concerned, and Jess squeezed her hand reassuringly. "Don't worry, Mom, he's the right man for me. We never had any problem with loving each other. It just took us a while to work out how to live together."

Tears welled in Constance's eyes and overflowed onto her cheeks. To Jess's amazement, Dan immediately came unstrung. He lost his usual glib charm, and started to babble. "Please don't cry, Mrs. Howington. We shouldn't have mentioned the divorce. Really, we do love each other and it's going to work out this time. I'll take the greatest care of your daughter, honest. I'm quite a respectable guy, these days. I write screenplays and one of my movies is just going into production and I have a lot of money in the bank. Well, not a *lot* of money, but it seems like a lot to me. We hope to get married again next weekend, or the weekend after. Maybe you could come to the wedding—"

Constance smiled through her tears. "Dan, enough! I'm convinced you're soul mates!" She dabbed at her eyes with a tissue. "Actually, I wasn't crying because of anything that happened between you and Lili." She reached out to grasp her daughter's hand again. "The truth is, I'm feeling very self-centered tonight, and I cried because it was so amazing to hear you call me *Mom*. My head's spinning, I can't take it all in." She turned to the doctor, half teasing, half serious. "Tell me I'm not dreaming, Ed. I'm not going to wake up in a minute and find Teresa hovering at my bedside, am I?"

"You're not dreaming," he said, getting to his feet. "But you should be sleeping. You've had enough stress over the past few weeks to test the strength of a stevedore. Therefore, I decree that it's bedtime. Doctor's orders."

"When will I see you again?" Constance asked Jess, not protesting the doctor's curtailment of their visit. "Are you . . . are you able to stay in the neighborhood for a few days?"

Her mother looked as if she were asking for the moon and stars, Jess thought. "Of course, we can stay. At least for a couple of days. And I'll come back very soon—"

"Your daughter and her husband are going to spend the night at my house, so you can talk to them to your heart's content tomorrow, over brunch," Dr. Foster said.

Constance shook her head. To Jess, it seemed that her mother was bemused with wonder. "So many treats all in one day. Honestly, Ed, I don't know if my constitution can handle so much happiness."

The doctor looked down at her mother with what Jess considered decidedly nonprofessional affection. "Get used to it," he said, smiling tenderly. "We're going to see that you have a lot more happiness to deal with in the future."

Jess felt better knowing that the medical director seemed to take a personal interest in Constance. She bent to kiss her mother's cheek. "Good night, Mom," she said. "Sleep well. I'm really looking forward to talking to you tomorrow."

"Me, too. Good night, Lili, and God bless." Constance briefly cupped Jess's face in her hands, her eyes bright with a mixture of smiles and tears. "I never thought I'd get to say that again in my lifetime. Sometimes, you know, miracles really do happen."

Jess was in such a state of emotional overload that she expected to pass a sleepless night. Instead, after a few restless turns in the strange bed, she fell into a zombie-like sleep that lasted a full ten hours. When she awoke to a sunny Thursday morning, her eyes looked out onto a world that had undergone a subtle shift in perspective. Or perhaps, as she explained to Dan over their cup of morning coffee, it was more as if she'd gone through her life with a mild case of mental astigmatism and had finally been handed the lens that corrected the blur.

Despite the strange sensation of viewing the world from a new angle, the topic foremost in her mind was her mother. Speaking quietly, because she wasn't sure where Dr. Foster was, she gave voice to her worry. "Dan, did you notice something really odd about our meeting with my mother last night? She seemed completely normal! What's she *doing* in that place?"

"I guess there are some forms of mental illness that don't manifest themselves at first acquaintance."

Jess scowled. "When you use that carefully bland tone of voice with me, I know you're covering up something unpleasant. What are you thinking? That the full moon turns my mother into a fiend who stalks the corridors of Merton House with a hatchet?"

"Nothing that bad, I hope. But you have to face facts, Jess. Your mother's confined to a maximum-security psychiatric hospital, and that doesn't bode well for her state of health. Mistakes do get made sometimes, I realize that.

But Dr. Foster didn't strike me as someone who would keep a woman incarcerated for no reason—"

"I appreciate the vote of confidence," the doctor said dryly.

Jess turned quickly. "Good morning, Doctor."

"'Morning. Mind if I join you for five minutes before I go to pick up your mother?"

Standing, Dan pulled out a chair. "Please do. We appreciate your hospitality, Doctor. Especially the pot of coffee waiting for us when we finally got up."

"Call me Ed," the doctor said, sitting down at the table. "I figure we're going to be spending quite a bit of time together in the future, so we might as well get rid of the pretense that I'm viewing this situation strictly as Constance's doctor. When you get to know her better, you'll both realize that Constance is a remarkable woman."

"But what's *wrong* with her?" Jess demanded. "If she's so remarkable, why has she been a patient at Merton House just about forever?"

"That's your mother's story to tell, not mine, and I want you to hear it from her," Ed told them. "What the two of you probably don't know is that I've only been the medical director at Merton House since April. I like to believe that if I'd been assigned here earlier, the misdiagnosis of your mother would have come to light much sooner than it has. And if that sounds arrogant, I apologize, but somebody should have picked up on the truth about Constance years ago. Your mother's mental state is undoubtedly fragile. What else could be expected after years and years in an institution? However, she should never have been held all this time. For what it's worth, I want you to know that on Monday, I intend to start the process that will get your mother released from involuntary confinement. After twenty-six years in a psychiatric institution, she's going to need a lot of help to make it in the outside world. But she's a strong woman, despite her fragile appearance, and I'm pretty damn sure she's going to succeed."

"Then she isn't mad?" Jess asked. "Not even a little bit?"

"In my opinion, she fails to meet any of the established criteria that justify involuntary confinement." Ed grinned. "And if that sounds like legalese, it is. Words like *mad* and *sane* scare the bejesus out of us psychiatrists. They're so clear-cut and definitive, and we specialize in waffle."

Jess decided that she was beginning to like Ed a lot. She took a sip of coffee. "Isn't it a strange coincidence that the papers my grandfather had hidden in his attic must have been found right around the time you took up your appointment at Merton House? It's as if there was a shift in the alignment of the planets, and suddenly the stars decreed that it was time for all our lives to head off in a new direction."

"A cosmic shift, or justice finally working its way through the universe," Ed said, his voice oddly savage. "Something else happened in April, too. The chief justice died and the president nominated Victor Rodier to fill the vacant seat on the Supreme Court bench."

"My father," Jess said, her breath catching. "Dan and I realized he'd be far too busy to listen to us until the nomination process is over. That's why we decided to approach you and my mother first."

Ed was silent for a long time. "I'm certainly not an unprejudiced observer," he said finally. "But I have to warn you that in my opinion, your father is not a good man."

"What do you mean?" Jess asked. The memory fragments she had concerning her father were bad, but she'd hoped they were distortions, childish misunderstandings of adult behavior.

"Based on things your mother has told me, I believe that your father treated your mother with unspeakable cruelty." Ed's voice was now grim.

Jess clung to fast-vanishing hope. "She might be mistaken—"

"I wish that was the case, but I think you're going to have to make a choice, Jess. You can have a sane mother or an honorable father. Unfortunately, I don't believe it's possible for you to have both."

It seemed to Constance that the sun shone more brightly, the birdsong was sweeter, the trees greener and the air fresher outside the Merton House grounds than inside the walls. Riding in Ed's car was an adventure. She couldn't work out how to fasten her seat belt, and she couldn't open the windows until Ed showed her the electronic buttons that made them slide up and down. She even found the dashboard extraordinary, with its glowing green display of digitalized computer readouts. Over the past year, she'd read voraciously and watched television with a hungry interest for news of the outside world. But one short car ride was enough to remind her that there were many things you could only learn by touching, feeling and seeing for yourself. She was aghast at the number of new skills she would need to learn, just to cope with the most mundane tasks.

"I know you're anxious to see Liliana again, so I'm taking you the quick way home," Ed said. "We'll take the scenic route back, through the old town center. It's quite pretty."

She couldn't imagine a route that was more full of interest than the one they were taking. *This is the regular world for sane people,* she thought, staring in fascination at the stream of cars turning into a giant shopping mall. She felt a sudden intense longing to walk into a department store and buy a frothy lace nightgown or a collection of ridiculously overpriced soaps and lotions as a gift for Lili.

"You're looking sad," Ed commented. "That's forbidden this morning."

"Seeing those stores reminded me of all the birthdays Lili's had when I didn't give her a present. Silly, isn't it, to regret something so trivial when I missed far more important occasions in her life."

He took his hand from the steering wheel and laid it briefly on her knee. "There'll be lots of birthdays when you can make up for past losses, Constance. And probably before too long there'll be grandchildren for you to spoil rotten with loads of expensive toys they don't need."

She smiled radiantly. "Grandchildren! I never thought of that." Blinking fiercely, she turned to look out the window again. They passed a McDonald's, and she watched a pair of little boys climb up brightly colored stairs and shoot down a tubular slide. She imagined herself, no longer confined to Merton House, taking a small grandchild to eat lunch at a fast-food restaurant with a playground like that. Her heart seemed to swell to the point that she wondered if it was capable of bursting with happiness.

"Thank you, Ed," she said quietly. "Thank you for giving me back my future. I still can't get used to the idea that I have so much to look forward to."

"I didn't give you back your future, Constance. You reclaimed it for yourself."

She pulled a face. "You make me sound a lot braver than I am. Do you have grandchildren, Ed? Do you have children, for that matter? You know more about my life history than anybody else in the world, and I know almost nothing about you."

"I have two children," he said. "And I guess you could say half a grandchild. My daughter, Becky, got married about six months before my wife died, and now Becky's due to have her first baby in November. We're all pretty excited about that. My son, Michael, is still in college and, last I heard, seemed to be dating three women at once."

"Doesn't that make life rather complicated?"

"Impossible, I'd say. But remembering back to my own misbegotten youth, it might only be routine idiotic behavior for a twenty-year-old male. And here we are. This is my house. I bought something fairly large so that the kids could come and stay without us tripping over each other every time we turned around."

In comparison to Merton House, his home looked tiny to Constance, but she didn't say so, of course. They drove into the garage and went into the house through the kitchen. Lili was seated at a table by the kitchen window with Dan, her ex- and soon-to-be husband, at her side. They looked good together, Constance thought. Their body language suggested friendship and trust, as well as sexual attraction. She wished them happiness from the bottom of her heart.

"Mom, you look great!" Lili said, jumping to her feet and giving Constance a welcoming hug. "Did you sleep well?"

"Surprisingly well, thank you." Lord, but she was gorgeous, this daughter of hers. Constance couldn't resist reaching out and ruffling her hair, which was still almost as golden and curly as it had been when she was a toddler. "I always wondered if your hair would get darker as you grew older," she said. "Now I can see that it didn't."

Lili pulled a face. "Mom, I hate to tell you, but my hair got darker as I grew older. Don't let Dan and Ed in on the secret, but this gorgeous pale blond shade is provided courtesy of my hairdresser."

She was laughing, clearly not caring in the least that Dan and Ed had both heard her admit to dyeing her hair. How amazing, Constance thought. Thirty years ago, women never acknowledged that sort of thing.

Neither Ed nor Dan seemed especially astonished by Lili's revelation. "Everyone must be hungry," Ed said, strolling toward the fridge. "I'll get busy preparing my world-famous, secret-recipe pancakes." He reached into the fridge and pulled out a carton of prepared pancake mix. "Voila, as they say in Spain."

"We'll lay the table," Dan volunteered. "Do you think it would be too hot to eat on the porch?"

"Not if we turn on both fans," Ed said, rolling up his shirtsleeves and setting a skillet on the stove.

"I'll get the silverware," Lili said.

"First drawer on your left. Table napkins are in the cupboard to the right of the sink."

"Where's the butter and syrup?" Dan asked.

"In the fridge," Ed said, putting oil into the pan and watching it heat. "There's a bowl of strawberries in there, too."

Constance watched in helpless silence as the three of them moved around the kitchen. She kept out of the way as much as possible, hoping nobody would notice how totally inadequate she was. Dan put four place mats and a pitcher of ice water into her hands. "Take those out to Lili, would you? I'll bring the orange juice and glasses."

Constance walked carefully to the porch, opened the door, walked down the step and crossed the brick-paved porch to where her daughter was laying the table. "Dan asked me to give you these."

"Thanks." Lili took the jug and the place mats with a warm smile. She put the jug in the center of the table and arranged a mat in front of each chair, adding knives and forks and napkins to each setting while Constance was still trying to orient herself to being in the porch instead of the kitchen. Dan came out carrying a tray loaded with plates, juice and glasses. He shut the screen door with his foot. Ed arrived moments later with a huge stack of pancakes. They all bustled around.

"Breakfast is served," Ed announced, unaware that, for Constance, watching them perform the simple, everyday task of preparing a meal had been a terrifying reminder of her own decades-long removal from the routines of normal life.

But, to her relief, Ed wasn't as unaware as he'd seemed. He forked a pancake onto her plate and passed her the syrup that she'd seen Dan warm in the microwave. The microwave that she hadn't the faintest idea how to work. "*Everything* will seem overwhelming at first," Ed said softly. "Trust me, Constance, this is going to get easier and easier the more time you spend away from Merton House."

And it seemed that he was right. Gradually, the feeling of drowning in new sensations faded, and by the time Ed suggested that she and Lili should start sharing their stories of the past twenty-six years, she felt mentally ready. In a way, telling the story to Ed had been a dress rehearsal, and she was glad she'd had some preparation for the ordeal of telling Lili the terrible things her father had done.

Dan didn't say much as Jess and her mother exchanged stories. Fortunately, they were too absorbed in mutual discovery to pay attention to him. But the longer he listened to Constance's shocking, mind-blowing revelations, the more frightened he became. Victor wasn't just a lousy husband, he was a monster, consumed by his own ambition, pathologically incapable of understanding anyone's needs other than his own.

Earlier this morning, Jess and Ed had been joking about cosmic destiny and the hand of fate. Dan was willing to accept that life was full of strange coincidences, but coincidence had become too feeble an explanation for what Jess had undergone recently. He kept lining up the facts of her situation, and however many different alignments he tried, he couldn't convince himself that the bomb explosion in her Denver office was yet another example of a random universe in action. She discovered that her whole identity was based on a lie, then somebody tried to blow her up, and there was no connection? Somehow, he didn't think so.

The bomb that killed Marla and destroyed the convention bureau had been sent in a package addressed specifically to Jess. It had been gussied up to look like a gift, and it had been marked Personal, both efforts likely to ensure that Jess would be the person who opened the package. But if Jess was the target, why take the risk, however slight, that Jess might not open the package, or even be in the office when the bomb went off? If a person wanted to be absolutely sure that Jess would be the person caught in the explosion, why wouldn't they send the bomb to her home address?

Dan easily found the answer to that question. If the bomb had been sent to her home, then everyone would have known Jess was the intended victim, and that would have precipitated a massive investigation of her life, her circle of acquaintances—and her past. By sending the package to her office, the bomber could hope that nobody would ever know that she'd been the designated victim. Of course, the bomber also took the risk that Jess wouldn't be the only person to die. But that, Dan thought, was not likely to deter a person crazy enough to send a bomb in the first place.

There was one thing the bomber couldn't have anticipated. It was outside the bounds of reason to have anticipated that Jess would be on the phone to her assistant, discussing the package Marla was opening, at the moment the bomb went off. The bomber's plans had gone seriously awry when Jess lived to tell the police investigators what the package had looked like, when it had arrived and who it had been addressed to. A totally unforeseen combination of circumstances—and one that the bomber wasn't likely to tolerate for too long.

Dan let the snake of suspicion glide sinuously through his thoughts. A month ago, Jess's life was turned upside down by the discovery of Magda Mizensky's letter. In search of information about the Pazmanys, she'd gone out to the Grants' old home in Hatterington. A home that, according to Constance, now belonged to Victor Rodier. Jess had told the woman who answered the door that her name was Jessica Marie Zajak. She'd asked the woman for information about the Pazmanys. Was it a stretch to assume that the woman had told Victor Rodier about the pesky visitor? Would that information have worried Victor, coming just when he reached the summit of his life's ambitions?

How could it not? Dan reflected grimly. Unlike his poor wife, Victor hadn't been drugged; he'd been in full possession of his mental faculties at the time Lili disappeared. He'd found Constance collapsed on the sidewalk in front of the Pazmanys' old apartment, so it wasn't unreasonable to guess that he'd known for years exactly what name his missing daughter had been raised under.

Then there was the phone call, supposedly from a private investigator, to Jess's adoptive family in Ohio. Was it sheer coincidence—that word again!—that the only thing the caller seemed interested in was the date when Jess would return to Denver? Or that the bomb arrived at Jess's office right after she was scheduled to be back at work?

Almost as if someone couldn't wait to be rid of her, Dan thought. Almost as if someone needed her out of the way as soon as possible.

"Help me clear a few of these dishes away, would you, Dan?" Ed interrupted the disturbing trend of Dan's thoughts.

"Here, let me help." Jess jumped up and started to stack plates onto the tray.

"Sit down," Dan said, gently pushing her back into the chair. "You and your mother still have a lot of catching up to do. Ed and I will take care of the dishes."

She flashed him a swift smile. "Hey, a new style of macho. I love it. Ordering me *not* to do the housework."

"Enjoy it while you can," he said. "This may be a one-time experience."

Constance, he noticed, was watching their banter like a zoology student hoping to understand the social interaction of chimpanzees. He dropped a quick kiss on the nape of Jess's neck—partly because it looked inviting, but mostly to reassure Constance that his teasing didn't mean he planned to lock Jess in a dark closet the moment they were alone.

In the kitchen, he scraped and rinsed, while Ed loaded the dishwasher. Dan wondered if he was going to sound like a full-blown paranoid schizophrenic if he suggested that maybe, just maybe, Victor Rodier would be more than happy if his daughter didn't live to see another sunrise.

Dan realized that he'd been so preoccupied that he hadn't said a word since he and Ed came into the kitchen. On the other hand, Ed had been equally silent. Dan searched for the best way to introduce the topic foremost in his mind.

Ed cleared his throat. "Dan, I have a problem, and I thought I'd run it by you before I mentioned it to either of the women."

Dan put his own worries on hold for a minute. "Sure. Go ahead."

"Hell, there's simply no way to make this sound like a reasonable accusation. The guy's about to become a Supreme Court justice, for Christ's sake!" Ed cleared his throat again. "The fact is, I think Victor Rodier may have tried to kill Constance the other day. Or at least tried to shove enough LSD into her system to fry her brains."

Dan could feel his expression turn blank with astonishment. Ed shut the dishwasher with a bang. "I know it sounds ridiculous, but Constance is trying to spare her daughter's feelings, and she's giving a very modified account of everything Victor's done to her."

"How modified?" Dan asked.

"Let's just say she left out most of the really horrific details. Like the fact that Victor raped her, for example. Like the fact that Constance has convinced me her ex-husband is more than capable of committing murder. Either Constance is crazy, or Victor Rodier is a monster—that's the choice."

Dan's head jerked up. "You really think that?"

Ed clearly misinterpreted the astonishment in his voice. "Yes, I really think that." He jabbed the sink with the dish mop. "Victor paid a visit to Merton House last week. He came to visit Constance, which is pretty remarkable when you consider all he has going on in his life right now. And I doubt very much that he took time out of his busy schedule just because he loves his ex-wife. He came to Merton House because he was worried by a report I sent him saying that Constance was showing remarkable signs of recovery."

"You believe he was scared that she might be filling in enough blanks in her memories to cause him trouble?"

"Yes. I saw Constance only minutes after Victor had been left alone with her, and she'd completely lost it. I'm sure Victor was hoping we'd all believe she'd simply suffered one of her periodic fits of psychosis, but since I don't believe she has psychotic fits, I have to look for another explanation." Ed drew in a deep breath. "I'm willing to stake my professional reputation on the fact that Victor slipped her enough acid to guarantee blowing her mind."

Dan gave a short laugh.

"I find nothing in the least amusing in what I've just said," Ed snapped.

"Neither do I. I laughed because I've been standing here, wondering how in hell I might manage to convince you that the bomb that exploded in Jess's office on Monday was sent by the esteemed jurist, Victor Rodier."

"What bomb?"

"You must have seen reports on the news. A bomb exploded in the offices of the Colorado Tourist and Convention Bureau early on Monday morning. Jess is the assistant director of the bureau, and the package that contained the bomb was gift wrapped, marked Personal and addressed to her. By sheer chance, the package was opened by Jess's secretary. The secretary is dead. That's why we have to get back to Colorado tomorrow. We have to be at Marla's funeral."

"Do you have any proof that Victor Rodier sent the bomb?" Ed asked.

"None," Dan admitted. "What about you? Do you have medical data that would stand up in court to prove that Constance was high on acid?"

"You'd need specific tests, which I didn't run," Ed said. "Besides, even if I had complete data showing Constance had taken LSD, I wouldn't have a shred of evidence Victor Rodier had given it to her."

Dan scowled. "If we go to the authorities with our accusations, they'll probably recommend locking us up with the other inmates of Merton House."

"If we keep silent, Victor is going to become this country's next Supreme Court justice," Ed pointed out.

"There has to be some way to confront him," Dan said. "Some way to force him to pay for what he's done."

"If there is, I can't imagine what it is."

"That's where it helps to have spent the past three years writing scripts for soap operas," Dan said. "The first requirement when you write for the soaps is *always* to have ideas on how to make characters pay for their past crimes. I think I know how we can confront Victor and force him to withdraw his name from consideration."

"Tell me," Ed said. "This is something I really want to hear."

"We're gonna talk money," Dan said. "If you mention a big enough sum, it's the one subject that always commands instant attention and total respect."

"Agreed, but we have no chance of proving that Victor's mishandled Constance's money. We just don't have time to do the research." Ed looked toward the patio where Constance and Jess were huddled together, deep in conversation. His expression darkened. "I want like hell to stop that bastard in his tracks. But if we're going to put a roadblock in Victor's path, we have less than four days to get our story in front of the public. Whatever the hell our story might be.''

''Basically, we're going to tell the simple truth,'' Dan said.

Ed snorted. ''You'd better have something more convincing to fall back on than that.''

''I have,'' Dan said. ''It's called the movie studio's PR machine. Allied Artists has a publicity department only slightly smaller than the federal government, and we're going to get them working on our behalf. I'll ask them to arrange a news conference for Monday morning in Washington, D.C. and tell them to make sure that the place is crawling with reporters.''

''And what are we supposed to say to all these reporters?'' Ed asked. ''That Victor Rodier is a nasty man and we don't like him?''

Dan grinned. ''You and I aren't going to say anything. We're going to send in Jess. And, trust me, she's going to nail Victor Rodier's ass to the wall.''

''That sounds like a worthwhile project, Dan, but it seems to me she's going to need long nails and a heavy-duty hammer. And maybe a chain saw in case the hammer doesn't work.''

At that moment, Jess came into the kitchen with Constance. ''My mother and I have been talking, and we both agree that Victor Rodier deserves to be punished, but we also agree that he isn't the sort of man who's going to turn and run at the first sight of trouble. He's more likely to pull strings, call in favors and get Ed dismissed as director of Merton House. Constance is afraid that once Ed isn't there to protect her, Victor will make sure that she's consigned to a maximum-security lockup for the dangerously deranged. And, in view of her past history, I can understand why she feels that way."

"So can I." Ed looked grim. "Victor is Constance's legal guardian, so her fear isn't unreasonable. I can take steps to void his guardianship, but he could do untold harm while I'm trying to untangle the paperwork."

"I'm begging you not to underestimate Victor, whatever you do," Constance said, white-faced. "If you attack him, make sure he's totally disabled at the first strike, or he'll lash back and destroy all of us. That's not a warning about vague possibilities—that's a certainty."

Dan cradled her hands in his. "Constance, we won't underestimate him, I promise. Thanks to you, we know exactly what sort of man Victor Rodier is, and he's finally going to come up against four determined opponents who've taken the full measure of him."

Constance tried to smile but didn't quite make it. "I guess I'm so frightened because all of a sudden I have so much to lose. You and Lili..." She glanced shyly at Ed. "Your friendship, Ed."

Ed put his arm around her. "Nothing Victor does can change the way I feel about you, Constance. Except, maybe, to increase my admiration for your incredible courage."

She blushed. "Well, thank you. But you all need to remember that Victor is very rich, very powerful and very connected. The past twenty-six years have taught me that truth and justice rarely win against money and corruption."

Jess sighed. "My mother's right, Dan. Her story is complicated, and we have to face the fact that a woman living in a mental institution isn't going to make a very convincing witness against the Honorable Judge Victor

Rodier." She gave her mother a quick hug. "Even though we know she's entirely sane and he's slime."

"Slime doesn't do well in the sunlight," Dan said. "And I'd say it fares even less well under the bright lights of a TV camera. But we're not going to subject your mother to the ordeal of exposing Victor's crimes. We're going to send you in front of the cameras, Jess—"

"But why me?"

"First, because you'll look great on camera."

She gave him a speculative glance.

He grinned, unrepentant. "And second, because you have an amazing story to tell. You're Liliana Rodier, missing for twenty-six years, presumed dead, and now miraculously reunited with her mother. That's the human-interest angle to the story. Then, as a bonus, you're the heiress to thirty million dollars, which should serve to catch the attention of any folks whose heartstrings weren't tugged by your return from oblivion. And finally, you're accusing Judge Victor Rodier, nominee to the Supreme Court, of stealing your inheritance and conspiring to commit murder. Not to mention sending a bomb that damaged a federal building and killed a woman. That combination packs enough punch to at least delay Victor's approval by the Senate Judicial Committee, and time is entirely on our side. The faster investigative reporters start running around, burrowing into records and attempting to disprove your story, the faster we're going to accumulate evidence that supports what we're saying. For once, telling the truth is going to be enough to ensure that justice triumphs."

Ed was already thumbing through his Rolodex. "I'm looking for Lewis Brokaw's phone number. He's a geneticist now, but we went through med school together. He owes me a couple of big favors. I might be able to persuade him to rush through some sort of preliminary blood test that would support the claim that Jess is Constance's daughter. Subject to more refined DNA testing, of course. It always helps if you can throw the press a piece of medical evidence.''

"Great!" Dan said. "That would be a big help."

Jess drew a deep breath. "You know, Dan, I'm almost beginning to believe this might work."

"We'll make it work," Dan said. "We're twenty-six years late, but we're finally going to nail the bastard."

Constance looked from Ed to Dan and Jess, and her mouth curved into a smile. "That," she said, "would be *very* gratifying."

Twenty

Victor could barely conceal his triumph. His performance in front of the judiciary committee this morning had been a *tour de force,* an opening statement of purpose that he was sure would go down in the annals of judicial history. Nestled within a brilliant summation of judicial restraint and moderation, he'd neatly brought in one quote from Shakespeare, two from Plato and three from the Constitution. He'd slipped in a deft allusion to John F. Kennedy and Ronald Reagan, thereby pleasing liberals and conservatives alike. And to gratify the doddery old senator from Idaho, who'd served on the judiciary committee for the best part of thirty years, he'd added a splendid line from the Old Testament and a pithy quote from the Acts of the Apostles.

His law clerks thronged around to congratulate him as the security detail had escorted them quickly along the corridors to the chambers that had been set aside for Victor's use during the hearings. The clerks were excited, scenting victory, buoyed by the increasing certainty that their careers were going to be advanced as they clung to Victor's coattails.

The Secret Service men pressed closely around Victor each time they encountered other people, as if it was vital to protect him from every possible threat of harm. Victor was so elated he felt as though he were floating six inches above the ground. Only someone who'd grown up bowing and scraping and kissing ass, constantly on the outside edge of the inner circle, could understand how great it felt to be at the very center of power.

He breezed into his office. His secretary handed him a sheaf of phone messages. "Here you are, sir."

"Thank you, Denise." Victor always liked to know that people had been trying to reach him. When you got more calls in a day than you could possibly return, you knew you were important.

"Congratulations, Judge, your speech was wonderful. We watched as much as we could." Denise nodded toward the television. "They're replaying highlights now, sir."

Victor cast a casual glance toward the screen and quickly turned away. "Well, since I know what I said, I dare say I can spare myself the chore of listening to myself all over again."

The entourage in his office laughed appreciatively, and he smiled at the assembled throng, uplifted by the knowledge that he was their wellspring, their focus, the man they all envied. "Thank you all for your help and good wishes. As you can imagine, I'm anxious to relax before the committee starts its questions this afternoon, so I believe I'll enjoy a sandwich in the solitude of my inner sanctum. Denise, would you be sure that there are no interruptions for the next hour?"

"Certainly, sir. You've earned some time to yourself."

He thought it impertinent of her to pass judgment on what he'd earned or not earned, but she was a good girl in many ways, and plain enough that she offered not the slightest temptation. Victor had his sexual needs under excellent control, but he prided himself on his forethought. He had no intention of allowing himself to be brought down by some late-night peccadillo, brought on by a fatal combination of boredom, fatigue and enticing opportunity. He'd seen it happen too many times to men who should have known better. A wise man made sure there was no enticement available to collide with opportunity.

Victor walked into the room designated as his private office. The furnishings were both elegant and comfortable, as befit his status. Most importantly, the room contained Washington, D.C.'s most ubiquitous device: a multichannel TV. Victor flung himself into the armchair, reached for the remote control and as quickly as he could, tuned to CNN. Ah, yes, there he was! God, he had a distinguished profile!

Victor sighed with pleasure, rested his feet on the ottoman and drank in the sight of his handsome self, speaking eloquently, being beamed by satellite into millions of homes and businesses all over the world. He hunched forward in his chair, listening intently, knowing he couldn't possibly have shared this wonderful moment with anyone else. He wanted to savor every successful phrase, admire every commanding gesture. If anyone had been in the room, he wouldn't have been able to devote his undivided attention to watching himself shine before the world's spotlight.

The commercials allowed him to pour out a cup of Earl Grey tea and eat a smoked-salmon sandwich. He was chagrined when he discovered the program didn't continue with further coverage of his opening statement, but switched instead to some dreary recap of a morning news conference. He muted the sound and poured himself another cup of tea, pondering some of the morning's better phrases.

He turned back to the TV just in time to see his former wife walk onto the screen. Good God Almighty! It was Constance, all right, but not the pale, shuffling Constance he knew from visits to Merton House. Somehow, she'd shed thirty years and transformed herself back into the woman he'd been married to years ago. How in hell had she managed to become a young woman again?

Victor searched for the remote control, fumbling for the mute button, his fingers not quite coordinated. Finally, he found the button and the sound clicked in. The screen was still showing Constance, smiling confidently, but whatever she was saying had been muted to allow for the voice-over of a commentator.

"Ms. Zajak acknowledged that her story is a bizarre one, but she insists that she is the long-lost Liliana Elizabeth Rodier, and that in making her claims against Judge Rodier, she has the full support of her mother, Constance Howington, the former Mrs. Victor Rodier. Preliminary blood tests confirming her identity have been performed, Ms. Zajak announced, and the results of those tests are available for scrutiny by the media. For the purposes of the civil suit she and Mrs. Constance Howington Rodier are planning to file against Judge Rodier, blood samples have been sent to one of the country's foremost laboratories specializing in DNA testing."

The voice-over faded and was replaced by a direct sound-clip. The young woman—not Constance, Victor realized, but her bitch of a daughter—looked straight into the camera, her gaze icy-cold, but her body language radiating the heat of vengeance. "While my mother has suffered for years, believing me to be dead, for every single one of those years, my father has been aware that I didn't die. Why didn't Victor Rodier ever tell anyone that his daughter was alive? A good question, to which there is a very simple answer—thirty million dollars. That's the amount of money left to me by my great-grandparents in a trust fund administered solely by Victor Rodier. That's the amount of money which he stood to lose the moment I stepped forward to claim my true identity. That's why Judge Victor Rodier has gone to great lengths for the past twenty-six years to make sure that I would never find out who I truly am.

"The purpose of my news conference today is to tell my father that he's failed. I know the truth, both about him and about myself. I'm Liliana Elizabeth Rodier, and my father had better prepare himself to face the consequences of more than a quarter century of deliberate, criminal fraud."

Victor continued to stare at the television screen, but he saw nothing through the steaming red cloud of anger that hung in front of his eyes. If he could have put his hands around Lili's neck at that moment, he would have squeezed the life out of her and taken the greatest possible pleasure in doing it.

My whole life, he thought. *My whole fucking life just went down the toilet.*

His intercom gave a low, discreet buzz. Victor ignored it. The intercom buzzed again. He stared at it, wondering why Denise was such a stupid fool that she thought he might actually answer her. She'd had the television in her office tuned to CNN. She must have seen the same thing he did. What the hell did she think he had to say to her?

A tap sounded at his office door. Victor didn't answer. Denise poked her head inside. "Sir... Your Honor... A woman who says she's Liliana Rodier is here. Her... her husband is with her.''

"That's why I have Secret Service people, Denise. Get rid of them.''

"Er... yes, sir.''

Victor risked a quick look at his secretary. In her face he read everything he needed to know. She'd seen Lili give her spiel, and she wondered if there might be some truth to what the bitch was saying. This afternoon, when he walked back in to the judiciary committee hearings, Victor knew he would read similar doubt in the face of every senator. Of course, they wouldn't ask any indiscreet questions in front of the TV cameras. But the moment he got through with the afternoon's session, his phone would be ringing off the hook with senators' aides demanding explanations. Instead of looking for opportunities to cut the hearings short and confirm his appointment, the honorable members of the committee would be looking for excuses to can his ass.

Denise was on the point of closing his door, when he suddenly realized what a terrible mistake he'd been about to make. "Wait!" he called out, having reached a momentous decision. "Denise, I've changed my mind. Send Lili in here, will you?"

In the tension of the moment, he forgot himself and called her Lili, acknowledging that her claim to be his daughter was true. Victor smiled. What the hell. It didn't matter anymore.

"I'll send her right in, sir." Denise sounded more cheerful, as if the stupid twit expected a five-minute meeting to put everything right, to undo the flood of disillusion Lili had rained down on Victor's moment of triumph.

Victor walked over to his desk and quietly slid open the center drawer. He pressed the latch that released the spring-mounted compartment concealed in the back right-hand corner of the desk and removed the two-thousand-dollar Swiss-made 9-mm SIG pistol from its custom carrying case. He accepted that his life was over, and he didn't intend to make a last-ditch attempt to pretend that it wasn't. But one thing he was sure of. He was going to take Liliana with him to hell.

She walked into his office, swift-footed, youthful, vigorous, full of righteous rage. The man she'd married and divorced was with her. Odd. In other circumstances, Victor would have wondered why. Today, he felt only indifference to this minor mystery.

It was a measure of how badly Lili had shaken him that he hadn't reckoned on the pair of Secret Service agents who accompanied Lili and her husband into the room. Of course, Victor reflected with silent irony, the agents were still sworn to protect their charge. The Honorable Judge Victor Rodier, Supreme Court nominee, couldn't be put at risk.

Lili stopped about three feet away from his desk, her husband at her side. He eyed this woman to whom he'd given life and felt a curious twist in his gut at the thought that she would have to die. She was beautiful, this daughter of his, and her blue eyes—so like her mother's—spoke of intelligence and passion. Victor admired intelligence and had always longed to feel passion. For a split second he wondered if he needed to punish her, if perhaps he might not spare her life.

Reason returned swiftly. She had destroyed him. Reviled him for all the world to hear and see. Ruined his chances of achieving the dream and goal of a lifetime. Death was too light a punishment for such a terrible crime.

She lifted her chin as she greeted him. "Hello, Father."

"Hello, Lili." Behind the cover of the desk, he looped his finger around the trigger of the gun.

"Let's get right to business, shall we? I've come to offer you a deal," she said. "If you withdraw your name from nomination and retire from the bench, my mother and I will drop our civil suit against you. You'll keep the thirty million dollars, except for an allowance you must guarantee my mother. Whatever you've been paying in fees to keep her locked up in Merton House will probably be more than enough for her to live on comfortably."

He laughed and looked her straight in the eye. "Surely to God you don't think I'd accept such a deal? Surely you don't think this was about *money?*"

"Wasn't it?" she asked.

"No, of course not." He wasn't quite sure why he told her the truth. "It was about the dignity and the respect money can buy for you."

"Money can never buy you dignity or respect. Those are honors you earn."

"That, my dear, is the view of a very young mind." He smiled pleasantly at each of the two Secret Service men. "I'd like to be alone with my daughter and son-in-law. There are some personal matters we need to discuss and I have to be back in the judiciary committee hearings in fifteen minutes. No doubt you've checked to make sure neither of my visitors is carrying a weapon. You can rest assured that I am not in any way at risk."

The Secret Service, thank God, trained its agents to have quick reflexes, not nimble brains. The pair exchanged glances. One of them spoke up, "Okay, sir. We'll be outside the door. Call if you need us."

It was the husband—Dan—whose sixth sense warned him that something was wrong. "Don't go," he ordered the men. *"Don't go!"*

The Secret Service agents hesitated just long enough to open up a split-second window of opportunity. Victor seized the moment. He pulled the gun out from beneath the desk and aimed at Lili, just as Dan threw himself at his wife. Dan grasped her around the hips in a flying tackle that sent her crashing to the ground. The bullet missed Lili, but one of the Secret Service agents spun around, clutching his shoulder.

He was a crack shot, Victor thought dazedly. Was it possible that he'd missed Lili by some deliberate command of his subconscious? He dismissed the idea as ridiculous. He didn't believe in the subconscious, and, of course, he'd wanted Lili dead.

No time for regrets. No time for thought. The agent was coming for him at a run. He turned the gun toward himself. In the mouth. That was how you did it when you were serious about killing yourself.

A missile hurtled through the air, slamming into his hand, knocking the gun from his grasp. A bullet exploded into the ceiling. The missile, a lead-crystal paperweight, shattered to smithereens against the edge of his desk. Victor scrambled to recover his gun, but Lili's ex-husband grabbed him by the scruff of the neck, pushing him back, pinning him against the wall, one arm across his throat, pressing against his windpipe.

Chest heaving, eyes blazing with murderous rage, Dan spoke through clenched teeth. "No, you don't, you miserable piece of scum. You're not taking the easy way out this time. For once in your life, you're going to face the consequences of what you've done. You'll stand trial for the attempted murder of my wife, and, by God, if there's any way I can pin it on you, I'll make sure the whole damn world learns that you were the bastard who sent that bomb through the mail and killed Marla Harries."

He wasn't going to die! Victor felt his body convulse with fear. He'd have to face the whole world, knowing that they were laughing at him, snickering behind his back, telling each other that he was just poor old Henry Rodier's boy, who didn't have two pennies to rub together, and would never amount to anything. He couldn't bear it. He couldn't live with the horror.

But Dan had him by the throat and wouldn't let him go.

Victor watched in silent disbelief as a Secret Service agent came toward him, gun at the ready. "Victor Rodier, I'm arresting you for the attempted murder of your daughter, Liliana Rodier. You have the right to remain silent. You have the right to consult with an attorney, and if you can't afford legal counsel, an attorney will be provided for you. Do you understand these rights?"

Victor started to laugh. They were asking the most brilliant judicial mind in the country if he understood his legal rights. He was still laughing when they put the handcuffs on him and marched him through the outer office, where a crowd of his staffers gaped as he walked by.

He was still laughing when they booked him and transported him to the local jail. He finally stopped laughing when two men in neat white uniforms rolled up his sleeve and injected him with a knockout shot of tranquilizer and supported him downstairs to the waiting ambulance.

CNN carried the story live.

By the bestselling author of *FORBIDDEN FRUIT*

FORTUNE
ERICA SPINDLER

Be careful what you wish for...

Skye Dearborn knew exactly what to wish for. To
unlock the secrets of her past. To be reunited with her
mother. To force the man who betrayed her to pay.
To be loved.

One man could make it all happen. But will Skye's
new life prove to be all that she dreamed of...or a
nightmare she can't escape?

Be careful what you wish for...it may just come true.

Available in March 1997 at your favorite retail outlet.

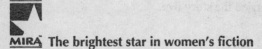

MIRA The brightest star in women's fiction

MESF

Cool warmth...fire and ice...

SNOW KISSES

by bestselling author

DIANA PALMER

Abby Shane has come home to Montana. It's to be a
healing period for Abby—a shelter from the nightmares of
Manhattan and the trauma that jeopardized her career.

She's also come back to Cade McLaren, and to the painful
memories of a long-over and far-too-brief love affair.

Maybe what they once shared was never really over....

Available in February 1997 at your favorite retail outlet.

Jake wasn't sure why he'd agreed to take the place
of his twin brother, nor why he'd agreed to commit
Nathan's crime. Maybe it was misplaced loyalty.

DANGEROUS
Temptation

by *New York Times* bestselling author

Anne
MATHER

After surviving a plane crash, Jake wakes up in a hospital
room and can't remember anything—or anyone...
including one very beautiful woman who comes to see
him. His wife. Caitlin. Who watches him so guardedly.

Her husband seems like a stranger to Caitlin—he's full of
warmth and passion. Just like the man she thought she'd
married. Until his memory returns. And with it, a danger
that threatens them all.

Available in February 1997 at your favorite retail outlet.

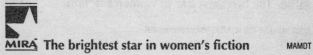

MIRA The brightest star in women's fiction

MAMDT

From the bestselling author of *Scandalous*

CANDACE CAMP

Cam Monroe vowed revenge when
Angela Stanhope's family accused him
of a crime he didn't commit.

Fifteen years later he returns from exile, wealthy
and powerful, to demand Angela's hand in marriage.
It is then that the strange "accidents" begin. Are the
Stanhopes trying to remove him from their lives
one last time, or is there a more insidious,
mysterious explanation?

Impulse

Available this March at your favorite retail outlet.